Ever After

Also by Kim Harrison

Books of the Hollows

A Perfect Blood

Pale Demon

Black Magic Sanction

White Witch, Black Curse

The Outlaw Demon Wails

For a Few Demons More

A Fistful of Charms

Every Which Way But Dead

The Good, the Bad, and the Undead

Dead Witch Walking

And Don't Miss

Into the Woods

The Hollows Insider

Unbound

Something Deadly This Way Comes

Early to Death, Early to Rise

Once Dead, Twice Shy

Holidays Are Hell

Dates from Hell

Ever After

KIM HARRISON

HARPER Voyager
An Imprint of HarperCollins*Publishers*

EVER AFTER. Copyright © 2013 by Kim Harrison. All rights reserved. Printed in the United States of America. No part of this book may be used or reproduced in any manner whatsoever without written permission except in the case of brief quotations embodied in critical articles and reviews. For information address HarperCollins Publishers, 10 East 53rd Street, New York, NY 10022.

HarperCollins books may be purchased for educational, business, or sales promotional use. For information please write: Special Markets Department, HarperCollins Publishers, 10 East 53rd Street, New York, NY 10022.

FIRST EDITION

Library of Congress Cataloging-in-Publication Data has been applied for.

ISBN 978-0-06-195791-8

13 14 15 16 17 ov/rrd 10 9 8 7 6 5 4 3 2 1

To the only man I'd make
butterscotch pudding for

Acknowledgments

I'd like to thank my editor, Diana Gill, and my agent, Richard Curtis, who have each helped shape the Hollows in uncountable ways.

Ever After

Chapter One

This is close enough. Thanks," I said to the cabdriver, and he swerved to park a block from Carew Tower's drop-off zone. It was Sunday night, and the trendy restaurants in the lower levels of the Cincinnati high-rise were busy with the March Madness food fest—the revolving door never stopped as laughing couples and groups went in and out. The kids-on-art exhibit had probably brought in a few, but I'd be willing to bet that the stoic pair in the suit and sequined dress getting out of the black car ahead of me were going up to the revolving restaurant as I was.

I fumbled for a twenty in my ridiculously small clutch purse, then handed it over the front seat. "Keep the change," I said, distracted as I tugged my shawl closer, breathing in a faint lilac scent. "And I'm going to need a receipt, please."

The cabbie shot me a thankful glance at the tip, high maybe, but he'd come all the way out to the Hollows to pick me up. Nervous, I readjusted my shawl again and slid to the door. I could have taken my car, but parking was a hassle downtown for festivals, and tawny silk and lace lost a lot of sparkle while getting out of a MINI Cooper. Not to mention the stiff wind off the river might pull apart my carefully braided hair if I had to walk more than a block.

I doubted that tonight's meeting with Quen would lead to a job, but I needed all the tax deductions I could get right now, even if it was just cab fare. Skipping filing for a year while they decided if I was a citizen or not hadn't turned out to be the boon I originally thought it was.

"Thanks," I said as I tucked the receipt away. Taking a steadying breath, I sat with my hands in my lap. Maybe I should go home instead. I liked Quen, but he *was* Trent's number one security guy. I was sure it was a job offer, but probably not one I wanted to take.

My curiosity had always been stronger than common sense, though, and when the cabbie's eyes met mine through his rearview mirror, I reached for the handle. "Whatever it is, I'm saying no," I muttered as I got out, and the Were chuckled. The thump of the door barely beat the three loud Goth teenagers descending upon him.

My low heels clicked on the sidewalk and I held my tiny clutch bag under my arm, the other hand on my hair. The bag was small, yes, but it was big enough to hold my street-legal splat gun stocked with sleepy-time charms. If Quen didn't take no for an answer, I could leave him facedown in his twelve-dollar-a-bowl soup.

Squinting through the wind, I dodged the people loitering for their rides. Quen had asked me to dinner, not Trent. I didn't like that he felt the need to talk to me at a five-star restaurant instead of a coffee shop, but maybe the man liked his whiskey old.

One last gust pushed me into the revolving door, and a whisper of impending danger tightened my gut as the scent of old brass and dog urine rose in the sudden dead air. It expanded into the echoing noise of a wide lobby done in marble, and I shivered as I made for the elevators. It was more than the March chill.

The couple I'd seen at the curb were long gone by the time I got there, and I had to wait for the dedicated restaurant lift. Hands making a fig leaf with my purse, I watched the foot traffic, feeling out of place in my long sheath dress. It had looked so fabulous on me in the store that I'd bought it even though I couldn't run in it. Wearing it tonight was half the reason I had said yes to Quen. I often dressed up for work, but always with the assumption that I'd probably end the evening having to run from banshees or after vampires. *Maybe Quen just wanted to catch up?* But I doubted it.

The elevator dinged, and I forced a smile for whoever might be in it. It faded fast when the doors opened to show only more brass, velvet, and mahogany. I stepped inside and hit the R button at the top of the panel. Maybe my unease was simply because I was alone. I'd been alone a lot this week while Jenks tried to do the work of five pixies in the garden and Ivy was in Flagstaff helping Glenn and Daryl move.

The lobby noise vanished as the doors closed, and I looked in the mirrors, tucking away a strand that had escaped the loose braid Jenks's youngest kids had put it in tonight. If Jenks were here, he'd tell me to snap out of it, and I pulled myself straighter when my ears popped. There were ley line symbols carved into the railing like a pattern, but they were really a mild euphoric charm, and I leaned backward into them. I could use all the euphoria I could get tonight.

My shoulders had relaxed by the time the doors opened and the light strains of live chamber music filtered in. It was just dinner, for God's sake, and I smiled at the young host at the reception desk. His hair slicked back, he was wearing his uniform well. Behind him, Cincinnati spread out in the dark, the lights glinting like souls in the night. The stink and noise of the city were far away, and only the beauty showed. Maybe that's why Quen chose here.

"I'm meeting Quen Hanson," I said, forcing my attention back to the host. The tables I could see were full of people taking advantage of the festival's specials.

"Your booth isn't ready yet, but he's waiting for you at the bar," the man said, and my eyes flicked up at the unexpected sound of respect in his voice. "May I take your shawl?"

Better and better, I thought as I turned to let him slip the thin silk from my shoulders. I felt him hesitate at my pack tattoo, and I straightened to my full height, proud of it.

"This way, please?" he said as he handed it to a woman and took the little paper tag, handing it to me in turn.

I let my hips sway a little as I fell into step behind him, making the shift to the revolving circle without pause. I'd been up here a couple of times, and the bar was on the far side of the entry. We strode through tables of upscale wining-and-dining people. The couple who had come up ahead of me were already seated, wine being poured as they sat close together and enjoyed each other more than the view. It had been a while since I'd felt that, and a pang went through me. Shoving it down, I stepped to the still center portion of the restaurant with the brass and mahogany bar.

Quen was the only one there apart from the bartender, his stance hinting at unease as he stood, not sat, with a ramrod straightness in his suit coat and tie. He had the build to wear it well, but it probably hampered his movement more than he liked, and I smiled as he frowned and tugged at his sleeve, clearly not seeing me yet. The reflection in the glass behind the mirror showed the lights on the river. He looked tired—alert but tired.

His eyes were everywhere, and his head cocked as he listened to the muted TV in the upper corner behind him. Catching the movement of our approach, he turned, smiling. Last year I might have felt out of place and uncomfortable, but now I smiled back, genuinely glad to see him. Somehow, he'd taken on the shades of a father figure in my mind. That we kept butting heads the first year we'd known each other might have something to do with it. That he could still lay me flat out on the floor with his magic was another. Saving his life once when I had failed to save my dad probably also figured into it.

"Quen," I said as he needlessly tugged his dress slacks and suit coat straight. "I have to say this is better than meeting you *on* the roof."

The hint of weariness in his eyes shifted to warmth as he took my offered hand in a firm grip to help me onto the perch of the bar stool. Tired or not, he looked good in a mature, trim, security sort of way. He was a little short for an elf, dark where most were light, but it worked well for him, and I wondered if that was gray about his temples or a trick of the light. A new sensation of contentment and peace flowed from him—family life was agreeing with him, even if it was probably also why he was tired. Lucy and Ray were thirteen months and ten months, respectively. As Trent's security adviser, Quen was powerful in his magic, strong in his convictions . . . and he loved Ceri with all his soul.

Quen made a sour, amused face at the reminder of our first meeting at Carew Tower. "Rachel, thank you for agreeing to see me," he said, his low, melodious voice reminding me of Trent's. It wasn't an accent as much as his controlled grace extending even to his speech. He looked up as the bartender approached and topped off his glass of white wine. "What would you like while we wait?"

The TV was just over his head behind him, and I looked away from the stock prices scrolling under the latest national scandal. My back was to the city, and I could see a hint of the Hollows beyond the river through the bar's mirror. "Anything with bubbles in it," I said, and Quen's eyes widened. "It doesn't have to be champagne," I said, warming. "A sparkling wine won't have sulfates."

The bartender nodded knowingly, and I smiled. It was nice when I didn't have to explain.

Quen leaned in close, and I caught my breath at the scent of cinnamon, dark and laced with moss. "I thought you were going to order a soft drink," he said, and I set my purse on the bar beside me.

"Pop? No way. You dragged me all the way into Cincy for a meeting at a five-star restaurant; I'm getting the quail." He chuckled, but it faded too fast for my liking. "Usually," I said slowly, fishing for why I was here, "when a man invites me somewhere nice, it's because he wants to break up with me and doesn't want me to make a scene. I know that's not the case here."

Silent, he tightened his jaw. My pulse quickened. The bartender came back with my drink, and I pushed it around in a little circle, waiting. Quen just sat there. "What does Trent want me to do that I'm not going to like?" I finally prompted, and he actually winced.

"He doesn't know I'm here," Quen said, and his slight unease took on an entirely new meaning.

The last time I'd met Quen without Trent knowing about it . . . Dude! "Holy crap, did you get Ceri pregnant again? Congratulations! You old dog! But what do you need me for? Babies are good things!" Unless you happen to be a demon, that is.

He frowned, hunching over the bar to sip his drink and shooting me a look to lower my voice. "Ceri is not pregnant, but the children do touch on what I wanted to talk to you about."

Suddenly concerned, I leaned closer. "What is it?" I said, a flicker of anger passing through me. Trent could be a dick sometimes, taking his "saving his race" quest to unfair extremes. "Is it about the girls? Is he pressuring you about something? Ray is your daughter!" I said hotly. "She and Lucy being raised together as sisters is a great idea, but if he thinks I'm going to sit here while he shoves you out of their life—"

"No, that's far from the truth of it." Quen set his drink aside to put his hand on mine. My words cut off as he gave my hand a warning squeeze, and when I grimaced, he pulled away. I could knock him flat on his ass with a curse, but I wouldn't. It had nothing to do with the fancy restaurant and everything to do with respect. Besides, if I knocked him down, he'd knock me down, and Quen had a spell lexicon that put mine to shame.

"Ray and Lucy are being raised with two fathers and one mother. It's working beautifully, but that's what I wanted to discuss," he said, confusing me even more.

I drew my hands back to my lap, slightly huffy. So I had jumped to conclusions. I knew Trent too well, and pushing Quen out of the picture to further the professional image of a happy, *traditional* family wasn't beyond him. "I'm listening."

Avoiding me, Quen downed a swallow of wine. "Trent is a fine young man," he said, watching the remaining wine swirl.

"Yes . . ." I drawled, cautiously. "If you can call a drug lord and outlawed-medicine manufacturer a fine young man." Both were true, but I'd lost any fire behind the accusations a while ago. I think it was when Trent slugged the man trying to abduct me into a lifetime of degradation.

Quen's flash of irritation vanished when he realized I was joking—sort of. "I have no issue in having a secondary public role in the girls' lives," he said defensively. "Trent takes great pains to see that I have sufficient time with them."

Midnight rides on horseback and reading before bed, I imagined, but not a public show of parenthood. Still, I managed not to say anything but a tart "He gives you time to be a dad. Bully for Trent." I took a sip of bubbly wine, blinking the fizz away before it made me sneeze.

"You are the devil to talk to, Rachel," he said curtly. "Will you shut up and listen?"

The sharp rebuke brought me up short. Yes, I was being rude, but Trent irritated me. "Sorry," I said as I focused on him. The TV behind him was distracting, and I wished they'd turn it down even more.

Seeing my attention, he dropped his head. "Trent is conscientiously making sure I have time to be with both Ray and Lucy, but it's becoming increasingly evident that it's caused an unwise reduction to his own personal safety."

Reduction to his own personal safety? I snorted and reached for my wine. "He's not getting his fair share of daddy time?"

"No, he's scheduling things when I'm not available and using the excuse to go out alone. It has to stop."

"Ohhhh!" I said in understanding. Quen had been keeping Trent safe since his father had died, leaving him alone in the world. Quen practically raised him, and letting the billionaire idiot savant out of his sight to chat with businessmen on the golf course probably didn't sit well. Especially with Trent's new mind-set that he could do magic, too.

Then I followed that thought as to why I might be sitting here, and my eyes got even wider. "Oh, hell no!" I said, grabbing my purse and shifting forward to get off the stool. "I am not going to do your job again, Quen. There isn't enough money in the world. Not in two worlds."

Well, maybe in two worlds, but that wasn't the point.

"Rachel, please," he pleaded, taking my shoulder before I could find the floor. It wasn't the strength of his grip that stopped me cold, but the worry in his voice. "I'm not asking you to do my job."

"Good, because I won't!" I said, my voice hushed but intense. "I will *not* work for Trent. He's a . . . a . . . ." I hesitated, finding all my usual insults no longer holding force. "He never listens to me," I said instead, and Quen's hand fell from my shoulder, a faint smile on his face. "And gets himself in trouble because of it. I got him to the West Coast for you, and look what happened!"

Quen turned to the bar, his voice flat. "His actions resulted in a bar burning down and the collapse of a US monument."

"It wasn't *just* a bar, it was Margaritaville, and I'm still getting hate mail. It was his fault, and I got blamed for it. And let's not forget San Francisco getting toasted. Oh! And how about *my* ending up in a *baby bottle* waiting for my aura to solidify enough so that I could survive? You think I enjoyed that?"

Granted, the kiss to break the spell had been nice, but the last time I worked for Trent, the assassins had been aimed at me.

Upset, I turned back to the bar's mirror. My face was red, and I forced myself to relax. Maybe Quen was right to bring me here. If we had been at Junior's, I probably would be halfway out the door looking for my car. Even angry as I was, I looked like I belonged here with my hair up and my elegant dress that made me look svelte, not skinny. But it was all show. I didn't belong here. I was not wealthy, especially smart, or talented. I was good at staying alive—that's it—and every last person up here save Quen would be the first to go if there was trouble. Except maybe the cook. Cooks were good with knives.

Quen lifted his head, the wrinkle line in his forehead deeper. "That's exactly what I'm saying," he said softly. "The man needs someone to watch him. Someone who can survive what he gets himself into and is sensitive to his . . . quirks."

"Quirks?" Frustrated, I let go of my clutch purse and downed another swallow of wine. "Dude, I hear you. I understand," I said, and Quen blinked at my word choice. "I even sympathize, but I can't do it. I'd end up killing him. He's too pigheaded and unwilling to consider anyone else's opinion, especially in a tight situation."

Quen chuckled, relaxing his tight grip on his emotions. "Sounds familiar."

"We are talking about Trent, not me. And besides, the man does not need a babysitter. He's all grown up, and you"—I pointed at Quen—"don't give him enough credit. He stole Lucy okay, and they were waiting for him." I turned back to the bar and the reflection of the Hollows. "He can handle whatever Cincinnati can dish out," I said softly, going over my short list of trouble. "It's been quiet lately."

Quen sighed, slumping beside me with both hands around his drink, but I wasn't going to fall for it. "I will admit that Trent has a knack for devising a plan and following through with it. But he falters at improvisation, and that's where you excel. I wish you would reconsider."

Hearing the truth of it, I looked up and Quen lifted his drink in salute. Trent could plan his way out of a demon's contract, but that wouldn't keep him alive against a sniper spell, and that's where the real danger was. My jaw clenched and I shoved the thought away. What did I care?

"I left the I.S. because I couldn't stomach working for anyone. That hasn't changed."

"That's not entirely true," he said, and I frowned. "You work with Ivy and Jenks all the time."

My eyebrows rose. "Yes. I work *with* Jenks and Ivy, not *for* them. They don't always do what I think is best, but they always at least listen to me." I didn't do what they thought was best, either, so we got along tolerably well. Trent, though, he *needed* to listen. The businessman made more mistakes than . . . me.

"He's doing much better," Quen said, and I couldn't stop my chuckle. "Yeah?"

"He worked with Jenks," Quen offered, but I could hear the doubt in his voice.

"Yes, he worked with Jenks," I said, the wine bitter as it slipped down. "And Jenks said it was like pulling the wings off a fairy to get Trent to include him on even the smallest details. No."

Quen's worry line in his brow was deepening. "Quen, I understand your concern," I said, reaching out to put a hand on his arm. It was tense, and I pulled back, feeling like I shouldn't have touched him. "I'm sorry, but I just can't do it."

"Could you maybe just try?" he said, shocking me. "There's an elven heritage exhibit at the museum next Friday. Trent has a few items on display and will be putting in an appearance. You'll love it."

"No." I faced the mirror and watched myself take a drink.

"Free food," he said, and I eyed him in disbelief through the reflection. I wasn't that desperate. "Lots of contacts with people with too much money," he added. "You need to get out and network. Let Cincy know you're the same Rachel Morgan who captured a banshee and saved San Francisco, and not just the witch who's really a demon."

I flushed, setting the glass down and looking around for a clock. Jeez, had I only been here ten minutes?

"I expect you would pick up a few legit jobs," he said, and I stiffened. I wasn't out of money, but the only people who wanted to hire me wanted me because I could twist demon curses. I wasn't that kind of a girl, even if I had the potential to be, and it bothered me that Quen knew who had been knocking on my door. Working a couple of easy chaperoning jobs for Cincinnati's elite would do wonders for my esteem.

Isn't that what Quen is offering me?

"There would be a clothing allowance," Quen wheedled. My pulse quickened, not at the thought of a new pair of boots but at being dumb enough to consider this. "Rachel, I'm asking this as a personal favor," he added, sensing me waver. "For me, and Ceri."

Groaning, I dropped my head into my hand, and my dress pinched as I shifted to turn away from him. Ceri. Though she had agreed to maintaining a public image with Trent, she loved Quen. Quen loved her back with all the fierceness of someone who never expected to find anything beautiful in the world. Hell, if it was nothing more than being a security escort, I could stomach Trent for a few hours. How much trouble could the man get into out at the museum, anyway?

"You fight dirty," I said sourly to his reflection, and he toasted me, smiling wickedly.

"It's my nature. So will you do it?"

I rubbed the back of my neck as I turned to him, guilt and duty pulling at me. Avoiding him, I sent my eyes to the TV. It was showing the Cincy skyline, which was odd since it was a national station. The banner THIRD INFANT ABDUCTED flashed up, then vanished behind an insurance commercial. *Act as Trent's security?* I thought, remembering Trent's savage, protective expression under the city when he downed that man trying to abduct me. And then how he looked on my front steps when he found Wayde carting me out of the church over his shoulder. Trent had spun a charm to knock the Were out cold with the ease of picking a flower. True, it hadn't been needed, but Trent hadn't known that.

My fingers spinning the footing of my glass slowed as I recalled Trent opening up to me and telling me about the person he wanted to be. It was as if I was the only person who might really understand. *And Quen wanted me to be the one to deny him that?*

"No," I whispered, knowing that Trent would count my presence as his failure. He didn't deserve that. "I'm not going to be his babysitter."

"Rachel, you need to put your petty grudge aside and—"

"No!" I said louder, angry now, and his words cut off. "This isn't about me. Trent can stand on his own. He's better than you give him credit for. You asked me, I said no. Find someone else to spit in his eye."

Quen pulled back from me, his face creased in anger. "That's not what I'm doing," he said, but there was a whisper of concern in his denial. "I simply don't want him out there alone. There's nothing wrong with someone having your back. He can stand on his own without having to be alone."

Behind him, the TV was showing the front of Cincy's hospital, lit up with lights and security vehicles. *Have his back?*

"I won't bring it up again," he said, shifting away from me, suddenly closed off. "I think our table is ready."

Confused, I slid from the stool, shimmying until my dress fell right. If I was there, Trent wouldn't see it as me watching his back. He'd say I was babysitting him. Quen had it wrong.

Didn't he?

"After you," Quen said sourly, gesturing for me to follow the man standing before us with two huge menus in his hand.

God save me from myself, maybe Quen was right. "Quen . . ."

But then my gaze jerked up to the TV over the bar as I caught a familiar phrase, and my thoughts of Trent vanished. With a sudden flash, I recognized the new Rosewood wing behind the newscaster on the scene. The Rosewood wing was simply a fancy name for the three comfortable house-like facilities they'd built for the terminally ill babies suffering from Rosewood syndrome. The cul-de-sac was damp from the earlier rain, and lights from the I.S. cruisers and news vans made everything shiny. The thought of THIRD ABDUCTION echoed through me, and I jerked to a halt. Behind me, Quen grunted in surprise.

"Turn it up!" I exclaimed, turning back to the bar and shoving past Quen to get closer.

". . . apparently abducted by a kidnapper posing as a night nurse," the woman was saying, and I felt myself pale. "I.S. officials are investigating, but so far they have no leads as to who is taking the failing infants, and why."

"Turn it up!" I said again, and this time, the bartender heard me, aiming a remote and upping the volume. I felt myself pale as Quen rocked to a halt beside me, both of us looking up. A phone buzzed, and Quen jumped, his hand fumbling to a back pocket.

"Because of baby Benjamin's miraculous progress in fighting the lethal disease, officials are not hopeful for a ransom demand—they fear that he was taken by unscrupulous biogenetic engineers trying to find and sell a cure."

"Oh my God," I whispered, fumbling in my clutch bag for my phone. They'd killed all the bioengineers during the Turn. It was a tradition both humans and Inderlanders alike gleefully continued to this day. That I was alive because of illegal tinkering didn't make me feel any better.

"Let's hope they find them soon," the woman was saying, and then the headlines shifted to the latest Washington scandal.

Head down over my phone, I punched in Trent's number. It would go right to his private quarters, bypassing the switchboard. I felt hot, then cold, my grip on my phone shaking. He wouldn't have abducted the baby, but he'd have a short list of who might have. The Humans Against Paranormals Association, HAPA, maybe, now that they couldn't have me. Trent had once promised that he'd give the demons the cure to their infertility, but after suffering through the chaos wrought by his father's saving me, I couldn't believe that Trent was looking to increase the number of survivors just yet.

The busy signal shocked through me, and I glanced up at the shadow of a man standing too close: Quen, his brow furrowed as he looked at his phone's screen. Blinking, I remembered where I was. Quen's lips twitched, and he held out his phone. It was smaller and shinier than mine. "He's on my line," he said with a thin, distant voice. "You talk to him."

Fingers shaking, I took the phone. "He'll know we're together, that we talked." Oh God, I didn't want Trent to know that Quen doubted him. He looked to him as his father despite the monthly stipend.

Quen shrugged. "He'll find out anyway."

Mouth suddenly dry, I answered the phone and put it to my ear. "Trent?"

The hesitation was telling, but he caught his balance quickly. "Rachel?"

Trent said, clearly surprised. "I'm sorry. I must have hit the wrong button. I was trying to reach Quen."

I held the phone tighter, my pulse pounding. His voice was beautiful, and I felt glad for turning Quen down. "Ahh," I said, glancing up at a stoic Quen. "You hit the right number."

Again Trent hesitated. "Okay?"

"We were having dinner." I explained nothing, and Quen's face became even more bland. "Quen and I. You saw the news? Do you know who did it?"

My worry came rushing back, crowding out my brief flash of pleasure for having caught Trent off guard. It happened so seldom. The host was still waiting, and when Quen shook his head, he smiled ingratiatingly and walked away, dropping the menus on the bar.

"No, but I'm going out there right now." Trent's tone was tight, and my idea that he was fixing Rosewood babies died. "Since you're with *Quen*, would you both meet me there?"

My lips parted, even as I heard the accusation in his tone. He wanted me there? With him?

"Rachel, are you there?" Trent asked, and I flushed, glancing at Quen before pushing the phone tighter to my ear.

"Yes. The hospital, right?" *Where all the news vans were? Swell.* I couldn't help but wonder if his invitation was because he wanted my professional opinion or simply to find out what Quen and I were doing.

"Rosewood wing," he said, his tone grim. "I doubt there will be any indication as to who took the infant, but I don't want evidence to be buried if the I.S. doesn't like what they find. If one of us is there, we will at least have the truth."

I nodded as Quen exchanged a few words with the bartender and slipped him a bill. The I.S. was an offshoot of the original FBI and local police forces before the Turn, responsible for hiding Inderland crimes before humans could find evidence that witches, werewolves, and vampires existed. Covering up the uncomfortable or unprofitable was in their blood.

"Rachel, may I talk to Quen?" Trent asked, shaking me out of my thoughts.

"Um, sure. I'll see you there." My stomach was in knots, and I held the phone out. "He wants to talk to you."

Quen looked at the phone, his expression never shifting as he reluctantly reached out. Turning sideways to me, he drew himself up. "Sa'han?" He hesitated. "Having dinner." Another pause. "Of course Ceri knows. It was her idea."

Ceri was in on this, too? Frowning, I forced my arms from my middle. Trent would be pissed. I knew I'd been when my mom and dad rented me a live-in personal security guy for a few months.

"No," Quen said firmly, and then again, "No. I'll see you there."

I could hear Trent complaining as Quen closed the phone, cutting him off midprotest. That wasn't going to go over very well, I decided, and when Quen gestured for me to head out before him, I meekly fell into place, my thoughts turning to the hospital.

Behind us people laughed and clinked glasses. Below, Cincinnati moved with her people, uncaring and unaware. It felt wrong now. Someone was stealing Rosewood babies. The "why" was ugly.

Quen was silent all the way to the elevator. He avoided my eyes as I handed him my ticket to give to the coat-check woman. I could have given it to her myself, but high society came with weird rules, and it was no skin off my nose. "You're not going to tell him?" I said, hoping he wanted to use the time it would take to get to the hospital to come up with some story other than Quen's asking me to babysit Trent.

Gaze distant in thought, Quen shook out my shawl and I turned around, my head lowered. "You might be right," he said, and I shivered as the silk settled over my bare skin. "I may have acted without thought."

It was an honest answer, but Quen might be right as well. Trent didn't need a babysitter, but everyone needed someone to watch their back.

Chapter Two

Q uen's car was warm, the seats heated and my vents aimed at me, making the escaping strands of my braid tickle my neck as we slowly wove through the twisty hospital campus. Feeling ill, I leaned toward the dash and peered through the curved glass, both anxious to get there and uncertain as to what I was going to tell Trent. It was starting to mist, and everything had a surreal glow. The tall main building looked foreboding in the rain, lights gleaming on its slick walls. That was not our destination. People got better—mostly—at the hospital. Where we were headed, the only healing was emotional.

The tires hissed on the wet pavement as we took a tight corner into a cul-de-sac. Three modest structures, identical apart from their color, were before us, I.S. cruisers and black Crown Vics parked in the drives and at the curbs. My lips curled in disgust at the news vans, bright lights spilling out along with heavy wires like grotesque umbilical cords running into one of the houses. It must have made their night to have their local story picked up nationwide.

The three two-story homes looked out of place in the otherwise institutional hospital setting. They were relatively new, the landscaping bushes still small and inadequate. It was Cincinnati's Rosewood wing where Rosewood babies were moved to, sometimes born here, but always dying here, never surviving. A lot of parents elected to take their baby home for his or her last days, but not all, and the homey atmosphere was a boon. Counselors were more prevalent than nursing staff. They hadn't had such a place when I'd been born, and as Quen parked his two-seater into a space too small for the official cars, I felt odd and melancholy.

Quen put the car in park, making no move to get out. I, too, leaned back into the plush seat, afraid almost. Blowing his breath out noisily, Quen turned to me. "I'm going to tell him we had dinner and talked about his security," he finally said, his eyes holding a hint of pleading. "I'm also going to tell him that I was asking your opinion if he was secure on his own merits, and that you said he was, but that if the situation changed that you would . . ."

My heart thumped as he let his words trail off into expectation, waiting for me to finish his sentence and tell him I'd watch Trent when he couldn't. That wasn't even mentioning the little white lie. I didn't know how I felt about that, and I searched Quen's expression. The shadow-light coming from the lit-up building made him look older, his worry clear. *Damn it all to hell.* "That if the situation changed that I'd be able to assist in keeping the girls safe," I said firmly, and Quen's expression became stoic.

"Very well, Tal Sa'han," he grumbled, and my eyebrows rose. Tal Sa'han? That was a new one. I would have asked him what it meant, but his voice had been mocking.

"Then let's go," I said, reaching for my bag. The little clutch bag felt too small as I got out, and my clothes were totally inappropriate for a crime scene. The cool mist touched my face, and the thump of Quen's door surprised me. Dropping my eyes to the damp pavement, I shut my door as well.

I took a deep breath and lifted my chin, starting for the door, already propped open for the sporadic flow of people in and out. I couldn't help but notice the opening was almost twice as wide as usual. I hated oversize doors—or rather, I hated the wheelchairs they alluded to. A sudden wish to be anywhere but here struck me. I had escaped dying from Rosewood syndrome. It had taken almost all my early life to do it and it shaped me in ways I was only now figuring out, but the reminder was bittersweet.

Quen met me stride for stride. "Are you okay?"

We had gained the paved walk, which artistically meandered to give the appearance of distance and interest. It just looked fake to me. "Fine," I said, my mood growing worse. I didn't want to be here—didn't like the memories being stirred up. Someone was stealing Rosewood babies, and what followed from there was enough to make my nights sleepless.

Head down, I stepped over the news van's cords, walking sideways to get through the door and flashing my ID to the I.S. guy. I think it was more Quen's and my fancy dress that got us in than my ID. The officer clearly didn't recognize me, but only someone who needed to be here would come dressed in formalwear. I'd have to remember that.

The cool night mist vanished, and I hesitated just inside the wide entryway, feeling Quen's silent, solid presence behind me. A set of stairs led up, probably to the nurses' quarters; the kitchen was behind the stairway, down a short hallway. There were two living rooms, one to either side of the door. Both of them were full of people standing around talking, but only one had the lights of the news crews. It was warm, even for me, and I didn't like the excited tone of the newswoman asking the distraught mother how she felt now that her baby—thriving against all odds—had been stolen.

"What a slime," I whispered with a surge of anger, and Quen cleared his throat. Someone had pieced together that the Rosewood syndrome was actually an expression of too much demon enzyme and was "harvesting" demon blood while the babies still lived. I'd be dead, too, if Trent's father hadn't modified my mitochondria to supply the enzyme that blocked the lethal action of the first enzyme that actually invoked demon magic. It was a mouthful that basically meant he'd enabled me to survive being born a demon.

Quen's hand cupped my elbow, and he gently pulled me out of someone's way. Numb, I looked for a familiar face—somewhere to start. My evening dress was garnering odd looks, but it also kept people away. That stupid newscaster was still interviewing the parents, and I.S. agents stood at the outskirts hoping to get some airtime. No one recognized me, thank God, and I felt guilty for being surrounded by so much grief—grief that my parents had endured and triumphed over. Damn it, I would not feel guilty for having survived.

"There he is," Quen breathed in relief, and I followed his gaze to the back of the living room to the hallway running from the nurseries to the kitchen.

"And Felix," I said, surprised to find Trent talking to the undead vampire. Or rather, he was talking to Nina, the young vampire that Felix currently liked doing his aboveground talking through. The young woman was looking thinner than the last time I'd seen her, better dressed and confident, but decidedly peaked, as if she'd been on too many amphetamines for the last four months. It was hard to see her behind the suave, collected undead vamp controlling her body, living through her for a few hours at a time.

It was about what I had expected. Serving as an undead master's mouthpiece wasn't safe for either party—the old vampire was reminded too strongly of what it was like to be alive and began to pine for it, and the young was given more power running through his or her mind and body to handle alone. It was a knife's edge that only the most experienced attempted at this level, and I was starting to think that the relationship had passed the point where it could be ended safely.

Concerned, I bit my lip, wondering if the I.S. was questioning Trent about the abductions. But as I watched, I decided that though Trent had proved he could be calm even while being arrested for murder at his own wedding, he didn't have the guarded air of someone being grilled for kidnapping. He was probably getting the real story, not the canned tripe they were feeding the reporters.

Trent's short, translucently blond hair next to Nina's thick shoulder-length wash of Hispanic elegance was striking. The woman herself had no political sway, but Felix was shining through, making the woman unusually sophisticated and in control—and slightly masculine in her mannerisms as she stood with her knees too far apart for her professional skirt and suit coat.

"Running into Trent and Felix at a crime scene is starting to become a habit," I said as I rocked into motion, moving slowly to avoid the reporters as we crossed the room. Seeing Trent, I felt my entire perception of Quen shift. Oh, both men had grace, but Quen's was born in the confidence that he could handle any situation. Trent's was from a lifetime of being listened to and taken more than seriously. They were both dressed well, but Trent's suit was tailored to every inch of his trim, sexy self, and it was growing obvious that Quen would rather be in his usual loose-fitting security uniform. Though I'd seen both men take down an attacker, Quen would always use the minimal amount of force, whereas Trent would be a conflict of visions—elegance coupled with savagery and a frightening grace, magic sung into existence.

Trent felt my gaze on him, his expression startled until he hid the emotion. Only after running his gaze up and down—appreciatively taking in my evening gown—did he touch Felix's shoulder to point me out. The young/old I.S. operative turned, beaming, the young woman's normal mannerisms gone as Felix took complete control.

"Rachel!" Nina said a shade too loudly and with an exaggerated slowness as Quen and I tucked into the marginally quieter hallway where we could still watch what happened. "I'm surprised to see you here. Is Ivy back yet?"

With a guarded air, I shook both my head and her hand. "Not until next Saturday," I said, pulling my hand from hers, not liking Felix's interest in my roommate. "I was at dinner when I heard the news and came over because . . ." I hesitated, my grip tightening on my clutch bag. *Because I wanted to know who was kidnapping babies who could invoke demon magic? Sure, that sounded good.*

Trent cleared his throat as the silence became awkward. "Because I asked her to," he said, reaching to shake my hand. It was missing the last two digits, but he hid their absence well until our fingers met. The glint of a ring twin to my own was still on his index finger, and I hid my hand behind my back, not wanting Felix to notice and ask. "Hello, Rachel. I appreciate you . . . changing your plans." The hesitation had been slight, but it was there. Beside me, Quen cleared his throat, clearly not wanting to explain in front of Felix.

I don't know if I want to lie to you anymore, I thought, warming at his touch and wondering if I had felt a faint tingle of spilling energy before our fingers had parted. "Who did this?" I said, trying to block out the woman sobbing on the couch. My God, didn't newspeople have any soul at all?

Nina laughed lightly, Felix apparently immune to the human tragedy.

"Let me consult my magic ball," she said, then sobered when both Trent and I stared at her. We weren't the only ones. That laugh had traveled.

"Quen, thank you for bringing Ms. Morgan out," Trent said as he inclined his head.

"It wasn't a problem. Sa'han . . ." Quen paused. "If I can have a second of your time?"

"In a moment." Trent beamed one of his professional smiles, and I slumped ever so slightly. As long as Felix was here, Trent would be the epitome of Teflon—knowing nothing, seeing nothing, accomplishing nothing—boring, boring, boring. He was also ticked. I could tell by the faint rim of red on his ears. He wouldn't talk to Quen until they were alone, and until then, he was going to believe the worst. Three days in a car was having unforeseen benefits. "I hope you and Rachel had a pleasant dinner."

That was catty for him, and I slipped my arm into Quen's, startling both men for different reasons. "He bought me sparkling wine. It doesn't give me a headache like most wines do."

Trent's attention lingered on my arm in Quen's, then rose to Quen's eyes. Slowly Quen pulled away, stiff and uncomfortable.

"Quen," Nina said as she looked at the reporters now asking the staff for their views. "Since you're here, could you give me your professional opinion on something?"

Quen blinked in surprise, his hands behind his back. "Me?"

Nina was bobbing her head. "Yes. That is, if Trent will let me steal you away for a few moments. You're well versed in a variety of security techniques both mundane and magic," she said, one hand reaching out to touch his shoulder, the other extended to escort him deeper into the building to the bedrooms.

"Personal security, yes. I don't see how I can help."

Drawn by the living/dead vampire, Quen brushed by me, leaving the scent of wool and cinnamon. "I'd be most appreciative if you would look at the security system here and tell me what would be needed to circumvent it," Nina said.

The man glanced back at Trent, and when Trent shrugged, Quen said,

"It would be my pleasure. Ah, I don't want to give testimony in court." He continued, "This is strictly my casual opinion," his voice going faint behind the noise in the front room as they walked away.

I couldn't help but smile. It was quickly followed by the sour emotion of envy. "Always a bridesmaid," I muttered as I shifted to stand shoulder to shoulder with Trent. No one ever asked *my* opinion of a crime scene. Reconsidering, I glanced at Trent. At least not before the vacuuming guys were done.

If I didn't know better, Felix had taken Quen away intentionally so Trent and I could talk. The feeling strengthened when Trent glanced at me and turned away, making me feel as if we were two wallflowers at a dance, left by our respective dates so we could "get to know each other," Trent in his three-piece suit that cost more than my car, and me in a slinky tawny number I'd probably never wear again ever.

Then the woman on the couch began sobbing again, and the feeling died.

"This is ugly," Trent said. The mask was gone.

He hadn't asked what Quen and I had been doing, and my shoulders eased. "How serious is the I.S. treating this?"

Trent's breath came out a shade too forceful, the small tell ringing through me. He was worried—a lot. "Not seriously enough."

That I could tell already, but Trent wouldn't be out here for just this. "How many babies are missing?" I said, wincing as the mother balled up her tissue in a tight, white-knuckled grip, her eyes red-rimmed and drained. "Other than this one, I mean. The press said three."

His gaze somewhere across the room, Trent whispered, "Eight total across the United States, but the I.S. is only admitting to those that get leaked to the press. The one just before this was a set of twins from a prominent political figure. They were over a month old. The parents are devastated. They don't know why their babies were surviving. Most of the infants abducted are male, which is odd since the female gender has a naturally higher resistance."

That was why he was here, and my eyebrows rose as he faced me, whispering, "It's not me. Someone has been giving them the enzyme that blocks the destructive actions of the Rosewood genes or they would never have lived even this long. Now that whoever is doing this knows that it works, he or she is coming back and stealing the infants who have been treated."

A sick feeling stole over me as I looked into the living room with its pain and guilt. "HAPA?"

He shook his head. "Felix says no."

That info was questionable at best, but I'd go with it until I heard otherwise. "Well, who else knows what these babies are capable of invoking?"

Trent gracefully turned to look down the hall as if wanting to leave. He was tired, but it was only because he was letting his guard down that I could tell. "Anyone can piece it together—now that it's common knowledge what you are." His gaze came back to me, an empty regret in them. "The sole survivor of Rosewood syndrome happens to be a demon? Perhaps we were lucky it took this long. That an enzyme can keep them alive, though?" His lips pressed together. "A handful know that, and most of them work for me."

Silent, I forced my arms to relax at my sides, the silk of my dress whispering.

"This isn't good," Trent said so softly I barely heard him.

"You think?"

A silence grew, not companionable, but not uncomfortable, either. The news teams seemed to be packing it up, and the I.S. operatives were getting noisy, a last-ditch effort to get the cameras on them before they left. I looked at Trent's jiggling foot and raised my eyebrows.

Grimacing, Trent stopped fidgeting. "You look nice tonight," he said, surprising me. "I can't decide if I like your hair more up or down."

Flushing, I touched the loose braid Jenks's kids had put my hair in, still damp from the mist. "Thanks."

"So did you and Quen have a nice dinner?" he asked, pushing me even more mentally off balance. "Carew Tower, yes?"

"As a matter of fact, it was drinks at the bar, but yes, it was Carew Tower." Flustered, I gripped my clutch bag tighter. "How did you guess?"

His feet scuffed, the small move telling me he was satisfied—and yet still ticked. "You smell like damaged brass. It was either Carew Tower or the deli down on Vine. The one with the old bar footrest?"

I blinked, lips parting. *Wow.* "Oh," I said, trying to decide what I could say. "Yes. We were at Carew Tower." I looked down at my dress, clearly not suitable for a deli.

Trent moved to stand next to me, so near I could smell his aftershave under the broken-green smell of him. Together we watched the newscaster finish her interview with a nurse, and him being that close was almost worse than his accusing stare. "You were discussing me," he said, his voice a shade high, his attention fixed determinedly across the room. The scent of spoiled wine and cinnamon joined the mix.

"Quen asked me to fill in for him when your schedules don't mesh," I said. "He knows you're planning the conflicts—did you think he would do nothing?"

His eye twitched, that's it, but I could see right through it. "Give the man a break," I said, and he finally gave up his false indifference to glare at me. "Quen cross-checked your prom date and took you to the DMV office for your license. He worries about you, okay?"

Unwilling to believe, Trent frowned. I could feel the reporters watching. His eyes flicked to them and slowly his hands unclenched. Exhaling, he forced a fake smile, but I didn't think he was fooling anyone now. He was ready to walk, and I took his elbow.

"Trent, I told him no," I said softly, and his gaze shot from my grip to my eyes. "I told him you don't need a babysitter. I told him he was selling you short and that you had the skill and dexterity to take care of yourself. He's trying to wrap his mind around it, but after a decade of keeping you safe, it's hard. You might want to ease up on the rebelliousness for a while."

Trent's anger vanished. "Rebelliousness?" he said, and we both moved sideways as the vacuum guys trundled out past us. "Is that his word or yours?"

"Mine," I said, relieved that I hadn't tried to lie to him. "I know rebelling when I see it. Come on," I cajoled, my hand slipping from him. "Let the poor guy come to grips with your independence before you go forcing it on him. That's kind of cool, you know? That he loves you so much."

Again he started, clearly at a loss. "Thank you," he said as his gaze canvassed the room behind me, but his smile was honest when it returned to me. "I never saw it like that."

My heart thumped when Trent ducked his head to rub his chin ruefully, and a funny feeling went to my middle. Behind me, the bright lights of the news crews pinned down the human tragedy like the African sun, exposing it in a distasteful savagery akin to lions ripping the underbelly of a gazelle. It was just as hard to look away.

I took a breath to tell him if he ever wanted someone to watch his back to give me a call, but I chickened out. Instead, I nervously shifted to stand beside him again. A wisp of separation drifted between us. "You're leaving."

"Ah, yes," he said, clearly surprised. "That newswoman has been eyeing me, and I don't want to give an interview."

I nodded in understanding. As soon as he left, I was going to beat a hasty retreat in the other direction in search of Nina. Maybe they'd let me into the crime scene if Felix asked them to.

"Rachel," Trent said suddenly, and I brought my attention back from the empty hallway between the kitchen and the bedrooms. "Be careful. It might be HAPA even if Felix says it isn't."

Angry, I nodded. Whoever was doing this knew I was a hard target, so they'd abducted babies instead. *Cowards.*

Trent was rocking forward to leave, and I stuck out my hand. "You be careful, too. If whoever this is knows about the enzyme, they'll know that you're the only one who can make the cure permanent." *Could I ever work for him?* I wondered as he looked at my hand and I recalled the satisfaction of bringing in Cincinnati's HAPA faction with him and the two-hour-long conversation with him over pie and coffee afterward. It had been wonderful, but I didn't think I could stomach taking direction from him, and I doubted he would ever learn to be anything other than what he was. I didn't know if I'd like him if he changed. *Damn, I liked him, and it kind of hurt admitting it.*

Trent eyed my hand for a half second, taking it only to pull me toward him. Surprised, I almost fell, my breath held as he gave me a quick, professional hug, our shoulders touching. My free hand went around him for balance, and the memory of kissing him flashed through my mind as my hand slid from his waist. "Thank you, I'll be careful," he said as my heart pounded and I stared at him. Then he let go and I stepped back, my face warming.

"Are you available tomorrow morning?" he asked, as if unaware I was now bright red. *Jeez Louise, what was with the hug? And in front of the reporters? Everyone can see me blushing.* "I'd like to talk to you about what this might mean," he said, his gaze rising to take in the entire ugly scene. "And I know Ceri and the girls would like to see you."

I hesitated. I hadn't seen Lucy and Ray for a few weeks. I was their godmother. Of course I wanted to come over, regardless of the reason. "Make it . . . ten?" I said, remembering that elves, like pixies, usually slept the four hours when the sun was the highest. "I'm, ah, usually not up before eleven, but I can swing ten . . . occasionally."

Oh God, I was blushing even more now, but Trent only bobbed his head, smiling at my red face. "We can make it eleven if you like," he said. "That's their usual riding time. Wear boots. We can talk on the trail. I'll see you then."

Calm and relaxed, Trent headed for the door, his steps confident as he timed his retreat perfectly to avoid the rising newscaster reaching for him. And then he was gone.

Crap on toast, I was gripping my clutch purse like a fig leaf, and disgusted that I'd handled that with the grace of a troll, I fidgeted where I was, feeling out of place in my tawny dress now that I wasn't standing next to a man in a suit. My heart was still pounding, and through the window, I saw a flash of light as Trent got into his car.

Hands swinging, I edged backward down the hall where Quen and Felix had gone. Quen would want to know Trent had ditched him again. I expected that the hallway led to the nurseries, and indeed, behind the first door I hesitantly peeped in was the expected double bed, two soft chairs, a rocker, TV, dresser, mirror, and a crib. There was a bank of white cupboards. I was sure they held lifesaving equipment, hidden like an ugly secret.

"Not here," I said to myself, starting to relax the farther I got from the noise and warmth of the living room. I pulled the door shut, then hesitated, looking at my fingers. They felt slippery, and I brought them to my nose, breathing in the smell of crushed leaves.

Pixy dust?

Pulse quickening, I went down the hallway, following voices. "Felix?" I called out, hiking my dress up so I could move better.

"In here, Rachel," Nina called back, and I froze at the tiny ultrasonic wing chirp of surprise that followed. I never would have heard it over the noise, except that I lived with pixies.

I spun back to the kitchen, my eyes widening. "Jax?" I blurted, seeing the little pixy looking at me from over the rim of the light fixture. "Jax!" I shouted as he darted down the hall and into the kitchen.

I moved. Dress hiked up, I stormed down the hall, blowing into the kitchen and scaring the two I.S. guys standing at the open fridge. The sparkling of pixy dust hung in the air.

"Pixy!" I shouted, and the two men stared at me. "Where did he go?"

Wide-eyed, they said nothing, the pie between them like guilt given substance.

"Where did the damn pixy go!" I repeated, my heart thudding.

"Pixy?" one of them asked, as if I were asking about a unicorn.

The sound of a vehicle starting came in through the open window, and I ran to the back door. Adrenaline surging, I shoved the door open. Cool night air hit me, misty with no moon—and the sifting silver dust of a pixy trailed like a moonbeam. It drifted to the sidewalk running past the Dumpster and vanishing around the corner.

Breathless, I followed the tracing of dust, my heels sending shocks up my spine as I clip-tapped around the corner. A squeal of tires brought me to a halt, and I put a hand on the Dumpster and watched as a blue Ford truck drove away, tires smoking. Anger sparked, but it wasn't until it hit a speed bump and the passenger door flew open that I was sure.

N-n-n-n-nick.

Chapter Three

The kitchen was bright with electric light, loud with the shrieks of pixies, and with a snap, I flicked the coffeemaker on before turning back to my sandwich. It was a rather large room, newly remodeled with stainless-steel counters, two stoves, and my mom's old fridge with the automatic ice dispenser right in the door. My spelling equipment hung over the center island counter, copper pots and ceramic spelling spoons making it look less like the industrial kitchen at the back of a church that it had started out as. Ivy's thick country-kitchen table where she did most of her research was depressingly empty. She'd been gone this whole week, out in Flagstaff helping Glenn and Daryl get settled in their new digs.

Standing at the counter in my evening gown, surrounded by cold cuts, condiments, and a half-empty two-liter bottle of pop, I clenched my teeth and wished the pixies would go away. They were playing war among the hanging copper pots, giving me a headache. Copper was one of the few metals that wouldn't burn them, and they loved banging into it. Telling Jenks about the abducted Rosewood babies had been bad enough, but bringing Nick into it had left us both in a bad mood that his kids weren't helping get rid of. Nick. If there was anyone who could irritate me by simply breathing, it was Nick.

The self-proclaimed thief once professed that he'd loved me, and I think he had, inasmuch as he could love another person. He loved money and the security he thought that it represented more. I honestly believed that he felt justified for all the trouble he'd heaped upon me. I hadn't trusted him for a long time, but when he had betrayed not just me but Trent in the same breath, I'd written him off. That he lured Jenks's eldest son, Jax, into a life of crime and hardship just pissed me off.

I'd not heard from Nick since he had spirited himself—and presumably Jax—out of Trent's high-security lockup. Only a demon could have done it. I frankly didn't give a damn if Nick had gotten himself indebted to a demon, but I *did* care about who might be holding his leash—and why he was again on this side of the ley lines stealing Rosewood infants.

The big knife Ivy left out to scare magazine salesmen was too big to comfortably cut my sandwich, but I used it anyway, setting it down on the counter with a thud when an unpopped kernel of popcorn zinged over my head and clattered against the wall.

"Jenks!" My shout sent a strand of hair drifting. "Your kids are driving me nuts!"

From the sanctuary-turned-living-room I heard him yell, "Get the hell out of the kitchen!"

Sure. That ought to do it. Frowning, I set the sandwich on a napkin, little drops of water from the lettuce making spots on it.

I reached for a paper towel as Belle edged into the kitchen, riding Rex like an elephant. The fairy had her feet snuggled in behind Rex's ears and she gave the cat a tap with the end of her bow when Rex threatened to sit down and spill her backward. Changing her mind, the orange cat twined about my ankles instead. Belle was an odd contrast of a pixy silk's bright colors and a fairy's naturally gaunt paleness. Never would I have imagined that Jenks would suffer to let a fairy live in his garden, but the small warrior woman had somehow become a part of the church—even if it had been her clan who had killed Jenks's wife. That the fairy was now wingless might have something to do with it, but I think he admired her grit.

"Your dad s-s-says to get outs-s-side," she lisped around her long teeth, her face turned upright at the noisy battle. "You shame your-s-s-selves!" With a disgusted snarl, she smacked Rex's flank as she purred and rubbed against me, hoping for a fallen morsel. "Get out!" she yelled at them. "Now!"

My head was exploding from their noise, but about half of them started for the hallway, flying backward and still shooting popcorn kernels at each other with slingshots. Someone shrieked when a seed punched through her wing, and the shouted threats got serious as the girls sided against the boys. There was a sharp ping when a seed hit my biggest spell pot and ricocheted into me, making my eyes narrow. Jenks was giving them a lot of latitude, knowing that as soon as it warmed up, half of them were going to leave to make homes for themselves.

"All right, you lot!" Jenks shouted as he flew into the kitchen, a faint red dust of annoyance spilling from him. "You heard Belle. Get out before I bend your wings backward! If you're cold, put on the long johns Belle made you, but I want you outside clearing the lines! Jumoke, get your sister a patch. You made it, you fix it. Do it nicely or you're going to do midnight sentry with Bis no matter how cold it is!"

I tossed my paper towel, exchanging a weary look with Belle as they flowed out of the kitchen with a chorus of complaints, going across the hall and up the flue in the back living room by the sound of it. Jumoke, Jenks's only dark-haired son, helped the pixy with the hole in her wing, stoically taking the verbal abuse the eight-year-old pixy was heaping on him. She'd probably be on her own next year, fully grown and ready to start a family. Why Jumoke hadn't left yet was obvious. Black-haired pixies were often killed on sight by their own kind. He, at least, would be staying.

Belle nudged Rex into motion, and she followed them out. It was too cold for fairies, but if she was sitting on Rex, she'd be okay. The cat door squeaked, and Jenks flew a red-dusted path to the kitchen spigot, where he could watch the garden and his kids dispersing into the damp spring night. His hands were on his hips and his feet were spread wide, but he seemed more worried about Jax than the noise.

Belle's touch was showing in surprising places, and Jenks wasn't looking so much like Peter Pan these days. He still had the tights and garden sword at his hip that he used to chase off birds, but his usual green gardening coat had been replaced by a flashy multicolored jacket with tails and a dark orange vest. Belle's work. With the hunter-green shirt, it made a striking statement with his curly blond hair, trim physique, skintight boots and tights, and that narrow waist and wide shoulders. His dragonfly-like wings blurred to nothing as he watched the dusty glows from his grown children in the garden. Though his feet never lifted off, the noise of his wings increased when the cat-size shadow of Bis joined them; then he relaxed.

"Thanks," I said in relief as I took my sandwich to the table. "They don't listen to me."

Jenks frowned as he flew over the center counter, spilling a sour green dust on the cheese and making it glow briefly. "They don't listen to me, either."

It was a not-so-subtle reminder of Jax. Nick's sudden appearance had us both in a stellar mood. Uptight, I shifted to try to make the dress feel more comfortable, finally sitting sideways to the table in the hard-backed chair. My clutch purse and shawl were at Ivy's empty spot, trying to make it look less . . . empty.

Suddenly Nick didn't seem so important, and depressed, I leaned sideways over the table as I took a bite of my sandwich, trying not to get any of it on my dress. The coffeemaker on the counter gurgled its last, but I didn't bother to get up. Jenks descended from the utensil rack, using his sword to cut a pixy-size chunk of cheese. Spearing it on the tip, he angled the short sword up to eat it right from the blade.

"So-o-o-o," he drawled, his dust shifting to a more normal gold. "You never did tell me what Quen wanted."

I froze, then took another bite to give myself time to think. Nick had been on my mind when Quen dropped me off: Nick, demons, Rosewood babies. Quen's request hadn't even been in the theoretical kitchen, much less on a back burner. "Ah, he wanted to know if I'd take over some of his security duties."

"Tink loves a duck, really?" It wasn't the reaction that I had expected, and my chewing slowed when Jenks flew to sit on the back of Ivy's monitor where he could see me better. "You told him no, right?"

I made a little huff, trying to forget that surprising hug. "Trent doesn't need my help. You've worked with him. Tell me I'm wrong. Quen is a nervous worrywart. Trent can handle anything Cincinnati can dish out."

His eyes fixed on mine, Jenks tilted his head and bit off a chunk of cheese. "Sure, like his best friend locking him on a boat and blowing it up. Demons possessing said best friend. Said demon's ex-familiar living in his home, mothering the child he had with the woman who tried to kill him last summer."

I sighed. "You think I should have said yes?"

Jenks shrugged. "Trent always pays his bills."

I stared at him. "Who are you and how did you kill my partner?" I asked, and a faint red dust of embarrassment slipped from him. Last year, he would have been insulting Tink with a brandished sword for my even considering the idea, but then again, he *had* worked with Trent to rescue his daughter.

Head tilting the other way, he plucked the last chunk of cheese from the tip and ate it, licking the crumbs from his fingers. "Cincy is a fickle woman. One day you're leading her in a waltz, and the next she's smacked you and is walking on your face. Round the clock would be an insult, but someone to watch his back, someone in a dress who looks like a pushover and isn't always telling him what to do? Yeah, he'd go for that." His eyes met mine. "Especially if it was you."

The sandwich went tasteless, and I set it down, two bites in. I'd worked with Trent three times: the first to steal a thousand-year-old elven DNA sample from the ever-after—which ended badly; the second to apprehend HAPA—which turned out okay; and the last at a museum fund-raiser— where the assassins were aiming at me, not him. And yet . . . "I can't do it, Jenks. I can't work for him."

"So work *with* him, not *for* him," Jenks said, as if that distinction was the easiest thing in the world. "Hell, if I can work with him, you can."

"Sure, because you're great at backup," I protested. "But I'm not a backup kind of girl." Jenks nodded solemnly and I slumped, shoving the tomato back into my sandwich. "Trent isn't either," I muttered. "*I'm* not going to change, and I'm not going to delude myself that I can change him. I don't know if I would if I could." Focus blurring, I gazed past the kitchen's blue curtains to the foggy night beyond.

"Good, because you can't." Jenks dropped down, his wings rustling as they lay flat on his back. "No one can change anyone but themselves."

My thoughts drifted again to the unusual hug Trent had given me, and then his request that I come out to talk about the abducted infants. I knew the subject of security would come up again. I could see it already, Quen forcing the issue and both Trent and I staunchly against it. I wasn't averse to spending time with Trent, and I liked kicking ass that needed kicking, but either I was in charge of his security and he took direction from me, or I wasn't. "People don't change," I whispered, silk sliding as I stood to get a cup of coffee.

"You did." I turned from the open cupboard to see Jenks smirking at me. "You're a hell of a lot easier to work with than you were a few years ago." He paused. "Tink's little pink rosebuds, has it only been a few years? It seems like three times that."

The sound of coffee chattering into the porcelain was comforting, and I smiled faintly. "He invited me out tomorrow to go over the abductions. If it's warm enough, do you want to come? I could use your take on things."

Jenks struck a pose as if shooting from the hip. "Pow! See? You never would have asked me that two years ago. Hell, yes, I'll come. Elf babies are almost as cute as pixy newlings. What time, so I can get Belle to watch my kids?"

Cup cradled in my hands, I leaned back against the counter and winced. "Eleven."

He snickered. "I'll wake you up at nine," he said, then flew to the counter, dust sifting silver and gold from him. "Felix knows about Nick, right? The I.S. probably has an APB out on him already. I bet that put slugs in Trent's roses."

"I didn't tell Felix," I said, eyes flicking to Jenks, and the pixy's eyes widened. "Quen didn't tell him, either."

"Why the hell not? He was right there!"

"What would be the point?" Avoiding his eyes, I came back to the table. "I can't prove anything. All I've got is a hunch." Admittedly, a pretty good hunch, but still just a hunch.

Jenks hovered at the coffeemaker to catch a drop in a pixy-size cup. "Like needing proof ever stopped you before."

Blowing over the top, I took a sip. "You're the one who said I was capable of change. Besides, if there's one thing Nick can do, it's disappear. He's long gone."

Sitting cross-legged on the coffeemaker with his cup, Jenks frowned. "And lie. He's really good at that." Wings slipping silver dust, he eyed me. "You should call him."

"Felix?"

"No, Nick!" Jenks looked at my clutch purse. "You've still got his number, don't you? It might still work. Ask him if he's involved. Even if he lies, you'll be able to tell. At the very least, you'll know if he's here or in the ever-after."

I sat for a moment and thought about it. I'd never bothered to take Nick's number out of my phone. I didn't know why. Maybe because I had so few friends whose number ever made it that far. Jenks made a get-on-with-it gesture, and I half stood, my dress pinching as I stretched across the table to reach my clutch bag. "Okay, I'm game."

Jenks flew over to eavesdrop, and I wondered if he'd suggested it in the hopes of finding out about Jax. I heard a stitch give when I fell back into my chair with my purse. Wings clattering, Jenks hovered over my open phone as I scrolled, his dust making the screen blank out until he moved away.

"Tink's panties, why do you still have Denon's number in your address book?" Jenks said, and I made a face at him. Not only was Denon no longer my boss, but the man was dead, entombed and burned to ash in one of Cincy's tunnels. I helped with the last part, but he got dead all on his own.

"You got a problem with that?" I asked him, and he held his hands up in surrender. Embarrassed, I punched Nick's number and put the phone to my ear. The hum of Jenks's wings was loud as he came to sit on my shoulder so he could hear.

"I don't think it's good anymore," I said, but then my bobbing foot stilled when the phone machine clicked on and an automated voice told me to leave a message. It was generic but familiar. The number was good. I finally got a beep, and I filled the silence with my attitude.

"Hello-o-o-o, Nic-*k*," I said, hitting the K hard. "You might want to consider getting a new number if you're going to be doing bad-guy stuff." Jenks flew backward off my shoulder, giving me a thumbs-up with both hands. "I saw you tonight—running away as usual. If I catch you, you will be in the I.S. lockup with a zip strip bolted to your forehead. That's a promise from me to you, you hear me, crap for brains? These are babies, not a piece of antiquated piece of history no one cares about. You are stealing someone's child, and I'm going to—"

The phone clicked. "Rachel."

The flat sound of my name cracked through me, and my eyes darted to Jenks, now standing on my plate. It was Nick all right, his tone dry and accusing. The image of his narrow face, scruffy stubble, and casual, unkempt clothes flashed through my mind, and my gut tightened. What had I ever seen in him? But behind his rough exterior was a wickedly clever mind, one that was going to get him in a hole in the ground.

"Oh," I said lightly. "So you have a pair after all, huh?"

"You left me with no recourse but to sell my soul," Nick said.

"Oh please." I stood, pacing to the other side of the kitchen with Jenks hovering by my ear. "You sold your soul all on your own. I never made you summon a demon. I asked you once, but you were summoning him already, so I'm not taking the blame for that. Besides, you don't belong to Al. Who owns you, Nickie? Is it Newt? You almost deserve her."

"There you go again," he said, his bitter laugh clear through the phone. "Jumping to the wrong conclusion. Listen to me this time. You left me with no recourse but to sell my soul. Thank you." My lips parted. "I never would have met Ku'Sox any other way."

Oh. Shit. My gut tightened even more, and Jenks dropped to the counter before me, pale and his wings unmoving. Ku'Sox was totally deranged and psychotic—along with coddled, endured, and hated by his entire race as their beloved and mentally unstable attempt to circumvent the elven curse that had made them basically barren. The lab-created demon had a tendency to eat people alive because he thought his soul was missing something. Maybe he was right. Nick stealing surviving Rosewood babies for him wasn't for the good of his species. He was up to something, something *really* bad. I had to call Algaliarept. My teacher had to know of this like yesterday.

"Son of a Disney whore," Jenks whispered.

I spun, hearing the silence of the church. "Listen to me," I said, and Nick snorted. "Ku'Sox is psychotic. He'll kill you as soon as he has everything he needs."

"Which is why I haven't told him how to make the enzyme that keeps his babies alive," Nick said, his voice distant. "God, you think I'm stupid?" He wasn't really paying attention, and that made me even angrier.

"You think you have something on him?" I exclaimed, and I heard pixy kids whisper from the hallway. "Nick, you almost deserve what's coming. Just stop. Okay? *Stop.* If you stop and go away, I won't have to hurt you. Better yet, put the babies back, and maybe I can get the rest of the demons to not kill you, too. You're not going to come out of this alive."

"You're not the only one who wants to cheat death," he said bitterly. "I'm hanging up now. Don't bother calling back. This number isn't going to work anymore."

I stared at the phone as he clicked off. "Son of a bastard," I whispered, knowing now why he'd gone to Ku'Sox. He wanted power and was hoping Ku'Sox would give it to him. "Sweet loving son of a bastard." More tired than angry, I leaned against the counter, my dress pulling tight against me. Head bowed, I set the phone down with an exaggerated softness. Nick was going to get himself killed, but not before he hurt a lot of people and broke the balance of power that kept Inderland and humans from open conflict. Ku'Sox was halfway to making his own army of day-walking demons— unless I did something about it.

My dinner sat on the table across the kitchen, the two bites out of it looking odd and disconnected—coffee and a sandwich when I'd been expecting to end my day with grilled salmon and tiramisu. "Where's my scrying mirror?" I said softly, and Jenks lit into motion, darting to the open shelving under the counter.

Lungs full of stale air, I leaned to get it. My dress tightened again, and with a smooth motion, I pulled the scrying mirror from between the demon textbooks and my favorite cookie book. Holding it tight to my chest, I sat back down in my chair and rested it on my knees. It was wrong side up, the flat silver back dull and mundane. "I'm calling Al," I said, though that was obvious. "He needs to know what's going on."

The red-wine-tinted glass sent sparkles through my fingertips and the tops of my legs as I arranged it right side up, the silver-edged etchings that I'd put in it catching the light and gleaming. The round, plate-size glass holding the demon curse had been scribed with the figures to make it into sort of an interdimensional cell phone. It was really beautiful, and the fact that I had made it was a source of guilty pride.

"Keep your kids out in case he comes over," I warned Jenks, but he had already chased them back into the garden, and I set my right hand in the center glyph. Tapping a line, I felt my mind expand as my awareness was dumped into the demon collective. I could still see the kitchen, hear the pixies playing outside, but I could also hear the faint whispers of a handful of conversations—demons in their chat room, I guess. It was uncomfortable, but it would ease if I could get Al to pick up.

Rachel calling Al, come in, Al, I thought sourly. It wasn't even midnight yet. He should still be up. Most demons kept to a witch's sleep schedule, and they did sleep. Al had given me his bedroom after examining the closet-size room I'd purchased from another demon. His old room had safeguards built into the walls, and he didn't trust I could take care of myself—yet.

Yo! Are you there, Your Immenseness? Come in, Al. I need to talk to you!

Jenks's wings were humming, and my move to look up at him was cut short when Al's thoughts slid into my mind, somehow maintaining the slightly dry, lordly tone of a British aristocrat that his verbal speech invariably had. *What do you want? We're busy.*

"We?" I said aloud, knowing that my verbal speech would carry through the mirror, reflected perfectly in my thoughts. Jenks wouldn't be able to hear Al's responses, but it was polite to include him as much as I could.

Ah, me, Al amended, his embarrassment making it through the attempted barrier that he tried unsuccessfully to erect between us. *What do you want? I'm busy. If it's about canceling your next lesson, forget it. Wednesday midnight, or I'll find you.*

I hesitated, getting the faintest impression of books and candles, but his thoughts weren't tinged with thoughts of the library. He was in his closet of a room, etching the walls with curses to make a new safe room. Paranoid, are we? "Ah, we might have a problem," I said, meeting Jenks's eyes and seeing his encouragement. "It's Nick."

How many nasty little men do you need, love? Isn't Trenton enough? Al thought, clearly distracted. *You can't have him. Ku'Sox would put too high a price just because it's you. Cut him loose. He's toad shit.*

My jaw dropped. Hovering across from me, Jenks's wings dropped in pitch as he reflected my shock, not knowing why. "You know Ku'Sox has Nick?" I said, warming. "And you don't care? You didn't tell me?"

Of course I know. And no, I don't care. His thought was distant, as if I was only getting half his attention, and I wondered what he was doing. *Why do you? If all you're after is abuse, I can give it to you far more deliciously than a human.*

I frowned at the wave of titillation he'd put in his words. "Do you have any idea what he's capable of?"

Ku'Sox?

"No, Nick!" I pressed my fingers more firmly into the glass. He was losing interest.

Oh, for the two worlds colliding, Al thought, clearly bothered. *Can this wait?*

"No!" I said, and Jenks crossed his arms over his chest to mirror my distress. "How did Ku'Sox get Nick? The two of them couldn't have met before."

That I knew for a fact. The timing was off. I waited, shoving needlelike thoughts of impatience at Al's mind, threatening him until he found out for me. Sure enough, he made a huge mental sigh, thinking, *Hold on a sec.*

I took a breath to complain, but he was gone. I shuddered—it felt as if I suddenly lost half my mind when the thousand half-realized musings that go on in the back of our awareness abruptly vanished. I hadn't lost my mind, of course, but Al and I had been sharing mental space by way of the scrying mirror, and I felt the loss of his background noise when he left.

"He's checking," I said, then jumped as my focus blurred briefly as Al came drifting back into my head.

Ah. Here it is, the demon muttered, and I pressed my fingers against the scrying mirror to improve the connection. *Ku'Sox won him in a bet. One concerning you, actually.*

I put my free hand to my forehead and massaged it. Jenks landed on the table beside me, his tiny features drawn up in concern. It was as I'd feared. Ku'Sox on his own was bad enough, but add in a thieving, magic-using human who didn't mind getting dirty, and we were in trouble. *Won him, eh?* I thought derisively. *This omnipotent crap you guys think of yourself is going to get you all killed. Nick is devious. Ku'Sox is worse. Together, they're really bad.*

Al's spark of amusement darted through me, alien and at odds with myself. *He belongs to Ku'Sox. That should be some consolation. Abject humiliation . . . blah, blah, blah.* He somehow gave the impression of leafing through papers. *It's all perfectly legal.*

"I doubt abject humiliation is what's going on. Nick is over here in reality," I said, and Jenks smirked. Frowning, I turned back to the mirror, seeing a very faint reflection of him in its reddish depths. I thought it interesting that the pixy showed up better than me. "Did you know Nick is stealing Rosewood babies?" I said shortly, and Jenks's dust pooling on the mirror shifted to a sick-looking blue. "Thriving Rosewood babies? Nick knows the enzyme to keep them alive. Stole it from Trent. He's injecting it into them, prolonging their lives, then stealing them. Eight so far."

Al's amusement only ticked me off. *Ah. You think Ku'Sox is making little yous? I don't blame him, seeing as you don't like him. Long-term planning. Good for him. It will keep the freak busy for a few decades. First thing the brat has done right since he got out of a test tube. I'm proud.*

Al's thoughts were going distant, and I pressed my hand harder into the glass until it ached with the thrum of energy running through it. "He's not doing this for the greater demon good," I said sharply. "In ten years, he's going to have a bunch of preadolescent, very powerful day-walking demons who look to him for everything right down to their continued existence. Nick knows the enzyme, not the cure. The moment they don't get the enzyme, they die. You think that little fact is going to escape Ku'Sox?"

Breath held, I felt Al consider that. A hint of worry colored his usual confidence. If he were actually next to me, I probably wouldn't have been able to detect it, but here, with our consciousness twined together, it was harder to hide. And just as I knew he was concerned, he knew I was deadly serious. *Mmmm,* he finally thought. *Is that coffee I smell in your thoughts?* With an abruptness that told me he was taking me seriously, he snapped our connection.

I sucked in my breath and jerked my head up, shocked. "Damn," I whispered, curling my shaking fingers under into a fist. The lingering energy swirled, hurting until it was reabsorbed. "I hate it when he leaves that fast. He's coming over." Fingers aching, I slid the mirror onto the table and stood, rubbing my hands together to try to rid myself of the lingering prickles of magic. "Scrying mirrors are like party lines. This is a good thing." *I think.* "You staying?"

Jenks casually cleaned his sword on a torn corner of napkin and nodded.

I smiled, carefully setting my scrying mirror beside my cooling coffee. "Thanks. He's easier to deal with when he thinks people trust him."

"Trust?" The pixy held the blade up to the light and squinted at its shine. "I trust him all right. Trust him to get away with whatever he can."

As if on cue, there was the barest tug on my awareness as Al gently misted into existence without even the hint of a shift in the air. Appearing in the threshold, he sniffed, his eyes going to the steaming pot of coffee. The demon was taller than me, his overdone buckled boots giving him an advantage. He was wearing his usual crushed green velvet frock coat with the lace at his throat and cuffs, having gone on to add a matching top hat, a scarf to protect against the night's mist, a cane he didn't need, and his usual round blue-tinted glasses. They did little to hide his red goat-slitted eyes, and I knew he didn't need them to see with. Al was all about show, and he liked the image of a bygone British nobleman.

"Rache-e-el," he drawled, eyeing me over his glasses as he loosened his scarf and came in, boots grinding leftover circle-salt into the linoleum. "Sweats at your trial, gowns in your kitchen. You simply *must* learn how to dress yourself properly. Or did you go all out for me?" His expression souring, he gave Jenks a disparaging glance.

Jenks wrinkled his nose in disgust at the rank smell of burnt amber now permeating the air. "Sweet ever-loving Tink," he said, rising up and holding his nose dramatically. "Haven't you learned how to take a shower yet? You smell like a burning tire."

"Stop it," I said, knowing Al couldn't help it. The ever-after stank like burnt amber, and it rubbed off on you. I still noticed it, but it didn't seem to have the same impact anymore, which bothered me for some reason.

"I didn't get dressed up for you," I said, hoping the pixies stayed out. "I haven't had time to change from my, ah, date is all."

Al pulled his bared-teeth smile from Jenks, mellowing as he turned to me. "Is that so?"

Wanting to improve his mood, I went to get him a coffee. Al propped his cane in the corner and sat in Ivy's chair by the door, knowing it was the throne of the room. Settling himself with a pompous air, he shook out his sleeves and took a deep breath to speak.

I spun when six pixies came burst in, shouting about something or other. Jenks rose up, but as soon as they saw Al, they flew out screaming. Jenks shrugged, and Al grinned to show me his flat, blocky teeth. "You *do* have an interesting life," he said, fluffing the lace at his cuffs. "Now, about Nicholas Gregory Sparagmos. Stealing Rosewood babies? How sure are you that he's not collaborating with Trent?"

Shocked, I almost sloshed his cup over. "Pretty sure. Trent seemed as angry as I was when we met at the crime scene."

"You wore *that* to a crime scene? No wonder they don't take you seriously." Al rolled his eyes dramatically, and frowning, I extended his coffee to him. His eyebrows rose at the rainbow mug, and in a huff, I sat down beside my uneaten sandwich and pushed it away. He was eyeing the cold cuts still out, and I gestured for him to help himself. Coffee I'd get him, but if he wanted a sandwich, he was going to have to make it himself.

Pinkie extended, he sipped from his rainbow mug, his eyes closing in what had to be bliss. "Oh, this is marvelous! Rachel, you have made a capital cup."

"Al, about Nick," I said impatiently, and Al set his coffee aside, rubbing his hands in anticipation as he went to the center counter. "Trent wouldn't help him. He doesn't want to see more Rosewood babies turning into demons any more than I do."

Standing behind the counter, Al shook water off the lettuce, looking odd in his silk and velvet. "Trent has been known to work with Nicholas Gregory Sparagmos before," he said, using his full name to denote his familiar status. "The tricky elf freed Ku'Sox from the prison we put him in. He allowed Nicholas Gregory Sparagmos to escape from his lockdown." Al put a gloved finger to his nose. "Sounds suspicious."

I frowned, chin lifted as I refused to let his doubt poison me. "Trent didn't let Nick go. He was abducted by a demon, probably one that Nick called for that very reason, and probably the same one Ku'Sox got him from."

"You sound proud of the little man," Al drawled, and my lips parted when, with a tug on my awareness and a cascading sheet of ever-after, the vision of a British nobleman vanished, replaced with a heart-stoppingly familiar vision of Nick.

"Son of a Disney whore," Jenks whispered, but I'd gone cold, seeing Nick with his thin build, shaggy mop of dark hair, and sparse stubble. Al even had the faded jeans, tatty sneakers, black T-shirt with the lumberjack-style shirt open and hanging loosely over his narrow shoulders. A chill went through me as he layered cold cuts on white bread, looking like Nick until he blew me a kiss and winked at me with his goat-slitted eyes with a confidence only Al could command.

"That's not funny," I said.

"Ahh, you do hate him." His voice was his own, and I shivered as Al put a last slice of bread atop his pile. Seeing me turn away, he sent a second shiver of ever-after over himself and was back to his usual appearance. "Good for you, Rachel," he said as he brought his sandwich to the table. "Hate is all that keeps us alive when love is gone. You're almost there. Not quite ready to let it go yet." Sitting, he took a large bite. "God slay me, this is good."

Shaken from the reminder of Nick, I crossed my knees. "So you believe we've got a problem?"

He bobbed his head, not letting go of his sandwich to take a sip of his coffee. "We might," he said, downing half of it in one go. "But you understand I *simply cannot* go to Dali with your scary bedtime story of killer demon babies."

Jenks's wings clattered in disgust. I, too, wasn't happy, my foot starting to bob.

"Ku'Sox hasn't done anything against the law. That is, *our* law," Al said, one hand holding his sandwich, the other his coffee. "Especially if these children are potentially demons. It's the first time he's ever shown a hint of an interest in seeing our species regain its health and should be applauded. As for Nick? He's just a human. Mostly harmless."

Outraged, I stood. "Al, you are underestimating the danger here. Yes, Nick is *just a human,* but he's not afraid to do things that might kill him if he thinks the risk is good. You can't fight something like that. Will you just listen to me? How come no one listens to me! Is it the dress?" I snapped, my anger misplaced but real. "Maybe the curves? If I shaved my head and dressed like Newt, would you take me seriously then?"

The demon's chewing paused as he sent his eyes over my shape, silent as he took a sip of coffee. "Now, now, no need to go to extremes," he said softly. "Where is the proof that he's planning mischief, itchy witch?"

My shoulders slumped. If he was calling me itchy witch, he believed me, believed the danger, and that was all I wanted. "I talked to him. He as much as admitted so."

Red goat-slitted eyes showing over his glasses, Al made a bland face. "You talked to Ku'Sox?"

I blinked. "God, no. Nick."

"Ahh." Clearly relieved, he took a bite of sandwich. "Then you have nothing," he mumbled around his full mouth.

Frustrated, I slumped back into my chair, my elbow just missing my scrying mirror. Jenks's dust sifting down seemed to fall through the glass, but I was too frustrated to care.

"Oh, very well," Al grumped with bad grace. "I suppose you'll be bad-tempered until I talk to Dali. I'll do it in the morning—he's crankier than you if he doesn't get his beauty sleep."

My head came up, and I smiled, glad I had him to go to. Then I wondered how I'd gotten to the point where going to a demon was a good thing. "Thanks," I said, meaning it.

Al stood, coffee in one hand, half-eaten sandwich in the other. "Indeed," he said, then vanished in a wash of ever-after. His cane in the corner went with him, and then my eyes darted to the counter when the coffeepot popped out.

"Hey!" I shouted, but it was too late. My fingers drummed once in discontent, but I could sympathize. You couldn't get a cup of decent coffee in the ever-after for any amount of money. I'd pick the coffeepot up Wednesday, but experience told me that a rank burnt-amber smell would taint the coffee for weeks.

"What an ass," Jenks scoffed. "He took our coffeemaker!"

Shrugging, I went to open the window. "I'll get a new one tomorrow on the way out to Trent's." The slider moved up with its accustomed ease, and

I stood a moment, listening to the pixies playing in the night as the stink of demons filtered out. My thoughts went to Nick, and my heart hardened. He had lied to me, misled me, and betrayed me time and again. I'd warned him, and I wouldn't feel guilty for whatever happened.

"You going to call Ivy?" Jenks asked, and I turned, my arms around my middle as I looked at her empty chair and her shut-down computer. Anything left open was going to smell like ever-after, and I bent to get the trash can out from under the sink. My first impulse was yes, seeing as she would like a piece of Nick's ass in a glass as much as me, but she'd tell Glenn, and Glenn didn't work for the FIB anymore. He had retired after finding out that HAPA had infiltrated the FIB, refusing to work for a company he couldn't trust implicitly and moving to Flagstaff with Daryl in the hopes that the higher elevation and cleaner air would help the nymph. Calling Ivy would only get them all in a turmoil.

Pinning the trash bin against the center counter, I ran my arm over the counter, throwing away the food that was open. "No," I said, and I met Jenks's eyes when he clattered his wings in disapproval. "It's the first time she's ever done anything healthy in her relationships," I said, not sure it was the right thing to do. "I'm not going to screw it up. She'll be back in a week."

Jenks's dust shifted from an uneasy green to a more neutral silver. "Yeah, maybe you're right," he said as he flew to sit on the windowsill to watch his kids.

But it didn't feel right.

Chapter Four

If I were to die and come back as a horse, I'd want to be a horse in Trent's stables. The stalls were large, the hay sweet smelling, and the layout set to funnel the wind from the pasture right through it all to create the sensation of an open pavilion. Tucking a strand of hair back under my hat, I gave Molly a pat, running my hand down her side to feel the swallow of air she'd taken in to inflate herself so the saddle wouldn't be so binding. I'd have to walk her until she released it before I tightened the cinch a final time.

"Molly, you're a sweet horse, but predictable," I said as I turned her around in the expansive box stall and walked her into the corridor. Around me were contented snuffs, grindings, and flicking of ears and tails. We weren't in the wing where Trent kept his racehorses. No, these were the animals he kept for the Hunt, and they were far more intelligent and level-headed.

My boots were silent on the sawdust as I headed for the north paddock. In the background was Ceri's high, serious voice going over our route with the stable manager. As soon as Jenks got back with Trent and Ray, we'd be taking the river path where we could stay in the shelter of the old-growth forest.

The late-morning sun was high and it was unusually hot outside, but the upper housing units caught most of the rays to leave the open stables cool. I couldn't help but be reminded of camp—though I didn't recall a lot of it, I did remember the stables. My endurance had been nil then, and the horses had made me feel strong. Though seemingly sure of himself, Trent had been anything but—until I told him to stop letting Lee bully him and stand up for himself. They found Lee in the camp well three days later. Maybe Trent listened to me more than I thought.

My faint caffeine headache was finally easing, and I grabbed my to-go cup for the last swallows. It had gone cold, and tossing the empty cup in the trash barrel, I came out blinking into the sun, Molly clopping behind me. Seeing Quen already there with Lucy waiting for us, I smiled.

Quen was standing sideways with Lucy on his hip, making a striking statement in his black-and-green riding clothes. A big gray horse hung his huge head over Quen's shoulder, snuffing at Lucy's bonnet. The little girl was sweet in her white riding outfit, the picture of privilege as her chubby hands reached up to the unfamiliar brim. Her expression was pinched in annoyance as she tried to pull it off so as to see it. The little girl had Trent's looks and Ellasbeth's attitude, and when the curious horse blew out his breath, the little girl squealed, reaching for his floppy lips.

"You need your hat today, Lucy," Quen said, moving before Lucy could get a grip on the horse. "We don't want to have to ask Aunt Rachel to spell your sunburn away."

Aunt Rachel. I liked that, and squinting despite my hat, I ambled forward with Molly. "I would, you know," I said, touching Lucy's soft-soled shoe and beaming at the little girl now shouting out nonsense, just to hear herself talk. "Even if it took a curse to do it." My gaze lifted to Quen's. "Shouldn't they be back by now?"

Quen peered at the height of the sun. "Give or take a few. Here," he said, holding Lucy out to me. "Your cinch is loose."

"I know," I said, then dropped Molly's reins as I found myself suddenly holding a squishy, surprisingly heavy small person. She smelled like snickerdoodles, and I laughed when she wiggled, almost jumping in my arms. "I was going to walk her to get her to exhale first," I said, scrambling to get my hat's strap out of Lucy's mouth.

"She let go already." Head lowered, Quen eased the cinch up a notch.

Molly flicked an ear, sighing. He gave her a pat and reached for Lucy, now patting my neck where my tattoo was. Realizing she was trying to say flower, I grinned. She was only a year old, but elves grew up fast. Not like witches, who Jenks swore were not able to be on their own until they were thirty. Ahem.

"They're just over the hill," Quen said as he took her back, his smile making his few wrinkles fold in and hide his pox scars. "Evaluating the three-year-olds practicing the gate."

"Oh." I didn't really know exactly what he meant, but I could guess.

"He's quite good at reading them," Quen was saying as I gazed over the nearby hill. "He's like his father there." Quen turned to the hill expectantly at the soft rumble of hooves. "Kal was extraordinary on a horse. He had a knack for knowing what it was thinking and countering it with just the right amount of force."

I looked up from playing peekaboo with Lucy, and Quen seemed to straighten. "That's him now," he said softly, then turned to the stables. "Ceri? He's back!"

My eyebrows rose at the informal hail, but being around horses tended to do that to a person. Big horses with jockeys looking like children on their backs were coming over the hill in pairs, high-stepping and sending up puffs of dust from the soft path. I didn't see Trent yet, but clearly practice was done.

The clop of hooves turned me around. Ceri was beaming as she looked up from adjusting her boot, the sun glowing in her hair caught back in a veil/hat kind of thing. She was utterly beautiful in her proper English riding outfit, sitting atop her horse with a happy air about her. Green eyes squinting, she was both breathless in anticipation and relaxed in the saddle. The voices of the jockeys became louder, and her mount backed up, nervous as the adjacent paddock filled with an aggressive energy.

"Do you have Lucy, love?" she asked Quen as she calmed her horse, and the older, pox-scarred man looked down at the little girl. His own mount didn't care about the spirited stallions and feisty mares, calmly twitching an ear at them.

"Down," Lucy whined, twisting until she could reach her hat. "Down. Down!"

"I'll take her," Ceri demanded, but Quen only smiled a private smile and handed her to me instead. It was then that Jenks showed up, and I almost dropped the little girl when Lucy squealed, reaching for the little funny man with wings who managed to stay just out of her reach.

"Jeez, Jenks!" I exclaimed, scrambling for a hold as the little girl wiggled. "If she ever gets a hold on you, I'm going to sell tickets. Back up, will you?"

"Awww, she won't hurt me," he said, but he hovered unmoving until I could hand the slightly squishy Lucy up to her mom. Or Ceri. Or whatever. Technically speaking, Lucy and Ray didn't share a drop of common blood, and the only thing that linked them were their perfect, uncropped, and somewhat pointy ears. But still.

Ceri was cooing over Lucy, adjusting her bonnet as I checked the cinch again and swung myself up. Immediately I felt taller as Molly took three steps to the gate before I pulled her back. Last-minute details were being sorted out as Ceri settled Lucy before her and talked to the stable manager—diaper bag, water, sunscreen, phones checked for a proper charge—but it was Trent my attention was on.

He had come in last with Ray sitting in front of him, and he was accompanied by a heavy, small man on a sedate quarter horse. Quite simply, Trent looked amazing on Tulpa, the same horse I remembered from camp. The tall black would be ancient by now, but being Trent's familiar had extended his life span, sort of a capacitor for high-voltage magic as well as allowing Trent to reach a ley line when surrounded by water.

His back to me, Trent discussed something with his manager. Seeing him there, Ray sitting before him, the picture of wealth and privilege, I felt something catch in me. It wasn't just that he looked good but that he was comfortable, at peace without the mask of perfection that he felt he needed everywhere else.

Molly flicked an ear at Jenks, and the pixy landed right between them. "Yeah, the elf looks good on a horse," he said dryly. "But he's mean to them."

My gaze jerked from Trent to Jenks. "Mean?"

Jenks nodded, using his heel to scratch Molly between her ears. "Mind games. Remind me not to piss him off. He's good at them. Little cookie maker."

I took a breath to ask him to explain, but he darted off to Lucy. The little girl was calling to him, shrieking at the top of her lungs for "Inks! Inks!" Ceri was looking harried, and I wondered how long it would be until she gave her back to Quen.

"Mind games?" I breathed, and Trent looked up as if hearing me across the distance.

His eyes met mine briefly in acknowledgment, then went back to the manager. "No, I want her across from Managed Detail, not out of his sight," he was saying, gesturing to a stable hand. "Where he goes, she goes three steps behind. We made progress, but it will mean nothing if she thinks the rules apply only on the track."

The stable hand lugged a bucket of water out, and Tulpa nosed him before dropping his head and sucking it in.

"I want Red right across from Managed Detail in a box stall," Trent said, his eyes again flicking to me. "He is to be lavished with attention for at least an hour starting now, and then special treats on the hour until sunset. I want her so frustrated and jealous that she does exactly what Ben tells her next time."

Mind games . . .

"Yes, sir," the manager said, squinting up at him, and we all looked at a fiery-tempered horse only now coming into the paddock. She was high stepping and beautiful, her jockey needing every ounce of his attention to keep her in bounds. Frustrated? I'd say she was that already. It was obvious to me she was pissed she'd been held back when everyone else got to go back to the stables.

The wailing of an ambulance drew my attention to the nearby service road, and everything became more serious. Seeing it, the manager sighed. "She's not a bad horse, sir."

"She's magnificent." Trent frowned as Red squealed and snapped at the horse next to her. "But if she doesn't learn that playing with others is more fun than playing alone, we will be the only two to know it."

"Trenton . . ." Ceri cajoled, a hand to her eyes. "The sun is getting hot, and the girls will be napping before we get to the woods."

Trent raised his hand acknowledging her, then turned back to his manager. "We're done with practice. Tomorrow take her and Managed

Detail on a ride and let them go. He has more endurance and can bring her to exhaustion. She'll gate next time." Pulling Tulpa together, he angled to the gate between the two paddocks. A stable hand ran to open it. Turning, Trent looked over his shoulder. "Treats every hour!" he reminded him. "Don't forget. And I want a call as soon as you know how Ben's collarbone is."

The manager jotted a note on his clipboard. "Yes, sir."

"And keep her away from everyone else. I want Managed Detail her best frenemy."

The older man smiled. "Yes, sir. Enjoy your ride."

Molly barely moved an ear as Trent rode up, but my heart gave a thump. Blinking, I looked away, pretending to fix my boot but taking sideways glances at him. Damn, he looked good, his trim physique—usually only hinted at underneath a suit—defined and definite in the jeans and button shirt he had on. I think normally he would be in full English garb but he had dressed down either for gate practice or me. I didn't mind. I rather liked seeing that wisp of chest hair and his muscles moving behind his shirtsleeves. Ray looked sweet beyond description in her sturdy pale green riding dress complete with white leggings, soft boots, and matching hat, happily playing with the bells woven into Tulpa's mane. Seeing her there only layered "paternal" over everything and hit just about every button I had. No. Working for Trent would be a mistake. *A big mistake.*

"Ready?" he said, the sun and wind in his hair, and Jenks snorted, rising up from Lucy and making the little girl whine.

"Rather," Ceri said as she nudged her horse into motion toward the far gate. A hand waited to open it for us. "Red is not suited for the track, dear. Why do you insist on tormenting that animal?"

Waiting for Quen to go first, Trent smiled. "You have to admit my methods have good results."

"Yes, but why?" Ceri insisted, her hand gentle on the reins as she angled her horse closer to me. "Let Red be who she is. She's better tempered to the Hunt and will make a magnificent courser."

Trent turned in the saddle to look behind him at the stables. "That mare is going to break women's hearts and men's fortunes, Ceri. I want the world to know her name. She will never be forgotten."

Confused, I turned to Quen. "Red?"

The man brought his eyes back from the edge of the woods where he'd been scanning, always on alert. "Her papered name is Kalamack's Sunrise Surprise. But we call her Red."

Really. I looked at Trent, his horse predictably out front. "Because of her color? That's original."

Quen leaned closer with a creak of leather. "No, her attitude. Red zone? Danger? We'd put a red collar on her if everyone didn't know to look out for her already. She bit Trent three hours after she was foaled."

Passing through the gate to open field, Trent looked at his hand ruefully, clearly having heard us. "Oh," I said softly, and Jenks snickered, coming to a landing on my saddle horn. Dropping down, he sat cross-legged, his wings glinting and his head drooping in the hot sun.

With a soft clicking, Ceri encouraged her horse to come even with Trent's and we went two by two. We were almost to the woods, and I was eager for the shade. "There's nothing wrong with anonymity if one is the best at their art," Ceri insisted. "The horse is a born hunter. Let her be."

They rode side by side, the girls they shared between them reaching out to touch each other. "If she doesn't gate tomorrow, I will let her be," Trent said, reaching across the space to kiss the top of Ceri's hand in a formal acquiescence.

Seeing them there, I glanced at Quen. His eyes were tired, but the only other emotion I saw was a fond pleasure that both Ceri and Trent were happy in their familiar but platonic relationship. He was secure in his love for Ceri, and it was obvious that though Ceri liked Trent, her heart belonged to the older man. Somehow it all worked. But even though the girls and their past bound them all together, I was dogged by the feeling that though Trent was a part of this, he would forever be somewhat . . . sidelined. His future demanded so much of him that love was a luxury his fortune couldn't buy.

And it bothered me, because I thought he not only knew it but accepted it as normal.

Smiling with the surety of the devil, Ceri drew her hand from Trent. "I would have a private world with Rachel, Trenton."

Jenks opened an eye, and I felt a sliver of concern at her soft confidence. *Private word? About what? What had I done now?*

"Just girl talk," she added, but her tone concerned me. She had something on her mind.

"Of course." Trent nudged Tulpa into a faster pace as Ceri drew her mount in.

I glanced at Quen, worried when his brow pinched. Refusing to look at me, he nudged his horse ahead. Jenks flew up, saying, "You're on your own," before he darted off to join the elves.

"I haven't done anything," I muttered, grimacing at his chiming laughter floating back.

Sighing, I looked over at Ceri, seeing the faint blush of anger on her as we slipped under the welcoming shade of the woods. The path was steep, and we said nothing as the horses scrambled up. Lucy was still in Ceri's lap, and the little girl was struggling to stay awake. Ahead of us, Trent and Quen rode with soft masculine murmurs drifting between them. Maybe her flush had only been from the sun.

"Lucy looks sweet today," I said, and her grip on the reins tightened. *Nope. Guess not.*

"Quen told me you refused to help keep Trenton safe," she said, coming right out with it.

My breath caught, and then I exhaled. Yeah, I probably owed her an explanation. "Trent doesn't need me to babysit him," I said, voice low. "And I won't insult him by doing so."

Her eyes widened. "Insult him? Rachel, we are teetering on the brink of extinction and you're worried that extra security will *insult* him?"

Lucy shouted, her voice echoing against the underside of the canopy as she mirrored Ceri's outburst. Wincing, I begged her with my eyes to lower her voice.

"His actions impact our entire species," Ceri said.

"Yes, but—"

"They're all looking to him now. Reclaiming Lucy solidified his standing. If he dies, it will be the Withons who chart the next fifty years, and they'd have us hiding in closets and cropping our ears again!"

I couldn't even catch her eye. I think Quen was laughing, the bastard.

"We can't survive another five decades hiding. We must come out, and Trenton needs protection. You think the vampires are happy about this?"

"No," I managed to get in.

"You think anyone is? You are a demon!" she shouted, and I flinched, looking up the path where Trent and Quen plodded along. Jenks rose up amid a sparking of gold dust and darted off at surveillance height, but thankfully no one turned around. "You are a day-walking demon, and as such you are the best person possible, save Quen, for keeping him alive! We all have our tasks, and what we want needs to be set aside to meet them. Why are you being so selfish?"

Selfish? I grimaced when Trent glanced back to make sure we were okay. I knew her anger was a mix of worry for Trent and her ironclad upbringing that personal desire was a distant second to political need, but seeing her spouting off when she had her happy ending, and Trent was being asked to sacrifice what he wanted for everyone else, rankled. "You just got done telling Trent to let Red be who she is," I said, allowing a hint of my own anger to show. "And now you're saying everyone should be what some big plan dictates?"

She was flushed, but I knew she enjoyed our shouting matches since I was the only one who would yell back at her. And if I was honest, I'd admit I enjoyed them, too. "Red is a horse, Rachel," she said pointedly. "Trent is poised to lead an entire society. He has healthy children, political and monetary advantage. Everyone from the vampires to the humans would like to see the elves die out. He needs protection. I don't care if he's insulted. A martyr won't save our species."

"I understand that," I said, knowing she wasn't angry at me, but that outside forces were threatening the one spot of peace in her long, heartbreaking life.

"Then why won't you do it?" she asked, her horse prancing because of her tension.

"I don't know what I want, Ceri!"

Ceri hesitated, and then her eyes widened. Sitting atop my horse, I went hot. *I don't know what I want?* Had I really just shouted that?

"What you want . . ." Ceri echoed, the clops of the horses silent beneath us. "By the Goddess, you *like* him! Mother pus bucket, when did *that* happen!"

Hearing Al's cuss phrase come out of her was a shock, and flustered, I scrambled for something to say. "Uh . . ." I hedged, praying that neither Quen nor Trent turned around. "I think somewhere between him slugging Eloy and pie. But it doesn't change anything."

"It changes everything," she said, her upright stance returning as she thought the possibilities over. All for the state, yes, but she was a romantic at heart, and I could see where she was going. Damn it, she was thinking again. I had to stop this, and stop it now.

"Ceri, look at me," I pleaded. "I've had four relationships in two years. One was a thief, one died as a political gift, one walked away because I was shunned, and the last is a slave in the ever-after. I know you think this is perfect, but I come with a lot of baggage, and it would be a mistake to work for him." I looked up, seeing the concern on her face as deep as her excitement had been. "He'd end up dead because of me, and you know it."

A wisp of pity showed in her eyes as she set Lucy's bonnet straight. "Maybe you're right."

It was what I wanted to hear, but it kind of hurt.

"It's simply that Trent is so important," she said, voice wistful as she stared into space. "I know he feels he can ward off any attack, but he needs to set his pride aside. He's more than he ever was, more than just himself."

There was a lump in my throat, and I wasn't sure why. Yes, Trent had always been more than just himself. But that wasn't what he wanted to be. I knew how that felt.

The flash of Jenks's dust over Quen and Trent caught my attention, and I wasn't surprised when both of them pulled their mounts up short. Concern pushed out everything else when Quen's horse nickered, feeling the tension of his rider. Trent was gazing into the canopy, and both Ceri and I urged our horses into a faster pace to catch up.

"There's something in the woods," the pixy said as we joined them, and a chill dropped down my spine. "The birds are agitated, and the small mammals are hiding."

Ceri held Lucy closer. "Quen?" she questioned, and he shook his head, clearly at a loss as he scanned the trees. I shivered, and the sun-dappled shadows became fraught with doubt. Reaching out, I tapped a line, filling my chi and then spindling enough energy in my head to make a circle around all of us.

"It's probably just Nick," I said, but Molly had felt my tension and was now stomping.

Immediately Ceri seemed to lose her concern. "The slimy little worm," she said sourly. "Quen, call security to dispatch him immediately. The thought of him here makes me ill."

"Ah . . . I talked to Al last night about Nick," I started.

Trent bobbed his head as if not surprised, but Quen turned in the saddle to face me straight on, an accusing look in his eyes. "And?"

"See, I was going to tell you all at once," I said, fidgeting with Molly's reins. Jenks had darted away, and both girls were wiggling to find him. "Ku'Sox owns him. Won him in a bet."

Tulpa pranced in place, giving away Trent's tension. "I wondered," he said softly, eyes on the canopy. "Nick gained the labs once. He could do it again. I know for a fact it isn't HAPA. *Damn.* He's making demons."

I didn't often hear Trent swear, and I nodded uneasily. "That's what I think, too," I said quietly. "In twenty years Ku'Sox will have at least eight day-walking demons who look to him for their very survival."

Quen glanced at Trent, and Trent nodded. "It's up to twelve now," Trent said, and Quen took Ray from him, the little girl settling in before her birth father with a serious air about her. "This is what I was afraid of. Ceri, I'm sorry but we are cutting our ride short."

"Trenton," she protested.

"You and Quen head back to the stables with the girls. If Nick is here, Rachel and I will draw him out. I'm the one he's after. I'm the only one who can make the cure permanent."

Ceri began turning her horse around, but Quen was unmoving, his horse blocking the path ahead of us. "It's not your place to draw out danger, Sa'han."

I, too, wasn't keen on this plan, but for another reason. "Ah, I don't think the cure is what Ku'Sox wants."

Trent pulled Tulpa up short, the black snorting at the rough motion. "If Ku'Sox didn't want the cure, Nick wouldn't be in the woods," he said, words clipped. "And yes, it's my place to draw out danger, just as it's Rachel's expertise to crush it." He looked at me. "We will continue on."

Oh, I was all for crushing danger, but this was moving too fast. Maybe

I'd picked up more of Ivy's cautious planning than I'd thought. "Jenks!" I shouted, and got a wing chirp back.

"Quen, it's only Nick," Ceri said, clearly wanting to get the girls out of the woods and possible danger.

But still Quen stood there. "This is an ill-conceived plan. We don't know if it's Nick. What if it's someone else?"

The corner of Trent's eye twitched, and he looked irate as Tulpa trotted in place under him. "You don't trust Rachel's skills?" he said, and I winced. "You went behind my back to buy them, Quen." Clearly angry, he added in a softer voice, "I can't risk any of you. Go. Let me do my job. Rachel?"

Easing up on his hold on Tulpa, he let the horse bolt. Quen jerked his horse back from following, his expression as angry and dark as I'd ever seen it. Before him, Ray was silent, but Lucy was wailing her distress. Shrugging, I gave Molly a nudge.

I glanced behind us to see Quen turning his horse back to the stables, Ceri sitting tall in her saddle with Lucy, waiting for her love to join her. I agreed with Trent. They had a perfect life, a perfect love when they'd both resigned themselves to having neither. It needed to be protected.

Trent was silent when I joined him, and we continued on. My shoulders were tense, and I listened to the wind in the tops of the trees, their new leaves pale green and rustling. Jenks was up there somewhere. He had my back. The silence stretched, and I glanced at Trent. His jaw was tight, and the sun caught his hair in a come-and-go fashion. Something other than Nick was on his mind, his fierce determination reminding me of his satisfaction when he turned that HAPA member into a deformed, twisted mockery of a demon. *Here, Nicky, Nicky, Nicky . . .*

Tulpa was a larger horse, and he was stepping out farther than Molly could comfortably walk. Trent was too distracted to notice. Jenks dropped down, and Trent absently corrected the uptight stallion when he shied. Used to it, Molly contented herself with flicking an ear.

"Something is in the woods, huh?" I said as Jenks landed on the saddle pommel. "Do you know how creepy that is?"

His sword was loosened in its scabbard, but he hadn't pulled it. "I don't know how else to say it, Rache. I'm going to do a Z axis until I see Quen and

Ceri make it out of the woods. There's nothing ahead of you for another quarter mile."

Trent shook himself out of his funk. "You couldn't have scouted a quarter mile that fast."

"That's right," Jenks said, grinning. "You just keep thinking that." He turned to me as he took wing. "I'll stay within earshot. Something isn't right."

"Thanks, Jenks." He zipped straight up to rise high enough to see when Quen and Ceri broke free of the trees, and I nudged Molly into a short canter to catch up with Tulpa.

Sighing, Trent drew Tulpa into a slower pace, the black horse snorting in impatience. "Thank you. I appreciate you doing this with me," he said, his low voice blending perfectly with the leaves, stirring in me like the wind in my hair.

And here I had just gotten done telling Ceri I wouldn't work with him. "You're welcome. If I hadn't, then Ceri would have refused to leave."

His profile showing his concern, he tucked a wayward lock of his hair away.

"You really should think about including a pixy clan in your security," I added.

Trent looked up into the canopy. "That's what you keep saying."

"Then maybe you should listen," I shot back. Tulpa had already resumed his faster pace, and it irritated me. "Or at least do a cost analysis or something."

Pulling Tulpa up short, Trent smiled with half his mouth. Molly stopped as well, and a sudden memory exploded in me, brought forth by the tension, the dappled sun, even the shadowed air drawing goose bumps. He had been lanky and insecure with youth, and I had been awkward and overly confident with the first hints of health, but Tulpa had been the same, and I had been irate that he'd gotten a larger horse than me and I couldn't keep up.

"What?" he asked, and I put a hand to my cold face.

"Um," I said, scrambling. "Ceri might be right."

Molly shifted under me, and Trent reached out. I froze as he tucked a stray strand of hair behind my ear, his fingers brushing the rim of my hat. "About what?"

My heart was pounding. "That you'd be good at being king of the elves."

His hand dropped, and I breathed again. Head bowing, he looked at his fingers laced among the reins. "I can be both what I need to be and what I want to be." But it was soft, and I wasn't sure he believed it.

"I tried that, and it didn't work," I said, the reins slipping through my fingers as Molly stretched to crop at the spindly grass surviving under the shade. "It didn't work for Batman, either." Trent didn't look up, and I blurted, "At least you have something worth fighting for. Trent—"

"I've been meaning to ask if you would like to choose a horse from my herd," he interrupted me. "One who would be designated as yours for when you ride with us. I still owe you a proper Hunt."

My eyebrows rose, more because of the change of subject than the offer. "We are sitting here in the middle of nowhere waiting to be attacked, and you offer me a horse?"

Tulpa sighed, making Trent shift his seat. "We can talk more about your conversation with Ceri if you like."

Oh God. No. "Sure. I'd love a horse," I said, feeling the need to give Molly a pat. "I'm not really into the Hunt, though." I remembered the sound of the hounds, the heart-stopping fear that they might catch me. *Is he nuts?*

He nudged Tulpa into motion, and Molly followed. "If you change your mind, let me know. Ceri would love another feminine presence on the field. She says we men lack style in running down prey."

I'll bet. "I might just do that," I said. "If only to get you to stop giving me Molly all the time."

Trent's smile warmed me all the way to my center. It was true and honest, and he was smiling at me. *Stop it, Rachel.* "What's wrong with Molly?"

"Nothing, but you keep giving me a horse I can't possibly win with."

His face lost all expression as he thought that over. Then his eyes narrowed. "You can't have Red. She's not in the herd you may choose from."

It sounded like a rather formal statement. The fiery horse was way out of my league, and I hadn't even been thinking about her. "Why not?" I teased. "She's sweet."

Trent stiffened, but he wasn't looking at me. Under him, Tulpa snorted, and with a sudden shock, I felt a huge drop in the nearest ley line.

Jenks pattered through the leaves, wreathed in a haze of silver sparkles. "Hey! Someone just made a huge bubble between here and the stables! It poked above the Turn-blasted trees."

I stared at Trent. "Nick can't make a bubble bigger than three feet."

"Ceri . . ." Trent whispered. "The girls . . ."

"Trent!" I exclaimed, my hand outstretched, but he'd already wheeled Tulpa around. With a word I didn't recognize, he urged him into a full gallop. In an instant, he was gone, the thudding of his hooves fading.

Molly snorted as I jerked her to follow, head tossing when I kicked her into a gallop. Hanging on low to her back and knees flexing, I pushed her down the trail.

I needed a faster horse.

Chapter Five

"C er-r-r-ri!"

Trent's voice raised in summons jerked my attention, and I yanked Molly to a halt. Just off the path was a clearing, the winding, shaded stream we'd been paralleling beyond it. The fresher wind shifted my hair, bringing the scent of burned grass and decaying vegetation—and spent magic, tingling like ozone before a lightning strike.

There were two ugly burn marks and a large circle pressed into the tall grass, and the line I was connected to seemed to hum with the reminder of an energy draw. The fast-moving stream chattered among the rocks and tree roots, and I stifled a flash of fear when I saw Trent crouched over Quen, Tulpa standing a watchful guard. It was probably the same stream that I'd stumbled through once to lose the hounds chasing me.

"Hie!" I shouted, giving Molly my heels, and she jumped forward, neck arching and hooves stepping high when her footing unexpectedly turned spongy. The low-lying area surrounded by craggy trees looked as if it flooded often; the grass that wasn't burned was tall. Three trees managed to survive the wet ground, but they were spindly and let a lot of light through, especially this early in the spring.

Jenks hovered over Quen, his dust seeming to melt into him as I came to a fast stop beside them. Ray sat in the crook of Quen's twisted body, her little hands clutching her father's jacket; she was too scared to cry. Quen was unconscious, no signs of attack but for a slight burn on his hands.

"His aura is intact," Jenks said as he darted to me, "but it's doing something really weird, shifting outside its normal color spectrum like it doesn't have a clear connection to his soul anymore."

Worried, I unfocused my attention to bring my second sight into play. Molly quivered as if feeling it, and I looked down. Trent's aura was its usual gold with sparkles around his hands and head, a deeper slash of red running in the thin spots and a new shiny white at the center I'd not seen before. Quen's was a dull green that mutated to red, then an orange as I watched. *Whoa.* Still holding my second sight, I looked away, shivering.

The sunbaked surface of the ever-after overlaid itself atop reality, a dry streambed and sparse grass running to the distant profiles of broken buildings where Cincinnati would be. There were no demons, no eyes watching, and I let go of my second sight, trembling as I maintained my hold on the ley line. "That's not right," I said, and Trent stood.

His eyes were haunted, and his hands cupped about his mouth. "Ceri!" he shouted again, but the silence was broken only by the sound of the water and wind. Ceri wasn't here, nor were the horses.

Jenks rose up on a column of purple dust as I slid down, my knees protesting. "How bad is he hurt? Is he okay?" I said as I crouched beside them. Ray made a sob that was too old for her, and I reached out as she leaned toward me, falling into my arms.

"No."

I froze where I crouched. Ray's grip tightened, and she twisted on my hip to see her dads. Still she didn't cry, red, wet cheeks under deep green eyes. *What had she seen?* Turning, Trent squinted into the surrounding woods. "Ceri!" he called again, his voice holding fear now.

I held my breath, listening. There was a burn mark on the closest tree, the part that hadn't hit it spreading out behind in a long trail. There'd been a fight—short but powerful. *Demons* . . .

"She's not answering," Trent muttered. His hair fell into his eyes as he looked down, cell phone in hand, and I stumbled to my feet when he shoved it at me. "Call the gatehouse. The number is there. Have them send the med copter. Stay with Quen. I have to find Ceri and Lucy. They could be hurt and unable to respond."

His leaving wasn't a good idea, and I resettled Ray on my hip when she reached for him, small sounds of distress coming from her. "Trent . . ."

Jenks's wings clattered. "Stay here," he said, hovering between both of us, Quen silent at our feet. "I can cover more ground faster than you can."

Trent looked awful, his grace mutated by fear. "No." Turning, he broke into a jog for the nearby trees. I took a hesitant step, but Jenks was faster, and before Trent could even get past the horses, the pixy was in his face, dripping a silver-tinted red dust.

"Hey!" the pixy shouted, and Ray's whimpering cut off. "I said stay *put*! Whoever did this might still be out there, Mr. King-of-the-World, and I can cover ten times more ground than you. You got me?" Wings clattering, he stared Trent down. "Stay here and call your ambulance. Quen's aura is freaking out. He needs help!"

My heart thudded, but Trent hesitated, and finally with a groan of frustration, he spun back to Quen, his head down to hide his eyes as he returned. He held his hand out for his phone, and I swear I felt a tingle of magic as he took it in his cold fingers.

"Do you know a healing charm?" I asked, not knowing one myself. I'd been afraid to learn, and Al wouldn't teach me lest I do something worse to myself than the burn or cut I would use it to fix.

"I did it already," he said, flipping his phone open as he dropped down to kneel beside Quen. "That's when his aura started cycling, but it did get his pulse to even out."

Not even a bird disturbed the silence, and, awkward with Ray on my hip, I knelt as well, reaching for Quen's wrist. "His pulse is thready," I said, and I shifted Ray's weight when I leaned to pull Quen's lids back. "Dilation is normal," I said, at a loss. My hand was tingling, and disconcerted, I pulled back. Ray began to protest, and I stood.

"It's Trent," Trent said into his phone, his voice iron hard, all hint of his fear hidden. "We've had an accident. I need the med copter out at the stables. Now."

"You have a medical copter?"

He didn't even look at me, his eyes scanning the nearby trees as if wanting to be among them searching. "Inform the university hospital we might be bringing Quen in. I suspect a demon attack. Yes, in the daylight. Ceri and Lucy are missing. I want the dogs in the woods running a rescue pattern as soon as possible. Focus on the river path." He hesitated, and I saw him struggle to keep his face steady. "I will be out of contact for several hours. Questions?"

He closed the phone, breathing raggedly. "Hurry up, Jenks . . ."

I stood, my shadow covering Quen's pale face. It made his pox scars stand out. I couldn't do anything. If he was bleeding, I could stop the blood. If he had a concussion, I could treat him for shock. If he was delusional, I could sit on him until help arrived—but this? I didn't know what to do, and I found I was rocking back and forth with Ray. She was silent, her beautiful dark green eyes scared.

"Maybe Ceri made it back to the stables," I said, turning to the burn marks. "The horses are gone."

Trent was taking Quen's pulse again. "I called before you got here." His voice was even, distracted. "The horses came in riderless. Ceri never would have left Quen."

And yet, she was gone. Damn it, Quen had tried to stop them. I should have been here. I could have helped. "It doesn't mean that demons took them," I said, flushing when Trent looked up, his anger obvious.

Ray turned, her eyes tracking Jenks as he darted back from under the trees. His dust was almost nonexistent. "I did a circle two hundred yards out," he said. "No sign of them."

"Then do a wider one!" I said, and he frowned.

"I didn't go out any farther because there's a circle burn. We're in the center."

Shit. Quen couldn't make a circle that big, even under stress. Neither could Ceri. It was demon made.

"If there's a demon circle, then they've been taken," he finished, and Trent's hands clenched.

Ku'Sox. I needed to talk to Al, and I turned to the horses, thinking of my scrying mirror, hours away. I'd been promising myself I'd make a compact version, and I cursed myself for having put it off. I was completely out of contact with the ever-after. "It couldn't be Ku'Sox," I whispered, just wanting it to be anyone else. "It's daylight, and he's cursed to stay in the ever-after."

"He's working through Nick." Trent stood up. "This is my fault."

Fault? It was no one's fault. "Don't start," I said harshly, and Jenks hummed his wings nervously. My tone brought Trent up short, and his eyes narrowed as he focused on me. "No, I mean it," I said, jiggling Ray on my hip. "Ku'Sox could have as easily been going for you. Maybe he didn't because I was with you, in which case it would be *my* fault they were taken." Oh God, Ceri and Lucy with Ku'Sox was too terrifying to think about.

"You don't understand. This is *my* fault," Trent said, his voice angry. "I never should have left them. I thought I was his target. I sent them into danger, not away from it." He looked at me, anguish in his green eyes. "He took them. Why? I was right there!"

"Because you're an emancipated familiar," I said, numb and almost sick to my stomach. "Ceri was freed, but you were emancipated. The papers had been filed and there was no way he could get away with it like he can with Ceri. Trent, give me a chance to look into it and get Ceri's papers signed and filed. Lucy is my godchild. I think that comes under the leaving-me-and-mine-alone deal we have." *I hope.* "We can get them back."

Teeth clenched, he turned away. Another look of guilt slithered over his face. "I'm the only person who can make the Rosewood cure permanent," he said, head down so the sun couldn't reach his eyes. "It should've been me. I was ready if it had been me."

His voice cracked and he stared at the river. It flowed uncaring before us, like the chaos that was running through his mind, always moving, never silent. I hovered over Quen as I remembered that hug last night. It had been unusual, especially in front of the newspeople. Had Trent known this might happen and had been trying to keep me from being a suspect? Up until recently, I would have loved to see him in jail.

"He took her to make me comply," he said flatly. "Rachel, I can't do that. I vowed to see to the survival of the elves. A resurgence of demons might be our end."

"Maybe not. There's the—"

"I can't!" he shouted, and I became silent. "I was ready to give my life to keep the secret of the demons' survival out of their hands. I was not ready to give theirs."

"We'll get them back," I said as I shifted Ray's weight, but even I knew it was only something to say. The doing would be harder. A faint thumping of a helicopter's blades sounded in the late morning air, and Trent looked at his watch, then the woods. I touched his shoulder, finding it rock hard. "It's going to be okay." He jerked from me, and my resolve strengthened. "I'm telling you, if Ku'Sox has them, they will be okay!" God, please let them be okay.

He spun, the sound of the chopper blades growing. "How?" he barked. "The demon is sadistic and psychotic! He does things because he enjoys it, not for power or money, but because he enjoys it!"

Then maybe you shouldn't have let him go from under the St. Louis arch, I thought, but to say it wouldn't do any good; he'd freed Ku'Sox to save me. "Trent, I've been where you are now. It's going to be okay. Give me a chance to talk to Al. We'll get the papers filed and get them back. In the meantime, they will be safe. Will you look at me?"

He finally looked up, the anguish he was trying to hide stopping me cold. I held Ray tighter, and the little girl began to fuss. "Pardon me if I don't share your trust of demons."

"Trust has nothing to do with it!" I shouted, and Tulpa flattened his ears. "I know he's psychotic, but he is not stupid, and he's not going to eat his bargaining chip!"

Trent glared up at the circling copter, ignoring me. *How would they even know where to land?* "Ceri knows demons," I said. "She will keep Lucy safe. She has her soul, and that makes all the difference. I promise I'll find out what happened. We have a space. We need to think. Please give me a chance to do something."

He wasn't looking at me, his jaw set and his manner closed. I didn't know if I'd made things better or worse. "Jenks," he said suddenly. "They will have to land in the pasture and walk in. You're the fastest person here. Will you tell them where we are?"

Frowning, I shifted Ray higher. We didn't have time for this. I didn't know what Quen's aura was doing, but it wasn't normal. "Are those trees important to you?" I asked Trent suddenly, and he looked at me blankly. Even Jenks hesitated. "Your dad didn't kiss your mom under them or anything?"

Trent shook his head. "No."

Jaw clenched, I pulled heavily on the ley line. Ray jumped as if smacked, but she wasn't crying so I narrowed my focus and pushed it into my hand. *"Adsimulo calefacio!"* I shouted, throwing the curse at the nearest tree, superheating the sap in an instant. The tree exploded, and I spun, shielding Ray with my body. Bits of bark and sharp splinters struck my back.

The horses scattered with the muted sound of hooves. "Hey! Give me some warning!" Jenks shrilled as the last of the branches fell back to earth, and Trent looked up from where he had hastily covered Quen. The tree was scattered over a twenty-foot circle, the last pieces still falling. It had only been Molly that had run away, and Tulpa stood at a four-posted stiffness, his neck arched and his eyes wild. He snorted at me, shifting his skin to shake off the bits of bark and leaves.

"Consider yourself warned," I said grimly, and after seeing Ray wide-eyed and quiet, I shifted her to sit more firmly on my hip and blew up two more trees. It was an ungodly mess, but there was room now, and better yet, the ambulance would know exactly where to land. Growing more angry, Tulpa withstood it all, held to the spot by Trent's will alone.

Trent was silent as he joined me in the new sun, squinting up as the sound of the copter blades grew closer. I felt ill as the imbalance for the curse rose up, lapping about me. I could feel it cresting, and with no regret, I lifted my chin. *I pay the cost for this,* I thought, feeling the smut slither across my soul. The sun didn't seem any dimmer, the sky was just as blue, but looking at the shattered stumps and splintered branches and wilting leaves, I knew my soul was a little bit darker.

But what was the point of a clean soul if Quen died and I could have helped?

"Thank you," Trent said, and then he darted back to Quen as the long medical helicopter began to land. What wasn't nailed down blew to the edges—and there was a lot. Ray began to wail, and I held her face to me, covering her head as I turned my back on the copter. Swearing, Jenks tucked in at my collar, and I stood there hunched and shaking, feeling as if I were at the center of a tornado.

Finally it was only bits of grass striking me, and I turned to see three men in scrubs jump out of the side, a stretcher between them. The blades slowed but didn't stop, and Trent stood over Quen, his worry coming back threefold.

"No spinal damage," one said, squinting at an amulet held against Quen's temple. "We can move him," and the other two manhandled him onto the stretcher, starting an IV and taking vital signs.

"Sir?" the one with the amulet asked, and Trent pulled his attention from Quen's face. His eyes looked better.

"Treat it as a demon attack," he said, voice raised against the wind. "Yes, it's daylight," he added when the man looked doubtfully at the sun. "He was possessing someone."

Jenks left me, Ray starting as the silver sparkles sifted down. "His aura is wonky," the pixy said, standing on Quen's chest to garner everyone's attention for a brief instant. "It's cycling through shades like it's ringing. It's getting worse, though. Five minutes ago, it was taking thirty seconds to cycle and now it's down to twenty."

Brow furrowed, the man put on a pair of glasses another handed him. His eyes widened, and his motions took on a new urgency. "Get him in the chopper. Now!"

"I didn't see it happen," Trent said as they counted to three and lifted the stretcher, the first man holding the IV bag high. "Morgan and I were out on another trail and felt the disturbance. I think they took Ceri and Lucy," he said, fear crossing his face before he tried to hide it. I could see it shimmering behind his every move.

With an efficiency of motion, they loaded Quen, the sound of the blades drowning out the new conversation between the two techs. Jenks had darted in with them and out of the wind, and Ray was watching for him to come back out—silent, so silent. Still beside us, the head guy looked at the pilot, motioning for a moment of time. Concern showed in his eyes as he leaned in to be heard. "Sir, I don't know what this is. We have to take him to the university hospital."

Trent looked up at the whirling blades, and I held Ray tighter to me. "Are you sure? I don't want a media circus."

But the man was shaking his head. "We're running out of time. He needs to be in a desensitization tank, and you don't have one. We can try a quiet room—"

"No." Trent looked inside, fear flickering over him like a second aura. "Go. Take him."

The man made a motion to the pilot, and through the glass, I saw him grab a radio. "We'll call ahead," the tech shouted. "They'll be ready for him. I think we're in time, but we have to move fast to stop the damage. I have room for one more."

Trent spun to me. His face was riven with a worry he was trying to hide with a cool efficiency. It all fell apart when he looked at Ray, then me and whispered, "Rachel . . ."

I couldn't hear him, but I could read his lips. Something in me twisted, and I shoved it aside. "Go!" I said, propelling him toward the door as the wind whipped my hair around. "I've got this! Call me when you know something!"

He kissed Ray's fingers, looking her firmly in her eyes. "I'll be back as soon as I can." His eyes rose to mine as the blades shrieked in the air. "Thank you."

I held Ray closer, letting her see as we backed away. Trent effortlessly got into the medical copter. Jenks darted out just before the door closed, whipped downward and out as if he were on a roller coaster. He streaked past me, swearing at Tink, but I figured he was okay.

One hand supporting Ray, the other holding my hair, I watched the pilot do a check before lifting up. Squinting, I held my ground as more sticks and leaves blew. Blades thumping, the copter gained altitude and vanished beyond the trees, heading for Cincinnati.

Slowly the leaves settled. Shaking, I looked to where we had found Quen. The grass was flattened. Ray's grip on my hair tugged, and I disentangled her, letting her soft, damp hand hold my fingers as I listened to the quiet, my ears ringing.

Jenks's wings sounded muffled as he started to land on my shoulder, then thought better of it and hung where he was, dust sifting from him in the leftover breeze. "He'll be okay. We got to him in time."

I didn't know. But I had an unusually quiet toddler on my hip and no horse. Tulpa had vanished. I didn't blame the animal, but I needed to get back to the stables. I heard the hounds bay in the distance and shivered.

"Quen is strong," Jenks said, his words fast as he fell into place beside me as I picked my way through the shattered vegetation. One of the trees

I'd taken out had been damaged by magic, all evidence of it destroyed. The I.S. would have a cow. Either that, or blame me for the attack.

"He's going to be okay," Jenks said again, and I walked into the shade on the path. Hoofprints were a sad reminder of how fast life could change, the marks going both ways and crisscrossing in a chaotic mishmash.

"He'll be okay," I agreed just to get him to stop talking, but I didn't know if I believed it.

Ray was still silent, leaning away from me to try to see Jenks flying over my head. I hadn't spent a lot of time with her, but enough that I was familiar. She was so different from her sister, quiet and reserved where Lucy was outgoing and demanding. My face twisted and my gut clenched at the thought of Lucy with Ku'Sox. I had told Trent everything was going to be okay, but the uncertainty as we waited for what Ku'Sox wanted was heartbreaking.

From above my ear, Jenks made an ultrasonic chirp. "Holy toad spit!" the pixy squeaked, and I stiffened, feeling as if something was crawling through me by way of the ley line. Ray, too, stiffened, her hand in my fingers clenching harder.

Then I sucked in my breath as I felt a huge tug from the nearest ley line. It felt like a sudden drop in the road you weren't expecting—a quick jolt and then back to normal. "What was that?" I said. The back of my head was hot, and I made a face as if trying to pop my ears.

"How should I know?" Jenks shrilled. "Listen, it's going to do it again. Oh God, here it comes!"

I froze, my feet planted on the path as the line hiccuped and became nauseatingly erratic. Hissing, I dropped the line from my thoughts as it raked through me. Silver-edged dust fell from Jenks so thickly that Ray reached for it. The memory of that itchy feeling scraped up my spine and lodged itself in my brain. Glancing at Jenks, I tentatively tapped a ley line, squinting as I let it flow through me, tasting it. It felt okay now, but something had happened. I'd have to ask Bis when he woke up tonight. He was more in tune with the lines than any person I knew. If I got home, that is. I didn't know if Trent would approve of me taking Ray home with me.

Jenks hovered before us, a weird, lost look on his face. "What happened?" the pixy asked, and I pushed into motion, wanting to get to a TV.

"I've no idea, but it can't be good."

Chapter Six

Ray fussed, threatening to cry as I inexpertly fumbled at the straps to buckle her into the car seat the nice-looking guy in Trent's garage helped me move into my little Cooper. "Don't start with me," I warned her, my unfamiliar tone catching her attention and distracting her. It might have been Jenks making faces at her from the rearview mirror, though, and I backed out of the car, blowing a strand of hair out of my eyes.

It was nearing three, I smelled like horse, and I had a cranky toddler who refused to go down for her nap. And it wasn't as if I hadn't tried. Trent's secretary had gotten me back to Trent's apartments to wait for him, but that had been four books, two songs, and three hours ago. Watching TV with Jenks had only made being stuck at Trent's big empty apartments worse. That line hiccup I'd felt wasn't just out at Trent's place, but everywhere, the entire United States and off continent, too. The lines were fine now, but the media was scrambling, interviewing specialists and wackos with little signs saying the end was near.

Jenks gave me a thumbs-up from inside the car, and I sighed. Diaper bag, extra food, change of clothes, blanket from her crib, and three stuffed animals she had pointed to when I asked her which ones she wanted. Yep, I had it all. It wasn't that I didn't appreciate camping out at Trent's apartments, watching his big-screen TV and raiding his fridge for fresh fruit and pudding, but I had stuff to do, stuff that I could get done while Ray napped. And boy, did she need to nap.

A sneeze shook me as I shut the door. My brow furrowed. If it followed the emerging pattern, I'd sneeze again in about ten minutes. Al was trying to get a hold of me, and my scrying mirror was across town in the Hollows. I'd tried stepping into the line that bisected Trent's estate and contacting him that way, but Al hadn't showed and I hadn't lingered since the lines felt sour somehow. I hoped it was only the uncomfortable state of the lines that he wanted to discuss, but I had a bad feeling it was more, and my eyes flicked to Ray in her car seat as I got in.

Jenks eyed me suspiciously as I settled myself, wiping my nose with a tissue I took out of my shoulder bag. "Bless you," he said sourly. "That's like, what, the twentieth one?"

"I lost count." Smiling at Ray, who was making *s-s-s-s-s* noises to get Jenks's attention, I headed for the bright square of light and out of Trent's underground garage. Worry flitted through me that I was taking Ray off the grounds, but Trent hadn't told me I couldn't.

Jenks went drowsy in the new sun, and I slowly wove my way past the employee parking lots and low buildings to the gatehouse. It was up about half a mile, and Ray was well on her way to snoozeville, too, when I came around a bend and slowed.

Trent had modified his gatehouse twice since I'd known him, once when I had blown through the simple metal bar on my way out, and again when Ivy had tossed me over his new wall when I was in a hurry to leave and he had wanted me to stay. The modest, one-story building was now a two-story edifice that straddled the road, officers on both sides to monitor traffic leaving as well as coming in. Parking lots were available on either side of the highly landscaped wall, the bushes trying to hide how tall and thick it was. It wasn't the five I.S. vehicles parked just this side of the bar that made me take my foot off the gas and coast in—it was the three news vans just past the gate.

Crap on toast, that hadn't taken long.

My sigh roused Jenks, and he whistled, bringing Ray's eyes open for a brief moment. I'd known the I.S. was out here, having seen the fax of the warrant sent to Trent's living room when they'd arrived. The I.S. I could handle. The news vans were another story.

"You think they saw you?" Jenks asked as I pulled into the parking lot.

"Probably. But I'm leaving with Trent's kid. I probably have to sign something," I said as I leaned to undo her buckle and pull the whining, tired girl to me. Leaving her in the car was not an option.

Both Ray and I sneezed on Jenks's dust as he shot out before us, and I took a clean breath as I stood beside the car, baby on my hip and blinking in the wind and sun. An anxious, nervous man in Trent's security uniform was gesturing for me at a glass door, and I headed for him, my bag over one shoulder, Ray gripping the other. Sure enough, a reporter on the other side of the gate shouted my name. I'd been spotted. Swell.

"Ms. Morgan, I'm glad you stopped," the man said as I came in and set Ray on the counter. Three walls were entirely glass, and it was like being in a fish tank. There was new activity among the press gathered, waiting for any tidbit the I.S. might let fall. Vultures, they were vultures. "We weren't aware you were going to take Ray off the grounds."

"Why?" Jenks asked snidely, giving the three other guards fits as he flew behind the counter and inspected the views from the security cameras. "You think you can stop her?"

"Well, actually . . ." the man hedged, and I took a pen away from Ray before she stuck it in her mouth and gave her from my purse a harmless charm that would straighten hair.

"Look, you," I said, a finger pointed, and I swear, Ray tried to mimic me, charm between her swollen gums like a teething ring. "Trent asked me to watch her, and I need to get home."

From behind the counter, a big fat guy in a uniform turned, his chair on casters. "Frank, she's on the list. Quit razzing her."

My eyebrows rose, my good mood returning. I was on the list. How about that? And then I sneezed, feeling a faint itch of a ley line pull attached to it.

"Bless you," Jenks said, and I swear, Ray echoed him, way off on the actual word but spot on as far as rhythm. Her little-girl voice was sweet, and charmed, I tickled her under her chin to make her squirm.

"Ma'am . . ." My smile vanished, and the man's became nervous. "Uh, you're on the list, but I need to see a photo ID and get a phone number we can reach you at, and we need to know where you're going, and when you expect to be back."

Oh. That was all right then, and I swung my bag up beside Ray, pawing through it with one hand as the other hovered over Ray's back in case she decided to move. The clatter drew Ray's attention, and she watched with a serious expression, not reaching for anything as I sifted past the splat gun, lethal charm detector, two sets of cuffs, handful of zip strips, breath mints, phone, and whatnot for my wallet.

"Thank you," he said as he took it to run it through their machine. It apparently liked what it found since he gave it back. Behind him, the news crew was setting up tripods and long-range cameras.

"I'm taking her to my church," I said as wrote down my cell number and I shoved everything away, Jenks laughing at the expression on the other officers' faces at the cuffs and charms. "I'll have her there until Trent picks her up or we run out of diapers."

"Thank you," the anxious guy said, and I swung my bag up onto my shoulder. Jenks hovered beside me, and together we looked at the news-people, hanging around in the hopes of a scrap of anything. I slid Ray onto my hip, motions slow.

"Think if I give them something they won't follow me?" I muttered, and Jenks snorted.

"Doubt it."

I doubted it too, but I headed for the door. If I kept my windows up, I could at least ignore them. Trent wouldn't be pleased about any photos they took of Ray, but it couldn't be helped.

The sun and wind hit me anew as I went outside. Jenks was close, and my steps were fast as I headed for the car. Shouts and calls for my attention got loud as I opened the door. *If you follow me home, I swear I'll let the pixies play in your electronic equipment!*

"Ms. Morgan! Is it true that Mr. Kalamack has been flown to the hospital and is in intensive care! Ms. Morgan!"

My back was to them, and Jenks, currently perched on the roof, winced. "It's not going to look good if you don't answer," he said, his eyes going to Ray and back to me.

"Ms. Morgan! Have you taken custody of his children because he's unconscious? Where is Ms. Dulciate? Has she been injured as well?"

I sighed, then shifted Ray higher. She wasn't fussy, happily gumming the charm. It wouldn't hurt to quash a few rumors before they got started.

The security people on both sides of the road were standing at their big plate-glass windows, watching. I'd get no help from them, and although Trent probably wouldn't thank me for putting Ray in front of the cameras, I'd found out the hard way if you didn't give the press something to chew on, they invented things that sold more papers than the truth.

"Ms. Morgan!" a woman shouted, and I turned, holding my hair to my head so the wind wouldn't catch it. I must look a sight, but at least I wasn't limping, beaten up, or bandaged.

The news crews had a spasm of delight as I let the car door shut and paced across the road to the gate they were clustered behind. Jenks hung back as the still photographers snapped their pictures and big guys with video cameras on their shoulders shoved for the best angle. They were all shouting for my attention. Jenks took refuge on my shoulder, and Ray hid her face, scared. My protective nature rose up from a tiny seed of maternal instinct I didn't even know I had, and I shushed her, rocking as I stood in the road, three feet back from the gate.

"You," I said to a woman in a white dress suit, her short hair hardly moving in the stiff wind. "Didn't I knock you down once outside of the mall?"

The woman grinned as her peers chuckled at her expense. "That was me, Ms. Morgan. Trent Kalamack was seen being transported to the hospital by helicopter, and unless I'm mistaken, that is his daughter. Something happened to the ley lines this afternoon, and the I.S. is on-site. Can you comment?"

From my shoulder, Jenks sighed. "You sure you want to do this?"

No, I didn't want to do this, but I wanted them following me home even less. "Trent Kalamack escorted one of his employees to the hospital after an accident that occurred while riding this morning," I said, smug when the woman shifted her gaze to her truth amulet ring, a nice steady green. They weren't legal in this situation, but hard to prove. "Mr. Kalamack didn't sustain any injuries, and I'm waiting for news just as you are."

"But the I.S.—" the woman blurted as a follow-up, and the rising questions subsided. "Were the ley lines damaged in the accident?"

"No," I said shortly. "I felt the lines sour well after the incident. The I.S. is here because the wounds his employee sustained are similar to those a demon might inflict." The noise rose, and I put up a hand, guessing their next question and wanting to answer it my way instead of needing to work around that truth amulet. "As you can tell, the sun is up, so logic says the I.S. is taking the opportunity to be nosy while Trent is away."

They liked that, scribbling on tablets or talking into their recorders.

"Ms. Morgan!" a man from the back shouted, his hand raised. "As Cincinnati's only day-walking demon, have you been questioned in the incident?"

"Told you this was a bad idea . . ." Jenks muttered, and I forced my smile to widen. A sneeze shook me, and Ray patted my shoulder.

"I wasn't an eyewitness to the incident," I said truthfully, "but I did blow up a couple of trees so the medical copter could land." I looked at the I.S. vehicles dramatically. "I'm sure they will blame me for something," I added, getting the expected laughs. This wasn't so bad. Making deals with demons had given me practice.

"Do you have an explanation as to what happened to the ley line?" a man in a sports coat asked, holding his mic out over the gate.

"No. I'm on my way home to talk to Al, actually, and find out if the demons know what happened," I said, then sneezed again. They were coming faster, and nervously I patted Ray on her back as she said "bless you" in a garbled baby talk. "So if there are no more questions?" I said into the suddenly awkward silence.

I took a step backward, and like lions on prey, they pounced. "Is that Ray? Can we have a picture? Are you taking her home? Where is Lucy? What has the I.S. learned so far?"

Jenks was laughing, and I reluctantly turned back around. I scanned the yammering reporters, finding one I recognized. "Mark," I said, and they all shut up. "You know I can't divulge what the I.S. finds, and besides, I've only seen the search warrant."

"Why are you taking Ray? Can we have a picture? Was Ms. Dulciate injured in the accident as well?"

I had three to choose from, and I took a step back. "Ms. Dulciate is currently occupied with Lucy. You can understand taking care of two little girls, twins, almost, is enough to drive anyone to distraction. I need to go. It's nap time."

"Ms. Morgan. A photo, please. Ms. Morgan!"

Ray was clutching my neck, scared. They'd already snapped pictures of Ray, so that boat had sailed, spent a week at the island, and returned to port for more tourists, but I didn't want Ray's fear to be what they walked away from here with. "A picture?" I taunted, and they clamored for one. "Maybe if you would all *shut up* for a moment!" I exclaimed. "You're yammering so loud that you would scare a third-grade teacher. Okay?"

They didn't know what to think about that, but they did quiet down, and sure enough, drawn by the sudden silence, Ray pushed herself from my front and turned, her big green eyes wide and looking sweet in the little pink-and-white dress I'd put her in to nap in.

I smiled at the adoring faces of the women as the cameras clicked. I'd give Ceri and Quen one thing—they could make very pretty babies.

But then my smile faded as I noticed a big black car that screamed money driving slowly up to the gate. It was Trent. I knew it. And here I was, showing off Ray like a prize.

"Now you're in for it," Jenks said, darting off my shoulder and making Ray jerk as she watched his angling flight to the black car.

"Okay, that's enough," I said, hoping that Jenks would put in a good word in for me. I waved cheerfully at the last shouted question as I added, "I gotta go. And if anyone shows up on my doorstep, I will file harassment charges . . . after I let the pixies into your vans. You got it?"

But they weren't listening, having figured out Trent was in the car as well. Head down, I hustled back to my car as they fell on his like zombies. If I could give him Ray right now, I could be home in thirty minutes and the press probably wouldn't follow.

Sneezing, I wondered if I could make it in twenty if someone from the I.S. ran vanguard.

A man from the gatehouse came out, waving everyone back, shouting that Mr. Kalamack would make a statement in an hour, and that they were welcome to wait at the gatehouse pressroom if they liked. In pairs and groups, they parted, and the black car moved slowly through the gate and turned into the parking lot where I waited.

Nervous, I leaned against my car, pointing Trent's car out to Ray and telling her that one of her daddies was in it. She was still gumming that charm when the car pulled to a halt two spots down. Immediately a back door opened, Trent not waiting for the driver to get it for him. Jenks darted out, shedding encouraging silver sparkles, but Trent was a great deal slower, moving as if he was in pain. Upon closer inspection, I decided he was just tired, his jeans creased and the sleeves of his riding shirt rolled up. There was a tuft of cotton and a Band-Aid inside his elbow, and I wondered if he'd given blood.

Squinting at the sun, he crossed the warm pavement, his hands outstretched for Ray. The little girl had begun to wiggle when she'd caught sight of him, and the smile that came over Trent caught in my heart. It didn't matter if this child was not his blood—she was his child. And Quen's, and Ceri's.

My smile faded. I had to fix this.

"Ray," he breathed, and suddenly I felt her absence keenly as he took her. "Your daddy is going to be okay, I think." His eyes rose to mine. "We got him there in time. Ten more minutes and they might not have been able to stop the cascading reaction." He blinked fast, then looked away. "That's twice you've saved Quen's life. Thank you."

I shifted from foot to foot, uncomfortable. "I'm sorry this happened."

"Me too."

Our eyes met for a long, silent moment. Ray jumped and wiggled as Jenks's dust sifted over her, and I flushed when Trent noticed what she was gumming, her little fingers gripping the charm so hard they were white. I sneezed, and I shook my head at Trent's unspoken question.

"Ah, I'm sorry about this," I said as the driver of his car began to move the car seat to the black Jag. "I hate coming home to find reporters in my driveway. I hadn't heard from you and I need to talk to Al. That's why I'm sneezing. Ray wouldn't go down for her nap, and I figured she'd fall asleep in the car." I hesitated. "You look tired."

"I napped during some of the tests," he said, and I wondered at the incongruity of us standing in the sun and talking as other people moved

Ray's things to his car. "I didn't want to leave until he was stable. They got his aura to stop cycling, but they don't know why he won't regain consciousness. Thank you for handling the press. One of the guards relayed what you said. You did pretty well."

My eyes dropped at his wry smile. "I've been dodging them the last couple of years. I know how much you have to give them for them to leave you alone."

Ray had fallen against him, her head tucked under his chin as she started to drift asleep, her eyes never leaving me. "Oh God," Jenks said from my shoulder, and her eyelids flickered. "Here come the vampires."

Sure enough, coming up the road on a golf cart were four I.S. officers. The grit ground under Trent's heel as he spun slowly to watch as they parked beside their cars and the one in the dress suit angled toward us.

It was Nina, or Felix, maybe. I could tell by the grace and slightly pained motion of the living vampire as she crossed the lot. The sun normally didn't bother living vampires, but Nina was channeling Felix by the looks of it.

Trent seemed to shed his fatigue like an old shirt, but I could see it in the wrinkles at the corners of his eyes. "They had a warrant," I explained, and he bobbed his head in acceptance. "The I.S. in your backyard is another thing I don't like coming home to. They've been on the grounds for the last couple of hours, but your security tells me they've been escorting them the entire time so they wouldn't wander. The hospital called them, probably."

"Thank you," he murmured, gently patting Ray as the tallish Hispanic woman in the black dress suit put a hand up to ask us to wait. "You did exactly what Qu— What should have been done."

I quashed the feeling of hurt. "I used to work for them. I know your rights."

"Trenton!" the woman boomed out, her voice too expansive and masculine for her slight frame. Clearly Felix was in her again, and I worried about her. It wasn't uncommon for the undead to use their "children" as moving walkie-talkies, but it was unusual that Felix kept doing it. But who tells an undead no?

"Good to see you again," Trent said, shaking the woman's hand with an expansive motion that he usually only used with men. "How much longer until you are off my property?"

The vampire smiled, setting a finger aside her nose in a gesture I hadn't seen anyone under the age of fifty use. "Rachel, is Ivy back from Arizona yet?"

"No." I shook Nina's hand, struggling with my desire to wipe it off. Her fingers had been cool and dry, but the man animating her bothered me. "Was it a demon attack?"

"It would be a lot easier to tell if you hadn't exploded three trees over the entire crime site." Nina squinted uncomfortably. "Can we move this inside?"

"No," I said again, shifting my bag up higher on my shoulder. "Can I leave, or do you want something?"

Jenks's wings shifted against my neck in warning. Okay, it wasn't smart to antagonize a vampire, especially a dead one, but Ray wasn't the only one tired here.

"I need a statement, if you would please. Before you leave."

I sneezed, my entire body contracting and the noise making Ray crack her eyes. Al was getting impatient. "I'm kind of busy right now."

"Then you shouldn't have obliterated the evidence," Felix said, Nina's beautiful white teeth bared at me in a threat thinly disguised as a smile.

"Oh. My. God," Jenks said, safely parked on my shoulder but his dust shifting a bright red. "Rache, they think you did it. Do you really believe the crap that is coming out of your mouth," the pixy added as Nina reflectively steepled her fingers as I'd seen older men do, "or do you just make shit up to see how stupid people might think you are?"

I knew I was filling the air with my anger, a close second to a vampire's favorite smell after fear. The wind helped, but by Nina's smirk I knew that she was picking up on some of it.

"You *are* a demon," Nina said, making Jenks's wings seem to hum in anger. "And yes, this has all the markings of a demon attack. It occurred in the daylight, meaning *you* are the only one who could accomplish it."

"That's dumber than Tink's dildo!" Jenks exclaimed, and I raised a hand to keep him from flying at her; the vampire might be quick enough to catch him. I doubted Felix truly believed I'd done this, or he would've had a dozen other magic users out here to bring me in. Unless he knew even that wouldn't be enough, and I'd been moved to the level of a banshee where they'd just kill me outright with a sniper's spell. *Grea-a-a-at.*

"Then there is option number two," Nina said brightly as I fumed, and she turned to include Trent. "Do you wish to start an investigation on the Withons?"

"Ellasbeth didn't do this." Trent's voice was soft because of Ray, but it had the sureness of wind and water. Slumped against him, Ray slept, at peace at last. Nina tilted her head as if unsure, and I agreed with Felix. Ellasbeth's family was one of the wealthiest on the West Coast. She had motive, opportunity, and the clout to buy a demon attack. I wished it *was* her. It would make my life easier. But with Nick involved . . .

Nina eyed Trent, a cruel twist to her lips. "Isn't that what you did to her? Steal her child?" she said as she held her hair against a gust of wind. "What's good for the goose, eh?"

Jenks's wings clattered, tickling my neck, and Trent frowned, letting a hint of his anger show. Beyond the gates, the press teams were coiling cords and packing away lights, but their long-range cameras were reading lips. "Ellasbeth did not arrange this," Trent said shortly, his back to them. "I stole Lucy with my own efforts under an arranged tradition older than your species, vampire. If Ellasbeth had come here and taken Lucy by herself, then I'd be angry for having allowed it. I wouldn't deserve her. But this wasn't Ellasbeth."

Nina swung back to me. "Which brings us back to you, Rachel."

Exasperated, I dropped back to my car, sneezing and trying not to look pensive. "Just because a demon can't come to reality doesn't mean that his influence ends at the ley lines. I saw Nick Sparagmos leaving the hospital in a hurry yesterday amid that media circus you instigated. I did some asking around and found out he belongs to Ku'Sox Sha-Ku'ru. Ku'Sox could have done this through Nick."

Not easily, but he could have.

"And why didn't you say anything earlier?" Nina almost purred, making me think Felix had known about it all along. Damn it, I hated when I fell into their mind games.

"Because up until today, Nick was stealing thriving Rosewood syndrome babies, not Trent's family."

Nina squinted, her guile replaced with a frown. "You think the two crimes are linked?"

I nodded, pulling my jacket tighter around my shoulders to make Jenks take to the air. Just as well since I sneezed again. Both the pixy and Trent eyed me in concern. "There's no way in the two worlds that you'll find him. You want his phone number? That's all I got, and it's probably not going to work anymore." I dug in my bag for a tissue. If I didn't get to my scrying mirror soon, Al was going to be pissed.

Nina's eyes narrowed. "I do not like you withholding information, Rachel Morgan."

I leaned forward to get into her face, emboldened by the news crews watching. "Then maybe you should stop accusing me of everything. I didn't have any evidence, and one thing I've learned is no one acts on what I believe, only what I can prove."

"I would," Trent said, and I smiled at him with a wash of gratitude. Jenks had moved himself to his shoulder, and he looked different with a baby on one side, a pixy on the other.

"I'm going to hold you to that," I said softly, and Nina's stance became antagonistic.

"I want a statement," she insisted.

"Am I a suspect?"

Nina sighed dramatically. "No-o-o-o."

"A person of interest?" I pushed, and she rolled her head on her shoulders as if stretching into a new skin and finding it unpleasant.

"No, not really," she said flatly.

"Then you can wait until I can come in tomorrow and give you a statement. Right now I have to talk to Al and find out what happened to the ley lines this afternoon. Okay? I'll even tell you what he said. Deal?"

Nina glared, brown eyes becoming black. I held her gaze, my heart hammering as I saw past the woman to the ugly old vampire speaking through her. Frightening ideas churned in him, whispers showing and vanishing like bursting bubbles of oil. He was old, maybe too old to adapt to the reality of demons among us and to make decisions to ease the coming chaos.

His attention bore into me, and I took it without flinching. Would he accept me and the possible demon baggage I might bring to reality, or forever keep me in the "them" category? The second choice was familiar, comfortable, but it would lead to their damnation. I thought he was smart enough to see it. The question was, could he sell it to those who looked to him?

"Very well. Tomorrow," the vampire finally said, and I exhaled as our eye contact broke, trying to make it inaudible but knowing that Nina could sense my relief easier than she could feel the wind in her hair. I hadn't gotten the full acceptance that I wanted, but rather a cautious maybe. It was enough for now. "Still, it would be easier if you hadn't obliterated evidence of the attack," she grumped.

"I was trying to save Quen's life," I said darkly. The news crews were finally going into the gatehouse pressroom. Soon as they left, I'd head home. "You did a moulage, right?" I couldn't see the imprint left by strong emotions, but vampires, whether they be living or dead, could. If Ivy was here, she could tell me, but she wasn't. I had an uncomfortable thought that she'd much rather be helping Glenn than our investigative firm.

Nina sniffed, clearly uncomfortable in the sun, but I leaned back against my car, enjoying the stored heat it was giving off. "Most has already evaporated with the sun," Nina said. "The evaluation is still being scored, but even though neither I nor Nina is rated for the courts it's obvious that there was violence, determination, frustration, and panic in large amounts. Mostly violence between two people."

"Gee, you think?" Jenks smart-mouthed. "You come up with that all on your own?"

Quen and Ku'Sox, I thought, seeing frustration cross Trent's face.

"It seems," Nina said, idly looking at her perfect nails, "as if Ceri did nothing. Perhaps she was knocked out or protecting the baby."

Trent turned away, the rims of his ears red in the sun. Jenks had taken wing, hovering protectively. Seeing it, Nina smiled like a cat who'd cornered a mouse. "I sensed three, maybe four auras present, but only Quen and one other were active. I'd be comfortable guessing that there was one person who abducted Ceri and Lucy, someone proficient in magic. Quen fought him or her, realized he couldn't overcome them, and the two females were taken."

How can she just stand there and say it? I thought, my frustration bubbling up. Lucy and Ceri were gone! Quen was possibly dying, having tried to save them. Trent . . .

I glanced at him, wishing he didn't have to deal with this. Demons sucked.

Nina was silent, reading the emotions as neither one of us said anything. Ray was slumped against Trent's shoulder, Jenks a silent presence of support I didn't understand. It was obvious that Trent had never admitted to himself how much Ceri and Lucy had come to mean to him. He might not even know it now, so wrought with the pressure of dealing with the present that he couldn't see clearly. He was suffering, though. He had no one. I didn't think he realized it yet—he wasn't angry enough. I could feel his realization coming. Maybe in a day. Maybe two.

Trent had always seemed to be alone, but he'd always had his assistant, Jonathan, as well as Quen. Then Ceri. Even Ellasbeth, though that hadn't turned out very well apart from Lucy. And now even Lucy was gone. Soon he would understand that the demons had taken everything but a child who would remind him of what he lost. Things would get ugly then as the worst parts of Trent warred with the best.

A chill went through me, and Nina looked at me in question, her eyes dilating in the strong sun as I shivered. Trent had power on multiple levels and he wasn't averse to using it. I didn't know which side of him would win. I'd seen both. There was little I could do. Except perhaps be there so he didn't feel so alone.

"Then you have nothing more to add?" Nina asked, her voice oily as she soaked in my sudden fear.

"No."

"I'll see you tomorrow, Rachel," she said, and I looked at her outstretched hand, refusing to take it. She might kiss it or something. "Trenton." Nina hesitated, inclined her head, and then spun slowly. Trent shifted to me slightly, and we watched her walk to the cars. You could tell when Felix left her: her head came up and she breathed as if coming out from a hole. As she paced faster, her heels clicked on the pavement until she got in a car.

Arms still over my chest, I watched her slowly pivot the big car back onto the road, headed for the gatehouse. I'd stopped sneezing. That was good, right? "She thinks I'm not telling her everything," I said, and Trent's shoulders slumped.

"Are you?"

I touched Ray's hair, smiling faintly. She hadn't let go of that amulet, and it was still in her tight little grip even as she slept. "I don't know. It's ingrained not to tell the I.S. squat."

I opened my car door to leave, and Trent lingered, Ray in his arms and the sun glowing on him. "Felix is teetering on insanity," he said, eyes concerned as he watched Nina's car go through the gate. "You'll be okay tonight?"

"Sure, unless they decide to blame it on me." I got in, finding my keys in my bag. Sitting there, I looked up at him. "It would be easier if Ellasbeth planned it," I said, wanting to believe that. I didn't like the woman, and by Jenks's scoff as he darted in to sit on the rearview mirror, I knew he didn't hold any love for her, either.

"I called her from the hospital," Trent said, a surprising tone of compassion in his voice. "She seemed shocked, and she doesn't lie that well. Even if it were ten against one, Quen wouldn't have—" His voice broke, and I felt a surge of pity when his jaw clenched and released. "He would have prevailed."

"I'm sorry."

His breath coming in was shaky, but it smoothed out when he exhaled. "Me too."

My chest hurt, and I watched him hold Ray. I knew he loved her, but the feeling that he had failed Lucy must be overwhelming. He had risked his life to find Lucy and bring her home, promised that she would be safe with him. "You're a good father," I said suddenly, and his lips parted. "No one can stop a demon when they make half an effort."

"You can," he said quickly, and Jenks made a pained sound from the rearview mirror.

The self-recrimination in Trent's voice made me feel worse. "True, but I'm a demon."

Trent blinked with a sudden thought. His shoulders eased, and the horrid tightness to his jaw let up. "You are, aren't you?" he said, as if I'd given him something new to consider, a fragment of knowledge that he could use as he began scheming, looking for a way to fix this.

"What?" I said, hoping he'd tell me what my words had sparked, but he shook his head.

"Nothing. Ellasbeth has promised to take Lucy from me, even if I can get her back. She's already filing papers."

I wondered why he was telling me this, even as my heart went out to him. "You will get her back. Ceri too." But I didn't promise it.

Still between me and my car door, he swallowed hard. I wanted to reach out to touch him, but didn't know how he'd take it. Putting the key in the ignition, I sneezed. Then I sneezed again, jerking so hard my forehead almost hit the dash. Scared, I looked at Jenks. His eyes were wide. *Shit.* I'd waited too long to get to my scrying mirror.

"Bless you," Trent said dully, not paying attention. My eyes widened, and I sneezed again. Mouth dry, I grasped his free wrist.

"Trent. I'm sorry," I said, knowing I couldn't stop this. He was going to lose me, too.

He stared at my hand, and then his eyes widened as I sneezed again. "No . . ."

I let go of him, sitting in my car afraid to move. I wanted to run, but I couldn't outdistance the summons. "I'm being summoned," I said, turning away to sneeze again. A nauseating, pulling sensation had started. It was soft right now, but if I didn't submit, it would grow until I had no choice. For a second, I panicked, thinking it might be Ku'Sox, but Al was the only one in the ever-after who knew my summoning name. *And Nick.*

The panic returned.

"Nick knows your summoning name!" Jenks shouted as he figured it out, too. "Rachel, fight it!"

But there was nothing I could do, and I shook my head, trying not to show my fear. I didn't have a choice. I had to go. At least the news crew couldn't see me. "I'm sorry," I said again, wincing. "This might be okay. I'll do what I can." I looked at Jenks. His face was white. "Give me an hour, then summon me back."

"No." The snarl of denial had come from Trent, and I gasped as he knelt and grasped my wrist. My head snapped up as the interdimensional pulling sensation vanished. Sitting in my car, I stared at Trent, shocked as the world seemed to revolve and settle. The tips of his hair were floating. As time seemed to stand still, Jenks began to softly swear.

Trent had stopped the summons? I hadn't known he could do that. I mean, I knew he could channel a crapload of ever-after, but this? This was incredible!

"Not you too," he said fiercely, and I smiled, grateful even as a sudden pain lanced through my head.

Trent cried out, and his hold on me vanished. Like the shocking snap of a rubber band breaking, the parking lot and my car vanished; Trent's aghast face was the last thing that I saw, Ray's startled cry the last thing I heard.

Chapter Seven

The scent of burnt amber pulled through my awareness first, dragging the rest of the ever-after behind it. I left the ley line gratefully, the harsh taste/sound of it making me shudder. Ku'Sox hadn't summoned me, or I'd be fighting for my life by now, and I sighed in relief as I decided that I was in the ever-after, blue sky, white sun, and salty-tasting wind notwithstanding. Nowhere in reality stank so bad. My nose had adjusted to the smell even before I finished coalescing to find myself standing on a round dais of white rock, two toga-clad demons before me like judges, a crowd of them behind me muttering like the mob they were.

I shivered, trying to throw off the wrong feeling of the line. I seemed to be in a Greek auditorium with rising benches of stone and stately pillars with white cloth strung between them to shade the demons from the fake sun. The horizon was lost in a stark white line, and I looked for the jukebox when I realized I was in Dalliance. It might look as if we were outside, but we were deep underground in the ever-after. The restaurant was a convenient meeting place, and I wondered why the demons were adhering to the dress rules since it was clearly not being used as an eatery, but rather . . . a courtroom? Irate demons filtered in, their varied clothing shifting to togas as they passed the threshold.

Al was beside me on the dais, and finding the collected, slightly bitter demon there was a relief. He was in a toga as well instead of his usual crushed green velvet frock coat, the fine cloth tied with a crimson sash so bright that it made me squint. His hair was in oiled ringlets, making his somewhat blocky face look even more so. Sandals peeped from under his hem, and I stared at his black toenails. That was new.

His manner was off as well, his red, goat-slitted eyes holding a sheen of nervousness as he gave me a quick once-over and frowned. This didn't bode well. He was always confident, even when he shouldn't be, and I followed his gaze to the long bench before us just on the other side of the shallow moat, making a pained smile at Newt and Dali. Not my favorite denizens of the ever-after.

"So you always talk to Dali in front of an audience?" I quipped, and Al grimaced.

"Stand up. Fix your hair," Al said as he smacked me into a stiffer position, keeping to his usual British nobleman accent though he now looked like a Greek councilman. "My *God*, what is that you're wearing? Jeans? You smell like horse."

"That's because I was on one," I said, becoming angry. "Someone from the ever-after stole Ceri and Trent's daughter. Three guesses as to who. And why."

My tone was sarcastic, but Al made a noise as if he didn't care, and I shivered as a cascade of ever-after fell over me, tainted with his aura. For a moment, the rising noise of the demons behind me muted, and then it returned as his aura fell away and I found myself in sandals and a homespun robe with purple silk lining. The moist wind tugged unfamiliarly at my hair, and I reached up to find a ring of wilting flowers. The entire outfit smacked of something that Ceri, Al's ex-familiar, might have looked good in. Me, not so much.

"There. Now you fit in." Al stiffened as he returned his attention to the two demons reclining on a long bench before us. There was an ominous wide ring of sunken ground between us like a barrier.

"You promised you'd never summon me," I said, nervous as Newt gave me a bright, evil-looking smile and toasted me with something red in a wineglass that didn't fit the time period. "We had a deal. I don't yank you across the lines, and you don't yank me." I tried not to complain, but I was still shaking off the adrenaline, and it was my God-given right to be bitchy. "I was trying to get to my scrying mirror, but I was across Cincy at Trent's." I hesitated. "Sorry," I added. "I really was trying."

Al didn't meet my eyes, instead gazing forward into nothing as he squared his shoulders. "*They* asked me to summon you, and since you failed to contact me, *I* complied."

They? He meant Newt and Dali, and I shifted uneasily, my sandals scraping. Better and better. Al took pride in refusing to work in the system—compliance meant we were up shit creek. Again. Nervous, I followed his gaze to the dais and tried to smile at the big bad demons smiling back at me.

Newt was the only other female demon in existence, possibly driven nuts because the elves killed her "sisters," but more likely because Ku'Sox had tricked her into killing the ones they'd missed. Slim and gender neutral, she was sporting a bald head again. Heavy black eyeliner edging her eyes was the only feminine touch beyond the spare curves showing past her toga. Her entirely black eyes traveled over me, and a turbanlike hat misted into existence atop her head, sliding her from androgynous to feminine. The demon had trouble remembering what she was doing, but she was powerful, sort of the crazy Wendy of the lost lord-of-the-flies boys. She seemed to do better when I was around, which made everyone nervous.

A good six feet away from her on the same bench, Dali reclined in apparent idleness. He was squinting at me in irritation, his decidedly round form half a civil servant, half a hanging judge. His toga didn't do a thing for him.

I glanced at the demons behind us, assembled either to watch or take part. I didn't know which, and the distinction seemed important. Some of the faces were familiar, demons who'd asked me to make everything from backyard pools to cars to chandeliers for them. I stiffened as I spotted Ku'Sox weaving his way to the front, earning disdainful looks from those he passed.

He has Ceri and Lucy, I thought, my hands becoming fists as I fought the urge to launch myself at him. I'd saved the tall, psychotic demon's life in the effort to save my own, and I trusted him about as far as I could throw a mountain. The admittedly attractive demon was the engineered child of the demons around me, created with both science and magic in an attempt to circumvent the elf curse that kept them tied to the ever-after and basically sterile. Except now he was chained here even more than they were—since I'd cursed him to be fixed to the ever-after day or night.

The more I got to know him and his kin, the more I wondered if most of the ugliness attributed to demonkind over the centuries could be lain at his feet. The wacko habitually ate people alive, believing that by doing so, he would absorb their souls; apparently he harbored doubts he had one. Even better, the demons had designed him with the ability to manipulate as much ley line energy as a female demon. That hadn't turned out very well, seeing as that was probably why Ku'Sox had tricked Newt into killing everyone who might have a hope of controlling him.

And now he was using Nick to drop into reality whenever he felt like it. It had to have been Ku'Sox who took Ceri and Lucy. He had enough reason. It was obvious, and I snarled at the demon working his way to the bottom of the arena.

Al was trying to turn me back around, and I tugged out of his grasp. "I know what you're doing, Ku'Sox!" I shouted as my face warmed, and several nearby demons elbowed each other to get their neighbors to shut up, hoping for some gossip.

The slightly gaunt, youngish demon in gray smiled at me, his charisma falling flat. "I doubt that," he said, his smooth, melodious voice not at all like Trent's. "You're not nearly scared enough," he added, shoving several demons out of his way with his foot so he could take a front seat.

"If you hurt one hair on Lucy's head, I'll throw you back into the ley lines from where I pulled your *sorry ass*!" I shouted, and Al tugged at me to be quiet. "You think I cursed you now, wait until I put your ugly face in a *jar*!"

Al smacked my gut, and gagging, I turned back around. "Al," I hissed as the arena began to quiet. "Ku'Sox is up to something."

"Ku'Sox is always up to something," Al muttered.

"He stole Ceri and Lucy!" Oh God. That murdering bastard had Lucy. Ceri could probably take care of herself, but if he hurt one chubby finger on the girl, I would tear both realities apart to make him pay.

Al sniffed as if he didn't care. "How? As you say, you cursed him to the ever-after, and even if he found a way past that, why would he?"

"Because he can't snag Trent, and if he has Ceri and Lucy, Ku'Sox has Trent's nuts in a vise."

"So-o-o-o?" he drawled, gazing up to the sky that had never seen a contrail.

"My God, Al, are you being intentionally blind? I told you Nick was stealing surviving Rosewood babies. Trent can make the cure permanent. If he gives it to Ku'Sox, he won't need you anymore. Any of you!"

Al's expression suddenly became worried. "You have more important things to think about than what Ku'Sox is going to do over the next hundred years," he said, a thick, heavy hand falling on my shoulder and turning me around. "We're on trial."

"Again?" I asked, shaking as I leaned past Al to eye Ku'Sox. "What, are we broke?"

"No." Al's voice was sour. "It's your damned ley line. It went wonky. Leaking like the bloody *Titanic*."

Remembering the increasingly caustic sound of the lines, I turned to face him fully. My line? Had it really gone that badly unbalanced?

Al's eye twitched. A spot of ice slid down my spine, making me stiffen. We'd been trying for weeks to get the line I'd scraped between reality and the ever-after to close or at least balance, but until I knew how to jump the lines by myself, it wasn't happening. The imbalance was slowly siphoning off the ever-after into reality, and the only reason that no one had said anything before was because it was only a trickle—plenty of time to fix it. That, and because I was the only female demon they might get some baby demons out of after they tired of the trinkets I could solidify into reality for them. They'd been losing maybe a cubic foot of their dimension a year, not much at all. "How bad is it?" I whispered, trying to smile as I looked at Dali, Al's parole officer.

"Bad." Al's voice was faint but resolute. "Stand up. Try to look sexy."

"In a bedsheet?" I complained, running my hands down it. "How can I look sexy in a bedsheet?" He cleared his throat, and I grimaced. "Never mind."

Frowning, I leaned past Al to glare at Ku'Sox again, certain that he was the reason my line had gone wonky. The demon's smile confirmed it, and suddenly I realized just how deep in the crapper we were. Ku'Sox had thriving Rosewood babies. He had the leverage to make Trent give him the permanent cure. He had a line—my line—leaking ever-after enough to be a real problem. He was going to kill the ever-after and blame me for it.

"Oh shit," I whispered, and Ku'Sox inclined his head as he realized I'd figured it out. I took a breath to shout out the truth, hesitating only because Ku'Sox seemed to want me to. There was more to this; I could see it in his face, feel it in the air, moist and heavy.

Frantic, I turned back to Al. "Al," I hissed. "Tell them he broke my line!"

"Right . . ." Al muttered. "We don't know that, and saying so will only get us in jail where you can't do anything."

"But he did it!" Crap on toast, this had gone from bad to worse, and Al didn't care.

"Don't say anything to get me in jail, love," Al breathed, hardly audible over the noise. "You don't have enough to get both of us out. We'll find out how bad the damage is and fix it."

I wasn't sure if Al meant damage to my line or damage to my credibility. Frustrated, I cocked my hip and fumed.

Dali, who'd been counting heads by the look of it, stood up, his hands raised to quiet the rabble behind us. "Quiet! Quiet!" he shouted, his resonant voice booming. The demon was used to being listened to, and the last of the demons hustled to find their places. Every demon was equal in the ever-after, but some had more power than others, and some had more money. Dali had both.

Beside me, Al jammed a finger into my ribs to make me jerk straight. "I'll do the talking," he said.

"If you can't shut your mouths and your minds in that order, I'm going to clear the room!" Dali bellowed. "None of you will have a chance to vent!"

Newt sniffed, curving her legs up beside her on the bench to look oddly sexy. "And by the Turn, you need to vent," she said, her soft voice carrying to the back of the stands. "It smells like goats in a locker room."

There was a smattering of masculine guffaws, and finally they all shut up. It was like living with perpetual sixth graders. Dali lowered his hands, moving his middle-aged spread gracefully as he walked to the center of the narrow stage. Demons could appear as whatever they wanted. I still didn't know what Dali found appealing in being a fortysomething, slightly overweight, graying civil servant.

"As Al's parole officer, I am responsible for keeping Algaliarept's be-havior within acceptable parameters," he said, and Al cleared his throat and made an elegant bow. "And you," Dali added, pointing at Al, "are re-sponsible for your student's."

That would be me, and I turned a smidge to show off my curves. So I wanted to appear attractive. So sue me. I was surrounded by perfection.

Al visibly swallowed back his ire. With a small breath, he seemed to gain two inches, again bowing with an overdone flourish and sending a foot to smack me to try to get me to do the same. "Assembled country-men," he said as he gracefully straightened. "May I say—"

"No, Gally," Newt interrupted as she took up her wineglass again. "You've talked enough. Your student's ley line has degraded to the point where we're losing enough ever-after to give me a splitting headache."

It might be the wine she was drinking, but I, too, had a soft throbbing at the base of my skull where there'd been none this morning. I had blamed it on whatever had been in Trent's fridge, but maybe it was more. Behind us, the demons muttered agreement.

"Why," Newt said as she fixed her eerie black orbs on Al, "haven't you taught her how to line jump so she can fix it?"

"You think I don't want to?" Al took a step to distance himself from me, and I felt alone. "Her gargoyle is a baby of fifty years, but he's bound to her already so we simply have to wait. And before you mention it, the scar tissue my student received from that *cretin* in the front row trapping her in a ley line prevents any other gargoyle from breaking through her aura to teach her instead."

It was true, and I winced when Ku'Sox rose up, looking lean and ele-gant. "Blaming *this* on me? How gauche." His expression turned mocking. "And typical, I'm afraid."

"Why not?" I barked out, unable to help myself. "You're behind *this*."

The demons around him eased back to give him more room, and an uneasy murmur rose. "Careful, Rachel," Al said as he leaned forward, blocking my view of them.

Jittery, I pushed his hand off me. "Ku'Sox kidnapped Kalamack's daughter and his, ah, common-law wife," I said, exaggerating. "And then the lines go sour? All of them? Doesn't that seem a little odd to any of you?"

Again, the demons whispered among themselves, very aware of, and not liking, Ku'Sox's genocidal tendencies. Al was a lot more direct, and I pulled away when he pinched my elbow. "Stop trying to distract them. It's transparent and obvious."

"Is it?" I said loudly to Al but talking to all of them. "Distraction seems to be working for him! Have any of you given any thought to *why* he might have kidnapped my former familiar's child and wife? My *elfin* familiar?"

The mention of their age-old enemies got the expected snarls, but Newt and Dali were listening. Their war had nearly killed all of them.

"I say we kill her and be done with it!" Ku'Sox said loudly.

Taken aback, I spun, the ring of flowers falling from me to land in the dry moat between us. "Kill me?" I said, unheard over the rising complaints. "Are you nuts?"

"I can't think straight, my head is ringing so badly from the lines!" one demon shouted as he stood, getting a round of agreements before he sat down in vindication.

"I was in the middle of some work, and I lost it all!" a second exclaimed. "You owe me restitution for a week's work down the crapper!"

Al's brow was furrowed. "My student is not responsible for your failure to record your curses in the collective," he said, and Dali nodded his agreement.

"We have a problem," a third said, a band of blue fabric draped over his shoulders. His voice was firm, and I wondered who he was. "The imbalance is impacting everything. It took two of you to summon her through the lines. Two! That's not normal. And it's getting worse!"

I took a step forward. "Well, that was because of Trent," I said, and Al jabbed me with his elbow to shut up.

Newt and Dali pulled their attention from the rising noise behind me. "Trent tried to block our summons?" Newt asked, her long legs showing from under her toga before she tugged it to cover them.

"It's never taken a collective to summon anyone!" the demon with the blue sash said loudly, enjoying the attention his claim had brought him. "The ever-after is falling apart!"

The sky is falling, the sky is falling, I thought derisively, and Newt shifted her feet to the floor, her expression seeming to mirror my thoughts.

"This is pointless," Newt said as she poised almost coyly. "Stay on track, gentlemen. Rachel, love, can you fix the line?"

I didn't like being called "love," especially not by her, but I let it pass. "No," I said sullenly.

"Of course she can!" Al shouted to drown out the immediate complaints, his hands raised pleadingly as he shot me a glare. "We need more time, is all."

"We have no time!" Ku'Sox asserted, aggressively riling them up. "She broke the balance. Killing her will fix it."

"It will not!" I exclaimed, but Al's wince and Dali's sudden deflation as he sat down made me wonder. "It won't, will it?" I asked Al softly, and the demon made a long, drawn-out, regretful noise of possibility.

Dali leaned forward, his elbows on his knees, ignoring the rising noise behind us for a moment. "Unfortunately it might," he said to me, giving the demons time to argue. "Lines created from a jump between reality and the ever-after are permanent, for the most part, but lines made from a reality-to-reality jump are not, and killing you might erase it."

"Might?" Panicking, I looked at Ku'Sox, hating his smug smile. "This is a setup," I said, wanting to retreat but there was nowhere to go. "The line was stable. Well, not stable, but it wasn't unzipping like this! Someone's tampered with it!" It was as close as I dared go without actually blaming him, and even so, Al lightly smacked me on the shoulder to shut up.

"We have nowhere to go if the ever-after collapses," Ku'Sox said, voice loud over the rising noise. "Kill her before it's too late!"

"Wrong!" I shouted, and Al sighed heavily. "*They* have nowhere to go. You do."

Ku'Sox beamed at me as if I'd played right into his hands. "Not anymore, but you do, Rachel. Perhaps *you* are trying to kill *us*."

"Me?" I stammered, mentally backpedaling as I realized why he was so smug. He was going to kill the ever-after and everyone in it—blaming it on me. He had a way around the curse. Had to. Or he knew a way to force me to remove it. Maybe Lucy and Ceri had been kidnapped to force my hand, not Trent's. Damn it all to the Turn and back.

"I didn't do this!" I spun to face the crowd behind me, then back to Dali. "I was on a horse in reality when the line started leaking this bad!"

Ku'Sox stood. "Then you admit it was leaking? And you never told anyone?"

Al was holding his head in his hand, and I wished I'd kept my mouth shut. "Just a little," I said, then had to raise my voice when they all began talking. "I was trying to fix it before anyone noticed!"

Al stood stiffly beside me as he fidgeted in subtle ways that only I could possibly see. "Will you shut up now?" he breathed, roughly turning me to face Newt and Dali.

"But he did it!"

"But you can't prove it!" Al mocked my whiny tone.

"There are thriving Rosewood babies being stolen, and he kidnapped hostages to force my freed familiar to make the cure permanent!" I shouted. "Doesn't that sound a bit odd to you?" But no one cared.

"Are you done?" Al muttered, his back stiff as he faced Newt and Dali.

Looking uneasy, Dali rose to his feet, hands raised to quiet them. "Rachel, as it is your line and you're the only demon who can survive free of the ever-after, we are understandably concerned that your intent is to destroy us *and* the ever-after."

My hasty breath to protest whooshed out as Al poked me in the ribs to be quiet.

"Much as I regret my decision," Dali said, moving to the front of the drop-off between us, "it's my recommendation that if Rachel admits that she can't balance her line, then perhaps her death is the best way to ensure our continued existence."

I couldn't speak. They weren't serious, were they? Ku'Sox had done something. I knew it by his smug expression as he listened to the demons call for my blood. Standing there, my heart hammered, and I backed up into Al. They couldn't. I hadn't done anything!

Dali looked at me, and I quailed. "If it's a choice between your life and all of ours, then you will die." He hesitated, then added quietly, "Even if you're not actually the one who should be blamed for it."

His eyes slid behind me to Ku'Sox, and my hope leaped. He believed me. I glanced at Al to see he realized it, too. And Newt, now toasting me with her wine. Proof. We needed proof. I could do that. I could get the damned proof. I just needed a few days.

"Gentle associates, gentle associates!" Al said, his voice rumbling through me from where I was pressed against him. "Of course she can balance her line." His breath was like brimstone against me, sharp and jolting. "Tell them, Rachel," he prompted, his voice low with threat.

"S-sure," I stammered, scared to death.

Al's eyes closed in relief. "We can fix it," he said as they opened.

"Then why haven't you?" Ku'Sox said softly, mocking us.

"My rooms are shrinking!" another called.

"We have nowhere to go. Kill her now before it's too late!" a third shouted, and it all started up again. I began to panic. Only Al's firm hold on my arms kept me from moving. He was not my jailer, he was my rock. Whatever happened to me would happen to him. I didn't altogether trust Al, but I trusted that.

"No." It was a soft utterance, and my eyes went to Newt, still sitting calmly on her bench, legs curled back up under her again. "I said no!" she said louder, and the noise behind Al and me abated. "I told you months ago that Rachel's line was unbalanced, and you all said I was crazy."

"You are crazy!" someone shouted from the back, and she smiled as if in benediction.

"Tru-u-u-ue," she drawled when they quieted again. "But no one listened. You will listen to me now. Call it your collective penance."

My heart gave a pound, and I tensed against Al. Was it a chance or a sentence?

Knowing all eyes were on her, Newt stood gracefully. "I will give you space from my own rooms to compensate your loss, Cyclarenadamackitn. I will compensate all your one-inch, two-inch losses because I know how *important every inch* is to you aged, decrepit men. But in return, I want to see if she can do it. It would be a skill worth having—don't you think? Being able to balance lines scraped from a reality-to-reality jump? In case we someday can return to reality and abandon the ever-after completely?" I swallowed hard as Newt turned her black, featureless eyes on me. "If she can't, then you may kill her."

There was a breath of silence, in which I could almost hear the demons thinking that over. Behind me, Al sighed, his hands gripping my upper arms easing. It was a chance.

I looked at Ku'Sox and his evident anger, but he stayed silent as the demons came to a consensus. I couldn't tell if Dali was pleased or irritated as he stood, frowning once at Newt's pleased smile as she beamed over all of them.

"So!" Dali said, bringing everyone's attention back to the stage. "Are we agreed? Rachel and Al have time to balance the line if Newt compensates everyone?"

Al held his breath as no one spoke, each waiting for the other to say something first.

"Ku'Sox?" Dali prompted. It was clear that the bastard child wasn't pleased, but if he continued to push for my death, it would be obvious that he wanted it.

His face empty of emotion, Ku'Sox turned on a heel. Pushing past the surrounding demons, he distanced himself, and then, with a soft breath of air replacing his mass, he vanished.

"I'll take that as a yes," Dali said as the rest of the demons began popping out in turn, a soft muttering of conversations rising and falling like surf.

I finally began to relax, turning to look up at Al as he let go of my shoulders. "Now what?" There was no way in hell I could balance that line.

Al wouldn't look at me, and I again wondered how I could have gone from fear to mistrust to understanding to reliance in so short of time. "We find a way to fix this," he said. "Or a way to blame it on someone else," he added, stiffening as Newt rose and made her way to us. Dali was busy with a few lingering demons, and I watched as Al seemed to shift and change, the mask he always wore sliding over him again as she came forward.

"That's it then!" he said cheerfully as he clapped his thick hands again. "I guess we'll be off to look at the line. See what we can do."

"Yes," Newt said, her smile chilling me as she took my hand and looked at it, noticing perhaps that I now had a metal pinkie ring instead of a wooden one. "You go balance that line. And in the meantime, Rachel's debt to me grows with each passing second."

I winced as I pulled my hand from hers, but what could I say? I did have some income here from the use of the tulpa I'd made for Dalliance.

Al was huffing and puffing, but I knew there was no deal we could get that was better than our continued survival.

"Al," Newt said sharply before he could protest. "If your student dies, that debt reverts to you."

Al glanced at Dali, and then back to her. "Looking forward to it," he grumbled, his hand on my shoulder tightening.

Newt's black gaze was on the wisp of my tattoo that showed, and I managed a nervous smile. "Thank you," I said as she turned to leave, and she spun slowly back to us.

"Don't thank me now, love. Save it till the morning after."

In a hush of inrushing air, Newt vanished like a Cheshire cat. Feeling ill and scared, I turned to Al. "Can we go home?"

"No," he said, simultaneously leading me down off the dais and waving to Dali as if everything was A-Okay, not Oh Shit. "But I agree we need to leave."

I hopped from the raised stage, and Al's hands left my wrist. I felt small as I looked at the stone bench Ku'Sox had been sitting on. "It's him," I said, and Al growled. "Ku'Sox has done something to the line. You know it, too. He's got those kids, and this is all an elaborate con to destroy the ever-after and blame me for it."

"If you can't prove it, it doesn't mean shit," Al said, but as I balked, he sighed and rubbed his head. "Fine," he grumbled as he took my arm as if to escort me. "The sun is still up, but let's go look at your line."

"How?" I said, knowing he couldn't be in reality when the sun was above the horizon, but it was too late and the soft ache of the ley line had taken me.

Chapter Eight

The red sun of the ever-after hurt my eyes, and I squinted, holding up a hand as I stood on dusty red soil made of pulverized rock and felt the gritty wind push at me. Al and I had come in on a slightly raised plateau. Before us snaked a dry riverbed. To our left was a slump of broken rock where Loveland Castle was in reality. Sprigs of waist-high yellow grass were scattered about, and a few stunted trees were all that was left of the woods that surrounded the castle in reality. Here in the ever-after, it was desolate.

Between us and the pile of rock, a ley line shimmered, more of a heat image than anything else in the sunbaked wind. The line was making me feel slightly nauseated, almost seasick. *The leak?* I wondered. As a gargoyle, Bis would know, but he'd be hard to wake until the sun went down.

Beside me, Al was again dressed in his familiar crushed green velvet coat, lace and all. Black boots with buckles scuffed the dirt, and he jauntily sported an obsidian walking cane and a matching tall hat. Dark round glasses protected his eyes, but I could tell it wasn't enough, as his expression was pained and the sun seemed to be picking away at our auras as we stood. The sun was one of the reasons the demons hid underground in vast caverns overlain with the illusion of the outside. The fact that structures tended to fall apart on the surface was another.

It was odd seeing Al, with his top hat and elegant grace, poking about with the tip of his cane as he found evidence of other demons. "No surface demons," I said. The hot air hurt my chest.

"The sun feels worse today." Al crouched to turn over a rock that someone had shifted.

I winced as the wind whipped my toga and tiny pinpricks of rock hit my bare legs. All around me were the telltale signs of other demons: a footprint here, a scuff there—an oval impression in the dust that looked like the bottom of Newt's staff. They'd been here, seen the damage, incidentally obliterating the evidence that Ku'Sox might have been here earlier to make the leak in my line worse. I sort of knew how the I.S. felt.

Al slowly exhaled as he stood, his expression blank as he looked out over the dry riverbed to the scrub and trees. His fingers fumbled in a tiny pocket, and he sniffed a pinch of brimstone. "It's a damn ugly place for a ley line."

"I wasn't planning on making one to begin with," I said, then shivered when a wave of ever-after coated me, falling away to show he'd changed me out my toga for head-to-toe black leather. No bra or panties, but at least the gritty wind wasn't scouring me like the sun was stripping my aura, and this outfit, unlike most, fitted me, not Ceri.

Oh God, *Ceri.* I was no closer to getting them back than when I'd got here.

Unaware of my thoughts, Al shoved a prissy pink-and-white lace parasol at me. "Here."

The frail thing clashed with the leather, but immediately I felt a sense of relief in its shadow. I'd seen Ku'Sox. He knew I was aware of what he'd done. He'd make his demands soon enough, and until then, I had to believe that Ceri and Lucy were okay. "Thanks," I said as I looked at the stack of rubble. "Shouldn't the line be over the rocks? That's where I came in."

Al began picking his way to my ley line, his cane knocking jagged chunks of rock from his path. "Lines drift," he said, his head down. "Move. They're like magnets repelling each other. They will shift across continents given enough time and impetus. They only appear to be stationary because they've balanced with each other ages ago. Yours here . . ." Al sniffed in consideration. "It likely won't move much anymore. Has it always been this size?"

I nodded as I came even with him and faced the barely visible shimmer in the air. The ley line the university was built on was wide enough that you could drive a team of horses down it for a quarter mile. The one in my graveyard was about four feet wide and twenty feet long, an admittedly small line. Mine here was about the same, maybe a little longer.

Al pressed his lips together, puffing his air out as he gazed at seemingly nothing, but he was probably looking at my line with his second sight. "You got out fast. The longer it takes, the wider the wound."

"Really?" So a small line was a good thing, which made me wonder who made the line in my graveyard. Then I wondered who had taken forever to get out of the one at the university. Al maybe?

Walking the length of the shimmer in the air, Al turned and strolled back, the line a haze between us. "A line this size can't be leaking this much on its own."

"It wasn't when I left it." I cocked my hip, feeling naked without my usual shoulder bag.

Al's focus landed on me. "Can you hear it?" he asked, and my lips puckered in distaste. "You're not using your second sight," he added, and I shook my head, tucking a gritty strand of hair behind an ear. But at his dramatic prompting, I exhaled and opened my second sight.

The ringing worsened, scraping across my awareness in a discordant jangle the way the red sun seemed to rub my skin raw. But as bad as it sounded, it looked even uglier. The line was the usual red shimmer at chest height, but there was a sharply defined line of purple at its center running the entire length, thickest at the center and thinning to nothing at the ends. It was almost black at its core, and streamers of fading red were funneling into it like bands of energy slipping into a black hole. I could actually see the leak as it sucked in everything around it, and it made my stomach twist.

"Is it safe to use like that?" I said to Al, looking distorted and red through the line's energy. Behind him, the rubble loomed ominously.

He shrugged. "We used it to get here."

Distressed, I put a hand to my middle and dropped my second sight. "Al," I said. "That purple core wasn't there the last time we were here."

"I know."

"What did Ku'Sox do to it?" I said, frustrated.

Hands on his hips, Al searched the line with his eyes. He reminded me of Jenks, somehow, even though he didn't look anything like him. "I don't know."

He believed me. Relieved, I eased my shoulders down. I debated walking through the line to stand beside him, then edged around it as he had done, my boots kicking rocks and pebbles out of my way. "So-o-o," I drawled, feeling small beside him. "How *do* you unbalance a ley line?"

Shifting his arms at his side, he glanced at me and then away. "No idea," he said, looking as if it had physically hurt him to admit it. "Tell you what. Toddle through it to the other side to reality and see what it looks like from there."

I backed up a step. "Seriously?"

Frowning, he gave me a once-over, the wind blowing his hair about his glasses. "Get in the line, will yourself through, and see what the line looks like from reality. If we're lucky, it won't be like this. Maybe it's merely a curse we can break."

I hesitated, then jumped when he swooped forward and took my arm, stepping us into the line together. "Hey!" I yelped as my stomach dropped and the sensation of an unending chalkboard scrape serrated over my nerves. Stiffening, I yanked out of his grip, but I didn't leave the line since he was still standing in it. If he could take it, I could, too.

Nauseated, I brought up my second sight. The purple line was so close I could touch it. My heart pounded, and little pinpricks of energy seemed to hit me. By all appearances, the line was sucking in energy, but the discordant jangle clearly showed it was giving something off as well.

"I'll stay here in the line," Al said, and I swallowed hard. "That way you can tell me what you can see. Do you think you are capable of that?"

"Sure." I licked my lips, then wished I hadn't as my tongue came away gritty.

"Now, maybe?" Al prompted as he tugged his sleeves down. "It's going to take me hours to get the sand out of my hair. And stay out of that purple shit."

I looked at the evil purple line, swirls of red vanishing at its black core. "Not a problem." Taking a slow breath, I closed my eyes and willed myself across the realities. It was different from using a line to jump, and demons seldom did it unless they were dragging an unwilling slave across realities—it was akin to taking a horse downtown when everyone else had a hovercar.

The whine from the line shifted, and I opened my eyes, seeing a ghost-like Al still standing beside me with a shimmer of red between us. The air lacked the bite of burnt amber, and the damned wind that always seemed to be blowing in the ever-after was gone. I could hear birds, and under my feet were weeds and grass. The sound of running water was faint, and tall trees leafed out for spring stood around me. Exhaling, I turned. Behind me Loveland Castle was whole again, albeit a dumpy little building falling apart—one man's dream of nobility crumbling from neglect. Noble ideas tended to do that when left alone.

"Well?" Al prompted, and I turned to him, catching my balance in surprise. The weirdness of the line was impacting everything. The vision of the dusty, sunbaked surface of the ever-after was superimposed over the lush greenery of the raised garden area of the castle, but the purple-and-black line looked about the same from this side as the other. *Ugly.*

I lowered the parasol and squinted up at the yellow sun. "It's hard to tell. Mind if I step away and see what it looks like from outside the line?"

"Hurry up about it," he grumped, and I took several hasty steps backward until the unsettling scrape across my nerves vanished. My soft headache went with it, and I took a breath of clean air. I was completely in reality, and I brought out the phone from my back pocket, checking the time. I had about fifteen minutes until Jenks summoned me, and knowing Al was becoming impatient, I texted Trent I was okay and to have Jenks give me another hour.

Unfortunately, the line looked about the same from this reality, though the grating whine that remained was a slightly higher pitch. Snapping my phone closed, I looked over the area to try to determine if anyone had been here. The weeds right under the line were all ramrod straight, as if they were being tugged upward. It was weird, and crouching just outside the line, I ran a hand under it, watching the grass spring back. The ground between the clumps of weeds looked as if it had been vacuumed.

I stifled a shiver and rose. Thinking my parasol must look silly, I closed it. They did have tours at the castle, occasionally. I could see no evidence that anyone had been here in weeks, and I stepped back into the line. Al seemed to relax as I became slightly more real to him, slightly closer to his reality. "Well?" he prompted.

I shrugged, scuffing my boots in the grass. "It looks the same, but the pitch of the whine is higher. The grass, though . . ." I kicked at a tuft. "It's growing funny. Straight up, like it's being pulled. Even the ground looks like anything not nailed down got sucked up into it."

"Maybe it did." Al ducked under the purple line, shuddering as he came up on the other side, closer to me. "The purple seems to be a physical manifestation of a heavy leak of energy."

"Where's it going?" I asked. "The energy, I mean?"

Al held his arms behind his back, adopting a posture of lecture that I recognized from our days and nights in his kitchen/lab. "When the sun is up, energy flows from reality into the ever-after; when the sun goes down, the flow reverses." His voice echoed, ghostlike. "The problem is that less is flowing into the ever-after than is going out. That purple line? I don't know what in the two worlds that is. It appears to disrupt the natural ebb and flow, sucking in energy like an event horizon. Making it worse than it should be."

Event horizon? I wish I'd paid more attention in advanced ley line physics.

Al sighed, and I willed myself back to the ever-after. The wind hit me like a slap, and I popped my parasol back open. "I'm sorry," I said as I walked around the line to join him.

"For what?" he said sarcastically. "You've done so much."

I fidgeted. "For making the line to begin with, I suppose. How did you balance yours?"

Al gave me an askance look before rocking into motion, distancing himself. "I tweaked it until it was within proper parameters, but we can't do that with yours because it is a reality-to-reality-based line. Besides, you need to know how to jump a line first."

My jaw clenched, then relaxed. Bis had to teach me, and he was too young.

"Even so," Al said as he waved a dry stalk of ever-after grass through the purple line, then inspected it for damage, grunting as if something pleased him. "I don't think knowing how to jump a line will help. No, this purple shit is different." He straightened and dropped the stalk. "We should be able to do something about it. Buy us some time. Put us back where we were yesterday."

The first faint stirrings of hope began in me. "What do you have in mind?"

He flashed me a quick grin, and I felt as if I'd done something right. "Stay here," he said, waving his white-gloved hands dramatically. "I'll be right back."

"Al?" I called out, but he'd vanished. Nervous, I gazed across the bleak, sunbaked earth and the dry riverbed, feeling the bits of windblown earth hit me. I didn't like being alone on the surface, and I twirled my parasol. My hair was going to be impossible to get through tonight.

Almost immediately he stumbled back in, his head down and back hunched. "Ah, here," he said, his goat-slitted eyes meeting mine from over his dark-tinted glasses. "Put this on."

It was a small black ring, and I looked at it in my palm, seeing there was a new lump of a circlet under his glove. Uneasy, I eyed him.

"I'm not giving it to you," he huffed. "It's a loan. For a few minutes. I want it back."

"It's a ring," I said flatly, not able to tell if it was black gold or simply tarnished.

"Sharp as a tack, that one," Al grumped. "You want to put it on, now? Pick a finger."

I spread the fingers of my left hand, and I swear, he made a small noise of dismay. I looked up to see his jaw clenched. "What does it do?"

Al grimaced, shifting from foot to foot. "I, ah, it's a life rope of sorts. That is, me in the ever-after to pull your ass out of the fire if I'm wrong, and you in reality, fixing it."

Fixing the line was the entire point, and I didn't mind having a safety rope. If it was a ring, then that was cool. Still I hesitated; the ring seemed to soak in the harsh light. It was heavy on my palm, and I had the insane desire to drop it into a fire and see if an inscription appeared. I set the open parasol down, and it rolled in the wind until catching against a large rock.

"The rings will allow us to function as a single energy entity across the realities," Al said, standing almost sideways to me as he looked out over nothing. "I think."

"You think?" I said, starting to understand. "Is that like a power pull?"

Al leered, the wind shifting the gritty lank curls of his hair. "If you want."

Head shaking, I extended the ring back to him. "No."

He rolled his eyes, looking at the washed-out sky and refusing to take it. "You are utterly without a sense of humor today," he said, and my hand dropped. "We will simply be able to borrow upon and find each other's chi with minimal disruption."

These were more than just rings, and I wanted the truth of it. "Al," I said forcefully. "What are these? You have one, too. I can see it under your glove."

Shoulders slumping, he showed me his back. "Nothing," he said, the wind almost obliterating his voice. "They're nothing now but a way to yank your butt out of the fire." He turned around, and his lost look surprised me. "Go through the line to reality," he said, gesturing. "You should be able to hear me whether you're in the line or not if you have the ring on. You'll have a better chance fixing it if you work from the reality you made it from." I hesitated, and he added, "Think of them as a scrying mirror, without the eavesdropping."

Unsure, I looked at the simple band of tarnished metal. A private line to each other's thoughts was a rather questionable connection—not a violation as such, but very . . . personal. It didn't help that they looked like wedding bands.

Against my better judgment, I slipped the ring on my index finger. Wavering on my feet, I felt my consciousness expand. It was exactly like a scrying mirror, but the connection was tighter, far more intimate. I could feel not just Al's presence, but sense his masculinity, his worry, his concern. I could sense the limits of his chi, and I knew to the last iota how much it could hold, the power he could wield. It wasn't as much as I could. It wasn't that he lacked. Female demons had a naturally elevated ability to harbor two souls behind one aura, as in having a baby.

"Mother pus bucket," Al said breathily. "You've expanded your reach, Rachel."

Apparently he could see my abilities as well. "Is it supposed to feel like this?" I asked, heart pounding as I flicked a quick look at him.

"This isn't a good idea," Al said, seeming as uncomfortable as I was. "We might be able to do this with scrying mirrors."

I jumped when he took my hand to slip the ring from me. There was a pain in the back of his eyes that had nothing to do with me. My heart pounded, and not knowing why, I curved my fingers to make a fist. Al's attention jerked up, and I knew I must've looked panicked as he froze. "Ah, I'm good," I said, tense. "That is, if you're okay."

His lips twitched. "I didn't expect it to be . . ."

"What?" I prompted when he faltered.

"Exactly the way I remembered it," he said sourly, and he dropped my hand. "Go. Let me know when you're in reality standing outside the line. As I said, they function much as a scrying mirror."

He turned away, waiting, and I hesitated. He was staring out at the broken landscape of the ever-after, thinking of someone. I could feel it in his thoughts, the longing for something he'd lost so long ago that he'd forgotten even that he missed it.

My feet scuffed, and he tensed. Spinning the ring on my finger, I stepped into the line, being careful to stay clear of the purple center. Immediately the harsh discord renewed my headache, but almost before I recognized it, the pain seemed to halve. Al had taken some of it.

"Sorry," I said, and he spun, coattails furling and heartache carefully hidden.

"That's what the rings do," he said, urging me away with his gloved hands. "It's not anything I wasn't expecting. Go."

Nodding, I took a breath and moved myself into reality. Again I breathed the fresh air, relishing the warmth of the yellow sun and the soft hush of the wind in the trees. It was no wonder demons were bad-tempered. They lived in a virtual hell.

Remembering Al, I toned down my thoughts of relief.

Good, they work, he thought, and I squirmed as his masculine, domineering presence solidified in mine. *I wasn't sure if they would between realities.*

"Good Lord, can you ease up?" I asked, feeling as if he was breathing down my neck, and I felt him chuckle.

Uncomfortable?

I looked over the fallow, weed-choked garden, seeing the outlines of a man's dream of a perfect spot of truth. "A little, yes," I said, then sighed in relief when the spun-adrenaline feeling he was instilling in me seemed to fade. He was everything masculine, and having it so close was unnerving. "Thanks," I said, backing out of the line and looking at it with my second sight. I could see Al watching me like a foppish ghost from a romance novel. "So, how do I fix it?"

I changed my mind. You watch. I'll investigate. I'm going to follow the purple line inward, see if there's an aura signature on it. Maybe I can plug it. It's clearly a manufactured flaw, and as such, it will have a beginning and an end with which to unravel it.

I smiled. "And with proof, they will go after Ku'Sox!"

I'd rather fix it, he thought at me wryly. *If we can't do that, we will all still die. That is, everyone but you and Ku'Sox.*

My attention came up from where I'd been scuffing the grass. "Then you think he has a way around that curse?"

He nodded, and my heart pounded. "But you said not to step into the purple line."

That was before the rings.

Distrusting this, I stared at him, the red sheen of a dimensional barrier between us.

There's nothing in either reality that will sever our connection through the rings, he thought, glaring at me. *If I get stuck, pull me out. Ah, without physically going into the purple shit, that is. If both of us are in there, what's the point of a lifeline?*

Still I looked at him, weighing his body language against the emotions I was sensing through the rings. He was better than me at blocking them, and I wasn't sure why he was nervous. *Al,* I thought at him, hands on my hips. *I don't like this plan.*

We don't have time to find a plan you like. His thoughts slipped into mine, oily with deceit. *Newt is paying for the volume lost with her own space. The sooner we get this hole plugged, the better. I just got my atrium back, and I don't want to lose it.*

He was moving toward the purple line, and fear slid down my spine, magnified by Al's own worry. "Al!" I cried out, hand outstretched.

Al stopped, turned, and gave me a last look. *Hold on to me,* I saw him say, hearing it echo in my thoughts as well. *Don't let go.*

And then, he stepped into the purple line.

I gasped—it felt as if an ice pick was hammered into my skull from the top right to the bottom left. I screamed, falling to my knees. Al's pain. It was Al's pain, and I floundered, forcing my eyes open. I couldn't see him, and I panted, almost losing him in my thoughts. Forcing the bile down, I closed my eyes and searched for him with my mind. I was swimming in a black cloud of acid, unable to open my eyes, arms outstretched and burning as I followed down a rising trace of agony like bubbles to find him.

"Got you!" I gasped, and I wrapped my soul around his.

I flung myself backward with him, crying out because it felt as if my thoughts had been ripped apart. My back hit the scattered tufts of grass, and I stared up at a perfect blue sky. The pain was gone. Al wasn't with me.

"Al!" I scrambled to my feet, realizing what happened. I'd tried to pull him into reality when the sun was up. It wasn't happening. I couldn't feel him anymore, and in a panic, I rushed back into the line, willing myself into the ever-after with wild abandonment.

The line burned, scraping across me like sandpaper. Even with my second sight, I couldn't see Al, and I wondered if he had been sucked into that purple line. If I physically went in after him, we'd both be lost. I had to stay where I was. But perhaps with the rings . . . Maybe I could find him with my mind and bring both his body and soul back?

I gave one last look at the broken, red-sheened world the demons were consigned to—a hell of their own making designed to entrap and kill the elves but that had only damned themselves. And then, falling to my knees, I closed my eyes and sent my mind into the line, letting it be pulled into the purple-black nothing.

My breath came out in a pained whimper, and I fell against the dry earth, my hands spasmodically clenching on the broken rock, my cheek pressed into the dirt. My mind was squished to a thin line, my thoughts reduced to a colorless state. My heart beat, and that hurt even more.

Al! I thought, and the pain redoubled as I found him, struggling to think, starved for thought under the crushing pressure. There were sparkles in my distant fingertips and toes. I was suffocating. If I didn't get us out of here soon, I was going to forget how to breathe and we'd *both* die.

My skin and thoughts on fire, I wrapped what I could of myself around the echo of emotion that was left of Al. With one last agonizing push of will, I sent us home, back to where my body jerked in convulsions in the red dust.

The harsh wind of the ever-after hit me like a slap. The heavy weight of Al slammed into me, and we both cried out as he slid to the earth. Sharp fragments of stone bit into my side, and I heard him take a sobbing breath of air. I tried to move, my scream of pain coming out as a whimper. My thoughts still burned, and I finally got my eyes open.

We were in the ever-after, the humming ley line still unchanged above us, still holding that core of purple nothing. Beside me, Al lay askew, his green velvet coat charred, mimicking the state of his mind, his aura. Pain-racked, I managed to sit up, tears running down my face as my eyes tried to clear. My clothes were untouched, and I wondered how much of this pain was mine and how much was Al's.

Al's body shifted as he took a ragged breath, and I touched him, my hand shaking and the ring glinting a bright silver white in the red air. It was black no longer, the tarnish burned away.

"Al?" I croaked. The sun hurt, but I couldn't reach the parasol, shifting back and forth in the wind that scoured me to my bones.

"I thought you'd . . . left . . . me."

I could barely hear him, and I leaned on his shoulder as I scooted closer. He gasped at the added weight, and the pain in my head doubled. "I couldn't pull you out into reality," I explained. "I had to move to the ever-after to do it."

"I'm out?" he said, and his jaw clenched as he opened his eyes. He'd lost his glasses somewhere, and his eyes were black—like Newt's. He closed his eyes at my fear.

"We're out," I said, still panting at the pain. We were out, but I didn't think it mattered.

"I'll get us home," he said, and then we both screamed as he tried to jump to a line. Fire burned down both our synaptic lines, and I fell back, groaning as I forced my lungs to keep working. If I was breathing, I was alive, right? How could it hurt so much? I was on fire. We were burning to death from the inside out.

"Oh God. Oh God," I moaned, looking in my hand in wonder. It looked the same, but it felt like it was burning, charring. "Don't. Don't do that again. Please."

"I can't jump us, Celfnnah. I'm sorry. Save yourself."

The heartache in Al's voice cut through the agony, and I focused on him, seeing him curled up against the pain. *Celfnnah?* "You want me to leave?" I said in disbelief as my tears started again, but whether they were to clear my eyes of the grit or because of Al, I couldn't tell.

Al groaned, and with a sudden jerk, he finally got the ring off his finger. My breath sucked in as the pain vanished. He took one last shuddering breath, and then he passed out, his entire body going limp. My hand flashed out as Al's ring pinged against the rock and I caught it.

Silence filled me, the cessation of pain almost unreal as the wind shifted a lank curl into my line of vision. There was only a fading ache, deep in my tissues as if I had been in a fever. "Al?"

I touched his shoulder, my hand coming away with a sheen of sweat bleeding all the way through his clothes. He still breathed, but he was out cold. "Don't you go to sleep, Al!" I shouted, shifting to kneel before him. "Stay with me!" I might as well be talking to the dead, and I put his ring on my thumb so I wouldn't lose it. Stretching, I reached for my parasol, holding it over both our heads. Damn it, we were in big trouble now.

My head jerked up at a clink of rock, and my heart seemed to clench at the skinny, raw figure silhouetted against the red sky, his tattered clothes drifting in the never-stopping wind, looking like the remnants of an aura as it fluttered. I tensed. Where there was one surface demon, there were many, and they only attacked the weak.

Yeah, we fit that category now.

"Al!" I hissed, shaking his shoulder, but he only groaned. "Wake up! I can't jump us. Damn it, I knew this was a bad idea!"

A huge shadow covered us and was gone. Looking up, I tapped my broken line, crying out and shoving it away as the discordant jangle cut through me. Either I'd damaged my aura, or the line was truly poison. Eyes on the empty sky, I scrambled up, not knowing if I could reach another line from here, but willing to try. But I froze when I saw what had made the shadow. It was a huge gargoyle—his skin gray and pebbly, and his leathery wings bigger than a bus is long. Slowly my panic ebbed to a cautious alarm, leaving me shaking and standing askew.

The surface demon had vanished, and I stared as the huge gargoyle made one last circle and landed where it had been, as if daring it to return. My gaze flicked to the sun. Either this gargoyle was very old or they went by different rules here in the ever-after.

My attention dropped to the heavy, notched sword he had in his claw-like hand, and I edged back to Al, feeling scared for an entirely new reason.

"Who are you?" the gargoyle said, his vowels sounding like rocks grinding, his consonants like iron shavings stuck to a magnet, sharp and pointy. "What are you doing to the new rift?"

His sword had drooped slightly, and I took a slow breath. Gargoyles were protectors. Either I was in big trouble or I finally caught a break. "We were trying to balance it. Please, can you help us? He's burned. We need to get out of the sun."

The gargoyle dropped the sword as if it were a worthless stick, and it pinged against the rock until it wedged itself. His craggy hind feet cracked the stone as he shifted his grip. "Balance the line?" he said, his voice rising and falling. "That's short term, but possibly the only answer that I will allow. For now. I know you. Your gargoyle is too young to facilitate fixing the new. This is your line. It rings with your aura. You let him break it. Why?"

Him? I thought, trying to shade Al with my body. He must be talking of Ku'Sox, and I wished a gargoyle's testimony would hold up in a demon court. "I didn't *let* him break it. He did it to blame me for destroying the ever-after. Do you know how I can fix what he did?"

The gargoyle yawned and looked at the sun. "Change damaged it. Change will fix it. In time it will fix itself, destroying everything here along with it."

From my feet, Al moved, whispering, "Newt. Call Newt."

My gaze jerked to him, glad he was conscious. "Newt?"

His eyes opened, and I started at his black eyes. "She can jump us," he breathed, clearly not seeing anything. "She'll be listening for you. She's worried about you, the insane bat." Wincing, he tried to move, then thought better of it. "Do hurry. I feel less up to par than usual."

Nauseated, I loosened my hold on my thoughts, searching for the demon collective. I'd never tried to contact anyone without a scrying mirror, but as he said, she was listening. "Newt!" I shouted, and the gargoyle lifted his wings in alarm. "Newt, I need you. *We* need you!"

The gargoyle made one leathery down pulse of air, then hesitated, his feet still gripping the ruins of the castle. "You won't find enough time to fix it before it fixes itself. The lines are failing. The world breaker wakes. We need to leave. Save who you can."

He jumped into the air, the wind from his departure making me squint and sending my lank hair blowing back. He circled once before becoming lost in the red sun. Desperately worried, I looked at Al, out cold again. The sweat had dried on him, and he was shaking.

"Maybe I should've asked him for help," I whispered, then spun at the clink of stone on wood. It was Newt, and I was struck dumb for a moment, reminded of the first time we'd met. She'd been a referee to see how long I'd last after the sun went down, marooned in the ever-after by Trent's "best friend." She was wearing a long, flowing robe like a desert sheik, her black staff in one hand, the other holding her robe closed against the wind. Her awareness, though, was clear this time, her step sure as she made her way to us with a new urgency.

"Help me get him home," I said before she had closed the gap, and I shocked myself with the knowledge that I'd pay just about anything for it.

Her long, somewhat bony hands were gentle as she crouched beside him, holding a hand over him as if testing his aura. "What did he do?" she asked tersely, then paused as her glance fell on the sword the gargoyle had left behind.

I sniffed, backing up a step with my arms wrapped around my middle. "He tried to find out if Ku'Sox made that purple line and fell to the bottom of it."

Newt spun, finding her feet in an instant. "And you *let* him?"

"He didn't say it was going to scrape his aura off!" I yelled back. "I got him out, but . . ." My words faltered, and I felt the prick of tears, hating them. It was Al, for God's sake.

"You got him out?" Newt blinked her black eyes at me, drawing herself up when she saw the ring on my hand. "Oh." She hesitated. "He gave you . . . Where is the other one?"

Nervous, I held up my other hand to show her my thumb. "He took it off. He took all the pain so I could call you."

Newt made a harrumph of disagreement. "He took all the pain so it wouldn't kill you."

Fidgeting, I came closer. Was she going to help or not? "Newt. Please. The sun."

Her androgynous face twisting to look more feminine somehow, she squinted up at it. "Indeed," she said sourly, twitching the hem of her robe off Al. "It's like breathing in acid."

The gritty wind gusted against me with a sudden force, and I closed my eyes, feeling the dust suddenly halt and drop away before it could hit me. It was Newt yanking me into a ley line, and with a nauseating twist, the horrid red sky winked out of existence.

My heart thudded once, twice, and still we hadn't reemerged anywhere. My lungs started to ache, and at the last moment, when I thought she might have forgotten me and I was going to have to scrape another line into existence trying to get out, she yanked me into reality.

Stumbling, I caught myself against the bedpost in Al's room. The oil lamp beside the bed was lit, making shadows at the edges of the smallish chamber. Browns, golds, and greens mimicked a primeval forest, and plush, sinking textures made it a close, secure space.

"Sorry about that," Newt murmured, looking matronly as she tucked the cover over Al, already resting in my, or rather, his bed. "It took me a moment to get around the room's safeguards. I thought one jump right to his bed would be better than sliding into the library and having to drag him."

"Yes," I whispered, suitably cowed. Al had told me his old bedchamber was absolutely foolproof, but apparently it wasn't crazy-proof. I let go of the bedpost, and Newt sat on the bed beside Al, looking like a bedside nurse. I couldn't see anything but his face, the rest of him lost in the voluptuous coverings.

Giving Al's cheek a little pat, Newt looked up, her black eyes taking in everything in a single sweep. "This is not Al's bedroom. It's far too . . . plush."

"It's mine," I rushed. "He gave it to me. Made me take it. He sleeps in the closet."

"You make him sleep in a closet? Very good. You might survive him after all."

I edged closer to look down at Al, the bed between Newt and me. "It's not really a closet. I just call it that. It's a tiny nine by twelve I got for making Tron that car."

"Oh." Her hand touched Al's, turning it over as if looking for the ring on my thumb.

"Is he going to be okay?"

Again, Newt blinked at me, her eyes looking almost normal in the dim light. "You care?" Her gaze was on the ring he had given me, and I hid it behind my other hand. My thoughts went to Celfnnah, but I wasn't going to ask Newt.

From the bed, Al's voice rasped out, "Of course she cares. I'm a god to her."

"Al!" I leaned forward over him, and he squirmed as if hurt.

"Mother pus bucket," he swore, running a sweat-stained, dirt-caked hand over his forehead. "I feel like I've been across a cheese grater several times in quick succession." His gaze sharpened, and he tried to sit up, panic edging him. "Where are my rings? My rings!"

"Here," I said as Newt forced him to lie back down, and I wedged both rings off my finger and thumb, dropping them into his waiting palm. He slumped, eyes closing as his thick fingers wrapped around them. His hand was shaking, and I remembered the pain we'd shared. Taking that doubled would have killed me.

"I let go of him," I said, backing up from the bed and feeling as if this was my fault. "I had to. I couldn't pull him through to reality while the sun was up. I had to let go so I could move to the ever-after to get him!"

"Stop babbling," Al grumped, trying to smack Newt's hand away as she tried to see his eyes. "It wasn't your fault. Let me sleep." He opened an eye to glare at Newt. "What is your problem, bitch?"

Newt stopped trying to lift his eyelids, and I shut my mouth.

"I'm not babbling," I said, sounding sullen even to myself.

Still sitting on the edge of the bed, Newt tucked the covers to his chin. "Good thought, bad implementation."

It looked as if he was going to be okay, and I wondered if Newt had seen the bottom of a purple line once and survived. "Can I do anything?" I asked.

"You? No," Newt said. "But I have an aura that I can give Al if—"

"No!" both Al and I exclaimed, and she looked insulted, standing up to smooth her robe.

"No need to shout. You'll just have to wait until you heal, then. Here, in Rachel's bedroom." Her eyes went over the ceiling. "Where all your *safe-guards* are."

I started to relax. It lasted all of three seconds until Al pushed Newt's hands off him again, muttering, "Ku'Sox did it." I stiffened, and he added, "The entire leaking line is a ruse to get us to kill Rachel for him. A very expensive, chancy ruse." He made a wry face at me. "Maybe you shouldn't have cursed him."

"It was him or me, and I like where I live," I said loudly, and Al winced.

Newt gave up on Al and stood with her arms crossed before herself. "I saw to the bottom of that purple line," Al said. "His aura signature is down there. He caused it, whatever it is."

I lifted the mass of my tangled hair and let it drop, wanting nothing more than a hot shower and a carton of ice cream. "So we can go to the collective and make him fix it, right?" I said, feeling good for the first time in . . . hours? Had it only been that long?

Newt had drifted from the bed, tidying little things here and there, snooping, and my hackles began to rise. "If he caused it, he can fix it," she said. "But he'll wait until after you're dead, then 'save' us so we are more indebted to him."

Al snorted. "A brat after my own heart. Minus the killing Rachel part, of course."

"But you know he did it!" I said. "We found the proof!"

Al said nothing, and my smile faded. "Al?" I questioned, and he sighed. Even Newt was avoiding me, and a spark of anger grew. "We can make him fix it, right? Al, you saw his signature in the leak."

"Unfortunately—" Al started, and I got in his face, waving my hand under his nose.

"No, no, no!" I exclaimed. "There is no *unfortunately* in your next sentence. We make him fix it! I'm not going down as the one who broke the ever-after!"

Al heaved a sigh, then shivered when a black-smeared coating of ever-after slithered over him. It fell away to leave him clean, the soft shape of an old-fashioned nightdress showing between his skin and the coverlet. Newt, obviously. "Rachel," he said as he studied his bare hands. "My aura is burned down to my soul. Will you wait a few days? Then we can go in, accusations and hidden barbs flying, okay?"

I scrunched my nose up, hating Newt when she laughed at me. "Ah, the vigor of the young," she said, making things worse. "If it were me, I wouldn't go even then."

"Why not?" I said, feeling another *unfortunately* coming on.

Newt touched a hand mirror that looked identical to the one I'd seen Ceri use. "Al's testimony will be suspect, even if he did nearly kill himself. No one will risk verifying the truth of it after seeing what it did to him. Al would be dead now if not for . . . you pulling him out."

She had been going to say "those rings," but I kept silent. Her word choice was telling. Frustrated, I loomed over Al, and he closed his eyes, ignoring me. "Al," I said forcefully, and he opened them. I hesitated at his black orbs, then rushed ahead. "I am *not* going to take the curse off Ku'Sox. It's the only reason I can sleep at night. Besides, I don't think he simply wants me dead, he wants all of you dead, too, or why bother with the Rosewood babies?"

Newt looked at Al, an unusual trace of fear in the back of her eyes. "I believe you," she said, her fingers tracing over the few things on the dresser. "But no one is going to help you."

"Why not?" I said in frustration.

"Because we know we can't control him, and we are cowards," she said. "It was your familiar who freed him, and thus it is your responsibility to control him. If you can't, we will give him you to placate him and save ourselves."

This sucked. "I got him back in the ever-after," I said, and she took up the hand mirror.

"Where we didn't want him," she said, and I slumped. "Best him, or we will kill you so he will save us. I'm surprised the collective gave you any time at all. They must like you."

I couldn't get the frown off my face if I tried. Like me, huh? Funny way to show it.

Al reached out to take the mirror Newt had brought to the bed. "Send her home," he said, sounding tired, and then he started at his reflection. "What the devil happened to my eyes?"

Newt took the mirror back despite Al's protests, oddly sexy as she sashayed across the bedroom to put it back on the dresser. "Will they return to normal?" he asked, and she shrugged.

"No!" I said loudly, and Al looked at me. "This is bull crap!" I added so he'd know I wasn't talking about his stupid eyes. "Ku'Sox is going to own up to this!"

"He'll say you went in on it together and are now backing out, love," Newt said.

My zeal evaporated at the moniker, and cold, I slowed my anger. I didn't like being "love" to a demon. It meant I was being stupid and foolish.

"Newt, send her home, please," Al said, his voice low in fatigue.

The demon inclined her head, and I waved my hands in protest. "Hey! Wait! Who's going to watch you?"

"I don't need watching," Al mumbled, burrowing deeper into the folds of goose down and silk. "Go home. Call me in three days."

Three days?

Al smiled, his eyes closed. "Newt?"

"Damn it, no!" I shouted, but my words caught in my throat as I was suddenly wrapped in Newt's awareness. I snapped a bubble of protection around myself before she could. *Send me home like a little girl, eh?* I thought, steaming in anger.

But, as reality swirled around me and I found myself standing in my sunlit graveyard, my church before me in the late afternoon light, I sobered. Ku'Sox could show up in my church day or night thanks to Nick. And there were Ceri and Lucy to think about, hostages in the extreme. I couldn't risk Ku'Sox taking revenge out on them, turning my potential win to a personal loss. Getting him to admit that I had nothing to do with that ugly purple line sucking in ever-after without compromising Ceri's and Lucy's safety wasn't going to be easy.

Immediately I found my phone, scrolling until I got to Trent's number. I ought to put him on speed-dial or something. Pixies were coming from everywhere, and I waved them off as I began walking to the church's back door, my head bowed as I waited for someone to pick up. "Your dad is fine," I said, glad when Jumoke chased most of them back to their sentry duty.

Three rings and a click, and my feet stopped when I heard Ray crying through my phone. It was a soft, heart-wrenching sob of loss that no ten-month-old should even be aware enough to make. Jenks was singing to her about blood-red daisies. "I'm back," I said even before I knew if it really was Trent. "Don't summon me."

"Did you see them?" Trent asked, his voice shockingly stark. I took a breath to tell him, my throat closing when I couldn't get the words out. My eyes welled up. For three heartbeats, neither of us said anything, and then softly, Trent added, "No, I guess you didn't."

"I think they're okay," I said, but it sounded like a thin hope even to me. My chest hurt, and I began to weave through the grave markers, one hand wrapped around my middle so it wouldn't cave in. In a soft sound of wings and dust, Jumoke sat on my shoulder. "Ku'Sox has them. He's going to use them to force you and me to do what he wants. Trent, give me some time to find a way to get them back. Ku'Sox can't do this. Ceri is a freed familiar. All I have to do is file the right paperwork."

"I don't have time for paperwork," he said bitterly, and then I heard him sigh as Ray finally stopped crying. I could hear her little-girl snuffles, and I figured he'd picked her up.

"Give me some time to talk to Dali then," I said. "I need a chance to explain what's going on to him, and then maybe he'll help."

"Why would a demon help me?" Trent said, and I looked up at the church, squinting to try to find Bis. There was another huge gargoyle up there, and I frowned.

"He'd be helping me, not you. And I'm not going to ask him to do it for free," I said, then softened. "Give me a few hours. Can you bring Jenks home for me? And maybe my car? Say after midnight? I should be done by then and will have more information for you."

"Midnight!" I heard Jenks shrill, then I frowned when Trent covered the phone. "Fine, midnight," the pixy said sourly when I could hear again.

"Trent?" I said cautiously.

"I'll see you at midnight," Trent said, and then the phone went dead.

Startled but not surprised, I closed the phone and tucked it away. Arms wrapped around myself and my head down, I stomped up the back porch and wrestled the screen door open. This was going to take a lot of planning.

I should have called Ivy.

Chapter Nine

Nervous, I wiped my fingertips off on a towel and tossed it on the counter. Almost before it hit, I was reaching for it again, carefully folding it to drape over the oven handle, right in the middle. Exhaling, I turned to look over my kitchen, dim with only the light from the living room across the hall and the small bulb over the sink. Demons and shadows seemed to go together, but they craved the sun like an undead vampire.

Ceri's teapot sat between two chairs at Ivy's farm table. The antique porcelain was warm with Earl Grey tea, two of Ceri's best teacups beside it. A candle on the stove made it smell like a pine forest. If I was lucky, it might even overpower the burnt amber stench. Maybe. I had an hour before Trent brought Jenks home. I couldn't wait any longer. I'd promised Trent results, and it was time to call the demon.

I turned to Bis atop the fridge. "Well?" I asked him. "Look okay to you?"

The cat-size teenager brought his wingtips up to touch over his head, his version of a shrug. "I guess," he said, his pebbly skin flashing the entire range from gray, to white, to black, and back to gray again. He was anxious. So was I.

I spun to the sink and closed the blue curtains, not wanting Dali to see anything more than he absolutely had to. For starters, the leather outfit that I'd come home in was on a hanger, hanging from a limb and airing out. "Thanks for being here, Bis."

"I'm not afraid of demons," he said, his high but gravelly voice giving him away.

Smiling, I leaned my back against the sink. I didn't like anyone with me when I contacted Al, much less an unknown like Dali, but Bis was involved up to his pointy ears, and when he'd refused to leave the kitchen upon hearing my plans, I'd let him stay.

"Demons aren't that bad when you get to know them," I said as I got a plate from the cupboard and arranged the store-bought petits fours around the pile of homemade gingersnaps in the shape of little stars. I didn't know what Dali liked, and variety was nice.

The church felt empty with Ivy still gone and the pixies asleep or out in the garden. I'd been dogged by a growing feeling of unease since I'd gotten back from the ever-after, and not all of it could be lain at the feet of my current problems. Something was brewing with the vampires. Felix had asked after Ivy twice. And I knew Rynn Cormel, Ivy's master vampire, did not like that Ivy had left the state, even temporarily. At least he wasn't sending assassins this time.

"You sure you don't want to wait until Jenks and Trent get here?" Bis said. "What's to stop Dali from just snatching you?"

"Nothing. That's why he won't try. Besides, he knows I'm Al's student. What would be the point? You sure you don't want to wait in the garden? It's okay."

Bis shook his head, trying to hide his slight shiver.

If it had been Ku'Sox I was calling, I'd have used circles, traps, maybe waited for Trent. Dali, though, was like Al in that he got a kick out of those weaker than him trusting him to behave—as risky as it was.

"I hope he knows how to help you," Bis almost whispered. "I don't like demons." His red eyes darted to mine. "I like you, just not them. I mean, if Dali knew how to get Ceri and Lucy back, wouldn't he have done it already?"

I smiled faintly and nudged the teacups back from the edge. "No." A sliver of unease slid into me. The demons couldn't control Ku'Sox. If I couldn't, then they'd give me to him as a bribe to save them. Yay, me.

Bis looked toward the curtained window, then me. Turning slightly lighter, he nodded, his clawed feet shifting. "Okay. I'm ready."

"Me too." Nervous, I pulled out a chair and sat in it, reaching across the narrow space to where I kept my scrying mirror under the center counter. It felt cool on my knees, the glass seeming to sink into me. The ache at the back of my neck became more pronounced as I rested my fingers on the wine-stained glass. I really needed to make a smaller one I could carry in my shoulder bag, and I vowed if I ever got a weekend where I wasn't saving the world, I would.

There was a faint, unusual tingling from my wrist, and I turned my hand over. The raised circle of scar tissue there tied me to Al, a visible mark that I owed him a favor for bringing me home the night we'd met. I'd never gotten around to settling it, and that it was tingling now was curious. Maybe it was responding to his ailment. Slowly my frown deepened. "Tell Ivy I'm sorry if this doesn't go well," I said as I placed my fingers on the proper glyphs.

"Roses on your grave. Right." Bis dropped to the chair nearest me, his craggy feet denting the back as he caught his balance. He really was a good kid.

The coolness of the mirror ached into me, and a new, slight discord blossomed into an irritating whine at the back of my ears. *Dallkarackint?* I thought in my mind, avoiding saying the demon's true calling name aloud. It wasn't that I had a problem saying it, but Dali wouldn't appreciate my speaking his name on this side of the lines, seeing as anyone who heard it would be able to summon him. Dali had taken great pains to keep his name secret.

Almost immediately the cloud of buzzing seemed to hesitate, part, and with a surprising suddenness, I had a second presence beside mine.

Rachel?

It was Dali, and I warmed in embarrassment. I didn't often talk to demons through my scrying mirror apart from Al, and having Dali in my thoughts was unnerving. Whereas Al used bluster and show to hide his true self, Dali was like a steel pillar, everything seeming to slide off him. "Um, I'm sorry to bother you," I said, my thoughts carrying through the mirror to him.

Irritation predictably joined my embarrassment in our shared thoughts. *I'm busy. Make an appointment with my secretary.*

He was about to break the connection. I was kind of surprised I'd gotten him at all and not one of his subordinates. "Dali, wait. I have to talk to you, and Al is . . ."

I stopped, not knowing who might be listening in.

Al is what? Dali asked, interest coloring his thought.

I hesitated, looking up at Bis's drooping wings. "I've made some tea," I started.

Outrage flooded me, and I almost yanked my hand from the mirror. *You're summoning me!* Dali exploded, and I scrambled to assert myself before he drowned me.

"I made some tea!" I said, trying to match his anger, and Bis's eyes grew round. "You want to come over here and drink it or not? It's Earl Grey. I don't particularly like it, but most men I know like bergamot. I don't give a flying flip if we do this here or your office, but if I have to bring the cookies over, they'll taste like burnt amber and I spent two hours on them!" I took a breath, feeling his anger subside. "I need to talk to you," I said softly, my thought mirroring the pleading sound I had. "My kitchen isn't much, but—"

My words cut off as I felt our connection shift, turning from the light, uppermost thoughts to a more enveloping, place-finding sensation. He was coming over, using the mirror to locate me. My eyes widened at the feeling, and a small noise of I-don't-know-what slipped from me, part alarm, part surprise, part sexual titillation as he drew a small trace of ley line through me so he'd show up next to me and not in the garden's ley line.

"He's coming," I said as I lifted my head, flushing because of that weird noise I'd made.

"Holy sweet seraph," Bis swore as a swirl of red ever-after coalesced in the corner of the room beside the fridge. I didn't have a formal circle to mark a spot to jump in at. Maybe I should remedy that if I survived the next couple of days.

"Earl Grey?" Dali's Americana businessman accent drawled as he shook off the last of the black-tainted swirls, showing up in a gray suit and a red power tie instead of a toga—thank God. He looked like a slightly overweight mob boss with his expensive dress shoes, tailored pants, and graying, styled hair.

Uneasy, I stood. Bis shrank back, his red eyes going wide. He held his ground, though, trusting my judgment. "Thank you," I said, wiping my palms on my jeans. Crap, I should have put on a dress, but it was my kitchen, and I'd have felt stupid wearing a gown—again.

Dali's attention had been running over my kitchen, but at my whisper, it returned to me. "You are far too quick in assuming this is a good thing." He glanced at his watch; then his red, goat-slitted eyes returned to the spell pots and the tea steaming on the table. "You don't have any wards protecting your spelling area?"

"I don't need it." I looked away, used to dealing with egotistical, powerful people who got a kick out of my apparent total disregard for the danger they represented. "You want to sit down?" I said, looking at the chair kitty-corner to mine.

My brow furrowed as he stepped forward and eyed the hard-backed chair. "It's probably more comfortable than it looks," he said as he gingerly sat, crossing his knees and trying to appear dignified, but he looked even more out of place than Trent usually did in my kitchen.

A memory of Trent standing at my counter making cookies with me flashed through my thoughts. That hadn't really happened. I'd been in a coma of sorts, and his mind had been trying to reach mine, but it had been real enough. So had the kiss that had followed.

Bis's nervous giggle made Dali frown. This wasn't going as well as I had hoped, but with the determination I might use on a badly begun blind date, I sat down and began pouring out the tea. "I'm only twenty-seven," I said dryly. "I've not had the time to gather much in the way of luxury possessions." It was starting to smell like burnt amber, and I wondered if I should've cracked the window and risked attracting the pixies on sentry detail.

Dali's wandering attention came back to me. "Speaking of time . . ." he said sourly. "You're rapidly running out of it. Or should I say, Newt is running out of room." His expression became wicked as he took a gingersnap. "You're going to make a pauper out of the ever-after's wealthiest demon. Congratulations. You should rent yourself out by the hour."

Not a good start. "I've been out to the line," I said, pouring out my tea now. "I have some ideas." Seeing as he wasn't taking his cup, I handed it to him. "This is Bis, my gargoyle."

Dali took a sip, his eyes almost closing in apparent bliss he tried to hide. "Bis," he said, nodding to him, and the gargoyle flashed an embarrassed black. "You're younger than I thought. Your lack of skill is excused."

"It's a pleasure to meet you, sir," Bis said, and I was proud of him.

"I'm sure it is," Dali said lightly, his attention on the cookies. "Are those petits fours?"

Silent, I pushed the plate toward him, and he took another gingersnap.

"Mmmm," he said, eating the star in one bite. "Where is Al? He has put a do-not-disturb note on his mirror. Are you thinking of changing teachers . . . Rachel?" His voice was sly, cruel almost. "Think I can save your life? Think again. You're not going to bankrupt me as well."

"Good," I said, trying to shift the conversation to where I wanted it. "You can go to your grave a rich demon. Al is busy renewing his aura," I said, and Dali's eyes widened in interest. "He burned it off while finding Ku'Sox's signature on that purple sludge currently taking residence in my slightly imbalanced line."

Dali took a third gingersnap, his stubby fingers sure and slow. "Al's findings cannot be used in court," he said, then bit the cookie in half. "He has too much to lose and isn't a reliable witness. I doubt you can convince anyone else to confirm it if in the doing he burns his aura off."

"I know that," I said, letting my irritation show. "That's why you're here. I want to talk to you about the legality of Ku'Sox abducting Ceri. The paperwork hasn't been filed, but she's a freed familiar. Ku'Sox is using her as leverage, and I want her and Lucy back."

His expression dry, Dali took another gingersnap. "Ku'Sox didn't abduct Ceri. He abducted Lucy. Ceri volunteered to come with her. When the cookies are gone, so am I."

"What!" I exclaimed, falling back in my chair in shock. I glanced at Bis, then back to Dali. My chest seemed to cave in as hope left me. It sounded exactly like something she'd do. Ceri wasn't afraid of demons. She was afraid of being helpless before them, and with her soul back, she was not. "But Lucy is my godchild!" I said, scrambling. "Ku'Sox and I have an agreement that he leave me and mine alone. Lucy is mine."

"File the paperwork for breach of contract, and I'll see what I can do," Dali said. It was like that, then.

"Ku'Sox is a touch . . . erratic. Newt and I are watching him." Dali's eyes rose from the plate of cookies. "We've known for some time that he was up to something. Hiding his plans from everyone else is the only thing postponing your death."

I thought about Newt's carefully worded question, becoming more frustrated. "Then why are you letting him get away with it?" I said, aghast. "You know I didn't cause that line to start sucking away ever-after that fast. Why are you picking on me? Ku'Sox did it!"

Dali wouldn't meet my eyes. "True," he said, "but he used your unbalanced line to do so. It's your responsibility. I'm confident that Ku'Sox knows how to control the leak. He's trying to eliminate you, making us miserable and reminding us of his power all at the same time, the little prick."

There were two gingersnaps left. I leaned forward, a ribbon of anxiety running through me. "Is that what you think?" I said, shoving my cup of tea away from me so hard that it sloshed. I hated bergamot. "You think he's going to *save* you after you kill me?"

Silent, Dali took a cookie. "Ku'Sox has threatened us before, but he's never gone through with it. He's young and angry. You cursed his freedom from him." Dali smiled, showing me his flat, blocky teeth. "Sibling rivalry. Maybe you should uncurse him."

"Don't think so," I said quickly, wondering how I was going to convince Dali the threat was more than he thought. "Look, letting me die would be a mistake. I'm not trying to kill you. He is, and I don't think that line *can* be shut down with that purple sludge in it, even if I am dead. And in case you haven't noticed, he doesn't need you anymore. He has Nick, who stole the enzyme that keeps the Rosewood syndrome suppressed enough to survive it, and then you stood by and hid the fact that he circumvented my protection of Trent—the only one who can make the cure permanent and able to pass to the next generation. Ku'Sox doesn't need you anymore. In ten years, he's going to have a bunch of demon-magic-using kids to play with."

"The Rosewood babies are not for him, they are for us." Dali washed down his cookie with a sip of tea, and I gaped.

"Y-you?" I stammered, and he nodded. One gingersnap left. *Thirty seconds.*

"They're life rafts, demon-magic-capable bodies that those loyal to him can slip into and escape a failing ever-after," Dali said, and I stared, not having considered that.

"And you believe him?" I said. "Seriously?"

Dali's eye twitched, telling me he didn't, but it did make it easier to understand why no one would help me. "Has it ever occurred to you that without a permanent cure, everyone who escapes on Ku'Sox's coattails will be completely dependent on him to stay alive?"

Dali's thick fingers were on that last cookie. Hesitating, he tapped it on the plate. "Which is why we're not forcing him to give Ceri back," he said softly. "We want the permanent cure."

I leaned back in the chair, hard-pressed to not pound my head on the table. "He's lying to you, Dali, to all of you. He's never going to allow any of you access to those children, and he's going to let the ever-after collapse whether you kill me for him or not. Now quit blocking me and give me Ceri and Lucy back so I can figure this out!"

Dali set the last cookie down and wiped his fingers. With a new stiffness in his manner, he shifted his weight. "You think his intent is annihilation?"

I nodded, and my shoulders eased. "Before Newt got us back underground, a gargoyle came to see who had been messing around in my ley line."

His carefully trimmed eyebrows high, Dali eyed me, but if it was because Newt helped us or that a gargoyle was involved, I didn't know. "In the daylight?"

"He had a huge sword that looked like it had been propping up a laundry line for the last fifty years," I said, angry. "He said the line would fix itself in time, but destroy the ever-after in the doing of it, and that they were going to leave and to save who they could."

"The gargoyles are leaving?" It was a soft but alarmed utterance.

"He also said I wouldn't find enough time to fix it before it fixes itself. If you can't give me Ceri, at least give me some time," I demanded. "Four days," I added, thinking of Al's burn.

Dali's intent gaze focused on me, considering it. Sighing, he crossed his arms over his chest and leaned back in the chair. "Do you have any idea what you're asking?"

Adrenaline jerked through me as I realized he'd probably come here with the intent to kill me and be done with it before he left. "I think I can fix the line," I said, scrambling to find something positive to take away from this. "I just need to borrow . . ." My words trailed off reluctantly, as if not wanting to divulge just what it was, not that I had no clue what I needed. "Something from Al," I finished, trying to appear cagey, not confused.

Dali peered at me, his mouth a thin line. "You don't trust me."

"Sure I do," I said, and Bis snickered, making a weird snuffing sound.

The older-looking demon frowned. "You don't have a clue how to fix that line," he said, but inside, I felt a tiny spot of hope. He was thinking about it.

Beside him, Bis cleared his throat. "I can see the lines," he said, flushing a heavy black. "I know I can help. I'm good at auras."

Dali ignored him, which made me mad, and I said, "Ku'Sox cursed my line. That purple sludge is demon made. I have yet to find the curse I can't untwist."

His face scrunched up, making him look like the benevolent uncle who *wanted* to give you the quarter of a million dollars to start your chinchilla farm, but those darn investors just didn't see the potential. "It's not that I don't want to believe you," he said, and I let out a loud, exasperated sigh as he continued. "But belief will be a thin comfort if we get sucked into oblivion waiting for you to figure it out. It's not like you have much to lose."

"If you don't trust me, we both die, Dali," I said, not dropping his eyes. "Even if the ever-after vanishes, do you think the coven is going to let me live after the lines disappear and there's no more magic? I don't."

Goat-slitted eyes unfocused, he nodded.

"Can't you choose what gets sucked into oblivion?" I said. "Try bubbling your rooms. Let it pull on the empty spaces for a while."

"Perhaps." Dali's knees uncrossed as he set his feet on the floor. He was ready to go, and he eyed the last cookie. "No one will want to if they're being reimbursed by Newt. We'd all like to see her brought down a decimal place or two."

"See if you can get them to think about it," I said, standing up and going to the counter where I had a bag of cookies for Ray. Dali might be a better choice. "I have an idea, but I need four days and your silence that we even had this conversation."

Dali's attention jerked to me. Bright eyed, he stood and took the cookies like the bribe they were. "Really?" he said, the plastic rustling softly. "Secrets, Rachel?"

I met his gaze squarely. "The fewer who know, the better."

Dali's head cocked suspiciously. "You *trust* me?"

My heart gave a thump. I didn't have a problem asking for things, according to Al, but in this case, I was asking for a lot. "You're a member of the courts," I said. "If I fail, go ahead and kill me," I continued, making Bis rustle his wings. "I don't want to be around to see the fallout when magic fails on this side of the lines. But if I succeed, I want all my debts slid to Ku'Sox." Dali began to smile. "Everything to date *and* any I acquire while resolving the mess he started," I said, feeling nervous. It was quite a lot. "Newt's debts accrued because of his tampering, too," I added. "I want that demon so far in the hole that if we survive, he will be spending the next thousand years as a busboy at your restaurant."

Dali chuckled, and I felt out of breath. "We," he said, and I blinked, not knowing why he'd said it until realizing I'd said it first. I had said *we*. I had lumped myself in with them, and it had come out as natural as if it had been *we* for a long time. "I like the way you think, Morgan. No wonder Al has risked so much on you."

"Well?" I asked, since it was obvious Dali was leaving.

His fingers tightened on the bag of cookies. "You have four days. More than that, and the ever-after will be too damaged."

Bis's ears pricked, and the sound of the front door opening echoed through the church. My gaze darted to the clock on the stove. They were early. "Four days," I said. Al would be able to tap a line in three. It would be close, but maybe by then I'd have this figured out.

"If it's not fixed by midnight, you die." Dali looked at his watch. "That's Friday," he said sourly as he squinted at Bis as if he had failed in something—and then . . . he vanished.

I exhaled, shaking as I went to prop the window open to let out the stink of demons. Dali had taken the cookies but left the petits fours. "Thank you," I whispered into the night, though he couldn't possibly hear me. Never underestimate the power of home-baked cookies. Bis's chair creaked as he eased his grip. Looking out at the dark graveyard, empty of even the glow of sleeping pixies, I felt my gut clench at the sound of Trent's steps in the hall. I had no idea what I was going to do next, but Trent wouldn't be happy with what I'd found.

"Pepper piss! It stinks in here!" Jenks swore as he darted in, fingers pinching his nose shut as he swooped a large circle through the kitchen and landed atop Bis's head. The gargoyle twitched his big fringed ears, and Jenks shifted to the top of the roll of paper towels we kept on the table. "He left? Just now? I wanted to talk to him."

I leaned back against the counter, glad the kitchen was clean. I think it was the first time Trent had seen it when it wasn't covered in spelling supplies. "Which is why I asked Trent not to bring you home until now," I said, smiling thinly.

Trent's nose was wrinkled at the stench, and worry warred with hope, showing in the way his brow was pinched. A long lightweight coat hid his suit. He looked wary as he held a hat to hide his missing fingers. The light caught his eyes as they traveled over the kitchen as if looking for a visible sign of Dali, but all that was left was the smell.

"Jenks said I could come in," he said, and my mouth went dry. I had no comfort to give him, and I stayed where I was with my arms over my middle. I didn't care if I looked pensive.

"Hi," I said. Jenks's wings clattered in surprise, but I didn't know what more I could say.

Looking polished and together, Trent came in another step. He nodded to Bis, and the gargoyle touched his wingtips over his head. Eyeing me up and down, Trent's hope slowly dulled and vanished. "That good, eh?"

I took a deep breath. Unable to meet his eyes, I pushed off the sink, my middle coming to rest against the center counter. The petits fours were sitting there, and the plate scraped as I pushed it away. "Dali's hands are tied," I said softly. "Ceri went willingly with Ku'Sox."

"What!" Jenks rose up on a column of dust, and Bis turned an apologetic shade of black.

Trent's face became ashen. "Ku'Sox took Lucy," he breathed, and I nodded.

"And Ceri went willingly to keep her safe," Jenks finished, now darting between Trent and me in agitation.

My head hurt, and I rubbed it. It was so simple, so devious. Trent's feet scuffed, and I pulled my head up.

"That's it, then," Trent said, every vestige of softness gone in the hard clench of his jaw. "If there's no chance at a political resolution, then I will use more drastic means."

I froze. A creak came from Bis's chair as he tightened his grip. *Drastic measures?* The last time Trent had instigated *drastic measures,* San Francisco was trashed and I ended up in a spell-induced coma for three days. "Whoa, whoa, whoa," I said, hand in the air. "You're *not* going to give yourself up in exchange. It's exactly what he wants." *What all the demons wanted.*

"Which is exactly why it will work."

I shook my head, but he wasn't listening, wasn't even looking at me as he stared at the wall two feet to my right. Cool and distant, he ignored even Jenks hovering inches before his face. "No fairy fart way, elf-man," the pixy said, a bright red dust spilling from him. "We talked about this, remember? You give yourself up, and then Rachel's just going to have to bail your ass out again, which means I'm stuck saving hers. I can't take it anymore. I'm not a young pixy. She's a demon, let her do her Tink-blasted job!"

Trent's iron-hard hold on his emotions cracked. Turning, he tossed his hat on the table. "If I call his bluff, he'll kill them," he said. "You know he will. Then he will steal someone else for leverage and it starts again. I *do* have feelings, Rachel. I *do* love people. I'm not going to let them die for me!"

"That's not what I meant," I said softly, and his glare fell from me. "We can't get them back through the courts, but in the meantime, I've got four days to balance the line."

Clearly frustrated, he spun away, his coat furling. "How does that help Lucy and Ceri?" he said, his back to me as Jenks shot me a look and landed on his shoulder.

Curious, I thought as Trent's shoulders relaxed at something Jenks said. Bis noticed as well. Clearly the two men had come to some kind of understanding. "If I can fix the line or prove that Ku'Sox made the hole, the demons will turn against him," I said, but it was really more of a hope. "Ceri and Lucy will be returned." I looked at the counter as if I could see the books on the shelf below. There was nothing in them about ley lines. Nothing in them, nothing in the library, nothing in Al's library. If there had been, we would have found it by now.

Exhaling loudly, Trent slowly sank down in a chair. The last of his mask fell away and he slumped, elbow on the table as he sat sideways to it. "I can't risk him killing Lucy and Ceri," he said, and a lump filled my throat. He was hurting. It wasn't my fault. He was the one who had let Ku'Sox out, but he'd done it to save my life, or rather, my freedom.

Jenks was making motions for me to do something, and I grimaced, finally moving around the center counter to stand there, feeling self-conscious. I wondered how long it had been since he'd eaten. "Al and I went out to look at the line," I said hesitantly. "He got burned pretty bad, but it did give us a better idea of what Ku'Sox did."

Trent didn't acknowledge me, making me feel more awkward as I edged back to sit in Ivy's chair. My eyes went to Trent's ring, and I remembered how it had felt to wear Al's. "I think I saved his life. Again."

"I bet that was a surprise," he said dryly.

Chuckling, I dropped my eyes. "It was. He won't be able to tap a line until Thursday. And since I don't trust anyone else over there, I'm stuck here until he heals. I know I can fix the leak in the line with Bis's help," I added, and the gargoyle bobbed his head, his tail whipping about to wrap around his feet. "If I can fix it, I can prove Ku'Sox is trying to destroy the ever-after. Ceri and Lucy will be the last thing on his mind if the entire collective is after him. None of them like him, anyway."

Trent said nothing, staring at the table. I wasn't even sure he had heard me.

My thoughts went to the demons and what Dali had said about them fearing Ku'Sox. Together, they could overpower Ku'Sox, but fear had made slaves of them. They were expecting me to take care of him, hiding behind semantics that it was a personal vendetta between us. Were they really afraid, or was apathy easier than survival? Maybe they just didn't care if they lived or died.

Trent still hadn't moved, and at Jenks's exasperated motions, I reached out across the table, putting my hand atop his. "We'll get them back."

Trent blinked as our hands met, not in shock, but as if bringing himself back from a deep thought. His expression was empty when his eyes touched my hand, and I gave him a smile and a slight squeeze before I pulled away. I could smell hospital on him, and I realized that's probably why my head hurt. I hated hospitals.

"How's Quen?" I said.

Trent eased back into the chair, his hand sliding from the table to fall into his lap. "He's not conscious yet, but his brain activity is good."

His relief made me smile again. "Good." I stood up, but I didn't know why other than I felt uncomfortable sitting across from Trent. "If there is anything I can do . . ."

He looked up as he reached for his hat on the table. "They tell me there's nothing anyone can do but wait. He's strong, and his chances are good."

I wanted to touch his shoulder in support, but I hesitated at the last moment, going to throw the petits fours away instead. "You believe he's going to make it," I said. Trent, too, had learned to believe in the eleven percent.

"Yes, I do." His voice was soft but determined.

"Give me a day or two before you start being noble, okay?"

He chuckled, and I hesitated, my thoughts spinning. I needed more stuff. He who has the most stuff in his toolbox wins. "Hey, you have a library, right?" I said as I turned back around. I'd moved too fast, and Jenks darted forward to catch one of the cakes as it slid off the plate. "Do you have any books about line energy?" I asked as I set the dish on the center counter, ignoring Jenks swearing at me as he brushed the frosting off his clothes.

Trent pushed forward, his hand reaching to touch a pocket. "I don't have anything in my library about the lines, no, but I know someone who does," he said, his hand reluctantly falling from his jacket. "Rachel, would you like to come to tea tomorrow?"

Jenks looked up from his soiled silk jacket, surprise in his angular face. Trent had stood, and I started at how fast it had been. He had a direction, and it changed everything. It was back, the power and certainty was back, and something in me shivered.

"Tea?" Jenks was standing next to the plate of petits fours. "You want to have tea? Are you nerking futs?"

The light caught the tips of his hair as Trent came up to the center counter, the fair strands beginning to float in his excitement. "I know of something you might want to read."

My pulse leaped. "Why not now?" I said, and Bis sniffed his agreement. If it was about the lines, he'd want to see, too.

But Trent was shaking his head. "Ellasbeth has it," he said, and I remember his aborted reach for a phone. "It was my mother's book, but I know she'll let us look at it. If she doesn't bring it, I won't let her on the grounds, and she's dying to yell at me in person."

We had a chance, and it was frustrating that we had to wait. "Okay," I said, hands behind my back so Trent couldn't see them tremble. "Tomorrow, then. Trent, when was the last time you ate?"

He was sideways to me, putting his hat on. His confidence was clear, his motions sharp. "I think something from the hospital vending machine." He looked up and smiled. Something in me fluttered again, and again I shoved it down deep. I knew what was going on, and I wasn't going to let it happen. It was a fantasy, and I was through with them.

"You're not going to do anything stupid without me, right?"

"I'm going back to the hospital for a couple of hours. Get another bag of salty snack food for dinner. Do you want me to tell Quen anything?"

My smile faltered. I wasn't invited, but I didn't like hospitals, anyway. "No," I said as I leaned to pull open a drawer and find a plastic bag for the petits fours. "But here. Run these under his nose. They smell like demons. They might snap him out of it."

Trent fidgeted, impatient to be away as I shook the cakes into a bag and tied it with a yellow twisty. Jenks landed on my shoulder, and I frowned when he whispered, "Go with him!"

"Here," I said, holding them out and flushing as Trent took them, the plastic bag looking both the same and different from when I'd given cookies to a demon named Dali. For some reason, giving Trent petits fours felt a lot more dangerous.

"Thank you. I'll let you know if they do the trick." He turned on a heel, then hesitated in the threshold. "You made the six o'clock news," he said, and my smile froze. "You did okay. Really good for what you had to work with. Thank you again for handling that."

I hid behind the center counter, more relieved than I wanted to be. "I'm sorry about putting Ray in front of the camera."

He shook his head, looking down at the bag of cakes. "No, it was worth giving them something positive to take away."

"Thanks."

He nodded sharply to Bis, and without another word, he headed down the hall, his thoughts already far away. Jenks hovered in my line of sight, hands on his hips and frowning. He gestured that I should escort him to the door, and I squinted, crossing my arms over my chest. "He shouldn't be alone," the pixy grumped, darting out after his fading footsteps.

I leaned forward as he left, the new quiet seeping in. "Maybe, but he shouldn't be with me, either," I whispered.

Even alone as he was, Trent didn't need me at all.

Chapter Ten

I'll be sure Belle gets it," I said, smiling at the wingless fairy standing on the wrought-iron garden table, her long white braid almost to her waist and her pale, angular features in a tight knot. Still the mistrustful, scary-looking fairy waited until I put the little packet of stitching into my shoulder bag beside her on the table. Jenks sighed, and she hissed at him, making me shiver.

Sure, she was only six inches high, but she looked like a tiny, silver-cloaked grim reaper with her raggedy clothes made from spider silk, her long fangs used to crack the shells of the insects she ate, and the bow and toxic arrows she carried to shoot me or Jenks if we did anything she didn't like. Her butterfly-like wings were gone, burned off when she and her clan had tried to kill me and Jenks last summer, and their lack made her far more mobile even if she was stuck on the ground.

Mostly, I thought as she shot a corded arrow into the canopy and climbed the string into the surrounding greenery, taking the packet of cloth that Belle had asked me to bring to her. It had that stitching that Matalina's daughters had taught her, the one that gave beautifully around the wings. True, the fairies in Trent's gardens were wingless, but their children wouldn't be. It was odd, seeing the first steps of understanding between two longtime enemy races. Jenks had come a long way.

Knowing we were being watched by a handful of lethal assassins, I leaned back into my chair and tried to look relaxed instead of uptight. Trent's glassed-in garden felt stuffy; the propped-open door leading to the exterior gardens let in very little air. Outside, the early afternoon sun shone thinly on the largely empty spring gardens, but it was here that Trent had brought me for tea—which I thought totally weird. I'd thought that "tea" had been an excuse, something he could tell people instead of the ugly reality that he wanted me to come out so he could show me some illegal black-magic books—and maybe that's all it was. But tea and cookies were on the table, and I was hungry . . . Besides, Ellasbeth had arrived late, and I had bowed out of going to meet her. Ellasbeth had thought I was a hooker the night we had met. Arresting Trent at their wedding probably hadn't helped.

The cord Belle's sister had climbed snaked upward out of sight, and Jenks sniffed, nervously adjusting his garden sword on his hip.

"I thought you were beyond that," I said, fingering my cup of cooling tea. It smelled like Earl Grey, but I could take a few sips to be social. Jenks's comment that Trent shouldn't be alone drifted through me.

Jenks edged to the silver tray, his steps hesitant and his unmoving wings catching the light. "I don't know her," he said as he glanced up into the potted fig trees.

"Well, knock it off," I grumbled. "You're making me nervous."

"I don't *know any of them*," he said again. "It's not like I trust her with my kids."

But he trusted Belle with them, I thought. Small steps could make large journeys, if admittedly very slow ones. Fidgeting, I lolled my head back to look at the plate-glass ceiling as I waited for Trent to return. Ellasbeth was an idiot. How long did it take to drive half a mile and get settled? There were three chairs here.

"I still think you should let the ever-after collapse," Jenks said, his knees up almost to his ears as he sat on the rim of the silver tray, then got up when he realized his pants weren't as good of an insulator as he had first thought.

Frowning, I stood to look at the orchid jammed into the crook of two branches. Jenks followed me, and the brush rustled as the fairies shifted to keep him in their sights. "Earth magic will work for a while before it fades," he said, demanding my attention as he hovered between me and the orchid. "A year at least. You could take down a reality-based Ku'Sox before that. Ivy and I would help."

A spike of fear slid through me, quickly shoved down deep. I'd survived Ku'Sox by the skin of my teeth—every single time. But as I counted the new blossoms yet to open on the orchid, the thought of the end of magic rang through me with a new clarity. *This* was why Nick was helping the psychotic demon. An end or reduction to magic would put humans back in the driver's seat. I couldn't believe that Ku'Sox didn't have a way to keep magic alive with the ever-after gone, doling it out to the highest bidder. Or maybe Dali was right and this was simply a way to get me dead and the rest of the demons kowtowing to him.

I sat back down in Trent's chair so I could watch Jenks now fussing over the orchid and the path. "I might not be able to hear you if magic fails," I said as I took one of the gingersnaps I had brought over for Ray. "Ever think about that?"

Jenks's eyes widened. "Tink loves a duck!" he exclaimed, his wings clattering as he carefully untwisted a stem.

The cookie snapped between my teeth. "Might be a good thing," I said, chewing.

Wing clatter dropping in pitch, Jenks slowly dusted the plant. It was nerves: he gardened, I ate. "I didn't think about that," he said.

"This isn't only about the demons," I said, making a face when I washed the cookie down with a swallow of that awful tea. It was tepid, and it sucked dishwater. "Having no magic would piss off the vampires, the Weres, and the witches. We'd all survive, but can you imagine? Everyone would be at a disadvantage. Everyone except the humans."

Jenks darted back to the table. "Yeah? There was magic before the ever-after."

I took another one of Trent's fancy cookies that smelled like almonds. "The ley lines in the Arizona desert are dead. The demons killed them when they made the ever-after."

Jenks looked into the canopy when someone hissed. Hearing it, he hunkered down, trying to look meek in a butch sort of way. I snapped through my cookie, recalling how the dead lines in the Arizona desert had been unusually close together, overlapping like pickup sticks. Maybe they'd been forced together in order to make a hole in reality, ergo making the ever-after. There was something here. I just didn't have the time to think about it.

"Maybe you're right," Jenks said, as if it pained him to say it. "I still say we'd be better off without demons."

I wasn't so sure. Demons were mean, cruel, untrustworthy, and just plain nasty. But the memory of Al sitting in front of his fireplace trying to remember what he originally looked like only made me pity them. The elves had cursed them for trying to kill their entire species, and the demons had returned fire. I wondered if either side remembered what the original insult had been. Hadn't five thousand years of war been enough?

There was a lesson here, too. I didn't have time to think about this one, either.

Impatient, I ate another gingersnap, rubbing the crumbs between my fingers before I leaned back and closed my eyes. Jenks's wings buzzed as he flitted from flower to flower like a hummingbird. "If it stays warm, we're moving back in the garden this week," he said out of the blue. "All of us."

"Great! That's great," I said, not opening my eyes. "Are you still in the garden wall?"

"Belle is . . ." he started, and I opened my eyes when he hesitated. Finding him at a nearby orchid, I saw him shrug. "Belle is going to move into the wall, too," he said quickly, his wings turning red and his dust evaporating before it could hit the plant. "She can have the spare room. We'd just be sharing a front door is all, like you and Ivy."

Ahh, I thought as I sat up. "That's good, Jenks."

"She gets cold fast," he said as if I had protested her moving in with him, but maybe he was really talking to her sisters in the foliage. "It would be easier to just have one fire."

Chair scraping, I moved the plate of cookies farther away from me so I'd stop eating them. "I'm proud of you, Jenks," I said, and he flushed, his wings going full tilt.

"Yeah, well, she's not cooking for me."

My smile was faint but sincere. "I'm still proud of you."

Jenks flew to the table, looking tall next to the tiny cups Trent was using. "She's okay, I guess. By the way, that gargoyle that showed up last night is still there."

Frowning, I put my elbows on the table and rested my chin on the back of my hands. I would've thought that it was the same one from the ever-after, but there hadn't been enough scars. "The one that looks older than the basilica?"

Nodding, Jenks speared one of the gingersnaps, holding it over his head like an umbrella as he twirled it. "I don't like it, Rache. Bis wouldn't tell me what they were talking about."

"And you didn't just spy on them?"

"You don't think I tried?" Jenks angled his sword until the cookie was at his face. His expression thoughtful, he nibbled a corner off the cookie, looking like Willy Wonka eating an umbrella. "The little turd kept spitting on me. All the way across the Tink-blasted garden. They have better hearing than even Jrixibell."

I squinted up at the glass ceiling, bored. "I'll ask him tonight when he wakes up." I hadn't wanted to interfere, but if he was still there . . .

"I think they're spying on us." Wiping his mouth, Jenks put the nibbled cookie back over his head, resting his sword on his shoulder.

"They have a right to be concerned." *Where in hell are Trent and Ellasbeth?* My foot began to bob. "Bis went ape when Al cut off his contact with the ley lines. Can you imagine what might happen if they collapse?" Foot slowing, I thought about that. Maybe I could ask for their help. They might know something the demons didn't, something that wasn't written down.

Spinning on a heel, Jenks took a breath to say something, then hesitated when the cookie sailed off the tip of his sword and smack-pattered into the surrounding greenery. There was a rustle and hiss of delight, and I wondered if he'd done it intentionally, tasting it first so they wouldn't think it was treachery.

"Piss on my daisies, we have to save the demons!" he said, his eyebrows high when my attention came back to him. "I'm not going to let Bis go crazy."

Ignoring his foul mouth, I set three cookies on the retaining wall. Seriously, how did my life get so screwed up that I was giving cookies to fairies and busting my ass to save the demons?

The faint *tap-tap* of shoes coming down the path caught my attention, and I sat up. "It's about bloody time," I whispered, moving back to my chair before they could round the corner. But it was only Trent, and I watched as his somber silhouette moved slowly through the greenery, his fingers reaching out but not touching the plants in passing like they were old friends. I don't think he even knew he was doing it. His stance was upright, and he managed a faint, worried smile. Something was different.

"Where's Ellasbeth?"

"Waiting for coffee," he said, his green eyes meeting mine for a bare instant. "She doesn't like Earl Grey." His fixed smile grew even more stiff. "I'd have rather looked at the book out here, but do you mind coming in?" He looked at Jenks. "Both of you?"

Immediately I stood. "Sure. No problem."

His smile was a shade forced, and he shook his head when I reached for the tray. "You can leave it." His focus came to me, and he took a cookie before he turned back up the path. "Is that a new outfit? It looks nice on you."

Startled, I looked down at my black slacks and linen top. I'd spent almost an hour in my closet, trying to find something professional and casual that Ellasbeth couldn't label "hooker."

"Ah, no, but thank you."

Still smiling, he gestured for me to go with him. "Ellasbeth woke up Ray when she came in, and now she won't go down. She's usually such a docile, biddable little girl, but she's been fussy since . . . her sister is away." He took a bite of cookie, mood introspective. "I never realized how she depended on Lucy to make her wishes known. She's had to speak up more. I suppose that's good."

The cookie I'd just eaten went tasteless. "Trent—"

His head dropped, and my words cut off at his sudden stillness. "Ellasbeth has been very cooperative. Dropped her petition for Lucy. I think she wants to try to make this work again."

I froze, almost choking. *Why is he telling me this?* "Ah, that's great!" I said, not looking at him as I spun to find my shoulder bag. "If you two get back together, then there won't be any issues with Lucy at all, right?"

Jenks took to the air, a sickening green dust sparkling from him. "What a little cat scrotum!" he said, and both Trent and I stared. From the bushes, three hissing laughs sounded and were shushed.

"Jenks!" I admonished him, and he hovered, his hands on his hips and a disgusted expression on his face. "What is your problem?"

"Nothin'." Wings clattering, he flew between Trent and me, headed for the door, a bright silver sparkle falling to show his path.

Okay, my first reaction had been not far from that of Jenks, but honestly, there was nothing between Trent and me, and never would be. If he could make it work with Ellasbeth, it wouldn't be simply the girls who benefited, but an entire demographic of politically motivated elves. "Sorry," I said as I fell into place beside Trent, our feet hitting the cobbles at the same time. "He just doesn't like her."

Trent was silent, and I looked at him questioningly. "Right," he said quickly, then ate that cookie he'd taken, but I wasn't sure what was going through his mind, and that bothered me. Jenks had told me little of what happened when he and Trent stole Lucy from Ellasbeth, saying it was privileged information, but Trent clearly hadn't appreciated having to steal his own child.

"This is good, isn't it?" I said, glancing back at the unappealing cold tea to see the fairies descending on it.

Trent looked sideways at me. "Yes, of course it is. It would make everyone's lives much easier."

Damn it, I couldn't read the smile he was giving me, and the nerves suddenly started. What if that book was useless? What if Ellasbeth had brought it all this way, and I couldn't figure it out? What if . . .

We paused at the door and Trent punched in a code on the pad. It was too fast for me, but I was sure Jenks caught it. There was a heavy thunk of a lock shifting, and Trent nodded, easily moving the huge, perfectly balanced door. "I'm anxious to see what you make of the book she brought," he said, and Jenks buzzed in ahead of us, ever curious. "I remember looking at the pictures when I was about ten. I don't know where my mother got it. Probably stole it from Ellasbeth's mom, seeing as she willed it back to her."

He chuckled, but I thought he might be serious as I followed him inside. The hallway was brightly lit and sported beautiful close-ups of orchids in the morning dew, but the air smelled stale after the rich scents of the garden.

"You're going to have to look at it in the girls' closet," he said as we started down the carpeted hallway, heading back to the great room.

"A closet?" I said, trying to keep up with him. "You keep your magic books in a closet?"

"You keep your splat gun in a mixing bowl."

True.

Jenks flew ahead as we entered the lower level of Trent's great room. To my right was the huge three-story window ward that Lee had made, letting in light and sound but little else. Beyond its faint shimmer was the highly landscaped outside living area with a grill/kitchen and swimming pool. At the far end of the gigantic room was a fireplace large enough to roast an entire elephant in. In between was the grand staircase up to Trent's apartments.

"Since learning my father's vault downstairs was not secure, we moved everything to the girls' closet," Trent was saying as he headed for the stairway. "Ceri put some kind of demon ward on all the upstairs rooms. They aren't holy, but it has the same effect. There's no way in or out but the door, which only Ceri, Quen, and I have access to. If you ask me, it's safer than my father's vault. But the reason Ellasbeth insists you look at it there is because it's temperature and humidity controlled and the book is ancient."

That Ceri had warded the girls' rooms sounded about right, and I touched the smooth finish of a couch as we passed. The ground floor here was basically a big party room. Past the stairway was a dark and silent bar area, and behind that the kitchen and underground parking. I knew, because I'd run through it more than once. Damn it, what was I doing having tea and cookies with Ellasbeth while Ceri suffered all that Ku'Sox was capable of?

Jenks dropped from the ceiling, an excited silver dust trailing from him. "Rache!" he exclaimed as he landed on my shoulder, his wings never slowing as they drafted my hair back. "You'll never guess who's here!"

"Who?" I asked, almost afraid.

From the third-story apartments, I heard Quen's distinctive gravelly voice say, "I'll speak to the chef immediately, Miss Withon."

"See that you do," said an imperialistic feminine voice, and I stopped short at the foot of the stairs.

Quen? He was okay? He was back!

Chapter Eleven

I spun to Trent. The smug brat was smirking. "Why didn't you tell me Quen was back!" I shouted, my urge to smack him hesitating when Quen dryly cleared his throat. Distracted, I looked up at the railing. Quen was there, his pox scars standing out strongly against an unusual paleness. Ray was in his arms, and the little girl clung to him. Both Quen and Trent were smiling. Ellasbeth was not.

Trent's hand went to my arm to lead me upstairs. "Why did you let me believe Quen was dead the morning he recovered from his vampire bite?" he said, and I jerked my arm away from him as we found the first step.

"I was a little preoccupied with Takata being my birth father," I said, heart pounding as I took the stairs two at a time.

Trent kept up, maddeningly graceful. "It wasn't my place to tell . . ."

My eyes narrowed. "Not your place . . . Are we even now? You little . . . cookie maker!" I exclaimed, knocking him off balance when we found the eight-by-eight landing for the first floor. Ellasbeth gasped, but Trent was laughing, even as he caught himself. Quen was here. He was okay. *Finally* something was going our way.

Seeing me lurch up the last of the stairs, Quen straightened to try to hide his fatigue. Our eyes met, and the older man nodded solemnly. On his hip, Ray gurgled happily. The little girl was in a sweet full-length jumper/

Indian-looking robe of some sort cut from a subdued orange-and-brown paisley, her brown hair braided and looped out of the way. Hearing Jenks's wings, she pushed from her father's shoulder to find him. She was a beautiful blending of Ceri and Quen, and again I was struck by the frailty of this small family.

"Rachel," Quen said simply, and I pushed past Ellasbeth in her cream-colored business suit and matching heels.

"That's not going to do it," I said as I pulled the older man into a hug, getting Ray mixed up in there somewhere. The curious scent of cinnamon and wine that all elves had mixed with the throat-catching odor of hospital. Under it was his masculine pull, a faint hint of controlled magic and ozone to give it some interest. *He smells different from Trent,* I thought. Trent's magic smelled powerful, but Quen's had a darker tang than Trent's shadowed glow.

Suddenly realizing Quen's arms had gone around me in what had probably been self-defense, I pushed back, embarrassed. "They let you out? When?" I said, wincing when Ray grabbed my hair and pulled me in.

The older man made a noise of admonishment, disentangling her fingers and then, unexpectedly, tugged me back to him with one arm, turning us both to the common living room visible through the wide archway. "They didn't let me do anything. I left. It's good to see you," he said, his voice rumbling through me. "You're the one who sent those damn demon-scented petits fours, aren't you? They woke me up at midnight, and I left at two."

I grinned as I slipped out from under his arm. He looked tired but good, the injuries to his nervous system obviously repaired enough to function. "Are you sure you're okay?"

"No, but everything will eventually come back," he said, and I gave him a light punch on his arm and wrinkled my nose at Ray.

"Tomorrow morning, probably," I guessed. Three days. That's how long it took to renew an aura so it didn't hurt when you tapped a line. What had Ku'Sox done to him?

Trent was making his way to Ellasbeth. Having seen our reunion—and not being a part of it—the woman had retreated to the small kitchen behind the large sunken living room. Four doors led to four suites—Quen and Ceri's, Trent's, the girls'. The fourth had been Ellasbeth's when she had been his fiancée, and by the sound of it, it might be again.

My heart ached at the toys scattered in the living room, and a crayon-scribbled picture of horses was pasted to a door, a sad two feet from the floor. This was the closest that Trent would ever get to a normal family life, and I was angry that Ku'Sox had spoiled it.

Suddenly unsure, I followed Quen and Ray to the sunken living room, having to wave Jenks's dust out of my way. The last time I'd seen Ellasbeth was when I'd arrested Trent at their wedding. I hadn't known she'd been pregnant with Lucy at the time, and I didn't know if it would have made any difference. The well-dressed, sophisticated woman looked broken as she sat at the small kitchen table, her expensive cream-colored slacks and coordinating top and jacket rumpled. She was tired, jet lag and worry having taken their toll on her perfect makeup and upright posture. Even so, I balked as her eyes found mine.

Her strawlike, straight hair looked fake next to Trent's wispy strands, and her build was too strong to have only elf in her. She was not full blood, and it showed. Money had a way of erasing that, though, and her family was almost as influential as Trent.

Jenks's wings shivered against my neck as he took refuge, and a chill went through me. "Oh, there's trouble with a high-end handbag," he said, and I agreed.

"Ah . . . hello," I said, feeling awkward, as if she'd come home and found me naked in Trent's tub. No, wait. She had once.

Ellasbeth stood in a smooth, controlled motion of grace, and I jerked to a stop. Quen gave me a "good luck" look as he continued into the lower living room area with Ray, and Jenks abandoned me, wings clattering. *Chicken.* But all she did was extend her hand, a stiff expression on her face. "Thank you for agreeing to help Trent get Lucy and Ceri back."

That was *not* what I had expected, and I cautiously took her unworked hand in mine. Her voice wasn't inviting, but it wasn't cold, either. My thoughts returned to Trent's words in the greenhouse. She wanted back into his life? Why? Power? Parental and social pressure? Lucy? I didn't think it was to spend the rest of her life with Trent, but it wasn't my business.

"Ah, it's the right thing to do," I said, letting her hand go and forcing myself to not hide mine behind my back. Her touch had been cold, and I maintained my pleasant expression. No, it wasn't my business, but Trent would tie himself to this woman if he thought it was what duty required of him. He'd do it for everything she represented despite her having nothing he wanted.

Her smile widened, but didn't get any warmer. "Still," she said, her hands clasped before her to look like a proper 1940s wife in her monochromatic dress suit and matching purse. "It's very noble of you to risk your life when you don't have a personal stake in the outcome."

Lemon-yellow dust sifted from the light fixture. Ignoring Jenks's silent comment, I smiled right back at her. "But I do. Lucy is my godchild, and Ceri is my friend. I freed her from the demons before, and seeing her cry over having a home, husband, and children when she never dreamed of freedom makes me a tad protective of her when some demon tries to take it away."

"I see."

I see? Did she say I freaking see? "Besides," I added when her eye twitched. "If I don't help him, who will?" My unspoken *you?* was obvious.

From Ceri's high-backed embroidery chair, Quen cleared his throat. Trent had his back to us, busy in the kitchen making coffee, and Jenks simply sent down another shower of sparkling dust, the crystal in the fixture tinkling as it shook from his laughter.

Inclining her head, Ellasbeth smoothly sat back down. "I'll make sure you're well compensated." My smile froze as I suddenly became hired help standing before her.

Damn, she was good. "I don't work for Trent," I said, suddenly feeling outclassed. Her eyes were on my pinkie ring, and I think she'd recognized it as matching Trent's. "I work *with* him."

Stop it, Rachel, I thought as I realized I was in danger of arguing with an idiot. *It wouldn't hurt you to be nice. She just lost her daughter, not once but twice.*

Exhaling, I leaned against the counter, forcing her to turn if she wanted to keep me in her sight. "Ku'Sox won't hurt either of them," I said as Trent passed between us to hand Ellasbeth a cup of coffee. "Ku'Sox wants something, and this is the only way he can get it. Hurting them will only piss me off, and Ku'Sox knows that."

Ellasbeth's beaming smile to Trent vanished. "Can we please stop saying his name?" she asked, and on his way back to the kitchen, Trent shot me a look to be nice.

"Why?" I crossed my ankles and leaned deeper into the counter. "It's not like saying it does anything."

"Coffee, Rachel?" Trent said as he shoved a cup at me, and I scrambled to take it before it sloshed over. A faint blush was showing on Ellasbeth. Maybe that had been a tad petty.

"Ah, you have a book for me to look at, right?" I prompted, then took a sip.

"It's in the safe room. Look at it in there." Chin high, Ellasbeth pushed away the cup of coffee Trent had brought her. Out of her sight in the kitchen, Trent hung his head, his free hand rubbing his temple.

Quen rose, his motions slow and pained. Ray was slumped against him, the little girl valiantly fighting sleep and starting to lose. "I'll show you."

Jenks peeked over the fixture at me, laughing. It made me feel as if I'd lost something. Damn it, I could be nice to this woman. I didn't have to be her best friend, just not smack her while we breathed the same air. "Thank you, Ellasbeth. This is going to be a huge help," I said, but it sounded forced even to me. "We're going to get them back. It's going to be okay."

She looked up. The worry and fear of the last two days pooled in her eyes as she met mine and held them. I don't think anyone had told her it was going to be okay, and upon hearing it—even if she didn't believe it— she began to break apart. Tears welled and she quickly turned away, her posture becoming more stiff, more closed. It must be hard when the only comfort you got was from the person you most disliked in the room.

Trent set his coffee aside, the cup hitting the granite loudly. "Quen, while you're showing Rachel the safe room, Ellasbeth and I will be in the gardens."

"Why?" Ellasbeth said in distrust as she fumbled in her matching purse for a tissue. "I can help."

Trent touched the woman's shoulder, and I shoved a twinge of jealousy away. "If you're open to it, I'd like to discuss the possibility of joint custody."

Ellasbeth's eyes widened. "Trent," she said breathlessly. "I don't want to have to need a joint custody agreement at all."

From the chandelier came a tiny "Eeeeewwww."

"I just want us to all be together as we are supposed to be," she said, gazing up at him, tears spilling from her. "I want my family! What if we can't get her back! What if . . ." Sobbing, the elegant woman dropped her head into her hands and sat alone at the table and cried. Uncomfortable, I glanced at Quen—who clearly didn't care—then to Trent. He seemed unsure, and I made a face at him to do something. Anything.

Grimacing, he pushed himself into motion, pulling her to her feet so he could hold her. That was even more uncomfortable, but at least she wasn't crying alone. "Shhhh . . ." Trent soothed, even if he did look a little stiff doing it. But awkward or not, they looked beautiful together. Sophisticated. "Ceri lived among demons for a thousand years," Trent said, holding the woman as she shook. "Lucy is resilient and brave. The demons won't hurt her as long as they have a hope I'll give them what they want."

My stomach hurt, and I looked away.

"We can talk in the garden," Trent said, starting to guide her to the stairway. Jenks dropped down from the light fixture, and my lips parted when Trent made a small finger movement to tell him to stay.

Oh, really? I thought, watching Trent help Ellasbeth down the wide stairs, a hand under her elbow as she continued to warble about home and family, and how she had been an idiot.

Idiot. Sure. My thoughts drifted back to her standing at the basilica's altar, furious at me for ruining her wedding day as I handcuffed Trent for suspicion of murder. I'd ruined *her* day.

Ray perked up at the sound of Jenks's wings, and she watched with sleepy eyes as he dropped down to me. "Tink's little pink rosebuds, you two are like dogs snarling," he said, and I scowled, looking at the top of the stairway.

"I didn't hit her, did I?"

He laughed, but I still felt ill. If Ellasbeth was going to be in Trent's life, I'd probably better start kissing ass if I ever wanted to see the girls again.

Jenks landed on my shoulder as I went to help Quen up the two shallow stairs. I was still wondering about that finger motion. "Is he seriously considering . . . that?" the pixy whispered as Ellasbeth's voice rose from the great room.

"Looks like it," I breathed. "If you ask me, she's nothing but bad news. But they look good together."

Quen grunted as he got to his feet, unbalanced from Ray and his injuries that he wouldn't tell me about. Shaking off my offer for assistance, he headed for the nursery, his left leg sluggish on the two stairs.

"Is that what you see?" Jenks said, jerking me back to my last comment. "That they look good together?"

I tried to eye him, but he was too close. "You don't think they do?"

Pushing open the nursery door with his foot, Quen shook his head. "The joining of the two houses would do a lot in bringing the two factions of our society together. I'm glad someone finally talked some sense into that woman."

He seemed genuinely pleased, but I couldn't help but wonder what would happen to Ceri, Ray, and Quen if Ellasbeth entered the family.

"Good thing the man likes frustrating women," Jenks said, and I tucked a strand of hair behind my ear to shove him off my shoulder. I could still hear Ellasbeth's tearful protests bracketed by Trent's musical voice. The farther they got from us, the more hysterical she was getting, and her voicing her doubts wasn't helping.

"She is wearing your ring, Trenton!" echoed, and then the door slammed shut.

We only had days, and despite Trent's confident words, I didn't have a plan; I had a goal whose solution revolved around a book I hadn't seen yet.

My heart sank as I looked over the dark nursery lit by a friendly, smiling full moon with cows jumping over it. *Oh God, Ceri and Lucy.* I'd get them back if I had to tear the ever-after apart line by line. "Was it Nick in the woods?" I asked Quen as he nudged a walk-'n'-ride out of the way to get to the closet door.

"On the outside," he said, and the little girl felt his tension and squirmed to turn around. "His speech patterns were Ku'Sox's." Quen shifted his shoulders painfully as he took a set of keys from his pocket.

"His combat patterns were Ku'Sox's as well. I'm surprised the human survived channeling that much power. But then he didn't have to do much once he got Lucy."

It must have been horrifying, and my eyes roved over the beauty here as he sifted through the keys: the well-thought-out toys, the books and figures waiting for pretend—the twin cribs, one messy, the other tidy, clearly not slept in, with a lonely giraffe waiting for Lucy's return. It about broke my heart, and feeling ill, I whispered, "I'm so sorry."

Silent, Quen held the keys up to Ray, and the little girl took an interest. Quen looked distressed. He knew Ceri would be okay, right? "I've been in contact with Dali," I said as Ray patted the keys. "We have some time before things shift. I'm sure they're both okay."

Quen's entire body relaxed. "It's what I pray to the Goddess for."

On the door frame, Jenks shrugged, but I didn't know what else to say.

Quen still hadn't unlocked the door, waiting for Ray to lose interest in the keys. I was all for letting children learn when the opportunity presented itself, but I did have a timetable. I took a breath to say something, then hesitated as I realized Ray wasn't playing with the keys; she was sorting them, her little fingers pushing them around until she found the one she liked with a pat.

"Abba," she said in her high, little-child voice as she touched the keys, and my eyes widened. I had no idea what Abba was, but it was very clear what she was trying to convey.

"Very good, Ray," Quen said, his voice soft and holding pride. "That's the one to get into the big toy box. Now will you go to sleep? Abba has to help Aunt Rachel pick out the toy that's going to get your mother and Lucy back."

The elf name for father? I wondered, vowing to ask Jenks about it later. *Guardian? Protector? Mom's Mr. Significant?* I didn't know, but it sounded like a term of affection.

Ray's face puckered. I thought she was going to cry, but when Quen raised his eyebrows, she thought better of it, turning away from me to cling to him.

"Oh my God," I said as Quen held her to him with one arm and fitted the key in the lock with the other. "You're teaching her to be a little you," I accused, and Quen flashed a smile, not looking at all guilty.

"Someone has to keep Lucy alive when I'm not around," he said as the door creaked open and he reached in to flick on the light. "Trent's daughter is entirely too trusting, and I doubt her days with a demon are going to change that. Go on in. I'm going to put Ray down. Ellasbeth already has the book in the cabinet, but this will just take a moment."

He turned back to the dim nursery, and I waved bye to Ray, the girl watching me over Quen's shoulder. "Abba," Ray warbled as Quen put her in the crib, and two little hands reached for him. Quen stooped down to reassure her, and I saw the love before the closet door arced shut. I couldn't help but feel good. Jenks sighed, and I jumped, having forgotten he was there. Obviously he'd seen the love between them, too. I knew he missed having newlings.

"Wow," I said as I turned away and took in the "closet." It was impressive, smaller than the vault Trent had been keeping his most precious secrets in, but more organized. Racks of paintings, shelves of knickknacks of various styles and eras, and one big glass-fronted cabinet with leather-bound books took up most of the room. Cabinetry and a small sink ran along one wall, and a library table with two wingback chairs filled the middle space. Underfoot was a rug that looked old enough to fly, and given the location, it just might if you knew the right word.

"Don't touch anything, Jenks," I said, and he scowled at me as he hovered before a rack of shiny ley line baubles.

"I won't break anything," he said, then spilled a flash of silver dust as something caught his attention and he darted to it. "Hey! Trent still has that elf porn statue you stole."

Eyes rolling, I came to see if it was as graphic as I remembered, but I lingered over the pair of rings below Jenks's feet. One was a simple gold band, the other heavy and ornate. They looked like mismatched wedding bands, reminding me of the rings that Al and I had used when we had shared each other's strengths. "Ah, Quen?"

Jenks had his hands on his hips as he looked over that nasty statue of three elves in the middle of a threesome. "Tink's titties," he said. "I suppose that's possible." His head tilted. "You'd need a lot of grease and two straps, though."

"Quen!" I hissed, and Quen pushed open the safe room's door, almost shutting it completely behind him. Ray was babbling to herself in the other room, but she'd probably drop off if we didn't talk too loudly.

"Let me get you the book," he said, limping past the library table to the tall cabinet.

I pushed close to ask him about the rings, and he handed me a pair of soft gloves lying out on the table. They looked too small, but I tugged them on, thinking they were likely Ceri's. Quen was putting on a second pair. "Thanks," I said, feeling the soft knit mold itself to my fingers. "Those rings by Jenks. How old are they?"

The hiss of escaping air from the temperature-controlled cabinet was soft, and Quen glanced at Jenks as he swung the doors wide. "Not sure," he said shortly. "Old. I can find out."

"Hey, Quen." Jenks circled the statue, avarice in his gaze. "Let me know if Trent ever wants to get rid of this. I have a spot in my front room it would look ace in."

I held my breath as I leaned toward the open cabinet, avoiding any possible demon stink. "Are they demon made?" I asked as I looked over the books, some so old they were falling apart.

Quen looked at me, suspicion in his eyes. "The rings? No. Elven. Why?"

"Al has something similar." I took a hesitant breath, pleased when I found only the honest scent of leather and decaying ink.

Quen snorted, the rude sound seeming odd coming from him. "I doubt that," he said as he scanned the spines. "They're chastity rings."

Jenks sniggered, coming to make annoying circles around me. "Too late for you, Rache."

Irked, I waved him off. I thought it odd that Trent would keep chastity rings next to his elf porn, but it wasn't like he used any of these things. I think. This was his father's collection, like some dads have stamps. Or guns.

Quen reached for a book set aside by itself. "More accurately, they're binding rings," he said, his face showing the strain as he stretched for it. "It creates a continuous bond between two chis so the wearer of the alpha ring can snuff the magical ability of the other if needed. They were used to keep younger, inexperienced elves from exposing themselves as magic users. They don't work, though. The charm in them is long spent."

"The books don't smell," I said as he set the book on the library table. "Bad, I mean," when he looked at me. No, they didn't smell, but there was a faint whine at the back of my ear, like a high-pitched echo of leashed magic that made me uncomfortable.

"None of them have been in the ever-after for at least five hundred years." His voice was distant as he stood over the book and carefully turned the yellowed pages until he got to a section marked with a black ribbon. The binding made a cracking sound as he shifted the last page, and I swear he winced.

Standing over the tattered book, I looked down to read "Ley Line Corruption and Manipulation" in big, squished loops that I sort of recognized. My eyes went up, and I squinted at Quen suspiciously. "That's Ceri's handwriting."

"No shit!" Jenks said, finally abandoning the statue to come hover over the text.

"I know." Quen's eyes shifted as he read the text. "We have six books here that Ceri has copied. A handful of other scripts. She doesn't remember doing them. Ellasbeth insists that the book stays here. You're welcome to spend the night if you want to read it cover to cover, but I believe this is what you want. I read it before it was returned to Mrs. Withon."

Sitting, I looked at Ceri's extravagant loops and swirls. I sucked at research. If he'd done it already, I was good with that, though I might come back and read it all later. "Thanks," I said as I tugged the book closer. Quen cringed, and I curled my tingling fingertips under.

"So how come it was at the Withons'?" Jenks said, his feet lightly touching the pages.

Quen sat in the chair across from me, motions slow as if he wasn't sure he was going to hold together. "Trent's mother and Ellie were good friends."

There was more to the story than that, but it didn't really matter. Jenks flew up when I shifted to a new page, and his dust spilled over everything to make the letters glow. Seeing it, Quen leaned forward. "Interesting . . ."

I met his eyes. "You didn't know pixy dust makes demon texts glow?"

"No," he admitted, leaning back and steepling his fingers.

Wondering if this was where Trent got his little nervous tell from, I went back to the text. "You're shooting yourself in the foot, Quen. Jenks has six bucks looking for property this spring. They can all read and they don't mind fairies."

"Hey!" Jenks said. "Quit trying to farm out my kids!"

"Just pointing things out," I said as I turned the page to a map of the dead lines in Arizona. A second map showed where the author thought they'd been before they'd been shoved together. Quen was right. There might be something here. It was all theory, but theory based on fact and observation.

Seeing me intently quiet, Quen asked, "Do you want something to drink? Eat?"

"No-o-o," I drawled, feeling like I was close to something.

Hesitating, Quen shifted his chair forward. "I'd like to go out with you the next time you look at the Loveland ley line."

I thought of his sluggish left leg. He probably couldn't tap a line yet either. I said nothing, embarrassed. He wasn't ready to battle demons again. Maybe next week. But next week would be too late.

Quen frowned at my silence, knowing what it meant. Clearly frustrated, he leaned closer until I could smell his aftershave over the characteristic woodsy wine-and-cinnamon scent. "I think I know how Ku'Sox made that event horizon."

I paused in my reading and looked up. "Event horizon?" Jenks asked, but that was what Al had called it, too.

"The purple line within a line sucking everything in," he stated, and I shuddered. No wonder I'd felt squished, even if it had only been my mind. Al was lucky to be alive. That the collective had something for him to pattern himself on was probably how he had survived.

Quen carefully lifted the book toward him, his eyes on the yellowed pages. "I think Ku'Sox made it by gathering up the small imbalances that already existed in the other lines, concentrating them in the leaking line you made," he said, carefully flipping back to the paragraph where the author mentioned the possibility of small line imbalances having no effect if the individual lines were spaced out enough and aligned to the polar forces of nearby lines.

I scooted my chair closer to Quen's and read the first passage again. "Al did say that the lines were balanced to within safe parameters, implying they all leaked to some degree."

"Must have been small leaks," Jenks said, hands on his hips as he hovered over it all, his dust bringing the print back to a new-edged brightness.

"That's just it," Quen said, his thick fingers tapping the table. "They don't add up to what's in the Loveland ley line."

"They would if they acted on each other exponentially," I said.

Quen's expression twisted in doubt. "Why would they do that?"

"How should I know? I'm shooting at fairies here." My fingers were starting to cramp from holding the book, and I took my gloves off to rub them. I had enough information to go on a fact-finding mission out at the line. I figured things out by doing, not reading about them. "Al told me that the lines push each other apart, like giant magnets," I said, unclenching my teeth. *God! Am I the only one hearing this whine?* "If the lines are positive, pushing away from each other, then maybe the imbalance is negative. Maybe you can't have a line without a little imbalance."

"Like those little black and white magnet dogs that don't like each other unless they go face-to-face?" Jenks laughed, but I thought he had it almost exactly right.

Quen adjusted his position, inadvertently telling me his hip was sore. "Lines don't move."

"Mine did," I said. "A good hundred feet from the second floor of the castle to the garden outside. Al said lines moved a lot when they were new, but they stabilized." Reaching over, I tapped the page with my naked finger, which made Quen wince. My head gave a throb, and I curved my fingers under, wondering if this might be why Al wore gloves.

"Maybe all the lines leaked at first like mine," I said, wishing I could ask Al about it. "But the farther apart they got, the smaller the leak became. And when Ku'Sox put the imbalances together again, bang! Big leak."

Quen's lips twisted in doubt, which made his hospital stubble more obvious. Jenks, though, was bobbing up and down. "Like one sticktight stuck to your tights compared to a ball of them."

"Or a bunch of dust scattered in a huge vacuum having no effect compared to the same amount balled up into a planet," I added, and Quen's expression smoothed as he considered it. "If that's how Ku'Sox got that purple sludge in my ley line, then all I have to do is divvy the imbalance back up again, and the leak will go back to its original pace. Clear the crud out, and anyone can see the curse that Ku'Sox used to break my line. They'd have to side against him!"

Jenks dusted an excited gold, but Quen still had doubts if his sour expression was any indication. "He'll simply break it again," he said as he closed the book and stood.

"Maybe," I admitted, feeling a stab of worry. "But I'll be waiting for him this time. If I catch him at it, then he's in trouble, not me. If I can prove Ku'Sox broke my line, they won't kill me but band together and make him behave." I frowned—they should just band together and be done with him regardless. *Cowards.*

The hiss of the door was less this time as Quen carefully put Ellasbeth's book away. It bothered me that Trent was with her right now, believing whatever drivel she was feeding him.

"And you know how to do this?" Quen said as the door sealed shut with a cold sound. "Separate imbalances?"

"No," I admitted. "But if Bis and I went out there, we might be able to figure it out. He's really good at separating line signatures."

Neither one of them said anything, Jenks sitting on Quen's shoulder and both of them eyeing me in doubt. "He is," I said in Bis's defense. "You look at him and all you see is a kid, but I've seen the lines through him, and he knows what he's doing. Besides," I added, "either of you *Abba*s got any other ideas? I'm all ears."

Quen flushed as I used the elf name he'd given himself, but Jenks flew almost into my face. "You're not going into that purple line. You saw what it did to Al." He spun to Quen, an alarmed gold dust making a sunbeam on the table. "It fried his aura, and they both almost died!"

Ignoring him, I chewed on my lip. "I'd be careful," I said, then stifled a shiver. What if I got sucked into it by mistake? Or Ku'Sox shoved me?

"You're not going out there!" Jenks shrilled, and Quen winced, looking at the closet door. "It's not safe, and you know it!"

"When is my life safe?" I said, trying not to get riled up. "Trent could spot me if I used Al's rings. Would that make you happy?"

Jenks dropped several inches before he remembered to move his wings. Still leaning against the cabinet, Quen seemed to stiffen. I knew being almost helpless bothered him. "Al's rings?" Jenks scoffed, coming down and kicking at the gloves I'd taken off. "You think demon magic is going to work with an elf?"

My eyes went to Quen. He was frowning in thought. "I don't know. You got anything on demon wedding rings?" I asked, but he was already at the cabinet, putting his gloves back on. "I yanked Al's soul out of that event horizon using a pair of rings," I babbled. "They sort of melted our minds together." Jenks made a face, his dust shifting green. "Not like that," I said. "It was weird, though, as if I could pull on his strength, and he could pull on mine."

"Without asking?" Quen reached high to pull down a slim volume. It was falling apart and had no title, so I figured it was a demon text. "You sure they weren't slave rings?"

Chastity rings sounded far more slavelike than Al's rings. "Pretty sure," I said as Jenks peered over Quen's shoulder. "The connection felt equal. Like a scrying mirror but more complex, sort of like the difference between a phone call and talking in person. Al said the rings made an unbreakable connection," I said, stifling a shudder at the memory of feeling his pain, then squishing the thought of what sex might feel like. Da-a-amn . . . Feeling two orgasms at once might be worth the invasion of privacy.

Quen eyed me in my sudden silence, setting the volume down before me and pointedly handing me my gloves. I put them on, my curiosity growing as Quen opened it to almost the last page. "I think what you want is here."

No matter how I tugged the gloves, they felt too tight, but I smiled as I saw the rough drawings. It faded as I read what the demon rings were actually for. Increased sexual pleasure was on there, but they were really created as an implement of war, allowing a sort of superdemon able to overpower elves and whatever more easily. There was no clear master or subordinate ring as there was in the elf chastity rings. How they decided what curse to war with was up for debate, but perhaps that never came up in the heat of battle? I thought it interesting that it was assumed that it took two demons to overpower wild, elven magic. One thing was clear, though. The two people wearing them had no defense against each other if there was treachery. Wedding bands, indeed.

"Look, there it is," Jenks said, his dust sinking through the pages to make them glow from underneath. "Demon use only. You don't make something your enemy can use."

He was right, but I wasn't going to give up on this, and leaning back in my chair, I racked my brain for an answer. "Well, why not use the chastity rings?" I said suddenly, and Quen started. "You said they made a bond. If it's tight enough to quash someone's magic, I bet it's tight enough to pull me out of trouble."

Hunched over the book, Quen's eyes came to mine. "Those are elven chastity rings, not demon wedding bands," he almost growled.

"Right." I pushed my chair out and went over to them. "But he could yank me back. Just like Al's wedding rings!"

They were both staring at me as if I was nuts, but I knew it would work. It had to.

"They're broken," Quen said, and Jenks bobbed his head up and down. "The knowledge to make new ones is gone. The women burned all the texts."

"Big surprise." Not ready to let this go, I looked at them on their little black saucer. One was tiny, like a child's ring, which made sense if it was to keep young people in line. "I know someone who can bring spent ley line charms back to life," I said as I picked them both up.

Quen made a small sound, and I jiggled them in my hand.

"Pierce!" Jenks exclaimed, his wings a harsh rattle. "You're talking about Pierce! He's Newt's familiar! Rache, what have you been putting in your coffee?"

Smiling, I looked at the rings in my palm. Quen was right. They were dead. Not even a whisper of magic.

"Don't put the little one on!" Quen said as I angled it to my pinkie to see if it would fit, and I hesitated. "That's the subservient ring. Once it goes on, it doesn't come off until the master ring allows it."

Oh. Thinking, I jiggled the rings just to watch Quen's reaction. "You said they don't work."

"You want to risk it? Go ahead. Put it on."

Jenks came to hover over them, frowning in disapproval. "Even if you could get the rings reinvoked, Pierce is in the ever-after," he said, kicking the larger one into the smaller. It made a ping that seemed to echo through me.

"Why are you two always Debbie downers?" I said, closing my fingers around them.

Jenks landed on my closed fist. "Just what do you plan to do? Call Newt and ask her to pop you over? She's nuts!"

From behind me, Trent's soft voice said, "She doesn't have to."

I spun, warming as if I'd been caught stealing his stuff again. Shit, how long had he been there?

"Sorry," he said as he came farther in and took his hand from the closed door. "I didn't want to wake Ray up."

Sure, that's what he said, but Jenks was smirking at me, and Quen seemed smug that I was the only one Trent had surprised. His manner quick, Trent held out his hand, and I dropped the rings into them. He smelled like the outdoors, and of Ellasbeth's perfume. I stifled a surge of pique. There was a new drive in him, a purpose. He could again be what the elves wanted, and I forced myself to smile.

Quen looked pained as he stood there, but I couldn't tell if it was because of his injuries or because Trent was behind me on this. "How do you propose she get there, Sa'han?"

Trent looked up, eager to explain. "My father's vault door."

"Perfect!" I exclaimed softly.

"Oh God," Jenks muttered. "They're at it again. I'm not going to get out of this one alive. I know it. I can see the web on the wall already!"

"Relax, Jenks." I took Trent's hand and turned it palm up so I could gently pry his fingers open. "You're not going." My eyes met Trent's, and I took the rings. "You either."

Trent's expression cascaded through about six different emotions, all finally vanishing under a cold calm. "I am a part of this," he warned me.

"Obviously," I said as I backed up out of his easy reach. He was still wearing the matching pinkie ring, and something in me felt like it was a victory. "I'll get the rings working, not you. I know you. You'll get over there, and you'll do something noble and throw everything off plan."

"I will not!"

"You will!" I affirmed. "Besides, if I'm over there slumming in the mall looking for Pierce, everyone will think I'm taking care of Al. If you're there, it will be noticed."

Looking as if he were eating slugs, Trent dropped his head, making his bangs fall into his eyes. He knew I was right, and it was killing him.

"Those are my rings and my door," Trent said, his head coming up and holding his hand out. "I'm going."

Chin high, I refused to back up—but my hand was in a tight fist, hiding them. I had a fleeting memory of having done something like this before involving a key and the counselor's locked office. "It's my old boyfriend, so you stay. I'll get the rings working, and then *we* can go out to the line and see what we can do. Deal?"

"Ah, Sa'han?" Quen interrupted.

At the *we,* Trent's entire mien shifted from frustration to sour acceptance. Backing off, he licked his thumb and held it out, a challenging slant to his expression. My heart pounded. "Deal," he said, and I licked my thumb and we pressed them together.

Quen hunched into himself in disgust. Jenks was on his shoulder shedding a weird purple dust, but I was ecstatic. "You won't follow me," I insisted, and Trent looked up from under his bangs again, making my heart stop with his half smile.

"I just thumb promised, didn't I?"

Yes, he had thumb promised, and that he wouldn't dare break. Or I'd throw him down the camp well and leave him there for three days.

Chapter Twelve

The last time I'd been in the room outside of Trent's vault, I'd been stealing that elven threesome statue Jenks was so enamored of to gain Trent's undivided attention. The outer chamber hadn't changed, the air still flat and unmoving, the floors and walls bare with no furniture. I stared at the blank wall, Jenks on my shoulder and Trent beside me. Quen was down the hall turning on Trent's magnetic imaging device. It would shift the ley line running through Trent's compound down into the earth. More proof that the ley lines functioned as magnets on some level.

Once the line was out of its natural course, I could enter the ever-after not through the surface, which not only sucked dishwater but had no direct access to the demon realm, but right into their underground mall. From there I could buy a jump to Newt's rooms. If she was there, we'd have a chat and I'd borrow Pierce for a few hours. If she wasn't, then I'd save myself a few bucks and talk to Pierce with her none the wiser. I was hoping for the latter.

"There it goes," Trent said softly, staring at the wall as if it were a big-screen TV, and feeling a sudden hiccup in my balance, I unfocused my attention and brought my second sight up. Sure enough, the red smear of a ley line now ran through the room at chest height, right before and through the blank wall. It would be an easy matter to step into it, will myself across, and be safe underground. Trent's father, Kal, had used the ley line as a way to have a temporary door to a doorless vault, accessible when the magnetic resonator was on, and completely impossible to enter when the machine was switched off. It had been off for almost a year now, since Nick and I had burgled the vault behind the wall. I agreed with Trent that having a vault full of precious artifacts where any demon could see them using his second sight was a bad idea, but then again, Trent's dad might have been using the room for another reason.

Nervous, I wiped my hands on my pants and turned to Trent, startled at his aura. It wavered over him like a gold sheet, like he was on fire. The slash of red through it hadn't grown, but there was a new hint of black to it that I thought might be the first visible signs of smut. The room with the resonator was fairly close. We had a few minutes until Quen rejoined us.

"Is an hour enough?" Trent asked, calm as ever as he looked at his watch, but I could see by a flicker of darker gold aura that he was nervous. I wasn't leaving until Quen was here to keep him from following me.

"You want to make it two?" I countered, not sure how long this might take.

Jenks flew from my shoulder, his rainbowlike aura trailing him. "How about five minutes?" he said tightly, and I pleaded with my eyes for him not to make a stink. It was daylight, and pixies couldn't stay in the ever-after when the sun was up, same as demons couldn't stay in reality.

"I'll have a better chance of success if I go alone," I said, then craned my neck to look through the low ceiling at the banners and dappled light patterns that the demons decorated their mall with. It was early yet, and there wasn't a lot of traffic, just a few harried familiars and disgruntled demons who'd been pressed into service to clear a debt. I thought I could hear '80s music being piped in, echoing against the flat places. It was weird standing so far underground and feeling as if you were outside, but the demons had had thousands of years to build their pretend.

Trent eyed me askance—making me wonder if he was checking out my aura for smut—then fixed his gaze firmly ahead to the shop sign visible through the wall, THE COFFEE VAULT. Someone had a sense of humor.

"We can turn the magnet on at fifteen-minute intervals," Trent said; then we both turned at a scuff at the door.

"Sa'han," Quen protested, out of breath but clearly having heard him. "The risk . . ."

Trent's pleasant expression never changed. "We can turn the magnet on at fifteen-minute intervals," he said again, and Quen nodded reluctantly. Satisfied, Trent turned to the humming ley line.

The sour whine to the ley lines throughout Cincinnati was getting worse. Seeming to hear it as well, Jenks hovered before the line, hands on his hips and glaring at an oblivious man behind the coffeehouse windows. There was no reason for the familiar to be using his second sight, and unless he did, we would be invisible.

I stepped forward, dipping a hand through the line and deciding it felt okay even if it sounded bad, the flow even and smooth. Perhaps Trent's dad had had a deeper relationship with demonkind than Trent wanted to admit. Being able to step through a ley line and into the demon mall and coffee shop was a little too convenient—even if it was going to save both our asses.

Ready to go, I ran my hands down my linen blouse. It was going to stink to high heaven when I got back. "Quen, don't let him follow me," I said as I took a step forward into the line.

"Rachel, wait!"

Trent's voice stopped me cold, and I turned, still in reality even if I was in the ley line. He was digging in his pocket, and I warmed when I realized I'd almost left without the rings. He held them out, and a spark of magic jumped between us as the rings fell into my hand. It was the ley line, not him, but I still shivered. "Thanks," I said sheepishly. Nodding, he stepped back with a quick, sharp motion, gesturing for me to go. Jenks's wings clattered, and with a final thin smile, I willed myself into the ever-after.

Nose wrinkling, I took three steps within the line, walking through the wall in reality and into the demon coffeehouse. I jerked as the muggy stink of ever-after and the echoing sound of a European band singing about red balloons hit me. *What is it with demons and the '80s?* I wondered, not for the first time.

The familiar looked up from behind the counter. "By the two worlds colliding, don't jump into reality in here!" he berated me, perhaps not even knowing about the door and thinking I'd jumped in. He looked oddly familiar with his green apron and cap. "I don't care how much of a hurry your demon is in for his coffee, if you mesh with the wall, I'm not paying for it."

I gave the guy a quick smile, backpedaling for the door. "Sorry, wrong store."

"Use the circles at the fountain," he said, eyes narrowed. "Stupid-ass newbie."

He looked like a Scottish lord from a romance novel, the bushy sideburns and thick blocky muscles not doing a thing for me, but as my scrabbling hand found the doorknob, he muttered an oath. "Hey, wait. You're Rachel Morgan, right?" he said, dropping his rag. "Hold on. I got something for you."

My hand slipped from the knob, and I turned. "Me?"

His head was down and he was rummaging in a bin behind the counter. "Yeah. My boss has a proposition you might be interested in."

Shoulders slumping, I sighed. Trent, Quen, and Jenks were probably watching with their second sight, and I did have a timetable. "Sorry," I said as I yanked the door open and the music got louder. "I'm not making tulpas right now. Saving the world, you know." *Again.*

"No, wait! Just take it. I'll give you a coffee on the house!"

I couldn't care less about the nasty coffee, but the guy at the fountain's jump-spot might, and I reluctantly took the envelope he was eagerly extending. It was thick, contract thick, and I shoved it in a back pocket to look at later. An ever-after job might be advantageous if Al and I ended up being strapped for cash. *Again* . . . Was my life truly this predictable, or did I just keep making the same mistakes over and over?

"Straight up black, right?" the guy was saying, hustling behind the counter for a to-go cup and filling it with something black and bitter. It wasn't coffee, but it was the best they had, and I took it just to get out of the place.

"Great. Thanks," I said, hoisting it. "Mmmm, good!"

"On the house," he affirmed, backing up and looking both nervous and pleased with himself. "Let me know about the contract!"

There was no bell to jingle as I went out into the mall, and after a quick look up and down the wide avenue, I headed to the central fountain and the jump-demons. Though demons could jump lines at will, familiars needed to buy them, and to facilitate ease of passage, demons convicted of minor crimes such as uncommon stupidity paid their debts by providing jumps. On the weekend there might be as many as ten jump-demons clustered around the center fountain moving people out, but this early on a Tuesday morning and with the impending line trouble, there was only one. Head down, I angled to him. He might have just been a demon waiting for someone, but the hat he was wearing said differently.

"Jump me to Newt's for a coffee?" I said as I got close, and he opened one eye. It was really weird. I knew I was deep underground, but between the shifting lighting, shadow, fitful breeze, and wide space, it felt as if we were outside on a cloudy day. A really hot, cloudy day.

"Newt's?" he said around a lazy yawn, then did a double take, pulling himself upright when he actually looked at me. A panicked expression raced across his face until it was replaced by mistrust. My eyes narrowed when he poked my shoulder as if trying to decide if I was real. "By the two worlds colliding, you really are Rachel. I thought you were Newt. Damn, girl! Wait until I tell my familiar!"

"Touch me again, and you'll really be in pain," I said, shoving the cup at him. "Newt's kitchen? You know it?"

He took the coffee and looked at the ceiling. "Costs more this week."

I forced my jaw to unclench. "Look, I'm trying to save your asses. You really think it's a good idea to try to skin me for a sliver of smut?"

The demon's gaze came back to me. "No. Look up there. The ceiling is down by about a foot from yesterday. Space is shrinking, and unless you want to end up in a wall, I need a gargoyle assist."

Shit, it is happening already. No wonder it is so warm.

"Well?" he said. "How bad you want in?"

If I didn't get these rings fixed, nothing was going to happen. I really didn't give a flying flip about the ever-after, but I wanted Ceri and Lucy back. "I'll take the smut," I said, and he grandly took his cap off to dust the nearest circle.

Two demons across the plaza had noticed me. Damn. One of them was

Dali. I gave him a bunny-eared kiss-kiss, and he vanished, leaving his friend to eye me in speculation. Great, this was going just great. "Can we make this fast?" I said as I stepped into the circle. It was taking too long.

Grunting, he gestured and the line iced through me, dissolving me to a thought and back to substance again. The line felt sour, but it was still even in flow. The gargoyle assist made the materialization smooth without the barest hint of unequal air pressures or misstep. I misted back into existence . . . in my kitchen.

"Hey!" I shouted, turning to him, but the jump was complete and I was yelling at my old refrigerator. My eyes narrowed. It was my *old* refrigerator, the one you could put a goat into, not that Ivy and I ever had. I'd blown it up almost two years ago on the solstice.

"I vowed if you ever put her image on your twisted bones again, I would not stay my hand, you foul carrion!"

I spun. "Pierce!" I shrieked as he came at me from across the kitchen, grabbing a knife from the counter as he ran. "Pierce, it's me!" My breath exploded out of me as I hit the wall, his arm under my chin and a knife at my middle. This wasn't my kitchen. The fridge was old. The light was wrong. The copper pots were too tarnished. "It's me," I choked, blood pounding. "Get off!"

But he only snarled, the scent of coal dust and shoe polish filling my senses.

"Hey!" I yelped when the knife pricked me, and I kneed him, getting my arms up and between his when his grip eased. "Get off!"

Clutching himself, he fell back. Pissed, I tugged my clothes straight and kicked the knife away. A wave of ever-after coated him, and I touched my side, my fingers coming away wet with blood. Damn it, he'd cut right through my shirt.

Pierce knelt on the floor before me in wool trousers and a colorful vest, looking like an actor from an early movie. His expression pained, he leaned back on his heels, his arms spread wide and his neck bared to me. "Go ahead!" he screamed, eyes shut as if daring me to strike him with lightning. "Rip my heart out, you foul beast! I could use the time off to plan your demise!"

I stared. He looked okay, other than the total surrender thing he had going on. His dark curly hair was down to his shoulders again, but his beard was gone, making him look younger. If he was upright, he'd be almost my height exactly, well proportioned and looking like no stranger to hard work. He opened one eye, and when I didn't say anything, a hint of confusion made him all the more appealing. I thought I might have loved him once, but he was too quick to use the black magic and he kept trying to kill the very people I needed to survive.

"Ah, Pierce?" I said, thinking this might have been a mistake. "You okay?"

His breath came in a heave and he scrambled to his feet. His face became ashen, then red. "Rachel?" he said, echoing my same hesitancy.

I looked over the kitchen, so clearly a mockery of mine now that I had a moment to look at it. *My God, it was hot in here.* "Newt isn't here, is she?" If Newt was making duplicates of my kitchen, then she was probably taunting Pierce with images of me as well. Either that or the man was truly off his rocker; by the horrified expression he was now wearing, though, I thought he was stone-cold sane.

"By all creation. It's really you!" he exclaimed, and I fell back to the wall when he rushed me. My lips curled up in a smile when he gave me a quick hug, my arms going about him to find he felt both familiar and different. Almost immediately he dropped back, pumping my hand up and down. "I am powerfully sorry!" he gushed, eyes bright. "I thought you were her. The hag appears as you to get a rise out of me when she's bored. Are you hurt? Did I bruise you? I should have known it was you. Gods, I'm a toad!"

"I'm fine," I said, hoping he didn't see the tiny cut. "Sorry about, ah, hitting you. Are you okay?"

He went scarlet, glancing at the floor where he'd prostrated himself on my mercy. "I'm of a mind I deserved it and more." Looking shamed, he fell back a step. "I agree my situation isn't ideal and a far cry from the pomp and circumstance of a coven member, but I understand the world here, unlike the one you live in, and every time I try to kill her, I get a little closer."

I came out from against the wall, both curious and afraid to see the rest of Newt's apartments. "Oh."

"I almost had the harlot the last time, but she turned into you." He gestured weakly, his eyes pinching at the corners as he tried to explain the last five minutes. "I couldn't do it."

"Pierce . . ." I started, my hand on the table so alike but not the same as the one Ivy had. Perhaps I should have tried harder to get him back on the reality side of the lines.

"It's who I am," he said solemnly, taking my hand and making me look at him. "I think she enjoys my trying to kill her." He winced, looking worried. "You're on her mind. Be careful. That's not a healthy place to be."

"That's why I'm here," I said, pulling away. "She's out, right?"

"Oh, aye, she's out on the surface. The ever-after is shrinking, and she's trying to talk to sleeping gargoyles." He leaned back, arms over his chest. We could almost be in my kitchen, if you didn't look close. "There's talk of killing you. Ku'Sox is petitioning for it in soft whispers." He pushed forward, eyes eager. "We can kill him, you and I. Rachel, is that why you're here? It is, isn't it! Why else would you risk it, especially now!"

"No. Pierce, I can't kill Ku'Sox."

He turned away, opening cupboards to show tools and instruments my kitchen had never had. "Not alone, certainly," he said confidently. "With my help, it's possible. Let me gather my things, and we will be away, that monster dead in five minutes."

Distressed, I felt the rings in my pocket. "Not even with your help," I said, and he glanced up from a drawer, frowning. I remembered that frown, and I stifled a surge of tired anger. "Pierce, I've fought him before, and he's too strong. Too fast. I'm not that good."

"Mmm," he grumbled, then shocked me when he opened the gas oven and pulled out a heavy lockbox. "I have a curse I was going to inflict on her next time I found her sleeping."

The box hit the floor with a thud, and I jumped. He wasn't listening. "Pierce."

"Here is the wicked thing!" he said, having opened it up. "That's a demon killer if I ever saw one!"

"Pierce, stop." He had stood, and I took his hands, folding them about whatever ley line charm he'd made. Eye to eye, he squinted at me in mistrust, and I slowly let go. "I'm not going to confront Ku'Sox in a test of magic. I'm not afraid of him," I said when Pierce took a breath to protest, "but everyone else is and I know my limits."

"Rachel . . ."

"I know my limits," I said again, silent until he brought his sour expression back to me. "I don't have to kill him, just prove that he's the one who unbalanced my line."

Pierce frowned, looking capable and disappointed in the fake sunlight coming in the window. It was foggy past the blue curtains. It would always be foggy. "Then why are you here if you're not seeking my help to kill him?"

Heart pounding, I brought out the rings. "These," I said, and he picked up the largest one. "I need to reinvoke them. You said it was possible."

"They're deader than a three-day possum," he said dryly, handing it back. "What do they do?"

"Create a bond between two people. They're elven chastity rings."

Pierce started, his blue eyes jerking from me to the rings and back again. Shoving the "demon killer" ley line charm in a deep pocket, he slid the box back into the oven. Smooth muscles moved under his thin cotton shirt, and I remembered the feel of them under my fingertips. He was a beautiful man, but I didn't trust his decisions, especially when they impacted my life in a big way. "Chastity rings?" he questioned when the oven door shut.

The rings felt heavy in my palm. "I think I can fix the line, but I need a spotter to pull me out if I get lost. And since the rings make a connection between two magic users . . ."

"An all-fire close one, I'd think," he muttered, his manner closed as he wiped his fingerprints off the oven door with the towel drying on a cabinet knob.

"Can you do it?"

His eyes flicked up to mine. "I'd rather kill him."

My sigh was heavy, and I waited. I needed his help, and I knew he wouldn't let me leave without it. I hadn't been able to love him, but he had loved me.

Head down, he gestured, and I jumped when a circle tinged with his green aura rose up around us. It was a great deal stronger than I remembered—his time with Newt had done him good. Perhaps I'd mis-judged him.

"Does she often make her kitchen look like mine?" I asked as I came closer, the corner of the center counter between us.

"Only when you're on her mind. I'm powerfully concerned for you, Rachel."

I wasn't embarrassed by asking for his help, but it was hard knowing that I meant more to him than he to me. "Thank you," I whispered as I put the rings on the counter.

"The trick is to not flood them," he said, ignoring my guilty look. "You can't use a ley line. That would break them for sure. Even your aura is too much when it's all together, but if you splinter it . . ." He picked up the rings, positioning the smaller inside the larger. "Fill them with one reso-nance before allowing the rest in, you can make a pie of it."

He set the rings in my palm, cupping his hands about it. A shiver went through me, and he smiled. "It's much like a rainbow is the sum of visible light. You first put in the red, then shift it to orange, then yellow, then green, and so on until you finally get all the colors singing together and they melt into a white light and the charm invokes."

He was standing close; his warmth and the scent of coal dust and shoe polish were bringing back memories, good but uncomfortable. "Show me?" I asked, and we both looked at the rings in my hand, his cupping mine.

"Push your aura off your hand," he said, and my head snapped up. "That's why the circle," he soothed. "Go on, do it."

My face puckered up, but I imagined my aura going thin at my finger-tips, peeling back from my fingers, soaking into my skin and vanishing to leave a huge gaping hole in my first line of defense. Cold pinpricks stabbed my hand. My aura wanted to return, but I held it off.

"Good." It had been a hopeful grunt of approval, and I caught back my adrenaline before I lost control. Before me, Pierce shifted his shoulders, clearly uncomfortable as well as he removed his own aura. The rings felt unnaturally heavy in my palm, and Pierce's loose grip around my hand, intimate.

"Now, I'm of a mind that your gargoyle, Bis, has been leading you in the practice of shifting your aura," he said, and I nodded, nervous. "Then simply tune the entirety of it to the clearest red you can imagine."

I met his eyes, seeing an unknown emotion. I couldn't see my aura, but he could, and flustered, I shifted it, knowing I had it right when he nodded. "Just so," he said. "Let a thin ribbon of it spill down into your hand. Mind you keep it a trace!" he exclaimed, and I backed off. It was hardly a whisper, but as it touched the rings nestled in my palm, I swear I heard them chime, like the ringing of a glass when you run your finger along the top. I could feel my aura like warm silk, tracing down the soft part of my arm and making a warm pool in my palm.

"You have a knack," he prompted, clearly pleased. "But even so, there's too much. It is an art, and you have to plan ahead such that it just fills the memory and no more."

I licked my lips, eyeing the rings and my aura echoing from them. "How's this?" I asked as I backed off until there was almost no "sound" at all.

"Perfect. But be of a mind that it's harder to remove it once given. Err on the side of hunger."

Smiling, I looked up. There was a happy contentment in his eyes. My smile faded. "Pierce, I can't do this."

"You're halfway there," he cajoled, and I shook my head, pulling my hand from his.

"No, I mean you! You're standing there, looking at me as if we just came out of that hole in the ground in Trent's woods. I can't do this! I can't ask you to help me when you think there might be a chance that someday . . ."

My words cut off. I was helpless to continue. Head shaking ruefully, he took my hand back in his own. "I know when I've been given the shrug," he said, tilting his head to keep me quiet when I rushed to explain. "You did well by me, and we both turned our attentions elsewhere. I'd be a cad to expect you to think of me as anything other than fondly. But a man can't help but remember. Now, hold the aura as it is and shift it to orange. What is needed of the red will remain within the charm. Easy now. If you can do this, then you can do the rest."

"Thank you," I breathed, hanging my head and closing my eyes because I couldn't bear to look at him anymore. *Orange,* I thought, shifting my aura as Bis and I had been practicing. This was easier than the melding of colors that we usually did, sitting at an outside café and trying to mimic the auras of people passing by, and Pierce's grunt of approval was like a wash of hope through me.

"Now to yellow," he prompted. "More than before since yellow is so thin to begin with."

I knew what he meant, and like hearing a partial chord of a song and knowing what came next, I layered another complexity over the rings, seeing it soak in as the excess orange melted away. The rings were starting to hum, taking on a note all their own.

"The blues and purples," he whispered, excitement in his voice. "You are a caution, Rachel. The demon you will be!"

I almost lost it, but caught myself, concentrating on the feel of his hands around mine as I added the last. Sweat trickled down, and I cracked open an eye at the funny tickle of feeling in my chi. My aura wanted to flood the rings with power, and I held it tight.

"My God . . ." Pierce breathed. "Easy, Rachel. Hint at a shadow of black. It should have invoked. It needs a harmony of something else, something dark. I've never charmed elven silver; it needs something else."

I was holding my breath, and I let it out as I turned my aura to an ultraviolet hue. It was as if smut snaked down my arm, but when it hit the rings, it pooled around them, refusing to join.

And then tiny cracks appeared in the cold, dead metal. *Shit.*

"Easy . . ." Pierce whispered as he stared at them. "Let it soak in."

My head was starting to hurt, and my arm felt dead. Pinpricks coated it, and I began to shake. The cracks grew, sending spiderwebs of instability through the surface of the rings. Panicked, I froze. There wasn't enough energy in there yet to rekindle the charm, but any more, and it would break. "Pierce?" I warbled, and his fingers around mine grew warm.

"I can't do anything," he said. "Rachel, you have to finish it!"

"It's going to break!" I said. "I can't hold it!"

"It's that damned elven magic," he said, and I caught my breath when his hands left mine. "Your energy is not mixing with the original maker's. Can you . . . think elf thoughts?"

Think elf thoughts, I mocked in my head, but the cracks weren't going away. I couldn't stop, and I couldn't move forward. I knew it would blow them to hell if I just let it go. "Elf thoughts," I muttered, frowning as I thought of Trent, tricky, proud, arrogant.

The skin of the rings seemed to shimmer, and I took a quick breath. The cracks were still there, but it felt right. My teeth clenched, and the memory of Trent's music as he sung my soul to sleep slipped into me, hazy from my subconscious. It was his plea to his goddess that he didn't believe in to listen, the source of his wild magic. It circled around and around in my head until I felt a somnolent nothing seem to take notice, hesitating in its glorious song, turning one of a thousand eyes to me. *Hear me,* I thought, begging. *See what I'm doing. Lend me your skill.*

Wild magic smiled at me, and the skin of the rings warbled. My last shining of aura reached for the rings, and with a ping of sound that echoed in my soul, the magic vibrated through me and became one. That simple, the rings reinvoked themselves and sealed.

I gasped, staring at the rings glowing in my palm like glory itself.

"Well, I'll be!" Pierce beamed as his protective circle flickered and went out. "You did it! First time out of the box!"

Elated, I clutched the rings. I had a chance now. I had a chance to fix the line, to free Lucy and Ceri. I looked at the clock on the stove before I remembered where I was. I had to get back to Trent. We had to move on this, and now!

"Thank you, Pierce, thank you!" I said, pulling him into an expansive hug, my clenched hand with the rings tight to his back. "I couldn't have done it without you. I can do something now. Thank you!"

He was smiling when I dropped back, his curls at his forehead damp with the heat, and my expression froze when he touched my hair. "You did it, not me," he said. "All of it. I only told you how. You never needed me. Even when you were but a young woman."

I let go of him, the memory of what lay in his eyes rushing back. "I did," I said, needing to be honest. "I did need you. I was strong with you. You helped me find that." Eyes down, I shoved the rings away. "I'm sorry," I said, knowing it was over, but not remembering why.

Pierce took a step back to put more space between us. "I demanded too much," he said, his sadness at himself, not me. "I see in your heart you found someone who makes you strong who does not hold too tight, who has learned that the pain of losing you to fate is more than the pain of you dying in a cage. Who is he?"

I looked at the clock again. "No one."

"Ivy?" he guessed, immediately shaking his head. "No. Someone new? No, someone old," he said firmly, his eyes going to my pocket. "An elf?" he guessed, then became ashen. "Kalamack?" he blurted, taking my shoulders. "Rachel, no," he pleaded. "I know I have no right, but he lies. He deceives. It is their nature. This is his plan, isn't it? That you come here, risking yourself instead of him?"

"It was my plan," I said, pulling back in anger. Oh yes, now I remembered why it hadn't worked. "It was all I could do to make him stay and not follow me here. He would've been recognized. I have a right to be here." I glanced at Newt's kitchen. "Well, not here, here, but the ever-after. Besides, would you've taught him how to invoke the rings?"

Damn it, he'd made me mad at him again, and I didn't want to be.

"He made you *think* it was your idea." Pierce pleaded, "Don't trust him. He's a Kalamack!"

"He . . ." I started, not knowing where I was going with my argument. Pierce had said I'd found someone new to love, and Trent wasn't it, but to say so sounded like I was protesting my way into a bag of truth. "There's no reason I can't work with him," I said belligerently, making a fist to hide Trent's pinkie ring. "Ku'Sox stole Ceri and his daughter. I can trust his hate."

There was a small circle on the floor where I'd popped in, and I stood in it, waiting for his help to get out of here. Nothing like needing an ex-boyfriend to slam your door for you as you make your dramatic exit.

"But he will spoil you, Rachel," Pierce said, and I stared until I realized he meant ruin, not overindulge. "He'll turn your heart hard and you will become as him. A shallow, self-indulgent shell of what you are now. Don't trust him. Let me help you. I have an arsenal. We can destroy Ku'Sox together. Right now. This very hour. Your strength and my charms. Our magics blend so well. With those rings, we can make a fist of it for sure!"

I looked him up and down, not surprised. "The rings are not for attack, they're a safety net for fixing the line. You keep telling me that Trent is going to change me, but you're the one who keeps trying to get me to kill everyone!"

"But it needs to be done," he insisted, and I crossed my arms over my chest.

"Send me to the mall, please," I said tightly. "I appreciate your help more than you will ever know."

"Rachel."

It was stifling, and I brought my attention down from the ceiling. Pierce stood before me, looking capable and strong, with his curls about him and his eyes promising me success. I remembered how thick his circle had become and imagined the skills he'd been honing since becoming Newt's familiar. Had she been training him for this? "Can you leave Newt's rooms without being detected?" I asked, already knowing the answer.

His head dropped. "No."

My posture eased and my anger vanished. "I'm sorry, Pierce," I said, touching his arm. "You'll jingle like bells in the forest, and I have to move with stealth. You've given me a tool that I didn't have before. *I can do this.* Thank you."

Jaw tight, he looked up, hearing the truth in it.

"Do you need anything?" I asked, not wanting to leave like this.

"Only that which you can't give. And I will not ask for it."

Yep, that's about what I thought. Sick at heart, I shifted foot to foot. "I have to go."

A savage light lit through his eyes, and his chin lifted. "Wait, there is one thing." Moving close, his expression became almost taunting. "Let me kiss you good-bye, for if fate allows that I see you again, you will not be you anymore."

"Pierce . . ." I whispered, but he'd taken both my shoulders and pulled me close. My breath caught, and as our lips touched, he filled my soul with the memory of his love. Tears warmed my eyes, and I didn't pull away, wanting just for a moment this perfect spot of what we might have had. Our auras, already sensitized to each other, mixed with swirls of pinpricked energy, sparking over our skin as our lips moved against each other, and his hands pressed into me with the memory of what had been.

Slowly he let go, and I wiped my eyes with the back of my hand, not ashamed for my tears. I could have loved him, but he demanded too much.

"I'm not going to change," I said, meaning several things at once.

Chin high, he let go and stepped back. "Elves are more evil than de-mons. They warp you to suit their needs and make you think it was your idea. You will always be in my heart, Rachel Morgan. Go, before my foul jailer comes back."

"Pierce."

He turned away and gestured. "Go."

I vanished, seeing him standing in a spot of sunlight that never moved, alone and apart, but wanting more.

I am not becoming Trent's tool, I thought as I misted back into existence at the fountain and the trite sound of synthesizers and cheerful lyrics beat on me. I was making my own decisions, not Trent's. Pierce was seeing the world through ancient glasses.

But as I pushed past the few meandering demons in search of the cof-feehouse, I couldn't dispel a faint whisper of warning.

Chapter Thirteen

Cool and carrying the hint of rain, the night wind pushed against me, sporadically sending my hair to tickle my neck. It brought to me the smell of early lilac and the sound of spring frogs and running water. Far in the distance was the sound of interstate traffic, barely a whisper. Behind me, Loveland Castle loomed dark, empty, and forbidding. Trent's snazzy black sports car sat parked in the dirt lot. My car was still at his gatehouse. The light from the camp lantern on the retaining wall behind me barely made it to the surrounding forest stretching around us— just far enough to make the place feel creepy.

Edgy, I shifted my feet into the gravelly scree of the lower garden path as I stood in the glow of the lantern, my hands on my hips and Bis on the crumbling retaining wall behind me. Four feet tall, it almost put him eye to eye with me. Together we looked across the tall grass at the damaged ley line stretching across the lower, long-fallow garden and waited for Jenks and Trent to return.

The ley line looked ugly with my second sight, worse in the lamp's glow than it had in the sun, with violet-purple streamers coming from the line to soak up the energy leaking through. But for all its nasty appearance, I was sure the line itself was fine apart from the original leak. Ku'Sox had moved all the minuscule imbalances from the other lines, concentrating them in mine to make an event horizon. It was an event, all right. The last one the demons would ever see.

I shivered despite the night's warmth, and Bis tightened his grip on the retaining wall, making the stones crack. I didn't want to let the little guy know how nervous I was, but it was hard with him so close. Trent's rings were in my pocket. I had refused to give them to him when I'd come back through the vault, afraid he'd come out here with Quen and do something stupid. Quen wasn't up to magic yet, and it had taken both of us to convince the man to stay with Ray tonight lest Ellasbeth take her to the West Coast for her own hostage demands.

Trent was helping Jenks canvass the nearby area for pixy intel, but I still felt naked knowing that Al wouldn't be able to save my butt if Ku'Sox showed. For the first time, I was really on my own. "Well?" I whispered to Bis, wishing they would hurry up. "What do you think?"

Bis shifted his clawed hind feet and bits of rock pattered down. "It hurts," he said, simply, ears pinned to his skull. Depressed, I went to sit on the stone wall beside him, scooting myself up until my feet hung above the lower path.

"But do you think we can separate the imbalances?"

He shrugged, looking lost as his ears perked up. I was asking a lot, and I edged closer, rocks pinching me. "Let me hear," I said, touching his foot so I could feel the lines resonate.

My teeth clenched as suddenly every single ley line within my reach sung inside my head. It was a heady experience—and why I usually had a bubble of protection around my thoughts when I touched Bis. This time, though, the harsh discord of my nearby ley line cut through the beauty, making my teeth ache and my head hurt.

"My God!" I said as I let go of him and stared at the line with my second sight. "How can you stand it?" *And how am I going to separate anything from that noise?*

The cat-size gargoyle shrugged, touching his wingtips together over his head. "I don't have a choice. Everyone is tired of listening to it. I've been told to fix it, and fix it now."

My thoughts zinged back to the three gargoyles I'd seen tonight before we'd left, perched on the roof of the church and spitting at the pixies to keep them out of earshot as they talked in low rumbles. I would've gone up into the belfry to eavesdrop, but I was afraid they might take Bis and move to another church. "You!" I said, surprised. "But it's my line!"

His red eyes glowed eerily in the lantern's light. "And I'm responsible for you having made it."

"Bis, this isn't your fault. Neither is Ku'Sox exploiting the tear to try to break the ever-after. Even if you hadn't left me, I would have scraped that hole trying to get out." I clutched my arms around myself, cold as I remembered it. I might have managed to jump the lines, but I'd damaged my aura and scraped a hole in reality in the process.

"But I left you," he said, unable to look at me.

Smiling, I bubbled my thoughts and touched his shoulder. "It was my fault, not yours, for trying to jump a line before I knew what I was doing."

He was silent, and I gave his shoulder a squeeze before letting go. I knew he still blamed himself. He'd changed a lot since then, waking up in the day for brief periods, becoming more somber, less prone to playing tricks on the pixies. He was getting older, and I worried that I'd brought an end to his childhood before its time. "Is this why there have been gargoyles on the roof with you?" I asked, not sure how much he'd be willing to tell me.

Immediately Bis brightened. "They're teaching me the vibrations of their lines," he said proudly. "Usually a gargoyle is taught by only one other gargoyle, but the lines aren't acting right, so they're taking turns by singing me only their line, the one they know by heart."

"D-demons?" I stammered. "You've been talking to demon-bound gargoyles?"

He nodded, almost going invisible as he flushed a deep black to make his red eyes stand out. "They're trying to teach me all the lines so that I can teach them to you. I only know a few, since most won't leave the ever-after and their demons. They want me to come to them."

He dropped his eyes, scared of the idea, and I frowned. "The lines aren't acting right," he said, clawed feet shifting as he looked at the line. "Demons aren't jumping on their own at all. Everyone needs their gargoyle, like they're brand-new to line jumping."

Remembering my jump from the mall to Newt's kitchen, I nodded. "They're teaching you line jumping," I said, and he grinned, a glint of light showing on his thick black teeth.

"Yup."

I looked at the line, then him. "So you know what some of the lines sound like?

He nodded, making a face. "I know what they're *supposed* to sound like. They're off."

"Because their imbalances are here in my line . . ." Fingers tapping the cold stone, I thought that over. "Bis, if you know what they're supposed to sound like and you can hear what they sound like now, then maybe I can find what's missing in my line here and shift it back. It's the misplaced imbalance that's causing the trouble."

Bis's eyes blinked slowly. "Maybe that's what they were talking about," he said, his heavy brow furrowing. "Pigeon poop, Rachel. Talking to those old gars is like talking to crazy old men. They never come out and tell you what they mean. Everything is spoons and two-legged chairs. What does a spoon have to do with a ley line? I don't know! Do you?"

Clearly he was frustrated. I could sympathize, having listened to enough wise-old-man crap to fill a wheelbarrow. "No," I admitted, "but if we can separate even one imbalance and put it back, it might make a big difference in the leak. Buy us some more time."

"Or Ku'Sox might show up," Bis said.

True. I exhaled heavily and turned in a slow circle, looking into the dark for the silver tracing of pixy dust. Jenks should have been back by now; Trent was slowing him down.

"Sounds kind of hard," Bis said, the tip of his tail twitching.

I turned to follow his gaze to the ugly, shrill line, slumping as my first excitement died. "I know," I said dejectedly. "I have no idea how to separate the imbalances."

Bis moved his wings, the hush of leather against leather making me shiver. "Why does it have to be hard?"

Bis's head turned. A second later, Jenks's wings' clatter became obvious. "It always is," Jenks said as he hovered before us, dusting heavily and clearly having heard Bis's last statement. Behind him, a black shadow strode out from the surrounding woods. It had to be Trent, or Jenks would be having issues. Besides, no one else I knew moved with that kind of grace.

"Well?" I asked Jenks, trying not to look at Trent as he rejoined us.

Pierce's warning was still ringing in me. I was not in love with Trent, and never would be—especially with Ellasbeth back in the picture and Trent on a mission to *save the elves.* True, we worked marginally well together. His unexpected surprises were annoying, but they did generally work out. And yes, he looked more than a little attractive in his sturdy black jeans, tucked-in stretchy shirt, and lightweight rain jacket. His fair hair was covered with a black cap to keep off the damp, and the black gloves were probably just for effect because I knew he wasn't cold. But to entertain anything more than a casual work relationship was laughable.

Seeing Jenks hovering over his shoulder, I was struck by how they managed to look as if they went together though they were nothing alike. "There isn't much here for pixies unless there's a tour coming through," Jenks said, his face glowing from the dust. "They remember you being here yesterday, and a bunch of demons before that, but not one on his own like Ku'Sox. We did a quick survey, and we're good for at least a quarter mile unless you count the raccoons."

I squinted at the line. "Okay. I'm going to take a look-see—"

"You're not getting in that line!" Jenks shouted, and Bis's red eyes widened in alarm.

"I'm not getting in the line," I said, glancing at Trent to see him watching me with the same intensity as Jenks. "You think I'm out here sniffing fairy farts? Bis knows what some of the lines are supposed to sound like, and by comparing that to what they sound like now, maybe we can find the imbalance, bubble it, and move it out . . ."

My words trailed off when Trent tilted his head. "That wasn't our original idea."

Jenks hovered right before my nose, wings clattering belligerently. "Yeah? Then what?"

I winced. "Maybe if I move it out, it might just get sucked back into place?"

Bis was making this weird noise, and we all turned to him. I think it was his version of clearing his throat, but it sounded like rocks in a garbage disposal. "Ah, bubbled imbalance won't get sucked anywhere," he said apologetically. "But if you tune the bubble holding it to the same vibration as its parent line . . ." His words trailed off and his wings shifted.

Trent's exhale was long and slow. It wasn't the immediate no I had expected, and seeing him consider it, Jenks seemed to become even more frustrated.

"Tink's little pink rosebuds," he grumbled, landing next to Bis and checking the sharpness of his sword. "Now I've got two of them to watch. Whose idea was this?" He looked up at Bis. "Yours?"

I waited nervously as Trent thought it over, his boots scuffing the gravel. "Tuning your aura to a line pulls you into it, so tuning a bubble, which is basically an aura-tainted field of force, will pull whatever is in the bubble to the line? It's worth a look, since we have the rings as a safety net." He turned to Jenks. "Jenks, what do you think?"

My eyebrows rose. *Asking Jenks for his opinion?* Maybe the time they'd worked together had made an impact after all.

"I think you're all screwy in the head," he said when Bis nodded his encouragement. "But go ahead. I've got Quen's number in my phone. I'll call him if you both explode in a flash of black underwear and money so I won't have to fly all the way home."

Bis made a snuffing snort of a laugh, but I was thrilled, and my heart gave a thump and settled. "Let's do it," I said as I turned to the line. "Bis? You want to sit on my shoulder?"

He nodded, and as Jenks crossed his arms over his chest and hovered over the wall, Bis made the three-beat wing flap to me, landing with his toes spread wide so he wouldn't gouge me when he landed. The lines flashed into existence at his touch, but prepared for it, I gritted my teeth at the tinfoil-like sensation. It was awful, seeing as we were so close to a line, and I could understand why the gargoyles on both sides of reality were having issues.

"Rache?" Jenks said suspiciously when my eyes closed in a strength-gathering blink.

"Fine," I said, then choked when Bis tightened his tail around my neck.

"Sorry," he said as he loosened his hold. The little guy was the size of a cat but had the weight of a bird, smelling like cold stone, leather, and feathers from the pigeons he ate.

"My God," I said as I stared at the line, a sharp pain starting just over my right eye. "This is awful. Bis, can you show me what one of the line signatures you've learned looks like?"

Trent cleared his throat. "You want to use that safety net, or keep it in your pocket, Ms. Morgan?"

I jerked, sheepish at Jenks's severe look as I wiggled the rings out and extended them to Trent on my palm. Bis wiggled his toes as they glinted in the lantern's light. "I think you'd have more control if you took the bigger ring," I said, and as Trent reached for it, I closed my fist. "No funny stuff," I warned, opening my fingers again.

Trent put his hand under mine to hold it steady, jerking back in alarm when the full force of the lines hit him through Bis. "Holy . . . ah, wow," he said, eyes wide in the low light, distress clear on him. "Is that what the line feels like to you?"

Bis's feet tightened on me. "It kind of hurts. Can we hurry up?"

Immediately Trent took the larger ring. I put the smaller one on my pinkie, but if it was like our practice run earlier, nothing would happen until he put his on. It bothered me that the only way I could take off my ring now was if Trent slipped his over mine, nesting them on my finger to remove them both at once. It had been a scary five minutes figuring that out.

"Here we go," Trent said as he took his gloves off, and Jenks frowned, still not convinced. The glint of the pinkie ring twin to my own caught my eye, and I wondered at the connections we had. I still wore Al's demon mark. Was it the same thing, or different?

My shoulders wiggled as the ring fitted about Trent's finger and a weird sensation of entanglement sprung up around me. Bis actually sighed in relief as the connection to the discordant line dulled. It was still there, but it felt diluted—the best I could put it was that the energy was now going through a maze of passages to find me. It was the chastity ring, and when I nodded, Trent eased the grip of it until the flow was again its normal self, almost as if he had lifted me above the maze and I could connect normally.

Trent's presence was faint in my uppermost thoughts, sort of like a teacher walking the aisles during a test. We were ready, and I closed my eyes.

"Okay." Bis loosened his tail about my neck and shivered. "Ah, I'm going to sing you Newt's line first."

My concentration shattered. "Newt's!" I exclaimed, heart pounding.

"Newt has a gargoyle?" Jenks exclaimed, and Bis's tail tightened until I nearly choked.

"Rachel, will you listen? I think I'm going to spew pigeon feathers. Newt's was the first one I learned, okay?"

I nodded, closing my eyes again, which made me feel dizzy. "Give me a sec," I said as I sat down in the puddle of lantern light, but then it only felt like the world was tilting.

"Rachel?"

Trent's voice was close, and I put my palms on the ground for balance. "Dizzy," I said, smiling at him. "We're okay."

Jenks's wings clattered. "This is as smart as sleeping outside in November," Jenks grumbled. "You sure you got her, cookie maker?"

"I've got her. Just watch the woods, pixy."

"Listen," Bis demanded as he resettled his wings, and I closed my eyes, feeling the pure ting of a rise and fall of sound, glittering in my mind's eye like a silver thread of light, a bare hint of jagged red and gray and silver, half a beat out of step with the glorious hum. It sounded sort of familiar, comfortable. Like the line in the graveyard . . .

"Got it?" he asked, and I *mm-hmmed*. "This is what it sounds like now," he said, and I jerked as if struck when the world seemed to hiccup. The feeling of the line I was looking at with my mind shifted slightly, and sure enough, the ragged half step was gone.

"No way," I whispered, and my eyes opened. Trent was standing guard with his eyes on the forest line. Jenks was hovering at my eye level, his angular features pinched. Behind him, the line glowed like a deranged fair ride, dangerous and unreliable.

"Rache . . ." he warned, and I held a hand up to forestall his next words.

"Trent has me, and I'm not going to do anything Bis doesn't want." I reached up to touch the gargoyle's feet. "Bis? You want me to try to find that ragged half step in the imbalance?"

Bis jumped to the ground before me. The expansive backdrop of the lines in my mindscape had vanished along with his touch, and my shoulders relaxed. Bis shifted from foot to foot as his tail whipped about until he curved it over his feet and sat like a little lion. "I'm sure this is how to fix the line," he said, and I heard a big unsaid *however.*

"I'll be careful," I said to Jenks, then looked at Trent. "I won't do anything until Bis tells me I can, okay?"

Jenks squinted at me, and when Trent nodded, the pixy gestured sourly to Bis to get on with it. A four-inch man ruled us all.

"Maybe you should bubble yourself first," Trent suggested. "In case Ku'Sox shows."

It was a good idea, but as I sketched a small, easy-to-hold bubble around Bis and myself, Jenks's dust went an alarmed red.

"Okay! That's it!" Jenks shouted, hovering before all of us. "I didn't like this before, and I like it less now! Rache, there has to be another way!"

Bis met my eyes, shaking his head so narrowly it was almost no movement at all. I looked past him to Trent, his stance stiff and his expression fixed. Ku'Sox was stronger than me. If we couldn't fix the line and prove that Ku'Sox had made it, then how would we ever get Lucy and Ceri back?

"Jenks," I said softly, and he hummed irately at me. "It's going to be okay. Trent will yank my butt out if I get stuck."

"I'm going to do a perimeter," he muttered. "You and Trent do your magic thing."

He buzzed off into the dark, and my gaze went to Trent. I didn't think Jenks was jealous, but it had to be hard to bear that I was putting myself in a narrow spot where anything bad could happen, and probably would.

"Circle?" Trent suggested, his expression holding both determination and frustration for not being able to do this himself. I didn't have a problem helping him. I loved Ceri and Ray, too.

Feeling odd, I reached a hand to the informal but securely scratched circle in the dirt. It was small, but I was sitting. *Rhombus,* I whispered within my thoughts, and a molecule-thin sheet of ever-after sprang up. It wavered as Trent tested his hold on me through the rings, and at my nod, the circle sprang up strong again. We were good.

Bis was well within my circle, and he fidgeted, a wingtip sliding out and back in through my bubble. He was the only person in two realities who could pass through my circle. It was why it took a gargoyle to teach a demon—or a witch, for that matter—to line jump. Gargoyles could hear the lines and tell those they were bonded to how to tune their aura so they would be sucked into the right line. What gargoyles got out of the deal was beyond me.

"Okay," Bis said as he reached out to take my hands. The harsh discord immediately fell on me, and I tried not to wince. His hands felt small in my grip, and I forced myself to smile reassuringly. "Take a look at your line here," Bis went on. "I'm going to focus on it, and hopefully the rest of the background noise will go away."

My breath came faster as suddenly the only thing I was hearing/seeing in my mind was my ugly ley line with the purple core screaming at me. I couldn't even hear the pure ting of energy behind it. It was disgusting. "Rachel?" Bis said in a pained voice, and I opened one eye a little. Behind him, Trent was scribing a larger circle around mine that could hold all of us. Wise man.

"Right." I turned my awareness to the purple sludge, careful not to get my thoughts near it and possibly get sucked in. Purple, everything was a blaring purple with fading striations of red, the sound of it rushing through me like ants, but the deeper I looked at it, the more I was able to listen past the purple coating to the twining colors behind it. Reds, blues, greens, oranges, and even browns and gold, just like auras, they swirled together but never mixed.

"Find Newt's imbalance," Bis whimpered, and I peeked at him again.

"Newt's!" Jenks shouted, and my eyes opened wide to see him sitting on Trent's shoulder, unable to stay away. "You telling me the line in the backyard—where my kids play—is Newt's?"

Bis's face was screwed up, and he nodded, the tufts on his ears waving. I didn't like the idea that the line I had claimed as my primary source had been created by Newt, either, but it was what it was. Trent looked a little ill, and I wondered whose half-a-mile-long line was running through his office, back room, and gardens.

Fingers holding Bis's, I resettled myself on the gravel path. It was obvious that this tight of contact with the line was hurting him. The discord was too loud, too painful.

Bis's grip on my hands tightened. "Now, Rachel."

I plunged my thoughts back in the line, ghosting through the purple haze, finding it easier now that I'd done it before, searching, discarding, sifting until I found the half step of red, tiny and lost among the rest. "Got it!" I whispered, heart pounding as I gathered it to me, struggling to pull it free of the rest. It was stuck like Velcro.

"Bubble it," Bis said. "Bring it out with you. With us."

With a curious flip-flop of thought, I bubbled the color/sound. My eyes snapped open as the connection broke and I suddenly found myself holding the memory of a mess of half-step red vibration in my mind. Trent was sitting before us, just outside the bubble with the line behind him. His eyes were wide, and I wondered how much he was getting through the rings.

"Whoa, whoa, whoa!" Jenks said, rising up on a dusting of blue. "That sounds like line jumping to me. Isn't this what you did to make your broken line to begin with?"

Bis was smiling, looking exhausted as his wings drooped. "She's just going to move the imbalance, not herself." He looked at me, his craggy brow furrowed in warning. "Right?"

My hair was tickling my face, but I didn't dare let go of Bis's hand to brush it aside. "Right," I said. "And besides, Jenks. I've got it already."

Trent's face was alight, and I nodded at his unspoken question. Yep, I had it. It was doing flip-flops in my soul, and I didn't want to think about what might happen if I accidentally let go of the bubble and the imbalance became a part of me, but I had it. It sort of hurt.

"Your line sounds better already," Bis said, his hand still in mine. "Do you remember what Newt's line sounds like without the imbalance?"

I bobbed my head, afraid to move. "Tune my aura to it?"

"No!" Bis shouted, startling me as his wings half opened. And then softer, almost sheepishly, he said, "Not your aura, just the bubble around the imbalance."

I fidgeted, embarrassed that Trent had seen the near miss. "Should I think about Newt?"

Bis's red eyes widened. "I don't think so."

"I wouldn't," Jenks said sourly. "Rachel, will you just dump that imbalance and get on with it? Your aura looks really creepy holding a chunk of Newt's."

Trent was nodding his agreement, so I closed my eyes to better focus on the bubble of imbalance trapped in my mind's eye. It was coated with my cheerful gold aura and a thin layer of demon smut, and I needed to shift it to . . . silvery gray red. Licking my lips, I screwed my face up as I tried to imagine silver pinpricks blossoming on my gold sphere, growing to encompass everything.

"Tune it higher," Bis whimpered, clearly in pain.

"I'm trying!" I said, tightening my focus. My breath sucked in as the bubble flashed silver, overfocusing to a solid black. With a curious sideways shuffle, I pulled it back to silver, imagining a shading of a pure tinge of red lined with gray. For one breathless moment I held it, feeling my entire soul chime with the sound of silver light . . . And then it was . . . gone. There was a faint tug, and then even that severed, my awareness snapping back with a twang.

"Rachel?"

My eyes flew open at Trent's call. He'd felt it. I thought he might. Heart pounding, I looked at Bis in the lamplight, Trent standing behind him with Jenks on his shoulder. The gargoyle looked as shocked as me. "Holy crap!" I shouted, my voice echoing back from the trees. "Did we—"

"You did!" the small gargoyle exclaimed, and I ducked as he made one push with his wings and was through my circle and airborne, flying loops with the bats and yelling in delight.

I beamed at Trent. We had done it. And if we had done it once, we could do it again and again until the line was fixed!

"You did it, Rachel!" Bis said, startling me as he skidded to a landing on the gravel path, peppering my circle with kicked-up stones. His wings were spread and his eyes wild. "You did it! Look at that line! It sounds better already!"

"*We all* did it," I said as I dropped the circle to put a hand on his shoulder. The glory of the lines flooded me, and yes, once I got past the discord, I could tell there was the faintest lessening of the leak. Relief filled me, and I swear, I almost cried.

"Nicely done, Rachel." Smiling up at Trent, I accepted his hand and stood. Our pinkie rings glinted together in the light, and I didn't know how to feel about it. My hands were shaking, but I was ready to put another imbalance back if Bis was.

Pulling my hand from Trent's, I looked for Bis. "Another one?" I asked, my intention obvious, and he nodded from the retaining wall, his red eyes glowing in the lamplight.

Jenks's wings clattered as he dropped down, shrilling something so fast I couldn't understand him.

"You surprise me, Rachel," came an oily voice from the dark, and I spun, heart pounding as I turned to the river. *Ku'Sox? Crap on toast!*

"It's Ku'Sox!" Jenks shouted, dripping an angry, frightened red dust. His sword was out, and his wings by my ear, harsh.

"Not in that you figured it out," Ku'Sox said, a small sphere of light blossoming in his hand to show his presence beside my screaming, damaged line, "but that you're stupid enough to be out here alone."

Bis landed on my other side, puffing up as much he could by sucking in the moisture from the air. The size of a large dog, he crouched beside me with his tail thrashing.

"She's not alone," Jenks spat, hovering at head height and brandishing his sword. "Back off, Cute Socks. I cut your nose off before, I'll do it again."

Ku'Sox's globe of light flickered, and with that as my only warning, I invoked my protection circle, still scratched in the dust around me.

Bis yelped at the energy I yanked through me, the gargoyle shrinking as a ball of greenish black bounced off Trent's larger circle, invoked an instant before mine. Ku'Sox's spell hit the nearby retaining wall and stuck, glowing a weird greenish light. I dropped my circle.

I stood, white-faced, and the ugly line hummed through me, harsh and dizzying as I pulled it in, trying to become stronger. "I cursed you!" I exclaimed as I stood behind a grim-faced Trent. "You can't leave the ever-after!"

"I haven't." Smug, he walked into the light of our hissing lantern, and my stomach clenched as my first thought was borne out. Nick. He had possessed him. A doppelgänger curse was easy. Demons did them all the time. Al had once possessed Lee to walk about in reality in the daytime. "You're fortunate that your boyfriend is rather light in the loafers when it comes to manipulating ley line energy," Ku'Sox said, confirming my thoughts, "or I would tear through your familiar's paltry circle and be done with you right now."

"He's not my familiar," I said as Ku'Sox halted before us. "And Nick is not my boyfriend. He is a mistake!"

Nodding absently, Ku'Sox poked at Trent's circle, evaluating the dimple he made as Bis continued to hiss and Jenks landed on my shoulder in solidarity. The demon was in a three-piece suit, and it looked dumb out here in the weedy garden at the foot of a homemade castle, whereas Al's crushed green velvet had somehow seemed right at home. The light coming from the spell that had hit the wall supplemented the lantern, showing his silvery-gray hair slicked back and reflecting off his shiny shoes. His expression was smug as he eyed me, running his eyes up and down my silhouette in a way I decidedly didn't like. "This body I'm in remembers what you feel like. Inside and out."

Trent stiffened, and the psychotic demon turned to him. "Your whore and child are alive. Come with me now, and they will stay that way."

I gripped Trent's arm, but he shrugged me off, the rising scent of cinnamon nearly overpowering the stench of ever-after Ku'Sox reeked of. "If you go with him, nothing will stop him," I said, and Trent's frustration grew until his circle hummed with it.

"Don't you think I know that?"

I wondered if he was wishing he'd never freed Ku'Sox. I knew I was.

Sighing dramatically, Ku'Sox rolled his eyes. "As entertaining as this is, would you mind if we flipped to the last page? I want that curse lifted you put on me, Rachel. I want Trenton Aloysius Kalamack to make me a brand-new generation of demons to play with, and I want the ancient demons dead. I want the ever-after dead so I may never be trapped there again, and I want it all in that order. Notice you are not on the list . . . yet."

His gaze traveled over the lines of my tattoo, and I stifled a tremor. Feeling it, Jenks lifted from my shoulder. "Are you fairy-farting kidding me?" Jenks said, and Bis's tail lashed through my bubble. "Rache, you don't actually believe this freak, do you?"

Ku'Sox almost snarled at the insult, but then his eyes lifted from Bis to Trent. "Working with elves . . . Really, Rachel. I think you should be commended for stretching your abilities, but Newt would be most displeased with you."

I pushed to the front of Trent's bubble. "Here's my list. We fix the line," I said as I carefully siphoned energy off the discordant line and filled my chi. "Then the *ancient* demons grow a pair and we all shove you in a little hole in St. Louis again. That's my list. I don't care if it's in that order, either."

Ku'Sox dramatically rolled his eyes. "My God, you are so like a woman."

"That's because I am one."

"Oh, this is tiresome," Ku'Sox moaned, and then he gestured, his hand glowing.

"Look out!" Jenks shrilled, shooting straight up. Both Trent and I instinctively crouched. Trent gasped as Ku'Sox's spell tore through his bubble, breaking it, and I threw a wad of energy at the incoming ball, deflecting it. The night wind shifted my hair, and Ku'Sox's energy pinged over my ley line and into the woods to die. There was a tug, and Trent's circle was up again. Ku'Sox jerked to a halt, so close the circle hummed a warning.

Trent's eyes met mine, and slowly we stood. I felt ill looking at the grim hatred in his expression. I didn't think it was the rings that had saved our skins. We just knew what to do.

"Curious," Ku'Sox said, walking the edge of our circle like a lion in the shadows. "Both of you together? Unexpected." His eyes slid to the ley line. "And potentially troublesome."

Satisfied, I stood straighter. A drop of sugar-coated anger slipped through my fear. "We can prove you did this," I said, and he rolled his eyes. "I'm going to Dali and—"

My words cut off as a wash of energy made Ku'Sox flicker. Trent moaned when it melted away to show Ku'Sox holding Lucy on his hip. The fair-headed little girl was only a year old, innocent of the monster who held her and happy with the world. Her little mouth curved up in a smile when she saw me, and then she cried out when she saw Trent, reaching with her hands for him to come take her.

"Rachel, I can't," Trent said, ashen. "She's my daughter."

"You'll go to Dali and what?" Ku'Sox said as he held her on his hip, his arrogant expression mocking. Beside me, Trent's breath quickened. *Shit, he might do anything,* I thought, and I grabbed his arm, refusing to let go lest he walk through his circle and break it. This was what had happened in the clearing with Quen and Lucy, and I vowed it would have a new ending.

"Down!" Lucy demanded imperiously when she saw Trent, then, "No! No!" when Ku'Sox tightened his grip.

"She's my godchild. You broke our agreement," I said as the little girl's pout drifted into the realm of a tantrum, and the clean-shaven demon in his three-piece charcoal suit smiled a perfect, evil smile.

"File the paperwork." Frowning, Ku'Sox jiggled Lucy, but she wouldn't be distracted, her hands extended to Trent and pleading for him to come get her. I didn't think I could hate Ku'Sox any more. Trent's hands were fisted, his breathing shallow. Bis's ears were down in indecision, and Jenks hovered at the top of Trent's circle, waiting for instruction. I didn't know what to do. Ku'Sox might hurt her.

Seeing us frozen, Ku'Sox turned the magic wreathing his hand inward. Making a fist, he opened it to release a dozen tiny winged horses, pink, purple, and red. "Love is such a fine weapon when utilized fully," he said as Lucy caught sight of them and was predictably distracted.

I stiffened when he set the wildly wiggling toddler down, but then he gestured, and the horses galloped into the dark, down the broken path and away from me. Shouting in delight, Lucy wobbled after them, her little riding outfit making her a darling of wealth and privilege.

Trent jerked, catching himself before I had to. If we broke the circle, Ku'Sox would have us at his mercy. Still within our sight, Lucy lost her balance and plopped backward onto her butt. Laughing at her own mistake, she crawled to a retaining wall and regained her feet. My teeth clenched, and my heartache turned to hatred. "I'll kill you if you hurt her."

"And then I'll kill you again," Jenks said, his dust an eerie black.

"If either of you touch her, I will eat her soul alive," Ku'Sox said mildly, brushing nonexistent dust from his shoulder. From somewhere in the dark, Lucy giggled.

"This could all be over if you agree to come with me, Trenton Aloysius Kalamack," he said as he stood before us. "Ceri is no good at fixing things," he added, looking scornfully at the small gargoyle when Bis hissed at him. "You need to learn some respect, goyle."

Lucy toddled up, the newly risen moon making her hair a silver halo. Shouting in glee, she threw herself at Ku'Sox's knees, a purple winged horse in her grip. Trent groaned, and my stomach twisted at Ku'Sox's fake smile. "Aren't you a love!" he said brightly as he took her in his arms and rose, giving me an empty black stare when the little girl looked away. Trent was beside himself.

"As you can see, I've not hurt little Lucy," Ku'Sox said, smiling. "I think elf children are sweet, actually. I don't have that grudge against the elves that my kin do. The new world wouldn't have that ugliness."

"Genocide is not a viable path to world peace," I said, seething. "I can prove you broke my line."

Seeing my anger, Lucy began to frown. The horse in her hand was dead, but she didn't let it go. Ku'Sox didn't seem to care. "Do that," he said, holding out a cookie to the little girl, but she'd have none of it anymore and wanted down. "I'll simply say we were working together and you backed out of the deal, leaving me to take the blame."

I thought of those life rafts in the form of infants. The panic I was holding seemed to shake its chain, gaining another few inches of freedom. They'd likely kill me for sure, four days or not. Dali was right. My silence was buying my continued existence.

Lucy ignored the cookie Ku'Sox kept pushing at her, holding her hands out to Trent instead. "Down!" Lucy shrilled, squirming and kicking him. "Do-o-o-own!" she howled when he held her tighter, throwing the cookie Ku'Sox was trying to pacify her with at him. She truly was Ellasbeth's daughter and had the vocal power to prove it. "D-a-a-a-addy!" she cried, reaching out to Trent, her little hands opening and closing. "*Daddy!*"

Ku'Sox gave her a little jerk, and she screamed at him, filling the night with her anger. Fear lit through me, and I swear he closed his eyes in bliss when he saw it. Lucy kicked furiously, howling and pinching his arm. Having endured enough, Ku'Sox gave her a shake, and the little girl vanished in a wash of ever-after. For a moment, her last cry of outrage echoed against the trees and castle, and then even that was gone.

"No!" Trent raged, a blur as he lunged at Ku'Sox. I gasped as he threw a ball of black-rimmed energy. It tore through his circle. Jenks was up and away in an instant, Bis hot on his dust trail.

"Trent!" I shouted as the cooler air rushed over me. Ku'Sox snarled, deflecting whatever it was right back at Trent. Every blade of grass, every leaf, took on a razor edge. I lunged for Trent but was jerked back by my hair.

"Ow!" I howled, my scalp on fire as Ku'Sox swung me around and threw me to the ground. I got my knees under me, and the demon shoved me down again, so hard my breath was knocked out. Just within my sight, Trent writhed on the ground, taken out by his own magic.

"You are troublesome," Ku'Sox said, and he sat on me, pinning me. There was a circle around us keeping both Jenks and Bis powerless, but I could still tap a line. I flooded him with it and he only sucked in his breath, enjoying it.

"Get off!" I shouted into the gravel, then screamed in pain when he wrenched my arm back, nearly dislocating it.

"Playing with elves?" Ku'Sox said, and the agony let up. He traced the outline of my tattoo with a soft finger, and I shuddered, breathing in the scent of carrion and trying not to throw up. This was *exactly* why I hadn't wanted to try to fight him. Why did no one listen to me?

"You kill me, and they will be looking at you to fix the line," I rasped in the dark, scared to death as I felt him fingering the elven chastity ring. "They know you're responsible for it."

"As you say," he drawled, and I felt the ring spin on my finger. "But we also both know they're cowards, and if you can't overpower me, then they'll kill you to gain my good graces again. Is this how you found the strength to shift the imbalance back to the proper line?" he said, tugging experimentally at the ring. "Ingenious, melding your abilities with an elf to best me. Tsk-tsk. Mustn't play with wild animals."

"No, wait!" I shouted, helpless, and he gave a tug.

Ku'Sox's cry of pain was like audible lightning, jerking through me. My arm thudded down on the gravel path, numb and unmoving as he was suddenly not sitting on me but writhing three feet away—his circle broken. It was the ring. It had its own safeguards, and they had just saved my ass.

"Rache! Get up!" Jenks was shouting, his sparkles filling my vision and lighting the night. Dazed, I sat up, dead arm cradled in my lap. "Get up!" he yelled again, and I staggered to my feet. Ku'Sox was picking himself up off the ground. He was between me and Trent, the elf still gasping at his own spell. For an instant, we froze, and with a snarl, Ku'Sox turned to Trent.

"No!" I shouted as the demon went for him, but it was too late, and I ran smack into Ku'Sox's circle. "Trent!" I exclaimed as I hammered on it, shocks of fire cramping my arm.

Ku'Sox had pulled Trent to his feet, and I was sure it was the last I'd see of him, but with his arm around Trent's neck, the demon bared his teeth at me. Teeth clenched, I pushed my fingers into his field. There had to be a weakness, a hole. Pinpricks turned to fire, and agony pulsed with my heartbeat as I pressed harder.

"Rache! You're burning your hand!" Jenks shouted, and with a cry of frustrated pain, I spun away, fingers throbbing. I couldn't do it. He was stronger than me. But I'd known that already.

Ku'Sox looked me up and down, evaluating. "Clever, giving your elf the master ring," he snarled, clearly out of sorts for the wallop he'd taken, his back hunched and his perfect hair out of place. "I'm willing to wager I can take this one," he said, wrestling Trent's arm up. Trent tried to wiggle free, and Ku'Sox flooded him with energy. I saw it dancing over him like ants, sparkling in the dark. Trent groaned and went still, his eyes bloodshot as he hung in Ku'Sox's grip, his hand with the chastity ring splayed open.

"You son of a bitch!" I shouted, burned hand cradled as he pulled the ring from Trent and let him fall to the ground, a slumped shadow in the dark. There was a quiver in my chi as the connection failed, but it didn't matter.

He was going to take him, I thought in anguish as Ku'Sox made a fist around the ring and let the twisted mass of metal hit the ground beside Trent.

"Mustn't play with demons, little elf," Ku'Sox mocked as he leaned over Trent and nudged him with a foot. "You'll end up dead, and I need you. Come with me of your free will, or I will cause you more pain, more heartache than you can bear."

"No-o-o," Trent breathed, the pain in his voice cutting me to my soul.

"I'm not going to let you do this!" I shouted, and Ku'Sox straightened, the lamplight making his expression on his long features ugly. Looking at him past the strands of my hair, my hatred grew. "I know how to fix the line, and we will stop you," I vowed. "This will see you dead. I'm done being nice."

Trent's head came up. With a lip-curling sneer, Ku'Sox dismissed my words. "Kill me? Chances are you won't, but no need to take chances."

I stiffened when the circle surrounding Ku'Sox and Trent fell, but he wasn't interested in me anymore. "You, I can take. Come with me," Ku'Sox said, pointing at Bis, and the gargoyle spread his wings in alarm.

"Bis!" I shouted as both he and Ku'Sox vanished in twin pops of in-rushing air. Shocked, I stared, unbelieving in the new silence. Ku'Sox had taken Bis? Why? But the answer was obvious. Without Bis, I couldn't fix the line, rings or no rings.

Ashen-faced, I stared at Trent. He was as stunned as I was. The lan-tern's glow fell upon the three of us, Jenks's dust shifting to a dismal blue. They were gone. *They were gone!*

I stared for three seconds at where Bis had been. "No!" I shouted, un-believing this had happened. "This is not fair!" I shouted at the sky, stag-gering three steps, but there was nowhere to go. "It's not fair," I said softer, then began to cry. I didn't want to, but the tears came.

Sobbing, I dropped where I was, curled my knees to my chest, and just cried. He had Lucy. He had Ceri. And now he had Bis. Bis. He had Bis, damn it. I was responsible for the kid. And Ku'Sox took him like plucking a flower from a field. I was so stupid.

"Rache? You okay?" Jenks asked from my shoulder, and I lifted my head, wiping my eyes only to get grit in them. Jenks was okay. I knew he would be. Ku'Sox must think he wasn't a threat.

"Ask me Saturday morning," I said, my resolve beginning to gather.

Jenks flitted up to my knee, his flight wobbly but growing more steady. "How are we going to get him back?" he asked, his face tight and his deter-mination obvious.

Moving slowly, I got to my feet, too numb to even look at Trent. He had lost Lucy again, and I didn't want to see that pain. "Plan C," I said. Trent had seen me cry. I didn't care. That butcher had Bis, Lucy, Ceri . . .

Jenks landed on my good hand, and my arm ached where Ku'Sox had pulled it. "What's plan C?"

Taking the remaining chastity ring off my finger, I threw it into the dark. Between me and the river was the broken line, and I looked at it, shaking. He'd taken Bis, Lucy, and Ceri. If I got the chance, I was going to kill him.

"You don't want to know."

Chapter Fourteen

The teakettle was whistling. It had been for some time. Angry, I shoved my chair back from the table, leaving the demon spell book open as I went to the cupboard. Muttering under my breath, I grabbed the first cup I touched, only to realize it had blue butterflies on it.

"Who in hell bought a mug with blue butterflies on it!" I shouted, slamming it on the counter beside the stove. "We are serious people doing serious things! I don't have time for butterflies!"

Chamomile. That's supposed to be soothing, right? I thought as I ripped the individual package open and dropped it into the cup. I didn't drink tea often, but it was getting late and I was going to have a hard enough time getting to sleep as it was. Gone. Bis was with that monster, and I was more than livid; I was panicked.

Unthinking, I reached for the teakettle, jerking my hand away and shaking it as the steam hit my fingertips, burned from trying to break Ku'Sox's circle. "Damn it!" I exclaimed, slamming drawers until I found the potholder and, more carefully this time, filled my cup. Bits of herbs floated up, and the fragrant steam bathed my face. Crap on toast, the bag was broken.

My shoulders slumped, and I stopped. From the hallway came the tiny whispers of the pixies—fresh from their midnight nap—watching my tantrum. Sniffing, I pushed my hair out of my face and tried not to cry into my tea as I imagined Bis trapped with Ku'Sox. The little guy was my responsibility. He was probably terrified.

Staring at my stocking feet with one hand over my middle and the other holding my forehead, I forced myself to breathe. Then I put my arms down, exhaling slowly. I could panic later. Right now, I had to concentrate. The sun would be up in a few hours, and if I didn't have a plan by then, I'd never get any sleep.

My hands shook as they encircled the mug. The ceramic was hot on my burned skin, and I changed my grip as I carried it back to the big farm table. I had to shove my spell and curse books to the side, and they threatened to spill off. There was nothing in them. I was coming up empty.

Depressed, I set the tea down with a soft thud. Elbows on an open book, I stared at the yellowed pages. The plop of a tear on the faded print surprised me, and I wiped it away, sitting up and away from it.

Bis was gone. Lucy was gone. Ceri was gone. Quen was with us again but unable to do magic. I had until Friday midnight to fix the line and prove to the demons that I could keep Ku'Sox from killing them. I knew how to fix the line, but I couldn't do it without Bis. If I told the demons what Ku'Sox was doing, Ku'Sox would turn everything around onto me. I didn't have any demon-magic-invoking babies for them to escape the dying ever-after with. They wouldn't help me. The truth didn't matter. It was all about perception.

I jerked, my head nearly exploding as, in shrill shrieks, six pixies skated in from the hall on my slipper. Scoot-the-shoe could usually make me laugh as five or six pixies jammed into my slipper; their screaming like they were on a roller coaster and being chased by an orange cat was hilarious. But tonight . . .

"Jenks!" I shouted, my frustration finding a convenient outlet.

Jenks darted in, his voice hushed as he corralled his kids, almost unheard as his kids complained, fussed, and finally left, flying my slipper out three feet above the floor. "Sorry, Rache. They'll leave you alone."

I looked up. He was hovering miserably in the dark threshold, a faintly glowing yellow dust slipping from him. Immediately a layer of guilt slathered itself over my already bad mood, making me even more depressed.

"I'm sorry," I whispered, my hand gesturing uselessly as it sat on the table. "Your kids are okay." God help me, I'd only made things worse.

He drifted up and down, looking as helpless as I felt. "We'll get him back," he finally said, then darted out when someone yelled at her brother to leave her alone.

I turned to the book, not seeing the print. Flipping a page, I felt the tingle of black magic stab my burned fingers. Hissing, I curled my hand into a fist and shoved the book away. I flopped back angrily into the chair, almost knocking myself backward. I knew how to fix the line, but not without Bis. I could get Bis back, but only if I fixed the line.

Jenks and Belle were in the hall, Belle's lisping whispers obvious but not clear enough to decipher. Depressed, I slumped. I was ruining everyone's day. Yay, me. I was still staring at the faded demon print when Jenks edged into the kitchen, looking as meek as a flying man capable of lobotomizing fairies in his sleep could. "Ah, how you doing, Rache?"

My teeth were clenched, and I forced them apart. "Fine." F'ed IN the Extreme, as Ivy would say. I should have called her yesterday, not three hours ago. She was on her way back, but it would take a bit.

Jenks hesitated, then dropped down beside me, wings flat against his back. "It's going to be okay," he said. I knew he meant to be encouraging, but it grated like fish scales.

I stared at the wall, my throat closing. Jenks's kids were soulfully watching from the hallway, sitting on the lintel with their dust like tinsel.

"I'm not Ivy, but I bet we can come up with something," he said.

I managed to dredge up a smile from somewhere. "I don't know where to start," I said as I closed the book. The binding cracked, and I didn't care.

"When was the last time you ate?"

I listlessly picked at the binding, then quit when I realized it was probably someone's skin. "I don't know. Last year, maybe?"

He chuckled, but it sounded forced. "I'll call for takeout. What sounds good?"

I knew he was trying to be helpful. It bothered him that he couldn't do anything for me or for Bis, and that the two worlds were about to collide in a big, kind of permanent way. I simply couldn't find the strength to meet his hesitant smile with my own.

"I'm not hungry," I said, and his dust faltered as his smile faded. I couldn't eat knowing that Bis was scared. My failings had put him there. Trent must be frantic about Lucy and Ceri. I didn't know how he had managed it, remaining calm when he drove me back home.

Silent, Jenks sat on the book, wings unmoving. My chamomile tea grew cold beside me. "I know it hurts," Jenks said, but I couldn't look up. "Remember when you told me I'd find a way to live without Matalina?"

My head jerked up. "Bis isn't dead."

"Bad example," he admitted. "But I didn't believe you, and I should have. It would have made those first few weeks easier. Rache, we will get him back. *Believe it.*"

But I didn't know how, and my helplessness welled up.

"Oh, thank God!" Jenks exclaimed suddenly, rising up on a column of gold dust and darting into the dark hallway. I wiped the back of my hand under my eye, then sagged again when I heard the bong of the church's front bell. The pixies clustered on the lintel peeled off one by one to follow Jenks to the front with the enthusiasm they reserved for elves.

"Swell," I whispered as I looked down at my socks, jeans, and black tee I'd changed into after crying in the shower. Turning in my chair, I eyed the clock over the stove. It was after four in the morning—just about my bedtime, but an elf would be bright-eyed and fresh. I had nothing for Trent or Quen. Nothing at all.

My heart seemed to quiver as I recognized the soft scuffing of Trent's shoes. I sat up and tried not to look so bedraggled as pixy excitement grew and Trent strode in, looking calm and focused in his long overcoat spotted with rain. He carried a take-out bag from a doughnut shop and a large paper bag with handles in one hand, a small briefcase in the other. Jenks was on his shoulder, looking as right as snow on a mountain. Trent had lost Ceri and Lucy and was keeping it together. If he could do it, I could do it.

"Rachel," he said, wincing at the noise the pixies were putting out. "I can't stay, but I had to come into the city to take care of some legal business and I wanted to drop these off and discuss something with you. I hope you don't mind me stopping in unexpectedly."

"No, that's fine," I said, glancing at where the coffeepot had been, wanting to offer him something. I still hadn't gotten a new one. Stuff kept interfering. My chest hurt, and I looked at the top of the fridge where Bis usually sat.

Jenks gave me a look to pull it together, then lifted from Trent's shoulder. "Let me get my kids out of here." His voice rose. "Hey! How many times have I told you to *leave* the *shoelaces alone!*"

Head going down, Trent shifted his feet and three pixies flowed out the door at ankle height, giggling and laughing. Jenks was tight on their dust, and the noise level dropped.

His relief obvious, Trent came farther in and set his briefcase down before placing the bag of doughnuts on the center counter and the paper sack on the table with a heavy thump. He was silent, utterly still, and I looked up. "Are you doing okay?"

I closed the demon textbook and shoved it to the center of the table. "No."

Trent dropped his rain-spotted hat on the table and began to unpack the leather-bound books of odd sizes from the paper sack. "It was a hard night."

I couldn't stop my sarcastic laughter. His daughter had been dangled before him and he had been given a horrible choice. A minor entrusted to my care had been abducted. Bis was only fifty years old. He shouldn't have even been there. The tears welled, and I held my breath, not wanting to cry in front of him again. "Look at me," I said as I dabbed at my eyes, trying to make light of it. "I'm such a baby. I can't stop crying."

"It's okay," he said as he stood by the table and carefully folded the paper sack.

"No, it's not," I protested, and Trent walked over to me and placed his hand on my shoulder. His shoes were untied, and I looked up, startled when he crouched to put our eyes at the same level. His eyes were dark with a shared pain. "I meant it's okay to cry," he said, and I remembered to breathe. "You're wound so tight right now, you need a healthy release."

I shook my head, glad he wasn't trying to convince me that everything was going to be okay. It wasn't. This was bad. Really bad. Knowing that he understood helped. He had lost his child. How could I even come close to his grief? His frustration? I thought again, *If he can function, then I can too.*

With a surprising touch on my cheek, he stood up and edged away. "We'll get him back. We'll get them all back."

I could feel a tingle where his hand had been, and I gazed at him, numb. "I don't see how. I can fix the line, but not without Bis. And no one will help me if the line is broken." It was a trap my mind kept circling, and until I broke from it, I was dead in the water.

Still in his coat, Trent pulled Ivy's chair out of the corner. His motions held a restrained excitement as he sat down to retie his shoes. "That's why I'm here. I've been thinking about tonight," he said, glancing up as Jenks flew back in.

"Me too." My voice was a dull flatness compared to his excited eagerness.

"Ku'Sox did a few things tonight to show what he's afraid of," Trent insisted.

"What does it matter? They engineered him to be stronger than everyone," I said, glancing at the books he'd brought. *More books. That ought to help,* I thought sarcastically, then I looked closer, sitting up and reaching for one. They all had library stickers on them—from the restricted section.

"Hey, these are from the restricted section," I said, taking one. "Did you steal them?"

Trent flushed, the rims of his ears going charmingly red. "No, of course not. They let me take them out."

My eyes slid to the brown paper bag he'd brought them over in. "Out of the restricted section? *Of the library?*"

"Yes, so please don't get anything on them," he said, moving my cup of chamomile tea to the center counter. "Oh, it's gone cold," he said softly, standing up and taking his coat off.

I still couldn't wrap my mind around the fact that they'd let him take restricted books from the library grounds.

Clearly discomfited, Trent dropped his coat over Ivy's chair. Reaching for his bag of doughnuts, he muttered, "It's amazing what they let you do when you supply a new roof for the children's wing and pay for the salary of the children's events coordinator."

"They let him take restricted books out," I said to Jenks, and the pixy shrugged.

Behind the counter, Trent rustled in his bag. "Ah, would you mind if I ate? I sent the staff home Monday and haven't called them back yet. Ellasbeth can boil water but she won't." He paused. "You don't want any, do you?"

The scent of fried doughnuts was strong. Tearing my gaze from the books, I eyed him standing behind the counter, his head almost touching the hanging utensils. His hair was darker than usual in the electric light, and his face was freshly shaven. Tall and unbowed, the calmness he radiated soaked into me, pushing my panic back to the edges so I could think again. "No, go ahead."

"Jenks, where are the plates?" Trent asked, and the pixy landed on his shoulder to point the cabinet out.

It felt funny with Trent in here, but the pixy kids were keeping it to a dull roar. The scrape of a plate was loud, and Trent put six pastries on it, taking a stark, plain doughnut from the pile when he set the plate before me and moved the books all the way back to the wall.

"Ku'Sox broke our rings," Trent said as if it was important, and I watched him take a bite from his plain doughnut, thinking it was odd seeing him here in my kitchen in his suit and tie at four in the morning. "I think that is significant. He didn't know we were using them as a safety net. He said 'meld your abilities to an elf to best me.' Ku'Sox thought we were using them to join our skills, to make ourselves stronger."

My stomach rumbled at the smell of the fried dough, and hearing it, Trent gestured for me to help myself. I shook my head, eyeing the one with the sprinkles.

"That's how the demons overpowered him before," Trent said, still standing in the middle of my kitchen. "He's afraid of us, demons, elves, anyone, working together. All his actions are to pull the demons apart, break alliances."

"I can't argue with that." Though Trent was clear across the kitchen, I felt as if he was too close, too accessible as he stood there looking good in my church eating a no-frills doughnut.

"And Bis," he said, making my stomach clench. "He didn't take him because he wanted leverage on you. If it was only that, he could have twisted the knife and gotten you to take the curse off right then and there."

I shoved my panic aside. "He took Bis so I couldn't fix the line," I said, and Trent nodded.

"Exactly my thoughts," he said, setting his doughnut with one bite out of it on a napkin from the bag. "He needs it broken. With purple sludge gone, everyone can see the curse he used to damage your line. That's why he can't allow you to fix it. But if you could move all the imbalance at once, you might get the same effect. Would you mind if I made something to drink?"

My lips parted at the new thought. "Sure, go ahead," I said, and he wiped his fingers off on a second napkin, turning to the fridge. Damn, I could move all the imbalance at once. I mean, I knew what my line was supposed to sound like. All I needed to do was bundle up everything that didn't belong and drop it into another line.

Silent, I jiggled my foot as Trent went to the fridge. Jenks was on his shoulder pointing things out. Trent came out with the milk, surprising me. *He likes milk with his doughnuts? You learn something new every day.* No, hot chocolate, I decided when Jenks darted around the kitchen and Trent followed, collecting sugar, cocoa, and salt.

"You think I can move the entire wad of imbalance without Bis?" I said.

"The hell she can!" Jenks protested, but I sat up, pulse quickening. "She can't line jump. That's what started this!"

"She isn't line jumping, she's moving imbalance," Trent said to Jenks, waving the pixy's dust from the two cups that Trent had pulled from my cupboards and filled with powdered cocoa. "She's already proven she can do that."

I stood up, coming to stand with the counter between us. "I know the signature of the line in the graveyard. I can dump it all there."

Trent looked up from pouring milk into two mugs when Jenks whistled. "Newt is going to be pissed," the pixy said, and my enthusiasm faltered, but only for a moment.

"Ah, is one of those mine by chance?" I asked, and Trent's smile widened.

"Yes."

Jenks hovered between us, a bright shimmer of red-tinted dust spilling from him. "I don't like this," he said. "It sounds risky."

"It's perfect," I said as Trent's spoon clinked, stirring them both. "Once it's moved, anyone can see the curse he used to break it."

"In which case he'll just say you were backing out of a deal?" Jenks prompted.

My shoulders slumped, and I chewed on my lower lip. "Maybe I could borrow Al's wedding rings and we could bind our strength together," I said hesitantly, and Jenks scoffed.

"They don't work between demon and elf," Jenks reminded me, but Trent had set the spoon on the napkin beside his half-eaten doughnut and had gone to his coat.

"We have options," he said as he triumphantly slapped a museum brochure before me. "That is, if you can reinvoke them."

Eyebrows high, I pulled the colorful brochure to me with ELVEN ARTIFACT SHOW emblazoned on it in a metallic mythological script. I knew there was no such collection at the Cincy museum. There was none anywhere. The elves had just come out of hiding. It was then that it clicked and I looked for the date. Quen had mentioned a museum outing at the end of the week. Sure enough, it started this weekend and ran for three months before going on the road.

"Jenks, would you get this for me?" Trent asked, standing before the microwave with his two mugs, and the pixy darted away, hitting the door button with a two-footed punch. Apparently the afternoon they spent together stealing Lucy had changed both their attitudes toward each other. They almost looked like friends. Finally the incongruity of a pixy helping a multibillionaire figure out my microwave was over, and Trent came to the table, the microwave a humming background to Jenks's wings.

I smacked the brochure down before Trent. "A museum show of elven artifacts? You arranged this?"

Jenks buzzed into the hall to settle another argument, and Trent ducked his head to look charmingly embarrassed. "Six months ago. As a show of solidarity and pride in our heritage. I've been slowly convincing the people I know that we need a public expression of our history, and it's gratifying what they have kept. Most of the magic artifacts are defunct, but it is an amazing collection nevertheless. Cincinnati will have the show for three months, and then it will be touring for the next three years while I build a new wing."

Standing at the counter, I opened the brochure. Colorful pictures and descriptions of ancient artifacts met me. Suddenly it looked like a shopping catalog.

Trent leaned closer, close enough that I could smell cinnamon and wine under his aftershave. "Tell me what you think will work the best, and I can have it loaned to you for a few days."

My eyes came up to find him deadly serious. "They will just give it to you? They might not get it back."

He nodded. "But if it does, it will be working. They'll risk it."

The microwave dinged, and needing a moment, I went to get it, eyeing the restricted library books in passing. Trent might be able to do that, yes. "You probably know better than I what these things can potentially do," I said as the scent of warm milk and chocolate hit me. My stomach rumbled when I reached for the two perfectly steaming mugs.

"Ah, I know what their owners *say* they're supposed to do," he said, and I hurriedly moved the hot mugs to the counter, shaking the heat from my burned and sensitive fingers. Seeing it, Trent seemed to go still. "You're burned?"

I hid my hand behind my back. "It's nothing."

"Nothing, fairy farts!" Jenks said, and I scowled at him. "She burned it trying to get through Ku'Sox's circle."

"It's fine," I said, but Trent was reaching for me. I stiffened, but he already had my wrist in his grip. "It's fine," I protested again, yanking away.

"Jeez, Rache. He's not going to bite you," Jenks griped, and Trent sourly held out his hand, head cocked and challenge screaming from his confident posture.

I wasn't going to show him, but as Jenks had said, he wasn't going to bite me. Feeling funny, I extended my hand. My demon scar was obvious, and I flushed when his eyes lingered briefly upon it before bringing my hand closer to him. I cringed a bit as his breath met my raw skin and he frowned. "It will be fine tomorrow," I said, and I exhaled in relief when he let go. "Here, drink your chocolate."

I pushed his mug to him, and he took it. His missing fingers showed; then he hid them again. Silent, we both took a drink, thinking our separate thoughts. I held the hot chocolate to my face, breathing it in before I tasted it, debating telling him that Quen had asked me to accompany him to the show. It seemed almost petty now.

"What the artifacts actually do is in the books. Somewhere," Trent said, and I met his eyes over my mug. Hot chocolate, sweet, rich, bitter, and warm, slipped down, warming me almost as much as Trent's sly smile. He was sticking me with the research, but I didn't care. For the first time since losing Bis, I thought we might be able to do this.

Nodding, Trent abruptly put his mug down and reached for his coat. "Just so. I'll leave the choosing to you then," he said as he gracefully put his coat on. "I need to get back. Thank you for the hot chocolate."

"You suck at research, too, huh?" Jenks said, perched on his mug and hazing the surface with his dust.

"Painfully horrible," Trent said, shrugging his coat over his shoulders and grabbing his hat and briefcase. His motion stopped, and he smiled faintly. "Let me know what piece you want."

"I will," I said, then started when Trent turned on a quick heel and headed for the hall. "Hey, what about your doughnuts?"

"You can have them," he said, already halfway to the sanctuary. "I'm not hungry."

At a loss, I glanced at Jenks, and he shrugged. Jolted into motion, I followed Trent, having to wave the pixy dust from Jenks's excited kids out of my way. "Trent, wait," I said, finally catching up with him at the door. "Thank you," I said, breathless when I almost ran into him when he turned at the old twin doors. "I think we can do this now."

Standing there in the dim glow of the light over the pool table, he hesitated. "Can I ask you something?"

"Sure."

Hands in his pockets, Trent looked totally unlike himself. "What would you have done with Dr. Farin?"

My smile faded. "Your geneticist? The one you killed?"

He nodded, opening the door to let a chill spring night breeze eddy about my ankles. "Now that you know everything, what hung in the balance, what was at stake—how would you have stopped him from going to the press and bringing about the end of everything that you'd spent your life trying to save? Life imprisonment such as a demon demands? Bribe him with even greater wealth, knowing you'd forever be his slave? Or would you end it cleanly, kill one greedy man to save thousands, maybe millions, from suffering?"

My mouth was dry, and I didn't know what to do with my hands. "I don't know," I finally said, and he nodded, deep in thought.

"That's a fair answer," he said lightly. "I'd wondered if you'd given any thought to the decisions I make and the possible reasons why."

I stared at him, thoughts racing through me. I didn't . . . I didn't know what to think anymore.

His expression blanked, and my sadness began to creep back. I knew where his thoughts had gone. "I'm sorry about Bis," he said. "I know it hurts."

And yet I managed to smile. He did know. He knew the guilt, the panic, and the strength it took to focus that energy on finding a way out. "Thank you," I said, refusing to cry in front of him again. He smelled like rain and leather over the scent of his aftershave, and my throat tightened and my vision threatened to swim again. "I'm sorry about Ceri and Lucy. I don't know how you can keep moving forward."

His eyes rose from my burned hand, and he unexpectedly tucked a strand of hair behind my ear, shocking me. "You were the one who taught me any chance is viable. If I didn't believe that, I would be a total wreck. I know how it hurts. Forgive me for my choices, maybe?"

Was he going to try to kiss me? I didn't know how I felt about that anymore. "I did that a long time ago."

Eyes holding an unreadable emotion, he hesitated, his attention running over my snarly hair. "Down, I think," he whispered, and making a sharp nod, he turned away.

I backed up, shoulder knocking the door frame as I misjudged and stumbled inside. Embarrassed, I shut the door before he found the sidewalk, but I watched him get into his car from one of the sanctuary's windows, his form blurry and wavy. Jenks's wings were a familiar brush of sound as he landed on my shoulder, and together we watched Trent's car lights flicker to life.

"What did he mean by that?" I said, feeling alone even as I could still smell him in my church.

Jenks's wings shifted fitfully. "I don't know."

Trent drove away, and I tried to look at Jenks on my shoulder, failing. "You called him," I accused. "You asked him to come over."

Red dust pooled down my front. "He was coming in to Cincy to talk to his lawyer," the pixy hedged. "I called him, yeah. I thought he might be able to help. It worked, didn't it? You're thinking again, right?"

I turned back to the window, staring out at the night-emptied street. "Uh-huh."

"With Ivy gone, you needed someone to ground you, Rache, and I'm not big enough to slap you."

I thought back to my frantic, useless state. He was right. "Sorry."

"Don't worry about it. Feel better?"

I put my burned hand on the window, the cool blood-red glass soothing my fingertips. Slowly I nodded. Trent had grounded me. How about that?

"The hot chocolate and doughnuts were his idea, though," Jenks said, then darted off to tend his children.

Chapter Fifteen

The faint ringing of the phone vibrated against the inside of my skull, and though I tried to incorporate the sound into my dreams of tiny purple hallways and black doors the size of acorns, it pushed itself into my conscious thought, shoving me awake.

The phone is ringing.

Eyes open, I stared at my clock glowing a steady 7:47. "Are you kidding me?" I whispered, and I rolled over on my stomach and put the pillow over my head. I'd only been asleep for a couple of hours and wasn't planning on getting up until noon.

I'd gone to bed late, not sleeping well with my dreams of shrinking rooms and being crushed in that singularity that Al had been trapped in making my sleep restless. That the sun was up seemed an insult, the bright rays making it past my curtain. Jenks would get the phone. It wouldn't be for me, anyway. No one hired a demon, and not at seven freaking forty-seven in the morning.

I sighed in relief as the phone finally quit. Then it started again. I groaned, wishing it would go away.

"Ra-a-a-ache!" Jenks's voice scraped along every nerve I had, and I propped myself up on my elbows.

"What!" I shouted, all the way awake now.

"My kids found Wayde's glue. I'm unsticking Rex's whiskers. Will you get that?"

"Are you serious?" I exclaimed.

"You want to hold the cat instead?"

I threw my pillow to the floor. Grumbling, I swung my feet down, jerking them back from the cold. "It's not even eight yet," I muttered, trying and failing to get my hair to lie flat as I looked in my dresser mirror. No, I didn't want to hold a hysterical cat who had had her whiskers glued together. God! I'd be happy when Ivy got home.

I reached for my blue terrycloth robe and jammed my arms in the sleeves. I couldn't find the slipper the pixies had been playing with yesterday, and staggering down the hall with a *scuff-pad, scuff-pad,* I tied my robe shut, ready to ream out the magazine salesman who was likely trying to work his way around our answering machine. Everyone important had my cell-phone number. If it was an emergency, they'd call me there.

I squinted in the brighter light in the kitchen, feeling ill from the lack of sleep. Trent's stack of books sat waiting. There wasn't a single pixy anywhere, and I wondered if Jenks had finally gotten them all out in the garden. It was spookily quiet.

"I'm coming!" I griped as the phone kept ringing, and ticked, I reached for the receiver. My heart seemed to catch when I saw the caller ID. It was Trent.

I picked up the phone, not knowing what was going on anymore. "Trent?" I said as I hesitantly put the receiver to my ear, not sure if I should be worried or mad. "What by God's little green apples are you doing calling me at seven forty-seven in the morning?"

There was a short silence, and then a familiar feminine voice said, "Sorry, wrong number."

I took a fast breath. "Ellasbeth?" I exclaimed, pushing the receiver tighter against my ear. "Is that you?"

Again there was silence. I could hear Ray crying in the background, and my spine stiffened. "Ellasbeth," I said softly, a hand to my forehead as I turned away from the bright kitchen window. "Trent and I have not slept together. Ever. I think you and he make a great couple. Can I *please* go back to sleep now?" This was ridiculous. Leave it to Ellasbeth to go poking around the first chance she got.

"I didn't know it was you," the woman said, the thread of fear in her voice waking me up faster than slamming a double grande. "You're the first number on Trenton's emergency list."

Ray was still crying. "Where's Trent?" She didn't say anything, and I hunched over the phone as Jenks came in, a worried gold dust slipping from him. "Look you . . . elf woman," I said, not wanting her to hang up on me. "I know you don't like me, but so help your trickster goddess, if you don't tell me why you're calling Trent's emergency numbers, I'm going to crawl through this telephone line and strangle you."

Jenks landed on the rim of my vat of saltwater, his expression becoming concerned when Ellasbeth took a frustrated breath. "He's gone! I think he went into the ever-after to get Lucy."

My grip on the phone tightened, and Jenks's wings hummed to life. Trent went off on his own? He dropped a perfectly good plan in my lap and went off and left me here? Son of a bastard!

Jenks darted out, and I stalked across the kitchen, waiting for Ellasbeth to take a breath, but she was well practiced, getting in three sentences belittling Trent before I could attempt even a word. "Ellasbeth, can I talk to Quen, please?" I asked, seething. He was gone. The smart-ass elf was going to get himself killed.

"I'm alone up here!" Ellasbeth shouted. "This baby won't stop screaming, and there's no one here to help me!"

Belle came in with Jenks, the fairy concerned as Jenks dropped down and smacked Rex's paw aside as he filled her in.

"Ellasbeth, stop having hysterics," I said as I met Jenks's eyes. "Where is Quen, and how long has Trent been gone?"

Finally she stopped. "I don't know. Quen is in the basement trying to open the vault."

Fear, thick and cloying, slithered out from the hopeful promises I'd been telling myself. "How long has Trent been gone?"

"I told you I don't know!" she shouted, and Ray cried all the louder, frustrated and forgotten in her crib by the sound of it. "The only thing I could get out of Quen was that Trenton used the vault door to get to the ever-after, but before he left, he set the machine to overload and it burned out the fuse. It's going to be days until we can get a new one. The last time I *saw* Trent was when he went to work this morning. That was about five."

Five in the morning—not long after leaving me. Son of a bitch! What was he doing going to confront Ku'Sox by himself? Alone? Damn it all to the Turn and back. I should have made him thumb promise. He was going to get himself killed. But then the thought occurred to me that maybe that had been his plan. He'd said he'd been at his lawyer's office.

Shit.

My eyes came up. Jenks was pale, waiting to see what I would do. "Ellasbeth, hold on a second," I said, interrupting her latest harangue.

"Don't you tell me to hold on, you little witch!"

I covered the receiver. "I think Trent went to confront Ku'Sox alone."

Jenks's face darkened. "The idiot!" he shrilled. "He promised me he wouldn't!"

"Yeah, he sort of let me think that, too," I said as I looked past him to the kitchen trying to decide the best way to deal with this. As a freed familiar, Trent had some immunity from Ku'Sox, but not if he attacked him. He'd only been there a couple of hours. Maybe he hadn't done anything yet.

My gaze dropped to my hand and the pinkie ring, twin to Trent's. The one time I'd used it, Trent had been pulled to me. The question was, had he been wearing it the last time I saw him? Ellasbeth had been razzing him about it, and I knew he was trying to appease her, make it work.

My heart pounded, and I put the phone back to my ear. Ellasbeth was still going on, clueless that I hadn't been listening. "Ellasbeth. Ellasbeth!" I shouted. "Shut up and listen to me!"

"How dare you—"

"I want you to take Ray," I said, my tone caustic. "I want you to pick her up out of that crib and I want you to give her a bath. I want you to bake cookies with her. I want you to read her a book. I don't care what you do, but you are *not* going to let her sit in her crib and cry. You got me?"

"You want me to read her a book?" Ellasbeth said in disbelief. "My fiancé is battling a demon, and you want me to read a child a book?"

My face burned. "You are going to read her a book," I said, my words slow so I wouldn't yell at her. "If I find out you put her in her crib to cry, I'm going to be pissed. Understand? When Quen comes up for air, tell him that I'm trying to yank Trent's ass out of the ever-after before he goes and does something stupid. Can you do that for me?"

Finally there was silence. "Ellasbeth?" I took a slow breath, trying to find a state of calm. "I'm not Trent's emergency contact because I look good in leather."

The click from the line being disconnected was loud. Lips twisting, I hit the button to end the call and set the phone back in the cradle.

"Well?" Jenks asked.

I tightened the tie of my robe. "Just a guess, but I think Trent got tired of waiting for results and went to talk to Ku'Sox."

I pushed off the counter, and Jenks took to the air. "Ah, Rache?"

"I'm just getting dressed, okay?" I said as I stomped down the hallway to my room, Jenks following me. "I can't fight the bad guys wearing a robe." I shut my room's door in Jenks's face, and the pixy simply darted under the crack in the door. His wings clattered in nervousness as I threw open my closet and started grabbing things. First Ceri and Lucy, then Bis. Now Trent. Thank God Ivy was on her way home. I needed her help. *Damn it, I am tired of this!*

"Rache?" Jenks said, coming to rest on a bedpost as I tugged on a pair of jeans, my nightgown riding up.

My heart was pounding. It was almost eight. He'd only been there a couple of hours. Maybe it wasn't too late. "Turn your back, or I'll ask Belle where you sleep."

Wings shifting tone, the pixy spun away. "Rache, I can't be in the ever-after after sunup."

His voice was scared, and shocked, I slowed as I pulled my nightgown over my head, snagging my hair. "I'm not going into the ever-after," I said, then covered myself when he almost turned back around.

"You're not?"

The cotton shirt rubbed my nose as I yanked it over my head. I couldn't help a faint smile at the amazement in his voice. "You think I'm crazy?" I said as I stuffed the shirt behind my jeans, then dropped to my knees to find my boots under my bed. "Ku'Sox is psychotic."

"Then what are you doing?" Jenks flew down to light the underside of my bed. Stretching, I snagged my boots and dragged them out. "You want me to call Felix? Bring the I.S. in on this?"

I sat on the floor of my room and tugged my boots on over my bare feet. "No I.S.," I said as I got the second boot on and looked at Jenks, my stomach empty and hurting. "But I am going to snatch that idiot out of the ever-after. If I'm lucky, he'll be with Lucy and Ceri, and we'll have them both." *Maybe that is his plan.*

The pixy's wings took on a bright silver hue. "Thank Tink's little pink—ah, rosebuds," he said in relief as I stood and reached for my door handle. "I thought you were going after Ku'Sox."

"Not this time."

My boots clunked on the hard wooden floor. I was not stupid, but I was angry. Trent had gone off without me. Right after we had a plan all worked out. Maybe the books were to distract me.

"She's not running off!" Jenks said brightly as he zipped into the kitchen ahead of me, and Belle turned from the kitchen window, her expression shocked.

"She's-s-s-s not?" she said, and I made a face at both of them.

"Good God, you think I'm stupid?" I said, then frowned when neither of them said a word. "Why should I go to the ever-after when all I want is Trent?" I said, holding up my hand so the light caught my pinkie ring.

"Hot piss on a toadstool!" Jenks exclaimed, and Belle waved at his orange sparkles in annoyance. "I forgot about that. You think it will work?"

My feet felt funny in my boots without socks between me and the leather, and I tapped a toe on the center counter's footplate. "Can't hurt to try." If it didn't work, I might try Newt. My gaze became distant as I remembered being bloody and beaten under Cincy's streets and using the ring to jump me out and finding it jumped the other person in. It hadn't been exactly what I had wanted, but that's the way wild elf magic worked.

It had better work again, I thought as I looked down at it, my knees feeling funny as I recalled the words to invoke the charm. *Ta na shay.* I needed to find out what that meant.

I took a breath. *Grown-up decisions,* I thought, thinking that Ivy would be proud of me. "One seriously angry elf, coming up!" I said, tapping the line out back and spinning the ring on my finger. "*Ta na shay!*"

But then my breath came in with a gasp as the ley line in the back reached out and yanked me into it.

"No!" I shouted, the last thing I saw before the line took me completely being Belle's and Jenks's shocked expressions as I vanished from my kitchen.

Chapter Sixteen

Wild elven magic coursed through my mind, electricity tasting of wine and music sparkling to my fingertips. The usual welcoming hum was a screeching din, and my stomach gave a heave when a wave of dizziness hit me, evidence of an unbalanced line. I was in a freaking ley line! *Bring Trent to me!* I wailed, promising the goddess that Trent didn't believe in everything and anything.

He needs you more than you need him tinkled through me, alien and wild, and I was shoved out of the line.

Arms flailing, I skidded on a white tiled floor. It shimmered under a cold electric light, and my nose wrinkled at the bitter bite of brimstone mixed with the acidic stench of burnt amber. I stood from my crouch, turning from the bank of electronic equipment and lab benches lining both the three sides and a short peninsula of the room to look behind me toward the muffled sound of crying babies. A glass wall stretched from waist height to the ceiling, showing what looked like a hospital nursery, complete with rolling bassinets and young women in uniforms tending them. There was no door. The women looked okay, and I wondered if they knew where they were or if they were borrowed familiars.

"Trent?" I whispered, glad that Ku'Sox hadn't felt me arrive. He had to be here somewhere. Stupid rings. I hated wild magic. It wasn't that there were no rules. I just didn't understand them.

My heart pounded when the familiar sound of a pen hitting the floor and a chair rolling joined the humming of machinery and Trent rolled backward out from behind the peninsula of shoulder-high machines. Shocked, he stared at me.

He was haggard, wearing a lab coat over his expensive slacks and linen pinstripe shirt as if it was a uniform. His usual tie was absent. Red-rimmed and haunted, his eyes blinked numbly at me. His hair was mussed, and his posture as he sat in that chair gave the impression of his insides caving in. He looked as if he'd been gone a year, not four hours. "What are you doing here?" he rasped, the music entirely gone from his voice. "Are you crazy?"

He needs you more than you need him echoed in my memory. "Maybe." I held up my hand with the pinkie ring on it. "I'm trying to get your ass back to reality. I thought we had some sort of understanding." Understanding. That wasn't like an agreement—which had definite expectations. Understanding was more nebulous, more dangerous. What was I doing, trusting Trent with an *understanding*?

His expression cleared somewhat, and Trent frowned. "I'm not leaving." He stood, so fast that his chair rolled backward. Lab coat furling, he scooped up his dropped pen, proving he could do businessman, playboy, and lab rat equally well. "You need to leave," he said as he jotted something into a lab book. "Go. *Now*. Before Ku'Sox finds you."

Go? Now? I wasn't a dog, but seeing as I had no easy way of leaving other than Jenks summoning me back, I crossed my arms and stared at him. Ku'Sox wouldn't know I was here unless he walked in the door or I tapped a line. My eyes went over the assembled machinery, all humming and clicking. Obviously he and Ku'Sox had come to some *understanding*. Damn it, I thought we had a plan. Must be the cost analysis had finally tipped the scales.

"Is that it?" I said, and Trent looked up, still standing hunched over his book, his back almost to me, stiff and cold.

"Is that what?"

I gestured at the instruments. "The machine that saved my life?" It was as close as I would go to an outright accusation of his helping Ku'Sox, and his ears reddened.

"No, it's better by about three generations," he said, still making notes. "Once I get the strand of DNA I want, I incorporate it into a mild-acting virus that targets the mitochondria. I'm not entirely happy with the strand I'm currently using. I didn't have a chance to clean it before proliferation." His pen stopped. Slowly he straightened and looked down at his lab book. "It has a seventy-seven percent perfection, which will cause problems in some of the subjects, but Ku'Sox is a butcher, and if twenty-three percent of his *children* die, then he will be happy with the seventy-seven remaining."

I blanched, turning to look at the empty bassinet and the rows of babies—eating, sleeping, crying. There had to be at least a dozen out there. "That's inhuman."

Trent gazed at the nursery, a lost expression on his face. "He would've been happy with twenty percent."

My lips curled. "You're helping him," I accused, and Trent's eyes narrowed. "You told me you'd never give him what he wanted!"

His eyes bore into mine. "Is that what you think I'm doing?"

"Hey, if the lab coat fits."

Making a low sound of discontent, Trent hunched back over his book. Thinking that might have been harsh, I went to the nursery window, my hand cold when it touched the glass. It was obvious that the women could see us, but they went about their business with a blind furtiveness that told me they knew they were alive on sufferance—until Ku'Sox didn't need them anymore. "He took their nurses, too?" I asked in guilt. I couldn't save everyone.

"In some cases."

His words had come from the back of his throat, and the hidden tight disgust in it made me take a second look. All the women had red hair. "Oh," I said, feeling uncomfortable. "Is there another way out of here?"

"I said I was not leaving."

The anger in his voice turned me back around. "Stay here?" I said, hand on my hip. "I thought we had a good plan. Thanks for nothing. Where's Bis? Have you seen him?"

Snagging his rolling chair with a foot, Trent expertly wrangled it around until he could sit. "He's fine," he said, so low I could almost not hear it. "The older gargoyles are very keen on talking to him when Ku'Sox isn't watching."

"Maybe they're teaching him the resonances of their lines," I said, wondering if there might be something good in this after all.

His head bowed, Trent kept writing. Ticked, I came to see what he was doing, and he looked up. "Bis knows the line in the garden," I said. "Where's Ceri and Lucy?" His jaw quivered, and I added, "Bis can jump us all out."

What in hell is his problem? I thought when Trent ran a slow hand over his face, almost ignoring me. "You keep saying you want to work together; well, how about accepting a little help? Trent, pay attention to me!"

Finally he looked up, anguish flashing behind his eyes before he whispered, "Ceri is dead. And Pierce."

My heart seemed to stop. I took a faltering step, my face cold. He had to be joking! But Trent's face was pale and his red-rimmed eyes had new meaning as I staggered back against a bank of machines. "Ceri and Pierce?" I whispered, looking through the wall as if I could see Pierce. I'd just seen him. Just talked to him. "Why?"

But then I figured it out. I'd *just* seen him. *Just* talked to him. Oh God, this was my fault. I'd talked to Pierce, rekindled his belief that he was a demon killer. *Ceri would help him . . .* Hand to my stomach, I tried to find something to say, my mind blank.

Seeing my understanding, Trent turned back to the lab book as if it was the only thing real left to him. "What happened?" I breathed. I already knew the why for everything: why Trent was here doing what Ku'Sox wanted, why he'd left with no warning, breaking the only easy way for anyone to follow, why he was closed and distant. Ku'Sox had called Trent's bluff. "What. Happened!"

My hand shook as it landed on Trent's shoulder. He didn't move, either to acknowledge my touch or shake it off. "She and Pierce got it into their heads they could overpower him if they worked together," he said flatly, and I closed my eyes against the heartache. This was my doing. *Oh God. Quen. Ray.*

"Ku'Sox told me they tried to kill him in his sleep and that in retaliation he had every right to burn Pierce alive with their own joined curse," he said, his tone frighteningly empty. "I have no reason to doubt that's exactly what happened. If Ceri thought she could take him, she'd try. Especially if he had been threatening Lucy. Ceri died several hours later. As best as I can gather."

I could hardly breathe, my chest hurt so badly. I wanted to rage that he was wrong, that Ku'Sox was tricking him into giving him what he wanted. But the memory of Ceri and Pierce working together to twist a black curse to kill fairies in my garden rose up, making my stomach sink. She'd been impressed with his skill, and Pierce had been trying to kill demons half his living existence and all of his dead. It had been all I could do to keep Pierce from trying to attack Ku'Sox yesterday. *Had it only been yesterday?* I thought, gazing at my burned fingers.

A tear brimmed and fell, splashing on them, and I made a fist. I didn't love Pierce, but it still hurt, still ached. *And Ceri.* She had been so happy, so alive. She finally had the family that she thought she never would. Now it was gone? She was dead?

My grief began to shift to anger. I could do things when I was angry.

"Ellasbeth didn't tell me any of this," I said, and Trent looked up, blinking as if he was rearranging his thoughts.

"Ellasbeth doesn't know," Trent said, his chest heaving with a sudden breath.

"Quen?" I asked, my voice rising at the end into a squeak. "Does Quen know?" Ellasbeth said he was in the basement trying to get the vault door open. If he managed it, he would be cut down in seconds, helpless without his magic.

Trent was writing in that book again, his numbers careful and precise. "Quen removed her body from my office," he said dully. "Ku'Sox left her there for me."

I thought I was going to throw up. Trent was calm, but I could see the rage underneath. Lucy had to still be alive. "Lucy? Bis?" I asked, and his writing hand faltered.

"Alive," he said, and my rapid breathing sounded harsh. "For the time being. You should leave before he finds you. Our plan can still work. You'll have to do much of it alone, though."

My anger bubbled over, and I pushed up from the machine, shaking. "Our *plan*?" I shouted, and he looked up, his expression horribly blank. "How can you sit there making notations! They're dead!"

Trent looked down at the book, his mutilated hand showing strongly on the lined paper. "He has a book mirroring mine. If I don't keep writing, he'll know something has captured my attention, and he'll come and see. You need to leave." Numb, he wrote the time and initialed it. The pen hitting the paper sounded loud, and he turned to look at me straight on.

Numb. He was numb, but there was a seething anger fueled by helplessness underneath. My mouth went dry as I realized he was on a knife's edge. He could do anything. He had vowed to keep his daughter and Ceri safe, and now Ceri was dead.

"Trent, I'm sorry," I whispered, and his eye twitched. "This is not fair."

"Fair?" he said, his anger showing. "When has fair ever entered into my life?"

I backed up as he struggled to take one careful, deliberate breath after another. "When fate levels the field," he said flatly, "the rich man finds himself struggling to survive while the man plagued with bad luck his entire life is ironically strong enough to prosper. I'm both, Rachel. I'm both." He hung his head, his fine hair hiding his eyes. "I wanted to believe that love could survive that which fate decrees, that love could remain when all is taken from you. But now . . . The Goddess has surely left me."

"I didn't think you believed in her," I whispered.

His eyes were empty when they met mine. "Chance can't build such a pit as I'm in. Only a god."

Trent rocked forward, and I jumped, startled. "There's no reason you can't carry on with our plan," he said suddenly, his voice holding a frantic determination. "I can't help you, even after you find something to bind multiple strengths together. I have to stay here and keep Lucy safe." He took my shoulders and gave me a shake. "I will not leave her. I'm going to do everything he tells me to. You have to find what you need, get it, and make it work. Understand?"

His resolve scared me, and I nodded. "Yes."

He let me go, and I breathed again. "Quen maybe," he said. "He will protect you when you move the imbalance, show the demons what Ku'Sox has done, and if they do nothing, I will be here to kill him."

I blinked fast. "K-kill him?" I stammered, my thoughts flashing to Pierce. "Trent, you are *not* a warrior poet. If Ceri and Pierce couldn't do it, what makes you think you can!"

Trent turned, looking furious. "Don't—" he shouted, a finger pointing to make me drop back, and he lowered his voice, his eyes still virulent. "Don't tell me what I can and can't do," he whispered. The scent of spoiled wine and broken fern grew strong.

Frustrated, I rallied my courage. "No one else will! I know you're upset. I'm upset. But you can't kill Ku'Sox!"

He walked to the nursery wall and stood looking out at his handiwork. "Your morals are going to be the end of two worlds."

Morals? I could not believe I was hearing this, and I got in his face, standing between him and the nursery. "This has *nothing* to do with my morals, and everything to do with *how strong he is*! You were there! You saw! I don't care if the one ring to rule them all is in that museum, we can't overpower him. You don't have a plan, you have an obituary! Ceri tried with the help of an experienced, powerful witch, and now Ray has only one parent!"

Trent's hands clenched. "You don't think I know that?" he shouted, and I could hear babies crying through the window. "Why do you think I burned out the fuse to the vault? You shouldn't be here, either. Why are you here?"

He was going to try to kill him. He was going to dump the task of proving Ku'Sox's guilt onto me, and if the demons turned a blind eye, he was going to sacrifice everything to save Lucy. Ceri's death and Lucy's vulnerability had tipped him over the edge. "Please," I said, taking his hand and forcing him to pay attention to me. "Promise me you won't try to kill him. You're right about everything you said last night. Give me a chance to make it work. Trent, you came to me asking for trust. It goes both ways."

Trent grimaced, his head down to look at my hand in his. His fingers moved against mine, his delicate touch skirting my burned fingertips. "You don't know how powerful he is," I whispered, pity surging in me, and he brusquely pulled away.

"I'm sorry," I said, trying again, and this time, he let my hand stay on his shoulder. It was rock hard with tension. "I'm sorry. I loved her, too. Just . . . breathe," I continued, and listening, he took a ragged breath, holding it. "It's going to be okay." I moved closer, the bitter scent of burned cinnamon mixing with the burnt amber stench and making me ill. "Stay here and do what you need to do to keep Lucy safe. I'll find something to allow us to work together. It's a good plan, and it won't get us killed." *I hope.*

For a moment, he stood before me, and then he slowly went back to his book, brushing his hair from his eyes before he made a hasty notation. "I thought I could do this," Trent whispered to the uncaring pages. "I thought I could sacrifice anything to save my species." He looked up, shocking me cold. "I can't. She's my child, Rachel. *I can't.* If I can't find a way to make Lucy safe, I will do everything he tells me to. I will fail everyone and everything. I will sacrifice even my species for her well-being. It's upside down, and I . . . I can't change it."

My heart went out to him. He had changed, and everything was painfully new. Now . . . he might understand me. "You aren't doing this alone," I said. I knew the anguish of knowing what to do but not wanting to pay the cost for it.

Heartache showed in his eyes. Behind that was a desperate need to believe. "No?"

There was the barest hint of air movement, and Trent's eyes shifted over my shoulder. His expression went ugly, and heart pounding, I spun.

Nick. At least I thought it was Nick. My relief was short-lived, adrenaline shoving it out for my hatred. "You!" I exclaimed, sure it was him when I saw his smug expression. He was in jeans and a casual tee, slippers on his feet, looking thin but satisfied, with a clean-shaven face and a haircut that showed every one of his scars. "Did you know Ku'Sox killed Ceri and Pierce?"

Nick leaned back against the window, his ankles crossed confidently. "Who do you think helped cover Pierce's absence from Newt long enough for them to attack Ku'Sox?"

My jaw dropped. For three seconds, I took that in, the awful truth sifting through my brain. He had . . . Nick had lied to Pierce? Pretended he was helping them kill Ku'Sox and then left them in the lurch? "You son of a bastard!" I screamed, launching myself at him.

Nick put up a hand to ward me off, shifting at the last moment to shove me into the wall.

I floundered at the change of direction, snagging Nick's shirt. I yanked him down with me. I had time for one good breath before his elbow landed on my middle.

We were a tangle on the floor, and my abdomen felt like it was on fire. Struggling to breathe, I grappled with him, slamming his back into the floor and straddling him. He pushed at me, and I pinned his arms with my knees. Grabbing a handful of hair, I thunked his head into the floor.

"You betrayed Pierce?" I wheezed, hearing babies start to cry, muffled from the glass. "He killed them! You helped him kill them! Ceri is *dead* because of you! Ceri and Pierce are dead, and I could have loved him!"

Twisting, Nick shoved me off, a nasty snarl on his face. "You could have loved me, too."

He jumped at me, and I rolled, my back crashing into one of the machines. I shook my head to get the hair from my eyes. Nick was still coming right at me, and I braced myself. We went sprawling again. Nick hauled me into a sitting position, slamming my back up against the machine. "This is for bringing that putrid witch of yours into my apartment."

My eyes widened and I gasped in pain as his open hand met my cheek in a slap that sent stars through my vision. Trent was yelling, the babies were crying, and my eye felt like it was going to explode.

"And this is for the hell of it!" Nick whispered.

I put a hand up to stop him, and he grabbed it. His other hand was coming at me, and I struggled, trying to *get him off*!

But before his hand could connect, he was yanked backward and up. Knees going to my chest, I tossed the hair from my eyes at the sodden thunk of fist meeting flesh. Nick reeled into the counter, his feet slipping on the tile floor until he went down. Trent stood between us, his back hunched and shaking the pain from a bleeding hand.

"Son of a bitch." Touching his bleeding lip, Nick got to his feet. I could feel him begin to gather power, slowly but gaining momentum as a weird keening from the damaged line he was pulling on grew in the back of my head. I stood, so frustrated that I was almost crying. Nick had lied to Pierce and Ceri both. Told them he was helping when he was really setting them up. How could I *ever* forgive that?

"Rachel!" Trent shouted as he dived in front of me. I jerked my attention from him to Nick. A ball of green-tinted aura was headed right at us. Without thinking, I flung up a hand.

"*Rhombus!*" I shouted, and Trent stooped as Nick's spell struck and slithered down to the floor where it bubbled into nothing.

Nick was grinning when I brought my attention back up, and I felt sick. Now I'd done it.

Trent was holding my arm. "Are you hurt?"

I shook my head. "I just rang the doorbell," I said, then added, glowering at Nick, who knew exactly what he'd been doing, "I tapped a line. Ku'Sox knows I'm here."

Trent stiffened, and then he spun as Lucy's childlike voice rang out in delight. "Daddy!"

Trent went down on one knee as if he'd been shot, his breath a quick gasp as he stared at Ku'Sox, Lucy on his hip. His expression was fierce with love and desperate hatred, and I don't think I despised Ku'Sox more than at that moment. He was going to pay. Neither Ku'Sox nor Nick had ever loved anyone, and they would pay.

My pulse thundered in my ears, and I forced my arms to remain at my sides as I backed up to stand by Trent. Dressed in a casual black kimono, Ku'Sox had misted into the room beside Nick before the nursery window. Lucy's dress mimicked his, and her hand reached for Trent, delight in her eyes. Bis was with him, too, and my jaw clenched as the little guy launched himself toward me, only to be snagged by Ku'Sox and tossed behind him like a kite.

The gargoyle spun through the air out of control, his eyes bright and cheerful as he found the wind in his wings before hitting the wall. I'd swear he was having fun as he changed his out-of-control spiral into a snappy landing on top of one of Trent's machines where he perched, glowing a bright black. He was all right. *He was all right!*

Guilt rose, and I shoved it away. I would not feel bad that I was happy for Bis when Ceri and Pierce were dead. Nick had betrayed them. Why? What had he gained?

"You, stay where you are," the psychotic demon said lightly to Trent as he rose, face awash with heartache. "I already took your second child's mother. Make a move I don't approve of and we will explore what else you hold dear. Understand?"

The scent of cinnamon became strong as Trent struggled with himself. He had admitted that he couldn't sacrifice his daughter. It made him both strong and weak. He knew what it was to love. Maybe he'd always known, and I had been too blind to see it.

"Down!" Lucy demanded, looking sweetly petulant in her Asian kimono, and Ku'Sox shifted her into a football hold, her little feet kicking behind her and her hands pushing at his arm as she made a face and squirmed. "Da-a-a-ddy-y-y!" Clearly not liking Lucy's frustration, Bis curved his tail around his feet, his ears going flat against his skull.

Nick's feet scuffed as he edged even with Ku'Sox, and the demon gave him a disparaging glance. "Wait your turn, Nicholas Gregory Sparagmos," Ku'Sox said as he shoved Nick behind him with one hand splayed on the man's chest. "You can beat Rachel when I'm done with her. Besides, I want to hear why she's here. She might, I don't know . . . want something?" Bis spread his wings, and Ku'Sox looked at him until the gargoyle eased back. "A cup of sugar? An egg, perhaps?" Ku'Sox said, struggling with an increasingly vocal Lucy. "Are you doing a little cooking this afternoon, love?"

My eyes narrowed. "There was no need to kill Ceri and Pierce."

A hint of a smile lifted Ku'Sox's thin lips. "Simple enjoyment." He glanced at the nursery. "What a marvelous woman she was. Al taught her so many, *many* things. She lasted the entire morning. I didn't even have to be careful. Ahh, that's so rare, so invigorating."

Trent's jaw was clenched, and my stomach twisted. Lucy had both hands out, craning her neck to see Trent as her fists opened and shut, struggling to reach him, little whines of frustration punctuating her loud demands. "You should have left," Trent said. I could see parts of him starting to reassert themselves, assessing the situation, deciding what would be cast aside as unrecoverable and what might be salvaged. I wondered which side of the scale I was on.

"Ku'Sox won't kill me," I said, my insides shaking as I shifted my feet to find my balance. "If he does, the demons will start looking at him to fix the line."

Ku'Sox's expression twitched. "Just so. Unless you give me provocation, it's best to leave you alone. For a few days." Now he smiled, and again my loathing fought with my fear. "Which begs the question of what you are doing here, Rachel? Rescuing your familiar?"

Ku'Sox was moving. My heart pounded, and I backed up. Trent, though, didn't move.

"As he has probably told you, he is here of his own free will," the demon said, stopping to keep Trent just out of Lucy's high-pitched, angry reach. "We're good friends," Ku'Sox said as he smacked Trent's cheek. "The elf freed me, and in return, I'm going to free him of everything that binds him, no ties to anyone at all. Aren't we, little Lucy?"

Trent was almost panting as he stood inches from his daughter, afraid to reach out.

Laughing, Ku'Sox turned away. Under his arm, Lucy cried her frustration.

"I'm not leaving here without Bis and Lucy," I said, and Nick, leaning against the window and nursing a swollen lip, made a noise of derision. "Lucy is my godchild, and Bis lives with me. I think that comes under 'not harming me and mine.' I get ignoring the me part since you're an ass, but you will *not* harm them."

Sure enough, Ku'Sox smiled. "Rachel, Rachel, Rachel, I have no intention of harming you—unless you attack me first, of course. No one will fault me for defending myself. Please, do try. Then I can drop this charade and we can all move on with our lives. That's what this is all about, you know. Getting others to kill you for me. But interpretation of the law is so-o-o difficult," he drawled. "As I told you before, get the proper papers filed, and I will gladly hand Lucy over."

I slumped where I stood, the machines clicking behind me to mark time in this nightmare. Trent's face was ashen as Ku'Sox struggled with Lucy. "Down!" Lucy cried. "Down, down, do-o-own!"

Giving the girl a little shake, Ku'Sox shifted her to his other side, and her cries went from frustration to hopelessness. Behind him, Bis was waving me off, his gray-skinned hands making the pixy signal to go to ground. He wanted me to leave? Standing at the outskirts, Nick saw the gesture, but Trent didn't, his attention on Lucy as he became more and more agitated.

"They know you're lying," I said so the demon wouldn't notice Bis talking to me.

"Of course they do." He turned to Nick, growling, "Get me that chair." His expression again pleasant, he smiled at me. "Is it not deliciously ironic? My lie is far more attractive than your truth. If they subscribe to my lie, they don't have to do anything about me—leaving it for you to handle or die. Which you will do if you persist."

His motions furtive, Nick darted between Trent and the machines for the chair. He looked like a bug, and my lip curled. "I know demons better than you do, Ku'Sox Sha-Ku'ru. They always bite the hand that feeds them." Nick trundled the rolling chair back to Ku'Sox, and it was all I could do to not reach out and kick him.

"Daddy! Down!" Lucy demanded, her eyes wet as she stared at Trent as if betrayed.

Ku'Sox held Lucy in front of him, looking scornfully at the little girl as she howled. "You've noticed that as well?" he said dryly as he sat with Lucy on his lap. She began squirming, her little feet kicking as she struggled. "My God," Ku'Sox said, his patience clearly wearing thin. "This child is intractable! I should have taken the younger one."

"Honor our agreement!" I said. "Or I will drag your ass before Dali right now!"

"Of course I will honor it. Go file the papers. Come back in three months." Ku'Sox's eyebrows were mockingly high. "Unless you want to settle this a different way?"

Trent paled, and in the corner, Nick shifted to make himself look smaller. If I could free Lucy, then Trent might be free to act when I got that line cleared of the sludge in it. "I'm a reasonable man," Ku'Sox said, bouncing Lucy, which made her cry even harder. "I'm sure we can come to a mutually agreeable arrangement. I want my freedom, Rachel. *Now.*"

I backed up, remembering the feel of Ku'Sox's breath on my skin, his grip on my body, the way his eyes touched me. I shook my head, and Ku'Sox smiled knowingly.

"Down, down, down!" Lucy raged, and his gaze never leaving mine, the demon let her slip from him. Immediately she got to her feet, running awkwardly to Trent. My heart seemed to break as Trent dropped down to meet her, holding her tight as his eyes closed, his hand covering the back of her head and his arm around her, lifting her to him. His eyes opened, and I saw his fervent surety that nothing short of death would ever convince him to let go of her again.

Son of a bitch, I thought, looking at Ku'Sox's soft smile of satisfaction.

We were his playthings, dancing to his whim. To say no now would start a bloodbath none of us would survive. Trent would never let Lucy go back to Ku'Sox again. "What do you propose?" I said flatly, having a pretty good idea. He had killed Ceri and Pierce. I wouldn't give him the chance to kill Lucy.

"Rachel!" Bis complained, wincing when Ku'Sox raised a hand.

Trent looked up, his arms still about Lucy. The little girl was complaining fretfully to him, her words unclear but serious. Behind Ku'Sox, I could see the women and children beyond the glass. *I'm sorry. I'm so sorry. I can't save you all.*

"I want my freedom," Ku'Sox said with a disturbing lightness. "I want that putrid elven curse you put on me lifted, and I want it lifted now."

"I want Bis and Lucy, and a trip home," I said, and he laughed, wiping a spot of baby drool from his sleeve.

"What horrid things babies are. Leaking from every orifice."

"You said what you want; well, I want Bis and Lucy!" I demanded again as Nick fidgeted behind Ku'Sox. Trent held Lucy tighter, standing up with her as if he would never let her go. He'd do anything for her. Anything. Kisten had looked at me that way once, and it had killed him. Ceri's death was both Trent's awakening and his downfall. He loved, he knew loss, and he would fight to keep what was dear to him, the rest be damned.

Ku'Sox told Nick to stop fidgeting with a sharp look. "Both? No. Trent is a nasty little elf. With Lucy gone, he will become most intractable. See? He's sullen already. And Bis? Well, that's obviously no. With him, your chances of preventing the end of the ever-after slip into the double digits."

Bis seemed to deflate in relief. I didn't like the way Nick noticed, and I cringed when Ku'Sox half turned to look at the gargoyle. "Don't think I don't know what you're doing, flying worm. You're talking to everyone's gargoyles and learning the lines because I see fit. When the demons die, their gargoyles go with them, and I will want someone familiar with the old lines so I can reinstate them."

Reinstate the lines? The words hit the pit of my being with a cold certainty. He was intending nothing less than complete destruction. This wasn't just to get the demons to kill me then return to business as usual. Ku'Sox was aiming at genocide.

"Then I guess we ought to just duke it out now," I said as I reached out with my thoughts and tapped the line. It filled me, screaming a discord that melded with my thoughts and flashed through me like grief. *God, please give me another way out.*

"I would consider giving you Lucy, though," Ku'Sox said, glancing at Trent's pinkie ring, and I froze, not believing I'd heard him right. Trent looked up, hope so deep in his eyes it hurt.

Nick stiffened in his corner. "L-Lucy?" I said, a part of my mind realizing that the scum bucket was afraid of me. *He was afraid!* My air came in with a rush, and I dropped the line, pulling myself straight and seeing Ku'Sox's fear in the way he held his head, squinted at the light. Lucy for his freedom? Two days ago I would have spit in his face, but now . . .

My gaze shot to Trent, his grip on his child almost frantic.

Smiling as if giving benediction, Ku'Sox inclined his head. "I will give you Lucy," he said softly, but his hem was shaking. "That is"—he looked at Trent, silent across the room with Lucy in his grasp—"if Trenton Aloysius Kalamack agrees to take the place of his daughter as my *familiar,* and you take that curse from me so I might see the sun again. I do so miss the color yellow."

Trent stood ashen-faced as Lucy softly complained of nothing. He knew what it was to be a demon slave. I had rescued him from it, and he had saved my life. Now he was going to give his own again to save his daughter, to save two worlds.

"Done," Trent rasped, his expression riven with grief as he pushed Lucy into my arms. "Take her, Rachel," he said, his arm stretched out to touch his daughter's hand as he stepped back, his eyes fixed to the little girl reaching back to him. She leaned toward him, whining, and I held her close, smelling the clean scent of her hair under the stench of burnt amber.

Take the curse from him? He could go anywhere . . .

"I say, done!" Trent shouted. "Send them home!"

Ku'Sox seemed shocked. I know I was. Things were moving too fast, and I jiggled her weight, settling her to me until it felt natural. "I thought elves were known for their patience," Ku'Sox said, and my gut twisted when he looked at me. "Rachel, is this acceptable to you, providing the elf holds to his end and I have him, body and soul?"

Crap on toast. If Trent was his familiar, he couldn't help me. That wasn't even considering that Ku'Sox would have access to everything on my side of the lines. But with Nick, he had that anyway. Torn, I jiggled Lucy. Oh my God. I was going to do it, and I felt light-headed.

"Take her, I beg you." It was Trent, and I took in his hope, his grief. "Take her," he whispered again. "I need to know they are safe, my girls."

"Oh, they will never be safe," Ku'Sox said, and Trent stiffened.

"They will, or I will not agree!"

Eyes rolling to the ceiling, Ku'Sox idly pushed his rolling chair back, gesturing lightly. "As long as you serve me faithfully, why not?"

Trent's grip on my shoulder tightened, his breath coming fast in the moment of success, but I was having doubts. My eyes slid to Nick, sullen in the corner. I took a breath to answer. Ku'Sox waited, poised. Nick was tense behind him, looking like a spider. Trent was energy chained—frantic. And Bis . . . I held my breath, trying not to be obvious as I watched him signal me to fly, go, flee . . . no, I think that particular motion meant fall back and circle around.

My heart pounded. Bis was learning how to line jump. And with Lucy safe with me, there was only Trent's life in the balance. He clearly was ready to sacrifice it. The question was, did I trust him enough to give him a chance to kill Ku'Sox? I needed help with my plan, and Quen and Al were still out of commission. I didn't know who to ask.

"Throw in a trip home for Lucy and me, and you have a deal," I whispered, and Ku'Sox clapped his hands, springing to his feet to make me drop back several steps, awkward from Lucy's weight. "But you will stay out of my church and the environs. Swear to it, Ku'Sox."

"Capital! I agree! I swear!" Ku'Sox said, looking amused, but seeing a black haze blossom on his hand, I bubbled us. Lucy and I weren't his target, however.

I spun as Trent hit the floor, choking as he grasped his throat. "Hey!" I shouted, backing up with Lucy, the little girl frightened and growing heavy. "You kill him, and all your demon babies are going to die!"

Ku'Sox strode over, and I backed up, breaking my circle. "That is my foot you feel across your neck," the demon said, leaning over Trent as he gasped. "Serve me without elven trickery, or it will crush your throat, and then I will move on to your children, your family, and everything you hold dear. Do you understand?"

Sprawled, Trent nodded, hatred burning in his eyes, his hand splayed out to show the missing digits that Al had taken from him. "If you harm them, nothing will save you," he rasped, and Ku'Sox straightened his kimono with a soft hush.

"Good," he said, looking down at him. "You have spirit. I'll enjoy it after the ever-after no longer occupies me." Making a sudden puff of distaste, Ku'Sox reached down, yanking Trent's pinkie ring off. My eyes widened when he made a fist, opening it to let a shapeless mass of black char ping dully on the tile floor. He'd melted it. Two in a row. "Get up."

His attention shifted to me, and I held Lucy closer, turning her so she couldn't see her dad pick himself up off the floor. My feet moved uneasily. I still needed to get home.

"My freedom?"

My eyes flicked uneasily between Trent and Ku'Sox. Lucy felt heavy in my grasp as she cried for Trent. It wasn't as if I could just pop out and conveniently forget to free him. The curse had been embedded into his DNA and wouldn't lift easily. The best I could do was modify it. Swallowing hard, I reached out and tapped the line again. I could feel the collective, hovering just outside my awareness, and I let a small portion of myself slip into it. I'd need the strength of them to make any changes, and I was disgusted when I found them waiting, quiet and still in a watchful unease. The sons of bitches knew. They knew.

My head began to throb behind my right eye as the discordant twang the collective had absorbed from the broken lines soaked into everything. Lucy's crying stopped, and I wondered if she was picking up more than she should. "*Si peccabas poenam meres,*" I whispered, the faint memory of a beating drum and stomping feet drifting through my memory as I began the curse anew. Tingles of wild magic sparked through me, and a hazy lassitude dulled my headache. There was an odd pulling sensation as the curse gathered itself within Ku'Sox.

Ku'Sox stiffened, his shoulders twisting as if something had struck his back. His eyes were alight, and his hands in fists. "Finish it. Free me!"

I licked my lips, my heart pounding. I couldn't look at Trent. He had taught this curse to me, learned it from Ku'Sox. It could not be untwisted, but it could be given away or modified. "I curse you, Ku'Sox Sha-Ku'ru, to be free of restraint, that you may freely travel between reality and the ever-after at your will for as long as you *leave me and mine alone!*"

The demon's breath sucked in, and he leaned forward, grimacing at the added restraint.

"That means you stay out of my church, you bastard," I said, relishing his anger. "You break it, and you'll find out how the Goddess rewards liars," I barked at him, heart pounding when a sleepy-eyed presence seemed to swirl through me, laughing languorously before dulling back to slumber. Crap on toast, elven magic was slippery stuff, and I gave a little jump to shift Lucy to a more comfortable position and hide my shudder.

Ku'Sox lifted his chin as if to denounce me. But when he nodded with very bad grace, I sealed the curse. *"Facilis descensus Tartarus."*

The curse was in Latin, but I knew it was elven magic by the tiny laugh of wicked delight echoing in my mind. It hadn't come from the collective, and Ku'Sox shuddered as the wild magic slipped reluctantly from me and onto him, the last bit twanging from my outstretched hand. My headache came back, pounding, and before I dropped the line, I felt the souls of the demons in the collective withdraw. They were somber and still, unusual for the usually vocal and self-assured demons. They'd agreed to this, but it had the transparent feeling of ambiguity.

Ku'Sox breathed slowly, and in the corner, Nick hunched into a small shadow of fear. "It will do," Ku'Sox said, and then his eyes became slate gray. "Leave. You smell like baby shit."

Lucy was starting to fidget, and I glanced at Trent. He looked crushed and beaten. "I told you I wanted a jump home. Al can't do it," I said, deciding he would refuse unless I gave him a reason. "He burned himself at the bottom of your purple sludge."

Ku'Sox looked me up and down in surprise. "And he got out? How?"

He wasn't wearing the smile I expected, and I patted Lucy, rocking like I'd seen parents in the grocery store line do. "Through his wedding rings." Ku'Sox's eyes went wide in amazement, and I shook my head, backing up. "Send us home," I demanded. *"Now."*

Trent's eyes closed, and I saw his lips move in a silent "Thank you," but if he was thanking me or the Goddess he didn't believe in, I didn't know.

"Go," Ku'Sox said curtly, and I tensed, slapping a bubble of thought around Lucy and myself as I felt his broken, slimy presence enfold us and push us from his reality. For a moment, I thought he might leave us halfway there and I'd have to chance shifting my aura myself, but then the stink of ever-after fell away, and the ground grew firm under my feet. The late-morning sun spilled through the new spring leaves, and I shivered, feeling winter in the spring damp.

"Home again, home again, jiggity jig," I said, patting Lucy.

"Aant achel!" the little girl said, laughing as she patted her middle. "Tickles!" I could only assume she meant the sensation of the line through her, but then her eyes widened as she saw the sleeping gargoyles perched everywhere. "Shhh," she said. "Biz-z-z-z nap."

I shifted her weight, not wanting to put her down and risk her trying to touch one. "That's right," I said as I headed for the church. "Bis is napping. Let's go call your abba." Oh God. Quen. Trent had been fond of Ceri, but Quen had loved her with the depth reserved for one who thought he'd never love at all. For once, I was glad he was injured and unable to do magic. If he had been otherwise, he'd likely be dead by now, too, having pitted himself against Ku'Sox.

"Abba!" Lucy crowed, wiggling in delight before she went still in thought. "Cookie?" she added hopefully, and my eyes filled as Lucy patted the dandelion fluff tattoo on my neck.

The sun was shining and I was home, but the reality of what had happened was falling on me anew. Ceri had died protecting Lucy. I'd make sure that Lucy knew that when she was older. "And a cookie," I said miserably as Jenks's kids found us, distracting the little girl and making her stretch for their clattering wings and bright voices.

I slowly trudged to the church through the pixy dust, wondering if the kitchen, at least, was baby proofed. I'd have to move my splat gun, bare minimum.

What had I been thinking? Ku'Sox was free. Ceri and Pierce were dead, Trent was a demon slave, again, and the son of a bitch was free.

Chapter Seventeen

The late afternoon sun was gone from the kitchen as I sat at the table, depressed as I stared at the defunct disguise amulet perched in my fingertips. I wasn't in the best of moods to be trying something so difficult as breathing life into a ley line charm that had been dead for more than ten years, but I wanted some practice before I tried this again with some rich elf's one-of-a-kind family heirloom.

I'd already found the charm I wanted from the brochure, checking the description and the owner's claims of powers against an account found in one of the books Trent had gotten from the library. Quen was going to bring it over when he came to pick up Lucy. He was overdue, and I hoped everything was okay.

"Rings," I said sourly, looking at the charm balanced on my hand. Why couldn't it be a sword or whip or something pointy? But no, elves apparently had a thing for rings, and the set I'd chosen seemed perfect, allowing a strong connection that would allow me to join my strength to Quen's or Trent's. It wasn't made for war, and I hoped that meant elves *and* demons could use it. That Al would be healed up enough to help me was nothing I wanted to count on.

"If, if, if," I muttered as I stared at the charm balanced on my fingertips. I was putting the F back in *if,* and I didn't like it. Time was stealing my buffer for when *if* turned to *no*. I was starting to hate two-letter words.

I'd thought that practicing reinvoking old charms would be a good idea. I just wished I wasn't blowing my dad's old charms to hell, one by one. It didn't help that I was trying to be quiet as Jenks read to Lucy in the back living room, or that a handful of pixies were playing in my dad's dusty box, giggling and whispering as they plotted mischief. Between the catchy rhymes from next door, the giggling whispers, and me thinking Jenks had hidden Pierce's old watch from me so I couldn't try to resurrect him, it was hard to concentrate.

Indecision had made me cranky, but I figured if Pierce was able to be summoned back to a temporary life, he would be changing my ringtones. My phone had been distressingly silent. Ceri and Pierce were gone, and my heart ached more than I could have imagined.

Stifling a sneeze from the dusty box, I exhaled, balancing the defunct disguise ley line charm and pushing my aura off my hand. The weird mental gymnastics needed to shift my aura to different shades was getting easier, but leaving my hand mostly bare of protection made it ache.

"Hey!" I shouted when the flap of the box flipped out, almost hitting me. Dust rolled up, and I sneezed, earning six high-pitched "bless-yous" from the pixies giggling inside. "Okay, everyone out!" They rose up, a charm between them as they apologized, begging to stay. "Out," I reaffirmed, holding my hand under the charm, and they dropped it. The tarnished silver fell into my hand, a pool of gold pixy dust seeming to warm it as they apologized again.

"Out, and stay away from Lucy! She's finally settled down!" I called after them, and they were gone, out through the flue in the back living room if the squeals of Lucy's delight were any indication. I relaxed a bit as I listened to Jenks's voice murmur in rhyme, soothing as I set the charm back in the box. Wiping my nose, I sneezed again, but it was only a sneeze. I didn't expect to hear from Al until it was too late. I was on my own, and I thought it ironic that elves were going to help me save the ever-after and all demonkind.

Exhaling, I emptied my mind of everything but the ring of metal perched in my hand, imagining the smallest whisper of red I could puddling under it. With just the barest nudge, I sent a tiny mote of aura up to the amulet. I held my breath as my aura drifted closer, the glyphs etched into the charm beginning to glow. My heart pounded, and I squinted as the ping of energy grew closer, closer, almost touching the metal. A glowing haze over the amulet moved faster, and when my aura touched the charm . . .

"Ow!" I shouted as my hand cramped up. Jolts of energy darted through my fingers as the full spectrum of my aura raced to protect my hand, and I dropped the charm. From the window came a tiny shattering of glass.

"You okay?" Jenks called, Lucy's voice rising as well, mimicking his tone perfectly though the words were nonsense.

"Fine!" I exclaimed, frowning when I looked at the window. The brandy snifter on the sill was busted, Al's chrysalis amid the thick shards. "Nice." Setting the defunct amulet aside, I stood, my nose wrinkling at the burnt amber smell coming off the chrysalis.

"Rachel?" Quen's voice called, strong but faint from the front of the church, shortly followed by the slamming of the door into the wall. "Are you in back?"

A bittersweet feeling took me, and I plucked the large chunks of glass out of the sink and dropped them in the trash. "Yes!" I exclaimed, and Lucy mimicked my call again.

A feminine clatter of high heels in the hallway gave me pause until I remembered Ellasbeth. I barely had time to run a hand over my hair before the woman skidded to a halt in the kitchen doorway, her eyes bright, her lips parted, hair a mess and her coat buttoned wrong. "Where?" she said, her eyes roving my kitchen and my empty arms.

"Abba?" Lucy called from the back living room, and Ellasbeth spun. "Abba!" It was demanding this time, and Ellasbeth bolted.

"Oh! My baby!" she said, but she was gone and I was alone, wondering how this was going to go over. Lucy probably didn't remember her. Sure enough, frightened, intolerant baby protest rose amid Ellasbeth's dramatic tears. "Lucy! Are you all right? I missed you so much! Look at you. You smell terrible, but I missed you so much. Oh, you got so big!"

I probably didn't smell all that good either, and I shoved the window open a crack to let the cool spring air pool on the floor. In the back room,

Lucy began to fuss in earnest, her complaints almost unheard over Ellasbeth. "It's going to complicate things," Jenks's voice came softly from the hall, mixing with Quen's footsteps. "We just have to be more careful."

Jenks and Quen came in as I turned from the window, Ray on Quen's hip, looking sweet with her dark hair and in her tartan kilt and hat. Ceri's death came rushing back, and suddenly tears blurred my vision. Damn it, I hadn't wanted to cry, but seeing him there with his motherless child and knowing that the girl would grow up without Ceri's love was almost too much to take.

"Don't," Quen said raggedly as Jenks hovered uncertainly at his shoulder, and I forced my eyes wide, sniffing the tears back. Quen's own eyes glistened, the limitless pain in his soul showing. "Please don't," he said stoically. "I'll grieve when the war is over. I can't afford it now."

I nodded, head down as I shoved my heartache away. *War.* That was about right. Quen looked capable in his short leather jacket and cap, like a bad boy grown up with a '79 Harley parked in a three-car garage and a huge mortgage. The child on his hip somehow worked perfectly. Grief shimmered under his tight jaw and haunted eyes. "I'm sorry," I said, feeling helpless as he came into the kitchen and set Ray on the center island counter, his hand never leaving her, steadying her as she sat upright and silently watched the pixies who had come in with them. "None of this was your fault."

"It feels like it is."

But it wasn't, and I leaned against the sink, aching at the sounds of Ellasbeth reuniting with her child. It hurt knowing Ceri never would. The pixies in the rack were taking turns dusting different colors, and Ray was riveted. Both Quen and Jenks began to look uncomfortable as Ellasbeth's noises became louder.

Quen steadied Ray, and remembering Jenks's cryptic comment when he had come in, I said, "So, what's up, Jenks? More trouble?"

Sitting on the faucet, Jenks frowned. "Jax is around." The draft from the window pushed his depressed copper dust from him like a wayward aura. "The kids heard his wings not five minutes ago. And where Jax is, Nick probably follows."

"Ku'Sox is trying to get around our agreement," I said as I went to get a paper towel from the roll we kept on the table, a must when living with pixies. Ku'Sox had Trent, body and soul. He was also uncursed, which meant he didn't need Nick anymore. That made the slimy man dangerous because he would be trying to prove to Ku'Sox that he was still worth something.

The rip of the paper towel was loud as I listened to Ellasbeth say, "Mama, not Abba. Mama, Lucy. Mama." I couldn't help my frown. Ceri was her mama, not Ellasbeth.

Jenks flitted to the counter, his wings still as he walked to the edge. "Don't worry, Rache. We won't let crap for brains or Jax close enough to know what's going on."

"Thank you, Jenks," I said as I dampened the paper towel and wiped the inside of the sink to get the tiny shards of glass. I had the beginnings of a plan that hinged on two rings I might not be able to use even if I could get them reinvoked.

Quen's guilty frown when I turned back around stopped me cold. "What?" I said flatly, and he winced. Jenks clattered his wings aggressively, coming to hover beside me. Together we made a united front, Ellasbeth's continued efforts to get Lucy to say mama an ugly backdrop.

Grimacing, Quen crouched with Ray, setting her on the floor, and gruffly saying, "Go say hi to your sister." Ray leaned forward into a crawl for the hallway, hesitating to study the feel of the circle I'd gouged out of the linoleum before crossing it.

"Ray!" Lucy crowed, and the little girl's feet disappeared with a gurgling giggle.

My faint smile faded as Quen rose, his eyes going to the scorch marks, then the ley line charms sitting next to the dusty box. "What aren't you telling us?" I demanded, and he clasped his hands before him.

"How badly do you need that particular pair of rings?"

Jenks rose up with a sound of disgust, and I threw the towel with the glass shards away, letting the cabinet door slam. "Pretty bad," I said tightly. "Why?" I couldn't tell if his grimace was because of the rings or because Ellasbeth was now crying at the girls' enthusiastic reunion.

"Ah, the family that promised their use won't give them to us now that Trent is missing."

Great. That's just freaking great.

Ellasbeth's soft, one-sided tearful conversation filtered in from the living room as Quen reached for a chair and sat down. It was unusual, but he was still recovering from the beating he'd taken Monday morning. He'd be on the cusp of having his aura back at full strength tomorrow. It sat sour in me that I'd be risking Ray growing up with no parent at all, but I needed someone to watch my back, and Quen would be shamed if I didn't ask him.

"I'll talk to them again," Quen said, clearly embarrassed. "Unless you want a different pair?"

I frowned. The only other pair that had any chance of making a strong enough connection between elf and demon was a pair that touted itself to be demon slavers. "I don't know how much it's going to matter," I said, frustrated as I started tidying, dropping my dad's old charms into the box one by one. "I'm having a hard time getting anything to reinvoke." Friday. I had until Friday night. "What do you mean they won't let me use their stupid rings?" I blurted suddenly, ticked. "Don't they know this is for the good of all elfkind!" Quen's eye twitched at Ellasbeth's ongoing passive-aggressive conversation with the girls aimed at us, not them. "Don't you have some kind of authority in his absence? I can probably move the imbalance, but without some power to back it up, I'm going to get smeared into a dark stain on an ever-after rock before any other demon can come out to verify Ku'Sox was behind it!"

Quen lifted a hand and let it fall, clearly at a loss. Jenks just shook his head and darted out of the room, his dust a bright silver. Yelling was getting me nowhere, and tired, I leaned back against the sink. Ivy would be back tonight. Maybe we could just go steal the damn rings.

Rex came in to curve around my ankles, and I ran a hand over my face.

"Can't you simply explain to the demons what Ku'Sox is doing?" Quen said. "They aren't stupid. Surely one of them can spot you. Al maybe?"

I never thought I'd *ever* see the day he would recommend a demon help me, and I smiled. It was short-lived, though. "No," I said flatly. "They're afraid down to the last one, and I'm not going to count on Al's aura being full strength in time." Quen's eyebrows rose, and I wiped my hands and leaned into the center counter. "They know what Ku'Sox is up to, better than I do. But the Rosewood babies Nick stole are Ku'Sox's bribes, life rafts for the demons who back him. They'll take a sure risk-free bet that might get them permanently in reality over standing up to Ku'Sox and possibly losing everything."

I hesitated, watching Rex make a slow, nonchalant way to the other side of the kitchen, her tail up and whiskerless face searching. In a fumbling, unbalanced jump from her lack of whiskers, Rex leaped onto the counter by the sink. I smoothly lifted her and set her back on the floor. The tip of the cat's tail twitched in displeasure as she stared up at the chrysalis. "I have to empty the line of the imbalances and survive long enough for the other demons to agree he broke it. Ku'Sox is stronger than me. Stronger than Newt. Really smart, huh? Making a child that no one can control?"

Quen exhaled in thought, and my stomach knotted. There were too many ifs. Too many maybes. I turned to the cupboard to get something to cover the chrysalis with. "If they don't give me the rings, I'm just going to go steal them."

The scrape of the glass going over the chrysalis was loud, and the silence grew as the pixies sang to Lucy and Ray, captivating them—and getting Ellasbeth to finally shut up. On a sudden impulse, I twisted Trent's pinkie ring off and shoved it under the glass with the chrysalis. Two days. Two freaking days. I didn't have the time to steal some dumb rings.

Jenks darted in, wincing at his offspring's noise. "You're overthinking this," the pixy said as he came to rest on Ivy's monitor where he could see the kitchen and a slice of the living room, too. "I say you get the rings, reinvoke them, forget the line, and just pop over to Ku'Sox's lair so you and Trent can kill the sucker."

"That's what Trent wants," I said, and Quen jerked his head up, clearly alarmed.

"Ah, Rachel?" the older man said, and I raised a hand.

"Relax, I'm not going to try to kill Ku'Sox," I said, though part of me cried out for revenge. A smarter bruised and battered part of me knew better. "I'm going to need your help, though, to hold off Ku'Sox after moving the imbalance. Will you be up for it Friday night?"

Friday night. Why did I always have to cut these things so close?

"Just try to do this without me," he grumbled.

Clearly unsure, Jenks dusted a dull gold, his wings blurring to nothing as he stood on the monitor. "Then that's the plan," I said, watching Rex pad out of the kitchen. "QED. Quite Easily Done." Or Quite Easily Dead, as my dad used to say.

It wasn't a great plan, but it was a plan, and the depressed silence in the kitchen grew until Ellasbeth began shouting at the pixies to get out. They were singing now, and Lucy was joining in, shrieking just for the hell of it. The woman needed help, but I wasn't going to go in there. Neither was Quen by the look of it, wincing from the shrill voices raised in rhyme and mayhem. Unable to take it anymore, Rex slunk past the kitchen, probably on her way to hide under my bed. Chaos. My life was chaos.

"So I guess the first thing would be to get the rings, preferably without Nick knowing?"

Jenks darted to the hallway to rescue Ellasbeth. "We're going to have to steal them."

Quen stood, his pox scars standing out sharp against his pale expression. "I'll talk to them again," he said, but Jenks was right. We'd have to steal them, and I stared at the ceiling, going through what I'd need. Rope, silence charms, something to remove aura residue . . .

"Worth a try," I said as Jenks yelled at his kids to get outside.

Finally there was only Lucy's loud "singing" as Jenks's kids left and Ellasbeth staggered into the kitchen, the weight of both girls nearly bringing her down. "Abba!" Lucy cried, her eyes alight as she reached for him. It about broke my heart, but in a good way. Quen immediately took her, having to forcibly pull the blanket-wrapped Lucy from Ellasbeth when the woman indicated he should take Ray instead.

"Coo ox! Coo ox!" Lucy crowed as she patted her blanket, then gently touched Quen's chin. "Abba, coo ox!"

My face warmed as Ellasbeth's eyes scanned my kitchen, lingering on the scorch marks, the water glass overturned on the windowsill, and finally to the dusty box. She said nothing, and I would have given a lot to know what she was thinking. Jenks whispered something into Quen's ear to make him blink, and she frowned. Ever stoic, Quen gently took Lucy's fingers and pulled them from his face. She was still going on about "coo ox." I had a bad feeling I knew what she was saying. Ellasbeth, though, was clueless.

"What does that mean, anyway? Coo ox?" the woman asked, clearly thinking our sudden silence meant we'd been talking behind her back.

"Ah, that's Ku'Sox," I said, and Ellasbeth's expression blanked.

"Coo ox!" Lucy crowed, making a show of smelling the blanket. Quen was mystified, but I winced as I figured it out.

"That's the blanket that Al gave me," I said. "It probably smells like the ever-after."

Horrified, Ellasbeth stood, her face red. "It *smells* like a *demon*!" she exclaimed, and ignoring Lucy's triumphant "Coo ox! Coo ox!" she snatched Lucy from Quen, pulling her out from the blanket and letting it fall to the floor.

Staggering under the weight of both girls, she settled herself in Ivy's chair. "Thank you for getting Lucy back to me," Ellasbeth said, her expression flashing into irate when she realized her coat was closed wrong as Ray patted the buttons.

Surprised, I stood straighter. "Ah, I just wish I could have gotten everyone out of there."

Ellasbeth's gaze came back from the window behind me. Pixies had plastered themselves against the kitchen screen, distracting the girls and making Jenks scowl. "Quen told me you bought Lucy's freedom at great risk to your own," she insisted. "I can't ever thank you enough. If there is anything, ever. At all."

I said nothing, a hundred things racing through my mind. She was going to be Trent's wife before too long, and something there really rankled me. He deserved better.

Jenks looked up at my silence, his motions to get his kids to leave faltering. "There is one thing," I said, and his dust shifted to an alarmed orange.

Ellasbeth blinked in surprise. "Name it," she said as if granting boons was her hobby.

Be nice, I thought, though it was hard, seeing her holding Ray and Lucy when Ceri no longer could. "I, ah, get that you and Trent are trying to make this work," I said, and Quen paled. "I think it's a great idea and all for everyone except Trent."

"Rachel?" Quen said, and Ellasbeth shot a look at him to shut up.

"Really? Do elaborate."

I knew it wasn't the polite thing, but no one else would say this, so I had to. "Do you think you could make half an effort to understand who he's trying to be?" I finished almost plaintively.

"I *beg* your *pardon*?"

Jenks winced, darting to the rack and out of range of anything. Quen also quietly stepped back. But hell, I had fought banshees and crazy vampires. If push came to shove, I could take her. Besides, what was she going to do with two babies on her lap? "He's great at being what you all need him to be," I said, gesturing at nothing. "Saving the elves and seeing you safe from the threat of extinction. But did it ever occur to you that he wants to be something else? Don't crush what he can keep for himself. That's all I'm asking. Let him have what he can."

Ellasbeth was white in anger. Lucy jumped in her lap blurting nonsense sounds, but Ray stared up at Ellasbeth and patted her trembling chin.

"Never mind," I said, dropping my head and sighing. "Go get married. Have more babies. Rule the world. You'll both be great at it."

"How dare you!"

I calmly watched her stagger to stand, and knowing it would infuriate her, I turned my back on her to get a glass of water. If she tried anything, I'd throw it on her.

"Quen! Take these children. Let me go!" she exclaimed from behind me, and I heard a scuffle. "Take your hands off me!"

The pixies at the window were watching with rapt attention, and I stifled a smirk.

"Don't do this," Quen said to her, his low voice gravelly.

"You will take your hands off me!" she insisted, and I let the water run until it got cold.

"Go wait in the car," Quen said. Then louder, "Go take the girls and wait in the car." Finally he shouted, "*Go wait in the car,* or I will stand by and let her say what she really thinks of you!"

I turned around with my glass of water. Jenks was watching from within a copper bowl hanging from the rack, a weird silty dust falling from it. Tense, Quen stood beside and a little in front of Ellasbeth. She was chalk white, her painted lips a bright contrast. I didn't care if she was insulted. It had needed to be said. I owed Trent that.

"I understand the strain you're under," she said, chin high as Lucy's hand patted her face. "So the door of friendship is still open between us. You mean a lot to Trent. He explained to me what happened at camp, and I understand your feelings for him."

My feelings for him? What happened at camp? What was she talking about?

Seemingly satisfied at my cautiously puzzled expression, she pulled herself straighter. "Please bring my fiancé home to us."

"That's my intent," I said dryly, and Quen tugged at her elbow. "But when I do, don't kill him slowly. Let the man breathe."

Eyes narrowed, she turned slowly under the weight of the girls and stalked to the hall. "Quen?" she said imperiously. "I will be waiting in the car. Call ahead and see that a bath is drawn for both girls by the time we get to Trenton's holdings. I want to stop on the way for an entirely new set of clothes for Lucy."

"It's only the clothes she has on that are tainted," Quen said, and the woman glared from the hallway.

"This entire church smells! She will have a new wardrobe!" she exclaimed, then *click-clacked* her slow, ponderous way to the door, the two girls calling in delight at the pixies waiting for them in the sanctuary.

Okay, that was probably going to come back and bite me on the ass, but I didn't care. Trent would thank me for it someday. Setting the water aside, I scooped up the blanket Ellasbeth had let fall and brought it to my nose. After three wash cycles, I couldn't smell anything, but I wasn't an elf.

Jenks whistled long and loud. "Damn, Rache, you sure know how to make friends."

Quen took the blanket from me, giving it a sniff as well. "Thank you for making the next forty minutes of my life hell," he muttered, clearly not smelling anything, either.

A tiny smile quirked the corner of my mouth up. "I'm sorry."

"No, you aren't," he said darkly. "You enjoyed it."

"Oh, you're just mad that I could say it and you couldn't." Taking the blanket back, I folded it up.

"Quen!" Ellasbeth shouted. "Come open this door! My hands are full with the children."

"I'll get it," Jenks offered, and Quen shot him a thankful glance. Immediately my mood swung back to melancholy as Jenks darted out, half-heartedly telling his kids to leave Lucy and Ray alone.

Still holding the faint remnants of a smile, I pushed away from the counter to give Quen a hug. Ceri was gone, and it hurt. My eyes closed as his arm went around me and the scent of burnt amber mixed with the smell of wine and cinnamon. "I'm sorry," I said as I stepped back, and his eyes took on a deeper shine.

"Thank you for bringing Lucy back to us," he said, and I shrugged with one shoulder.

"I wish I could have—" My throat closed. Damn it, how could Ceri be dead?

"It wasn't your task," Quen said, and I forced myself to look up. "It was no one's fault."

"But . . ."

He smiled, the pain thick in the new wrinkles around his eyes. "She'd tell you to mind your own business and to not blame yourself."

My head dropped. Probably in loud, small words so I wouldn't run the risk of misunderstanding. "She would at that," I said, and he touched my shoulder as he turned away.

"Quen," I said, and he halted. From the front of the church came a loud boom of sound as the door shut, then blessed silence. I looked at Quen. I had things I wanted to say, that Trent was braver than I had thought, and foolish. That I trusted him, but I also knew there were limits to magic and luck. That I didn't see a happy ending to this.

"I don't think Trent is planning on coming back unless he can kill Ku'Sox," I said flatly, and Quen's lip twitched. "That Lucy is safe has given him more freedom to act, but unless we can convince the other demons to band up against Ku'Sox, I don't see a happy ending to this." I lifted a foot and rubbed the back of my calf to hide my trembling.

Quen's expression gave me no clue as to what he was feeling. "You think he can do it?"

My breath came fast. "Kill Ku'Sox? Frankly, no. Not alone. All the demons together were only able to shove the psycho in a hole in reality. It might be different now." I looked at the ceiling, avoiding his eyes. "Sorry about Ellasbeth. I don't know what came over me."

Quen chuckled, his shoes scraping as he put a light hand on my shoulder again. "Thank you for trusting Trent," he said, his eyes heavy with emotion. "Not many do, and even fewer for the right reasons." He looked toward the front of the church. "I should be able to manipulate line energy tomorrow. It would be my honor to help you at the Loveland line."

My heart pounded, and a wave of relief took me, even as I worried it might end in more grief, more pain. "Thank you."

"But I have a favor to ask."

My head snapped up. Elves asking for favors was never good. "What?" I said flatly.

Quen's gaze dropped, then came back to mine. "I asked this before, and I'm asking you again."

Shit. "Quen," I whined. "I'm not going to do your job. Look at that woman out there. You think she will let me anywhere near him again? And that's even assuming we all make it out of this alive."

Taking my hand, he turned it over so the demon mark on my wrist showed. His eyes were filled with grief as they met mine. "Rachel, I didn't mean it to happen, but I have someone else I have to protect now. Someone besides Trent."

I remembered Ray on his hip and Lucy's hands eagerly reaching for him. It was the right thing to do, but still . . . panic slid through me. "Quen, I don't even like him. I mean, I do, but I live here, and you live there, and how am I supposed to keep track of him when I've got my own stuff to do and that woman—"

"Please." Quen's expression was pained. "I'm not asking you to do my job. Just . . . understand that I can't be what he needs anymore to survive. I can't devote myself to him. Ray—" His voice choked off. It was low when he spoke again. "Ray needs me. All of me, not the thin sliver of me that's left when Trent needs help. She won't be safe until Ku'Sox is dead, but after that, I am hers, not Trent's. You don't have to work for him, just be there when he needs it. That's all I'm asking. And maybe don't let Ellasbeth snuff everything he wants to be."

My pulse was hammering. I recalled Trent pulling Nick off me, the power that had flowed through me when he'd broken the charm hiding me from Al, waiting until I knew what I would lose if I turned my back on my future, and finally that kiss we had shared. It had only been a kiss—no feelings behind it but my own selfish pleasure. Then I thought of Ellasbeth. He had a duty there, one I knew he would sacrifice everything for. "But . . ."

"I wasn't sure until now, but I know you'll be what he needs."

What he needs? "What about me? Who is going to risk their life for me?"

Quen's eyes came back to mine. "He will, of course."

His voice was confident, and I could do nothing but stare with my mouth hanging open.

"I have to go before she learns how to drive," he said, seeing my confusion. "I'll talk to the owners of that charm again."

"I haven't said yes, yet," I said, and Quen turned in the threshold, not in the kitchen, not in the hall.

"It's said that the reason the elves and demons began their war is because of a broken alliance," he said, the world-weary damage to his face making him look wise. "I've always found it to be true—that the best of friends make the bitterest of enemies. Elves and demons, forever fighting. Who is to say that demons weren't the slaves of elves first?"

My eyes were wide as he inclined his head, spun slowly on a heel, and went down the hall. "Don't worry about reinvoking the charms," he said loudly, his steps going faint. "Your dad was a good man, but cheap. The silver is too frail. You'll be able to fix the good ones."

I dropped back against the counter, crossing my arms as I listened to him pass through the sanctuary and into the late afternoon sun. Work with Trent? With that dragon in the background watching me? Was he nuts?

Chapter Eighteen

My boots thumped dully on the sidewalk before the church, and with a bag of groceries on my hip, I smiled as I passed the red Mercedes parked at the curb, looking gray in the new dark, but still sexy. Ivy was back early.

Ivy didn't have a car, much less anything as flamboyant as a red Mercedes, but Nina did, and if Ivy had caught an earlier flight, Nina would have offered to pick her up at the airport. Which was good, seeing as my car was still at Trent's gatehouse.

The sound of kids playing in the dusk a block over was comforting, but when something ghosted over my head, I instinctively ducked, spinning to follow the shadow floating between me and the sky, still holding the pink of sunset. Slowly my pulse eased as I recognized the shape of a small gargoyle swooping through the spring-narrow leaves, large wings beating heavily as he or she came in almost vertically to land on a tombstone. Yellow eyes swiveled to me, and then her shape melted into the darkness.

My steps had bobbled, and knowing they had heard it, I quickened my pace. There had to be at least a dozen that had flown in since sunset, most on the tall wall surrounding the graveyard, but a few of the smaller ones sat in the neighborhood trees like huge vultures. None of them was on the church, which I thought telling. Jenks had talked to one yesterday, and apparently they were watching Bis's church to make sure Ku'Sox didn't damage it while he was in the ever-after.

It both pleased and worried me.

God help me, I had so much to do between now and Friday. *It will be easier with Ivy back,* I thought as I took the wide stairs of the church fast, shifting the reusable tote so I could get the door. But it opened as I reached for it, and Ivy stood before me, her silhouette sharp in the light pouring onto the stairs.

"Oh thank God you're here," I said, shifting the bag to my other hip so I could give her a hug right there on the stoop. "On top of everything else, we have to lift two elven rings from the museum."

"I should leave more often," she said, as her arms went briefly around me, her low, throaty voice an audible version of the vampire incense now pouring over me like fragrant oil. Giving her a last squeeze, I stepped back, beaming. Though clearly glad to see me, she was tense and furtive. Her jeans and black sweater were more casual than usual, and her hair, too, was free from its typical ponytail. The new boots she was wearing had a distinctive western feel to them, but she made it work with her sophisticated, trendy jacket.

A tight band eased about my chest as I breathed her in, her vampiric incense laced with the stale plastic scent of air flight and rental cars. Under that was the sweet honeyed smell of Daryl and Glenn's masculine scent. They were fading, though, and Nina's expensive perfume was by far the strongest outside influence. Ivy's hand on my back trembled, and I let her completely go, thoughts of Jax and Nick making my smile falter. I could hear Nina inside, talking to someone. Jenks maybe? Or on the phone, perhaps.

"You should have called me sooner," Ivy said, her tone accusing as she stepped back into the church. But then her posture slumped, and pain slipped into her black eyes. "How's Quen doing?"

Mood darkening, I followed her in, waving the new pixy dust aside as Jenks's kids dove into the bag to see what I'd brought back. "He's fine, meaning he's holding everything in, letting it fester."

She said nothing, and I looked up, reading the concern in her eyes. She had liked Ceri, too. "How are you doing?"

A hundred answers rose up, a hundred frustrations, a hundred raging cries at the world. "I'm fine, too," I said flatly.

Ivy's new boots scuffed on the sanctuary's old floor, her hair falling to hide her face as we headed to the kitchen. Nina's excited and cheerful voice—no sign of Felix—stood at dark odds with my thoughts.

"So how are Glenn and Daryl?" I asked, and her chin lifted. Concerned, I pulled her to a stop at the top of the hallway. "Ivy?" But she wouldn't bring her eyes down from the rafters, a hint of emotion welling up as she bit her lip. "Shit," I whispered, flushing as I realized what I'd done. "I shouldn't have called you."

Her eyes flicked to mine, and she shook her head. "I was already on my way back."

She tried to push past me to go into the hallway, and I got in her way. "What happened?" I demanded. "Did he dump you?"

Ivy's eyes went pupil black, but I didn't back down, even when her lips parted to show her teeth. Finally she dropped her head, saying, "Someone tried to sideswipe us on the expressway yesterday." The way she said it precluded that it was an accident. "Glenn handled it," she added, voice low as Nina laughed, oblivious to us. "Apparently he's had some defensive driving classes. Almost as good as the vampire who tried to kill us."

Her voice was light, but I was too befuddled to do anything as she pushed past me with the intoxicating scent of angry vampire, the complex cocktail plinking through my brain to make my skin ache. I'd thought it was a mistake for her to leave Cincy, but I knew how badly she'd wanted the relationship to work.

"Cormel told me not to leave. I stayed too long. His lapdog is back in the fence," she said bitterly, halfway down the hall. "He was right. I was wrong. Everything will be *fine* now."

She'd given me a reason, but something else had happened out at Flagstaff, something she didn't want to talk about but probably needed to. Groceries on my hip, I followed her into the brightly lit kitchen. I'd mention it to Jenks. He could push her a lot further than I could, seeing as he couldn't get bitten.

Nina looked up from Ivy's computer as I entered, a slim finger running down a search engine list. Jenks hovered over her, clearly interested in the screen. "What will be fine?" Nina said as I dropped the bag on the counter, and the pixy kids flew out, startling me. I'd forgotten they'd been in there, and I exhaled, trying to get rid of the flash of adrenaline.

"Everything," Ivy said. But her mood seemed glum when she strode to the window and shoved it all the way open. Cool evening air tasting of sunset seeped in, shifting my hair.

Nina wrinkled her carefully powered nose. She looked exceptionally polished tonight, wearing a versatile black pantsuit and functional low heels. Her makeup was light but exquisite, accentuating her fabulous cheekbones and dark coloring. If I hadn't known by her voice and cadence, I would know it was just her, not Felix, by the color in her cheeks, even if her pupils were edging into a dangerous black. Her eyes were bright and eager as she typed her way through a questionnaire with a speed that was borderline impossible.

"Secrets?" the woman said good-naturedly, her red lips curving up in a smile. Nose wrinkling again, she glanced at me, then away. Oh God, I hadn't had a chance to shower since coming back from the ever-after. I probably stank. That was why Ivy had shoved the window open, not to get rid of the scent of her anger or my flash of surprise.

Ivy sashayed over to her, and startled, Jenks rose up, wings clattering. "Secrets," Ivy breathed as she leaned over Nina's shoulder, her lips inches from her neck. "Always and forever, Nina. It's what keeps us alive."

Her eyes on the screen, Nina reached up to touch Ivy's cheek, hardly noticing.

Embarrassed at my apparent stink, I unpacked the bag. Organic raspberries for an illegal doppelgänger curse, white thread since the pixy girls had absconded with mine, a new coffeemaker . . . Ivy watched in question as I set it clunking on the counter. Her eyes went to the empty spot beside the toaster, and I shrugged.

A faint wish for hot chocolate lifted through me as I took the coffeemaker apart and squirted a splat of soap into it. Filling it with water, I realized my old scar was tingling. Suddenly a lot more awake, I reached for a dish towel and turned. The coffeemaker could wait. Having my back to two amorous vampires was not a good idea.

Ivy was still hunched over Nina, a pale finger tracing something on the monitor, and I felt a pang of loss when Nina smiled beautifully up at her. Nina was on top of the world. It was right about then when things usually fell apart.

"That's the school Wayde used," Jenks said, hovering between Nina and the wall as he pointed to a link on the search engine's list. "He said the rates were high, but the equipment was state-of-the-art, and that's what you want, right?"

Nina pulled back to see Ivy. "Well, Ivy? You, me, and fifteen thousand feet next Friday?"

I almost choked. "Skydiving?" Ivy hated taking unnecessary chances. "Like two days from now?"

Still bent over Nina, Ivy met my eyes. Maintaining our connection, she found her full height before turning to the fridge. "The week after. You want to come?"

Nina froze. Realizing I'd be a third wheel on a bicycle made for two—or whatever—I turned back to the sudsy coffeemaker. "No, thanks." It would be all over one way or the other by then. Ivy moving on was a good thing.

Ivy's motions were intentionally slow as she came out from the fridge, frowning at Nina. She'd caught that jealous stiffening as easily as I had. "We're out of orange juice," she said as the door shut hard enough to make the cookie jar rattle.

"We didn't expect you back this soon," I said as I rinsed the coffeemaker and set it to dry.

"They have juice at the corner store," Nina offered. "I'll run down and get it. I could use the fresh air." Her nose wrinkled again.

Because I'm stinking up the kitchen, I thought sourly.

Ivy glanced at Jenks with a pleading look, and the pixy brightened as Nina reached for her purse. "Hey, ah, I'll come with you," he said, making me more than a little curious. "I've got to, ah, stretch my wings. See if we're the only church on the block with gargoyles on it."

We were the only church on the block, period. That wasn't why he was going with her, but content to wait and see, I leaned against the counter and dried the coffeemaker as Nina gave Ivy a quick peck on the corner of her mouth. Ivy's hand was on her shoulder, the first softening of her mood showing. Whatever was bothering her wasn't Nina.

Nina strode confidently from the kitchen, Jenks right behind her, his dust a hot silver as he yelled to his kids that Belle had the conn. *He's guarding her?*

I put the coffeemaker back together as Nina's footsteps grew faint. Her voice rose pleasantly as she said something to Jenks, and then there was silence. The door boomed shut.

Ivy's jaw was tight and her head was bowed.

I exhaled long and slow. It had been a while since we'd been alone together. I hoped whatever it was, it wasn't too late. "Nina is in a good mood," I fished. If Ivy wanted to talk, she would.

Ivy pushed herself into motion. "She should be," she said, a hint of pride in her as she went to her stack of mail and began sorting. "On the way home from the airport, she shoved Felix out of her mind."

"No!" I put the coffeemaker back in its spot and levered myself up to sit before it. "I didn't think she had any say in the matter." Maybe this was why Jenks was with her. Felix would be pissed.

Ivy lifted a shoulder and let it fall, focused on her mail. "If he'd been conditioning her from adolescence, she wouldn't even think to try, but she grew up without him. Their relationship is only a few months old." She frowned at the duplicate catalogs from Vamp Vixen. "He's been relying on her willingness until now, and Nina has a very strong core of self," she said, smiling faintly. "It's the first positive step she's taken to become less dependent on him." Her smile faded. "He uses her too much."

Unease trickled down my spine. Though *no* was in a vampire's lexicon, it was only to give the other words like *sex, hunger,* and *violence* something to bump up against. "You encouraged her to do this?" I said, and a delicate flush crept over her cheeks. "Damn it, Ivy, do you know how dangerous that is? To flaunt your independence before a master?"

Her fingers faltered as they sorted, and I slid from the counter. "Yes, you do," I said, glad now that I smelled like burnt amber and that the window was open. "Fine. Play with the master vampire. But don't do it here. I put you back together once. I'm not going to do it again if you go out looking for it!"

Somber, Ivy turned to me, her hair swinging. "I—"

"Don't tell me you know what you're doing," I said, angry that she'd knowingly pushed Nina into something that might get Ivy hurt. "He's a master vampire, and he's not even yours!"

"Since when do you have anything to say about what I do!" Ivy exclaimed, her eyes flashing black.

I stood even with the center counter, measuring the space between us. Worlds, there were worlds there. "Since I am your friend," I pleaded, letting go of my anger so my concern could come forward. "I know I said to try to help her, but goading her master like this? Proving he doesn't have control? He's going to be furious. Cormel can't protect you from everything. He's pissed you left!"

Turning away, Ivy ripped open an envelope, sorting everything into keep and toss piles.

"Ivy . . ." I pleaded. "You've come so far. Why? Is it because you love her?"

"I don't know!" she said, her eyes black, not in fear, not in hunger, but in heartache. "It didn't work out between me and Glenn and Daryl, okay? We tried, and it all fell apart. Bad."

I slumped. This was where her turmoil was coming from. "Your needs are not wrong—"

"Then why couldn't I make it work, Rachel?" she shouted, and I drew back. "Why did they have to move halfway across a continent to get away from me?"

Throat tight, I crossed the room to her. "Because you need someone who needs you, and I don't anymore," I whispered. "Ivy, I'm sorry."

Her shoulder under my hand trembled, and she backed out of my reach. "There's no reason to be," she said softly, hair falling to hide her face. "I have to do this. I like Nina. She's alive, smart, always moving but never toward anything that doesn't have meaning. The way she loves life reminds me of you, and she is good at making me do things that I'm afraid to do. But what Felix is doing to her . . . It draws me to her as much as it disgusts me. She's so much like a master, but innocent."

Eyes bright with unshed tears, she looked at the ceiling. "I left for a week, and I came back to find he's in her thoughts almost every waking moment the sun is up, and half the time at night, filling her with power and desire as he sucks in the memory of the sun and love. He won't leave her alone. I don't think he can anymore." Again she looked at her fingers among her mail, shifting them aimlessly. "The man is using her like a drug. He's not tapping her for blood anymore, which might mean she's become an extension of himself in his mind. Nina is balanced on a fine edge of control."

"And you like it."

Head down, she nodded, tucking a strand of hair behind her ear. She felt better for having told me. I could tell. Or maybe it was because I was asking about what she could do, plan . . . fix. "She's as dependent upon him for control as he is on her for stimulation at this point. He can die twice for all I care, but I don't want her to pay for his mistake. The only chance Nina has to survive is to take control and tell him no for as long as she can. Even if it puts her in more danger."

And it would. I could tell. This wasn't good.

"Nina's control when alone and under stress is almost nil," Ivy said, eyes lowered toward the table. "That's why I asked Jenks to go with her, to buffer any conflicts. I know I can help her learn control if I can keep them apart long enough." Her head came up, meeting my eyes fully. "She has a chance. If she really wants it, she has a chance."

I managed a smile to match her own tremulous expression. Ivy had a tremendous need to give, to lift others above the muck she had pulled herself out of. Watching Nina innocently and willingly slip in over her head had been hard. Accepting the challenge to help her was even harder. "Be careful," I said as I reached across the distance between us and touched her arm. "I'm proud of you, Ivy."

Her smile slowly vanished, and her dark eyes drifted aimlessly over our kitchen, touching parts of our lives as if she'd never seen them before. "Felix is going to be looking for her tonight. I have to get her to a safe house, but I'll be back to help plan the museum job." She took a deep breath, her chin lifting as if she was taking on a new responsibility—or maybe accepting that I wished her well. "The hell they put us through," she whispered.

I didn't know what to say. I could tell she was about to leave.

"I should probably go," Ivy said. "Jenks won't be able to do much if she loses it. I didn't want to bring up the safe house while she was in the church. She thinks she's got the world by the tail."

Yet another trait that Nina and I shared. "That's usually when you get bitten," I said, and Ivy smiled. Nina was far away and distant from me, but there was enough there to make an easy comparison. Ivy might not know it yet, but she was falling in love again.

Ivy reached for her purse, then hesitated. "Are you sure you'll be okay for a few hours?"

My gut hurt, and I smiled widely. "Oh, hell yes. Nick is around somewhere, but I'll be fine, especially with all those gargoyles. Ku'Sox won't show, afraid the curse will bounce back at him. Go."

Still unsure, Ivy started to back up to the hallway and out of my life. "Stay on hallowed ground until I get back, okay?"

She knew the kitchen wasn't hallowed ground. "You got it," I said, turning to look out at the silent, damp garden. "And Ivy? I know what I said, but I will always be here to put you back together. If it should come to that."

Her smile faltered as she stood in the threshold. "I know. Thank you."

Head down, she turned away, the keys to Nina's car jingling. Her footsteps were slow as she made her way through the dark to the front of the church. The boom of the door shook through me.

Arms wrapped around my middle, I smiled even as the tears threatened. This was good. This was very, very good. It had to be if it hurt this much.

Chapter Nineteen

Ms. Morgan! Why is your church the only one with gargoyles?" the woman on my front stoop was saying as I smiled and waved at the camera guy, waiting for the last pixy to come back in before I shut the door in their faces. "What a bitch!" the newscaster added as I bolted it, probably not aware that voices carried through the wall of the church well enough that we didn't need an intercom.

A peephole would be nice, though, I thought as I put an ear to the door and listened to them pack up and head back to the news van. The camera guy was talking about going down the back street to get a shot of the graveyard and the gargoyles perched on the tombstones, but the woman was in too bad a mood to care about aesthetics. It wasn't that I didn't want to talk to them after they misaligned, misinformed, and generally blew everything out of proportion when it came to my life—but that I really didn't care to speculate on local TV as to why every single gargoyle in the Cincinnati area was now perched on my church's wall and in my graveyard.

Sighing, I headed back to the kitchen with pixies in my hair, wishing I'd taken the time to take my apron off before I'd answered the door. I was a mess from spell prep, bits of green stuff and ground herbs marking me. Pixy dust was everywhere, and the ugly red stain on my sleeve from the organic berries looked ominous. At least I wasn't barefoot.

Boots clunking, I headed for the kitchen, my pixy escort going before me in swirls of cheerful color and noise. Though the night was warm, they were all back inside to avoid the gargoyles. I'd been spelling for hours, and I had to clean something before I could make anything new.

As I ran the water into my spell-grimed pots, Jenks flew in smelling like garden and sounding like wind chimes. Cutting a startling image, he landed on the center counter beside my drying charms. No longer in his usual gardener green, or even his alternate thief-black, skintight ensemble, he all but strutted a few steps, clearly liking the sound of the bells that Belle had sewn into the top of his new boots that she'd made to go with his new black jacket and pants.

Silver and ebony meshed in a sharply angular pattern that never seemed to repeat and, indeed, seemed to change with the light, making a mesmerizing pattern that would get anyone to stare even if Jenks didn't look like a million bucks in it.

"You sure you don't want me to harvest more of that yew?" Jenks asked as he came to stand on the spigot. "The gargoyles out there don't bother me."

I smiled and ran the now-warm water into the nested spell pots. "No. I'd rather wait. Friday sunrise is the equinox."

Jenks nodded, jingling his bells when Rex padded in with Belle on her shoulders. "Je-e-enks-s-s-s," she hissed, her angular features drawn up in annoyance. "I told you to take that off. Those are not fighting clothes-s-s."

"It's black, I'm wearing it," he said, his wings blurring to invisibility. "I don't have anything else to put on."

That wasn't entirely accurate, and I hid a smile and moved the gradu- ated cylinders and mortar to the sink, piling them in the sudsy spell pots. Wringing out the saltwater-soaked rag, I began wiping down my spell-prep area, thinking it rather useless when half of Jenks's brood was up there, dusting heavily.

"The tails-s-s are too long. If an enemy catches it, he will have you at a dis-s-sadvantage," she said. "The buttons are too large. They glint in the light. The bells-s-s will give you away."

I nodded, agreeing with her, and Jenks began to look worried. "I can muffle the bells," he said, tugging the coat straight. "I like it, fairy woman! I'm wearing it!"

"Your vanity will be your death," she hissed at him, and Jenks put his hands on his hips.

"Yeah?"

Scowling, Belle nudged Rex toward the door, but the fluffy yellow cat purred her way to me instead, coming to twine about my feet and beg for some attention. Seeing her intent, Belle slipped off, shaking her clothes straight and adjusting the bow across her back.

Jenks flew to the center counter where Belle couldn't see him from the floor. "Are you sure all this is going to work?" he asked, looking over the assembled charms and spells.

"As long as I can keep your kids' dust out of them," I said, then bent down to pick Rex up. "Hi, sweetheart," I crooned, trying to distract the cat from the pixies arguing over the gumdrop they had found left over from solstice cookie decorations. "I can't pet you right now. I'm still cleaning the kitchen."

Jenks rose up on a column of muddy gold. "Everyone out!" he shouted, and the handful of pixies in the rack whined their disappointment. "Go play in the belfry or something!" he added, and the complaints turned to delight. "We're spending tonight inside!" he added when half of them darted out. "You hear me? I don't want any of you out there pestering the gargoyles! They might squish you before they know you're there. Jrixibell! You hear me?"

"Yes, Papa!" the little pixy moaned, then darted out, her dust a bright red of mischief.

"Thanks, Jenks," I said with a long exhalation, then glanced out the window at the dark garden, the gargoyles' eyes winking eerily. The older ones looked huge this close to the ground, wings as big as sails stretching in the shadows. No wonder Jenks had corralled his kids back inside for the night. Creeped out, I rinsed the ceramic spoons and set them aside to soak in my saltwater vat.

Rex, who had hid under the chair with wide eyes and flattened ears at the noise from the departing pixies, came out, meowing up at me for an early dinner. Jenks's wings began to glow as he took to the air. "I don't like leaving the lines this vulnerable, but Nick isn't going to show with those gargoyles out there. They probably hate Ku'Sox more than you do."

I made a sour face. The fact that my line was the only one on the US continent that wasn't screaming probably had something to do with them being here, too.

"I don't trust my kids," Jenks said as he rose up, wings clattering and limbs stretching. "I'll be on the steeple."

"I'll join you," Belle said, resettling her bow. "I don't trus-s-st your kids, either."

Jenks hovered where he was, dust pooling under him. "You want a ride up there?"

Shocked, I stared. Belle, too, seemed taken aback at his offer. "Do you think you can handle my weight, little man?"

"Tink's panties, yes."

I watched, amazed as Jenks darted over, picked her up from behind by the waist, and rose, Belle hissing in delight. Wings humming, they flew into the hall, a line of descending silver stars marking their path.

"By the Goddess, you're more maneuverable than I ever was," I heard faintly, then even the sound of Jenks's wings was gone.

"Huh," I said softly, feeling good. "How about that?"

Smiling, I turned back to the sink. Past the blue curtains and Al's chrysalis, the hunched shadows of gargoyles were thick among the tombstones, but I could imagine it a month from now with the early flowers blooming and pixies out there instead of in here. I hoped I was here to see it. I had gotten rid of most of the ifs, but it would only take one to bring it all crashing down. *Please be okay, Bis.*

Slowly the silence soaked in as I finished rinsing everything and set my spelling supplies to dry. My smile faded, and the feeling of being watched pricked through me. There was nothing outside but the low rumbles of the gargoyles. But I knew Nick was out there somewhere—becoming frustrated.

The hair on the back of my neck rose, and even knowing Jenks was on the steeple, I felt as if I was being watched. The air was thick with the scent of vampires, evidence of Ivy and Nina, and nervous, I ran the tap to warm the water as I messed with the soap, head down as I tried to scrub the burnt amber stink out from under my fingernails.

Goose bumps rose, and I couldn't say why. "Stop it, Rachel," I whispered as I turned, shocked to see a young, thin vampire standing at my table.

Holy shit! I thought, panic icing through me, first that he might know what I was doing, and then because there was a undead vampire standing in my kitchen and I hadn't heard him come in. "Who in hell are you?" I said, heart pounding. No wonder I'd felt as if I'd been being watched!

For an instant, I thought he looked like Kisten, the same blond hair falling about his eyes, and when he tossed his head, I almost forgot to breathe. But it wasn't Kisten. This vampire's face was thinner, younger, less worldly wise. His frame wasn't nearly as bulky, giving him a bookish, intelligent mien. His black suit fit him perfectly, a dull white shirt, paisley ascot, and handkerchief finishing his polish. His shoes looked as if they'd never seen the dirt before today.

"I startled you," he said, hands clasped innocently behind him, but I wasn't fooled.

"Ivy isn't here," I said cautiously, thinking that word she was back got around fast. "I can give her a message." *And then you need to get your ass outta my kitchen, dirt nap.* Talking to undead clients in the unsanctified back rooms was standard practice, but they usually knocked first. Damn, this one was old if he could get past Jenks and me without my even hearing him.

"A message will do," the man said, and I moved to put space between us. I knew it made me look scared, but I wanted to be able to react if I needed to. Slowly his voice filtered through my memory. I recognized it from somewhere, or rather, I recognized how his voice pulled at me, the cadence both mesmerizing and soothing, unnervingly so. Suddenly I was a lot more concerned.

Breathing in my alarm, he moved, the silk of his suit rustling against itself as he tucked a foot behind the other, just the tip touching the floor. His eyes flashed black, and I froze. "I want Nina returned to me," he said, and that fast, swirling madness entered his eyes.

Shit. "Felix," I whispered, and he inclined his head, never taking his eyes off mine. This was Felix. He was out of his hole. I was looking at him, not a willing mouthpiece. Ivy had called him out by encouraging Nina to rebel, and he had come. Looking for her.

My fingers slipped from the stainless-steel counter. Felix moved. I got a gasp of air in, and he was on me, pushing me back until I found the wall beside the archway. His arm was under my throat, his breath was on my skin. Delicious tingles sparked through me, and I shoved them aside, refusing to let him take me this way.

"Where is Nina . . ." he began, and I pushed him off me.

He stumbled back, clearly shocked that he hadn't bespelled me. I was shocked, too. The guy looked like he was eighteen. I didn't sense any magic keeping him this way. He had died young.

"I'm only going to tell you one more time, Felix," I said, trying to pull myself out of a defensive crouch. "I don't care what you want, you will keep your hands *off* me. Got it?"

Oblivious to my threats, he licked his red lips, gaze darting over the ceiling. "She was here. I can smell her." Eyes closing, he breathed deep, exhaling to fill the room with the sound of desire. "She has been willful. She needs . . . gentle correction."

This time I had a bare instant of warning as his eyes met mine before he lunged. "*Get off!*" I shouted, tapping the line out back as one hand gripped my shoulder and the other twined in my hair. He jerked my head back to lay my neck bare. Energy sizzled as it raced from my chi, running down my hands and burning as it flowed through ever-smaller pathways until it found my palms. I cried out as it burst from me, arcing to him with a tiny pop of sound.

Snarling, he flung me away as it struck him. My back hit the wall, and I stumbled, falling into Ivy's chair. Tossing the hair from my eyes, I scrambled to my feet, heart pounding. He stood a good eight feet back, almost to the sink. The imprint of my hand showed clearly on his jaw and neck, and he touched it gingerly.

"You said what you wanted. Get out," I threatened, moving farther into the room so he could leave without getting any closer to me. Where in hell was Jenks? And what was it with the gargoyles letting this guy through? Apparently undead vampires weren't on their watch list.

But Felix only tugged the sleeves of his suit coat down, clearly trying to calm himself. It wasn't working. Ivy had been right. This guy was halfway off his rocker.

"Ivy put Nina up to this disobedience," he said, voice smooth and persuasive, but I wasn't buying it. "I need her. Directly. Tell me where she is, or I'll take my needs from you."

My eyes narrowed at the threat, but I was spared threatening him in turn when Jenks darted in, blade drawn. "Who the hairy-ass fairy are you?"

"You all need correction," Felix said, and I swear he swallowed back his saliva. "Especially Ivy. I've heard about her, been warned she could satisfy me. Bring me to my knees."

"I can bring you to your knees right now," I whispered.

"Felix?" the pixy shrilled. "What's the point of having gargoyles in the backyard if they let this crap through? Troll turds, I'm sorry, Rache."

My eyes never left Felix's. He was fast. Faster than Jenks. Still, was I a demon or not? "No need to apologize. Felix was just leaving. Weren't you?"

"No." Felix had lost his smile, his youthful features tight in anger that I might be able to stand up to him. It was starting to smell really good in here, but I could ignore it. Mostly. "Give me Nina and I'll leave you alone for a time. She has it coming."

How many times had I heard that? How many times did the abuser blame the abused?

"Ivy is trying to help you and Nina both," I said, keeping my eyes away from the floor and the circle etched into the linoleum. If I could get him two steps closer, he'd be in it. "You are dangerously dependent on her. Let her go. It's going to kill both of you."

"Kill me!" he shouted, and Jenks's wings clattered. Still, Felix remained outside the circle, pacing like a predator afraid to take the bait. "Nina is what is giving me *life*! She is mine to do what I want with. Mine. Ivy is hiding her. If you won't give me Nina, restitution is mine to claim. *Where is she?*"

Fingers crooked into claws, he jumped at me again.

This guy is out of his friggin' mind! I thought as I stood where I was, eyes screwing up against the impact. Jenks darted up and away, the ringing of his sword echoing through me, mixing with the unreal sound of Felix's anguish.

My eyes flew open as his bone-crushing grip knocked us back into the wall again. Again I poured the line through him.

His fingers tightened as he screamed his frustration, and then he was gone, whirling in anger eight feet away, his black eyes pits. Blood dripped from his face just under his eye, mirrored on Jenks's sword.

"I will have *someone*!" Felix shouted, and my lips parted as he crouched, preparing to jump me again. *Is he trying to get me to kill him?* I thought, shocked when a low sound of hatred rumbled forth, growing as he slid closer, dancing to music that maddened him. "I will have someone . . ."

"Felix, we're trying to help!" I cried, then traced an informal circle about myself. Seeing it, Felix lunged, arm reaching. Instinct pushed me back, and my heel broke my circle even as it formed. I gasped, then stared, shocked as a shadow from the back living room flew into the kitchen, jerking Felix from me and spinning him into the corner by the fridge.

"Ohem!" a voice boomed from the short, stocky man somehow standing between us. "Find yourself!"

"Holy crap, it's Cormel!" Jenks shrilled, and I fell back against the wall, hand on my throat as I realized it was Rynn Cormel, probably here to talk to Ivy.

"That one needs punishing!" Felix pointed at me, pacing back and forth before him, totally out of his mind. "She is mine. Mine!"

Rynn Cormel's jaw was tight as he raised a hand. His felt cap lay on the floor, and his coat smelled of cashmere and vampire. "Let go of the thought of her, sir," he said calmly, and I pulled myself straight, grimacing. I'd filled the air with my fear—I'd known better. Jenks, hovering at the ceiling with a bloody, bared sword, was tense enough for both of us.

"The demon witch encouraged my scion to defy me . . ." Felix's voice was softer now, more calculating, scaring me.

Rynn Cormel shook his head, his Brooklyn accent sounding odd as he firmly said, "This is mine, not yours. I punish her, not you."

No one was going to punish me, but I was smart enough not to say anything. My heart pounded, and I was glad Cormel was here. Felix was out of his mind.

Felix's angry pacing slowed, and Cormel's outstretched hand shifted to one of welcome. "You are in need, sir," he said respectfully. "Distraught, and drunk on the sun. Let go of this idea and turn to a new one before my ward kills you. She's not for you. She's not for me. She is for Ivy."

"Ivy . . ." Felix snarled, and I held my breath as Felix thought that over.

His youthful face was twisted into an ugly mask of anguish and fear, his eyes black and showing a lack of control I'd expect from the newly undead, not one older than Cincinnati's tunnels.

"I am drunk on the sun," he said suddenly, his beautiful voice cracking. "Oh God." He said the words with anguish, falling back against the counter as if having abruptly found himself. "What have I done? What . . ."

Jenks dropped from the ceiling to my shoulder, and I jumped.

"What am I doing?" Felix lamented, his head bowed until his hair hid his eyes. He was shaking, and only now did Cormel glance back to make sure I was okay.

"You think it's wise to turn your back on him?" I said as Cormel came to me, a cold hand landing on my arm to push me into the hall. He was wearing a tidy suit that made him look like a middle-aged politician, and his smile that had saved a world was now focused on me. It wasn't working. I was scared shitless.

"I'm sorry you saw this, Rachel," he said, and I slid out from under his hand on my shoulder. "The diseases of the undead are not easy to understand. Might I have a moment alone with him?"

Head shaking, I backed up into the corner. "Not in my church, no." My eyes flicked behind him to the undead vampire. Felix looked crushed, beaten as he slumped against the counter and threatened to slip to the floor. Was this what happened when vampires got old? They slowly lost their mind until they walked into the sun?

Cormel's eye twitched at my defiance. But it wasn't until Jenks clattered his wings that he turned back to Felix.

"I can't," Felix said, his voice wispy and beaten. "Nina showed me the sun, and I stared too long. I can't bring myself to forget again, now that I know what that looks like."

I took a breath to say something, my words forgotten when Felix brought his gaze up and I saw the agony in him. He had come here looking for me to kill him. He wanted to end it, but walking into the sun took too much courage.

"Let Nina be," Cormel said, turning his back on me. "Let her have her time."

Felix was shaking like an addict in withdrawal, and maybe he was. "I can't. I can't," he said, his voice broken. "The sun pulls me. God, it's too easy to just . . . and then I'm alive through her. I am alive." His face became animated, almost too beautiful. "Do you remember being alive? I do. I didn't get enough when I was alive, taken too soon. Why are you stopping me? You don't know! How can you?"

Cormel had crossed the room, and I watched, unbelieving, as the younger undead comforted the old. "You know it will never be enough," he said, a hand on Felix's shoulder. "You're lost to the sun. If you don't let it go, it will kill you. Nina is too bright."

Felix licked his lips, confusion slipping into his eyes. "Nina loves me."

"You're killing her," Cormel said, and I wondered if I should have left when I had the chance. "Ivy is right in teaching Nina control. Let Nina live her time."

Felix took a huge breath. "I need her!" he shouted, and the hum of Jenks's wings increased in pitch. "Who are you to say no to me! You are a pup!" He strode back and forth, never getting any closer, never any farther. "A squalid, puking whelp snuffing along the edges of the birthing box, unable to see the depth of pain beyond it!"

"Perhaps." Cormel inclined his head, standing very, very still. "But I, sir, know not to look. I believe the lie, and so I survive another day. You can't have Nina anymore. I will not give you justification on Ivy or Rachel. The darkness will warm again if you turn your back on the sun. Sir. Please. It's not too late."

Felix spun into an ugly hunch, the hem of his beautifully tailored suit quivering in his anger. "It is my right," he hissed, his gaze starting to dip back into madness. "I hunger because of her; she alone satisfies me . . ."

Frightened for Ivy, I moved, Cormel's back-flung hand stopping me.

"You may not claim justice on Ivy," he said firmly. Something had shifted. His voice was still respectful, but the subtle subtext of subordinate vampire was utterly gone. And by Felix's reddening face, I think he recognized it as well. It was too late for him. He couldn't let go; he couldn't become what he had once been. There was only the task of seeing it to the end now.

"Your favored child is stealing from me. I demand compensation!"

I exchanged a look with Jenks, seeing he had seen the shift as well.

Felix was no longer a functioning undead vampire, but one who was ailing, one to be humored and lied to. He was old, forgetful, lacking control. He had done it to himself, and I pitied him, remembering seeing the controlled, confident vampire through Nina's eyes not three days ago. He had known what would happen, and he had done it anyway, all for the chance to see the sun.

"I'll give you compensation, but you will *not* have Ivy or Rachel," Cormel said, and I pitied Felix as he all but whined.

"Ivy could satisfy me," he wheedled, looking ugly as he tried to hide his emotions, but he was broken and couldn't be fixed.

Cormel shook his head. "Rachel is going to find our souls with her, and Ivy needs to remain untouched. She will find our souls so that the sun may find us again and end this lie we live. Will you wait with me for that day?"

Felix's ugly gaze slid to me, and I held my breath. "That's fallacy," the younger-looking, aging, sun-addicted undead vampire said.

"Still, you will leave me to my fantasy and shun Ivy and Rachel as I ask." Cormel shifted to open a way for him to go, incidentally placing himself even more firmly between me and Felix. "My car is out front. The driver will take you wherever you wish. It would be my pleasure to show you my children if you will wait but a little."

Felix straightened at that, almost finding his old bearing. "I am so hungry," he whispered. "The blood doesn't help anymore. There's never enough."

Cormel's head bowed. "I'm sorry. Give me a moment with Rachel? I'll join you soon. My children will slake your thirst. I will stand beside you and be sure of it."

My God, it was enough to turn my stomach, but it was what they were down to. I stiffened as Felix shuffled out past me, a slight tilting of his head the only indication that he knew I was there, and I shivered when a black eye watched me from under his shifting bangs. Jenks followed him out, staying just below the ceiling as a quiet guard.

"I am not yours," I said hotly to Cormel before the back door clicked shut.

In a wash of incense, Cormel moved swiftly to the archway, leaning to look down it into holy ground. His lips were pressed in anger, and I marveled at how alive he appeared. Practice, practice, practice. "You are. I just saved your life."

"I could have taken him," I shot back, and Cormel's irate gaze finally came to me. His eyebrows went high in a mocking question. "I just didn't want to hurt him."

"No doubt. I think you killing him was his plan. And then what? You would be accused of murder as no one but you saw him ailing. You could flee to the ever-after, but we all know how you feel about that—Rachel."

He was right, and it irked me. "You make me sick," I said instead, pushing around him to get out of my corner. "The two of you going off to a blood orgy together, offering your children to him like they're candy. There's no love there, no caring. Ivy was right. Why should I help you find your souls?"

Cormel stooped to pick up his hat and dust it off. "Because I am here saving your life." I huffed in disbelief, and he turned to give me his full attention. "I'm joining Felix in his bloodletting so he doesn't kill my children in his grief for the sun. I am there so he won't take too much or be too brutal for their desires to withstand. I doubt very much I'll enjoy watching an old man gum his food." His gaze became distant. "There will be no finesse, no beauty there. I had hoped that he was still recoverable, but it won't be long now." His eyes met mine. "They failed to tell me that caring for the old as well as the young would be my responsibility when I took this job."

It was as I had thought, then. Felix had faltered and was failing fast, dragging Nina down with him. This was so ugly. "Ivy is trying to save both their lives," I said softly, and Cormel's bad mood seemed to hesitate as he saw my own soften. "Doesn't that count for something?"

"She still broke the rules. He is mad, Rachel. He is mad, and no amount of blood can save either of them, but Ivy broke the rules by interfering. Ohem is already lost but for his final walk into the sun and leaving Nina to lose control." Cormel leaned to look down the hall, his thoughts already in the car and the remainder of his night. "They'll have to shoot her down like a dog to stop her once she starts to look for solace. As it was, he would have only taken himself and one other, but your Ivy wants to love again, and so we all suffer so that you might save her soul, save all of ours."

Jenks arrowed into the kitchen, bringing with him the scent of ash from the fireplace. He looked agitated that Cormel was still here, and the undead vampire raised a tired hand to tell him that he was on his way. "My children will suffer indignities and pain tonight because of you," he said, and my gut tightened in guilt. "All my children are paying the cost for Nina's possible survival. All to keep one vampire happy." Cormel put his hat back on and buttoned his coat. "I pay it willingly. But you will give me what I want, Morgan. *And soon.*"

My chin lifted, and Jenks's dust turned a glittering gold. "That sounds like a threat."

He smiled from under the brim of his hat. It was the smile that had saved the world, and it was ending mine. "It was supposed to." Cormel stepped into the hall, then paused. "I know you're occupied with repairing the lines, so I'm willing to wait, but Rachel, I will not end up like Ohem." His expression darkened, his pupils going wide and his eyes black. "I will not be a shell of myself, pitied and grasping for the sun when I know my soul is lost to hell. If Ivy leaves Cincinnati again, I will kill her myself. Tell her that for me."

Cold, I wrapped my arms around myself.

"I want my soul back. Find it."

Between one breath and the next, he was gone, the door squeaking shut the only sound marking his passage. Shaking, I sat down in Ivy's chair.

If Ivy leaves Cincinnati again, I will kill her myself, he had said.

Don't think so.

Chapter Twenty

Junior's was frighteningly busy, the clientele mostly human at the early hour, stumbling about in search of their first cup of coffee. Either humans appreciated their coffee more than the average Inderlander, or Mark's marketing gamble of claiming to serve coffee that demons crossed the lines for was paying off. I couldn't help but notice that the floor had been repainted with circles and spirals, and I wondered if the lock access to the back door had been changed as well. The talk was loud, and the music cranked decibels higher than normal made my head hurt. I truly sympathized with the rare Inderlander accused of eating humans. They were annoying and obnoxious when they thought no one was listening.

My mood couldn't be entirely blamed on the noise and early hour—seeing as I'd not gotten to sleep until Ivy had come home, and then gotten up at an insane seven in the morning to get here by 7:35 exactly. But if my mood was bad, Ivy had me beat, glowering in the corner of the darkest booth we had been able to snag. The three beatniks bemoaning the unfairness of life and the publishing industry had been taking up the spot when we'd arrived, but after Ivy stood over their table with her grande and bad attitude, they'd packed up their double-spaced pages and red pencils and moved to a sunnier table.

Ivy was better now that most of her drink was inside her and her head was down over the museum blueprints, but if my evening with Felix and Cormel had been disturbing, hers spent getting Nina into a safe house had devolved into terror. As Ivy had expected, Nina had gotten angry at the mere suggestion, and without Felix to steady the overwhelming sensations, clarity of perception, and power that he'd gifted her with, she'd quickly spiraled out of control. Ivy had gotten her to the safe house just in time.

The morning was bright and chill, and Jenks was warming himself on the light fixture. It was just us three, the way I liked it, and I had a suspicion that we were at the very same booth where we had made our agreement to go into business together. I wondered at all the changes in our lives since then. We were all better, weren't we? I wasn't so sure anymore. I'd loved and lost. So had Ivy. So had Jenks. There was good stuff too, wasn't there?

Ivy checked her watch, folded up the map, and shoved it away.

"Is she here?" Jenks asked, his dust an odd light blue edged in gold. I'd never seen that before, and I wondered if his extended life span was giving him a wider repertoire.

Ivy shook her head, casually pulling her coffee to her with long, pale fingers. Silent, she stared out over the patrons at nothing as she tried to put her night in perspective. Her hair was perfectly arranged, and her short jacket made her look like a model. People were eyeing her in envy. She looked like she had everything. *Looked* was the keyword. Her eyes were red with worry, and fatigue pulled at her like a cur.

"I would rather have done this at night," I said, thinking that the idea to just walk in, grab the rings, and walk out was great if you were fourteen and trying to steal a candy bar, but not twenty-seven and aiming for a piece of irreplaceable elven heritage. Then again, the oldest tricks worked the best.

"Security is impossible at night," she murmured.

"Ana 'eesides, 'ache," Jenks said as he dropped down, his words slurred as he chewed one of the nectar and pollen balls Belle had made for him. "Ee don't 'ave time to plan ah 'eel job. Ou'll 'e great!" He swallowed a chunk. "It's not that much different from legit work. You get busted for doing that, too, half the time."

Resettling my scarf, I eyed him sourly. His cheek was still bulging like a chipmunk's as he furiously chewed. Belle had made his travel food her size, not his, and his kids had had giggling fits this morning when the fairy had gruffly given them to him in a paper sack she had folded herself. Jenks had only said thank you, even as he'd gestured for his kids to leave off. I was proud of him.

"Piece of cake," I whispered, wanting to ask Ivy for the map.

"Easy as pie!" the pixy said, his fingers now sticking to a napkin. Frustrated, he lifted off the table, taking the napkin with him. His dust shifted to an irate red, and Ivy pinned the paper with her index finger. Wings clattering, he drew his sword, and with three frustrated motions, he rose up, a piece of napkin drifting down under him.

"If you two don't relax, I'm going to jump Rachel's jugular," Ivy muttered, and I slumped into my chair, taking my double shot grande, Italian blend, skim milk, shot of raspberry, no foam coffee with me. Al liked whole milk, but I thought it was too rich that way.

"Sorry." It bothered me more than I wanted to admit that we had to steal the stupid rings. Involving an innocent kind of bothered me, too. But as Jenks had said, there hadn't been enough time for Ivy's usual beauty-in-planning. We had to go in dirty and fast. Get in, move to the secure area where the pieces were being held under the cover of a distraction, do a little light-fingered shopping, and leave a pair of fake rings before walking out the front door with what we'd come for. It was that skinflint elf's fault—going back on an arranged . . . arrangement. Trent was still in the ever-after, and it bothered me. A lot.

I fiddled with my cup of coffee, feeling the silence become uncomfortable. "I'm glad you're back," I said, and Ivy's eyes flicked to mine. "It's been quiet."

Her brow furrowed and she looked away. "I'll try not to make so much noise."

Anger flickered and died, and I watched her pupils dilate and return to normal in response. She'd had a difficult night. I could cut her some slack. "I didn't say you were being noisy. I said it's been quiet. I also said I'm glad you're back. I'm sorry you had such a hard night with Nina. Is she going to be okay? Felix was . . ." I hesitated, my anger vanishing as I remembered his hunched shadow, as he stood anguished in my kitchen in a moment of lucidity, his eyes rolling as he looked for me to kill him as a way out of his new hell. "I don't like undead vampires, the way they use people like tissue and discard them, but seeing him broken like that and losing his mind?" I looked up, seeing her own pain. "I feel bad for him."

Ivy's eyes were haunted as she watched her fingers encircle her cup.

"Hey, ah, I'm going to check out the perimeter, okay?" Jenks said, then darted off through the drive-up window, scaring the crap out of the barista managing it. Though the sun was bright this morning, it was too cold for him to be outside long. He'd be back.

Chicken, I thought, but I didn't blame him. Ivy exhaled, still avoiding me. Either she would talk or she wouldn't.

"Maybe I shouldn't have interfered," she said, and I strained to hear her over the noise of "background" music and conversation. Ivy's eyes came up, heartache mirrored in them. "People suffered for me last night, good people. Not just my friends at Piscary's who fed that monster, but the ones at the safe house, too. Nina agreed to this arrangement with Felix. Who am I to try to help her?"

I leaned over the table, and Ivy flinched as my hand covered hers. The cup was long cold, but her fingers were warm. "Nina did *not* agree to *this*. She bought into a lie, one coated in power and euphoria. People suffered for her, but they did it knowing it was to help one of their own come back. If Nina can survive, if you can bring her back from where Felix filled her with ecstasy and then dumped her, then there's hope for them. That's why they took your pain. You gave them hope that they might survive, too."

Ivy looked away in guilt, and I remembered the wild abandonment I'd seen time and again at Piscary's under Kisten's management, living vampires going there to lie to themselves that life was good and they had the world on a string. They needed knowing that there was a way out, perhaps more than they knew.

My eyes were warm with unshed tears, and Ivy blinked fast when she pulled her hand out from under mine. She wanted to believe, but it was hard for her to accept others sacrificing for her.

"Keep Nina safe," I said, hiding my hand under the table. A resolve had filled me somewhere between finding Felix in my kitchen and Ivy stumbling home last night crying over someone else's pain. I couldn't let Ivy suffer the hell I'd seen Felix trapped in. I had to find a way to save her soul. *I had to.*

"Thank you," Ivy whispered, her motion slow as she balled up her eco-friendly napkin. Taking a deep breath, I could almost see her focus on the "now." "It was a rough night. It took six of us to hold her down when the bloodlust hit her. If this goes okay, I'm going to try to be there when she wakes up so she knows I'm . . . okay."

She couldn't look at me, and I wished she wasn't so ashamed of what we had to do to survive. We all fell. What mattered was what we did after that. "Tell Nina for me that she can do this, okay? That it's worth it." *That you're worth it.*

"I will," she whispered. "Next time I see her. Thank you."

Tears pricked my eyes, but I was smiling and so was she. Nina was strong. She would survive. I never would have thought that Ivy would ever be on the other end of the addiction, and I was proud of her.

Ivy's gaze flicked past me. She didn't move, but something shifted in her, a predator's quiet breath slipped in and out, and I suppressed a shudder. Just that fast, everything changed.

Reaching for a napkin, I pretended to dab my mouth as I turned to the line. "Is that her?" I said, seeing a blonde with her sweater cut low and her spring skirt cut high. She was in a tight jacket, and she seemed to know everyone behind the counter, talking loud and cheerful as she flirted, waiting for her turn.

Ivy was already reaching for her purse. "Yes," she said, standing up and not looking at her. "Five minutes to eight. Right on time."

Jenks dropped down, his wings giving me a bare instant of warning. "She came in in the blue Mustang," he said, still picking napkin from between his fingers. "I think it's new since the cover is open. It's too cold for that unless it's your first convertible. I'll get you the keys, Ivy. You're going to want that top closed."

"Thanks," she said, giving me a soft smile before she turned away and breezed out, coming within inches of the woman.

I stood as the blond woman shivered as if chilled. "Chicken," I berated Jenks as I moved to get in line right behind her.

"You think I'm going to get involved in that heart-to-heart women crap?" he said as he snuggled in behind my scarf. "Hell, no! Aw, she's sweet! You sure we have to lock her in the trunk?"

When I'm done with her, she's going to be more pissed than a cat in a well, I thought as I took a quick step back from her as she ordered. I was afraid if I got too close, I might catch whatever cheerful bug had infected her. It was too early to be that sickeningly bouncy, but I suppose if your job required you to dress as a professional distraction, a happy disposition might be an asset. Right now, she was making me ill on smile overload.

"Holy toad piss," Jenks muttered. "This woman is even bouncier than you after you've got some, Rache."

"Shut up, Jenks."

"I haven't seen you like that in . . . hell, how long has it been?"

"Shut up!" I muttered, tightening my scarf until he called uncle, laughing at me. It had been a while, and even worse, it had been with Pierce. Everyone I had sex with died. Except Marshal, and that had only been because he left in time.

Adrenaline hit me when Ms. Bouncy-Hair finished her transaction, catching my eye as she moved to the pickup counter. She must have heard me telling Jenks to shut up, but being the crazy woman would only help, and I gave her a neutral smile and hitched my shoulder bag higher. Sweet or not, she was our fast and dirty ticket into the museum and behind security doors. I hated locking people in their own trunks. Except for Francis. That had been fun.

I was still wearing my smile as I stepped up to the counter. "Ah, two grandes, black. A skinny chai tea tall, and a vanilla grande with a shot of pumpkin in it if you still have it." I knew they did. The drinks I ordered were was the exact same ones Ms. Bouncy-Hair had ordered, right down to the size. "Oh, and can you put it all in a to-go bag? Thanks."

"Got it," the barista said, never looking up, never noticing it was a duplicate order. Junior would have, and I was glad he wasn't here.

I handed the barista a bill to cover it, turning around to see the blue Mustang in the parking lot, the top still open to the sky. "Thank you," I said around a yawn as he gave me my change. Eight? Was it really eight? Adrenaline or not, this was an insane time to be up. That was humanity's problem right there. They were brain damaged from the early sun.

"Ah, Rache?" Jenks whispered, poking me in the neck, and I jumped, giving the barista a faint smile as I moved down.

I stood just inside most people's personal zone, and sure enough, Ms. Bouncy-Hair noticed, shifting down a smidge. My pulse quickened. I couldn't help it. Maybe I was as bad as Ivy. When the woman's order slid onto the counter in one of those paper trays, I was ready.

"Thanks, Bill!" she called out cheerfully, reaching for it as I leaned in as if going for it too. The woman got there first, her hands full of hot coffee as she turned, smashing right into my upraised hand. It would have gone all over me, but I was the one planning accidents, and with a little flip, it went down her front instead.

"What the fuck!" the woman exclaimed, staggering back with her entire order spilled on the floor. Well, not all of it, and her pink V-neck sweater was now an ugly brown.

"Ooh, mouthy," Jenks said, and I heard him take to the air, wings clattering.

My shock was fake, but it looked real enough. I'd had plenty of practice. "Oh, my gosh!" I exclaimed, standing there with my eyes wide and hands up in the helpless-me position. "I am so-o-o-o sorry!"

The baristas were already moving to mop it up, and she dropped back to the tables and chairs, disgust swamping her. "Bill, can I have another set?" she said, and then muttered at me, "Why don't you watch where you're going," as if embarrassed for the F bomb she'd dropped.

She was on the defensive, and that was fine with me. It didn't make the guilt any less, but it did tend to put it off till later.

"Oh my God, I'm so, so sorry," I said, grabbing napkins like mad and shoving them at her. "Here, let me give you my address," I said, head down and fumbling in my bag as she took them, dabbing at her front until she realized it was useless. Jenks was at the ceiling, and I dumped my bag out to distract her when the napkins hadn't done it. "I've got a card in here somewhere. Send me the bill for your cleaning. Oh, that's got angora in it, doesn't it? I can tell."

"Seriously, it's okay," she said, but she was watching me now, not Jenks in her purse. Hell, everyone was watching me. Ivy and Jenks had helped me stock my bag, and the tampons, diaphragm, jumbo condoms, and fuzzy cuffs that Jenks had picked out were garnering snickers.

"I am such a klutz," I said, snatching up the pen Ivy had given me from a Hollows strip joint. I scribbled the downtown bus depot's address on a matchbook.

"No, really, it's okay," she said, hand up to keep me at arm's length. Her expression was a mix of disgust and contempt. I was a doofus, and everyone could tell.

"Please, just take it," I said, and she finally did just to shut me up. "I must have been half asleep." My order came up in its bag, and the woman realized she was going to have to go home and change. I could see it in her eyes. Behind her in the parking lot, the top was almost closed. "At least let me pay for your drinks!" I said, reaching out as if I was going to take her arm.

She backed off fast. "I already paid for them," she said, bouncy no more. Grimacing, she plucked at her sweater and looked at her watch. "Bill, I gotta go. Forget the coffee."

"Catch you tomorrow, Barbie," one called, and I almost choked. Barbie? Really? Was that legal?

But the car again had a roof. "Wait! Your coffee!" I exclaimed, taking my own bag of duplicate brew and following her.

"Look, it's okay!" the woman said, starting to get angry as she headed for the door. "I have to go home and change. Just forget it, okay? Accidents happen."

I hesitated, a forlorn expression on me as she stormed out. Accidents do happen, especially when you plan for them. The chimes jingled merrily, and my eyes fell to my feet. "Well, I tried!" I said to everyone, then darted back to the counter and shoved everything back in my purse.

Hustling after her, I stiff-armed the door open. She was almost to her car, and she jerked when she saw me. "Really, it's okay!" she said as if knowing I was going to follow. I almost smiled. My gaze slid to the nearby Dumpster, looking for a leprechaun catching a smoke beside it. Today I might risk accepting a free wish.

Jenks dropped down, and I fluffed my scarf as he snuggled in. "Hey, you think it's gotten colder?" I asked him as we *click-clacked* to her, more to be sure he was watching his temps than any need for conversation.

Jenks tugged the scarf tighter around himself. "Dropped two degrees since this morning. We'll be inside tonight."

Adrenaline flowed, sweet and beautiful. She was standing at her car, fumbling for her missing keys in her cluttered purse. It was so easy to take someone. Really, it was astounding it didn't happen more often. She was so frazzled she didn't even remember the top had been open when she'd gone in.

"Here, take some money!" I said, arm out to her as I came forward. "I owe you for the drinks."

"I said it was okay!" she shouted, clearly pissed. Still no keys in hand, she got in her car, thinking it was safer. The door slammed, and I stood there, tapping on the window. "Leave me the fuck alone!" she shouted, open purse on her lap. "My God, are you trying to pick me up?"

Ivy sat up from the backseat, a pale arm sliding around her neck. "No, we're trying to abduct you," she whispered. "There's a difference. You'd have more fun if we were trying to pick you up."

The woman took a breath to scream, and I tapped on her window, shaking my head.

"I wouldn't," Ivy breathed, her eyes a nice steady brown.

"Yeah!" Jenks shouted through the glass at her as he hovered at her eye level. "It will only get her excited. You won't like her if you get her excited."

"Unlock the door," Ivy demanded, and Barbie fumbled for the lock, scared.

I opened the door, smiling now so she wouldn't be so frightened, but it kind of backfired. "Slide over," I said, gesturing. "Go on. You're skinny. Get in the passenger seat."

"Money?" she said, white-faced. "You want money? I don't have any brimstone. Here, take my purse. Take it!"

"I've already been in your purse," Jenks said from the dash. "You don't have any."

"Just slide over," I said, concerned someone was going to notice me. "Now, Barbie, or I'll turn you into a frog."

Jenks's wings clattered, his dust a happy silver. "She'll do it!" he warned. "I used to be six feet tall."

Ivy rolled her eyes, but the woman awkwardly moved over the console. "You really need to stop making up stupid names for people you come in contact with," the vampire muttered, shifting with her. "It's not respectful."

Mood improved, I flipped the seat to put the bag of coffee on the floor. "That's her real name," I said as I got in, and Ivy winced.

"Sorry."

"Please don't hurt me!" Barbie said, really scared now, and I felt bad as I took the keys Ivy handed over the seat and started up the car with a satisfying rumble.

"Hurting you isn't in the plan," I said as I carefully backed up and put it in drive. "So please don't do anything to change it. All we want is your car for a few hours, and then we will drop you off in downtown Cincinnati with a story that will get you a ghostwritten novel and a movie of the week. Okay?"

Barbie licked her lips. "You're Rachel Morgan, aren't you," she said, eyes wide.

I met Ivy's eyes in the rearview mirror, not sure if I should be flattered or not. Ivy shrugged, and when Jenks snickered, I turned to the woman, smiling my warmest.

"Yep, and you're going to help us save the world. What's your parking spot, Barbie?"

Chapter Twenty-One

But I want to help save the world!" Barbie said plaintively as I helped her into the backseat of the cab, my hand on her head so she didn't hit anything. Her hands were bound with those fuzzy cuffs, and it made her balance chancy. "I can help. Oh God, don't leave me here. It smells like bad tacos!"

My nose wrinkled, and I took her ID tag from around her neck and stuffed it in a back pocket. "Larry gets one of the no-frill blacks, Susan the pumpkin, and Frank the chai, right?"

Jenks hovered over the roof of the cab, impatient. "You're gonna be late for your first day," he warned.

"Yes, but I can help!" she insisted, and I leaned back in to wiggle her shoes off. I hadn't worn the right heels, and the doppelgänger charm would only glamour me to look like her. It would be more convincing if we were the same height.

"Trust me," I said as I shifted out of the backseat. "You're helping. Really."

I stood and looked over the empty park, hoping no one was watching from the town houses across the way. Ivy was bent over talking to the cab-driver, giving him a wad of cash and a peek at her cleavage as she told him to take the woman to the hospital—the mental hospital. By law, they had to give everyone who was dropped off an exam, and with the story Barbie had, they'd give her the long version. It was the best I could come up with on such short notice, not very nice, but better than stuffing her in the trunk of her car or leaving her tied up somewhere.

"Good?" I asked the driver, and he met my eyes through the rearview mirror, nodding.

"Wait!" Barbie cried, as I shut the door and she pounded on it with her fuzzy-cuffed wrists. "How will I know?" she shouted, muffled but understandable through the glass. I motioned for the driver to roll the window down, and she leaned toward me, breathless. "How will I know if you save the world?"

The really, really long version. "If we're all still here Saturday, then it worked," I said, then patted the top of the cab to let him know we were done.

"I want to help!" the woman cried as they drove off, and Ivy crossed the pavement to stand beside me. Jenks flitted close with a strand of Barbie's hair, and using it, I primed the doppelgänger charm. The ley line up here was barely usable on the best of days, running right through the manmade ponds and under the Twin Lakes Bridge, but now, with the lines unbalanced and screaming in discord, it was awful.

I shuddered as I invoked the charm and dropped it into a pocket. Jenks made a long whistle, and Ivy nodded. I looked at my hands, seeing nothing different, but obviously they could. Even my voice would sound like hers. Illegal. Everything we were doing was illegal, and not for the first time, I wondered how I'd gotten to this place, doing illegal things to help Trent. Help him save the world.

Maybe I should be the one in the cab going to the hospital.

Seeing my mood, Ivy put an arm over my shoulders and turned me back to the cars. "You were nice," Ivy said as we crossed the night-cooled pavement. "Nicer than I'd have been. She'll have an interesting morning and be home for lunch. Don't beat yourself up about it."

"I don't like involving her," I said as we came up to Barbie's car. "And trying to be her is going to get us caught. I can't be a real person."

"Yeah," Jenks said as he checked himself out in the side mirror. "She's too bouncy."

Frowning, I opened the door and sat down, my feet still on the pavement. "Have you ever tried to be someone you're not?" I said as I pulled off my boots, tossing them into the back, and put on Barbie's heels.

"All the time." Ivy wasn't looking at me, her eyes on the Hollows across the river.

"That's not what I meant," I said, then used *Barbie*'s keys to start *Barbie*'s car. I didn't like this. Not at all. But I needed those rings, and this was the only way to get them.

Ivy looked at me through the open window. I could still smell Barbie's perfume, and it made me uncomfortable. "You okay with this, or you want to scrap it right now?"

Jenks hovered behind her, and I put the car in reverse to back out. She knew as well as I there was no choice. Still, I stewed over it all the short drive to the art museum, becoming more and more angry. The only reason we were trying this on such short notice was because I was familiar with the layout. Nick had worked here, and he'd given me a private tour on more than one occasion. The entire basement was a maze of storage and offices, and that's where the showpieces would be until the night before the exhibit opened.

Ivy was behind me in her mom's blue Buick as I pulled into the museum's parking lot. Knowing it would be what *Barbie* would do, I parked in a spot where no one would scratch the paint, finding a place that would be in the shade come noon. Ivy slowly drove past, headed for a spot closer to the door. She was going in as a patron and had a sketch pad and folding chair. Once I got downstairs, Jenks would give her my ID and she'd come down in the far elevator, clearing our exit en route.

The coffees were cold when I picked up the bag and slid out, and after locking the car, I crouched to put the key on the front wheel where I had promised Barbie I would leave it. Not wanting to ruin my story with cold coffee, I reached for a ley line and warmed them up with a charm, my thoughts firmly on the dark, bitter brew so I didn't warm up, say, the radiator of the car. Ceri had taught me this one, and thoroughly unhappy, I stomped to the main entrance, the unfamiliar heels making me trip on the curb.

I didn't look up as Jenks rejoined me, having ridden to the museum with Ivy. Silent, he worked his way past my hair, now down like Barbie had hers. "She'll be fine," Jenks said as he resettled himself behind the curtain of my hair.

I didn't like that I was telegraphing so much, and I said nothing. Barbie probably wouldn't come to work in black slacks and a sweater that covered her cleavage, but I had an excuse for that, too. Late, I took the stairs at a mincing hurry, fumbling for my ID.

"These heels are killing me," I muttered to Jenks when I got to the top and the security guy cracked open the door for me.

"Relax, Rache. You're sweating."

Yes, I was sweating. I didn't like this. I had abducted a woman and was pretending to be her. It was daylight. And I couldn't shake the feeling that Nick was somewhere watching me.

"Hey! Hi! I'm late!" I said cheerfully, trying to match Barbie's bouncy attitude when I reached the door. "Some witch spilled her coffee all over me and I had to go home and change."

Larry—by his name tag—smiled and held the door as I slid in before him. "You got five minutes," he said, and I hesitated just inside the echoing space. Crap, I'd forgotten which one he was supposed to get.

"You'd better hustle, though," the man said, eyes alight as he took one of the tall, no-nonsense black coffees. "Bull is on the warpath."

My brief relief that he knew which was which died. *Bull?* I thought, then juggled the remaining coffee to get my ID to show. "Thanks for the heads-up," I said, rolling my eyes because it seemed the right thing to do.

"Thank you." He hoisted the coffee in salute, hiding it behind his security podium when a masculine shout echoed from somewhere deep inside.

I gave him a last smile, then turned away, heart pounding. Barbie worked the information/security stand just across the lobby, but there were two, and I wasn't sure which one to go to. The elevator to the basement was through the Great Hall, but there was a stairway across from Larry's post that only the employees, and their ex-girlfriends, knew about. My heels clacked on the marble floor, and I angled to the woman watching me from the information booth. I was willing to bet that was Susan.

"Barb!" a high, masculine voice called, and I smiled at Susan when our eyes met.

Jenks's wings tickled my neck. "Ah, Barbie?" he prompted, and that first call registered.

Feeling out of control, I spun to the guy in the tweed vest hanging out of the museum gift shop. "Girl, where's my chai!" he called good-naturedly, and I reversed my direction. I was guessing this was Frank.

"Sorry!" I gushed as I hustled to him, my voice raised in the echoing space as Jenks darted off my shoulder, zipping up and into the ductwork to find the main security junction. "I am so ditzy this morning. Some witch at Jun—ah, at Mark's spilled her coffee all over me and I had to run home to change. I haven't been able to think two straight thoughts in a row since!"

Frank took the chai tea, a smile on his face. "Thank God . . . ," he drawled, running an eye up and down my outfit. "That swill they serve in the cafeteria sucks. Honestly, I don't know why you don't wear black more often. It's classic, and with that figure of yours, you can get away with it. Go on now. You'd better make with the busywork. He's on the warpath. Some tight-ass is jerking his chain, and we peons get the horns."

My smile took on an honest warmth as he took a sip, waving me off. "Thanks," I said, guessing they had a good friendship, and he smiled right back and sipped his drink.

"Damn, girl!" he exclaimed dramatically. "How did you get it here so hot!"

Larry was opening the doors to the public as I hustled to the last woman. Her polyester navy-blue suit with a white blouse screamed tour guide, and her eyebrows were high at my black outfit. "Susan," I blurted before she could say anything. "Oh my God! You wouldn't believe the morning I've had." Nervous, I slid behind the counter, praying I was doing this right. "How's the Bull?"

Susan took the pumpkin latte, and I exhaled in relief, glad I got to keep the straight-up black. "He's on fire," she said, making an *mmm* of appreciation and wiping the foam from her lips. "Something about that new elf exhibit. Thanks, this is good this morning. Black is a new look for you. What's up?"

I shrugged, not wanting to sit down and claim the space until I knew it was mine. "A witch dumped her coffee on me. You like the purse?" I lifted my shoulder bag for her inspection. "It doesn't match, but I was in a hurry." Susan shrugged, and I set my bag on the counter beside my coffee. "Elf exhibit?" I prompted, scanning the security cameras at the ceiling for Jenks's dust. We'd had zero time to plan this, and though I liked working by the seat of my pants, I didn't want everything to come tumbling down because of new security.

Coffee in hand, Susan eyed the first people coming in. "Something about the security not being adequate. Here they come. Is it Friday yet?"

"Don't push it," I whispered. Hand to my middle, I fell back, not wanting to do a tour. Just inside the door were two moms and three kids. They were getting their strollers and diaper bags arranged as the kids hooted, listening to their voices echo. Behind them, Larry gave Ivy's sketch bag a cursory glance. She got the all-clear, and the stately woman strode by the young moms with their kids with a tight-jawed stance at the lack of planning, but under it was a wistful need.

"I don't feel so good," I said, still standing behind the information counter as if I belonged. Susan seemed to think I did, and I was going to go with it.

"You look awful," Susan said, eyeing me in concern. "Sit, will you? You're making me nervous. I'll take the first tour."

"Thanks," I whispered, sinking down.

"And while you're there, organize the brochures, will you?" she added cheerfully, grabbing a map and going out to meet the moms, now trying to get their kids and move forward.

I gave her a sour look when she simpered at me over her shoulder. It was the right thing to do, apparently. Ivy was gone, and I looked to the hallway that led to the stairs and employee break room. I was anxious for Jenks to get back. The less I had to play tour guide Barbie, the better.

"Good morning!" Susan said, maps in hand as she approached the two women. "We're gathering a tour up in the Great Hall if you're interested. It takes about forty minutes and is free. I'll be along in about five minutes if you want to wait."

Jenks dropped down, scaring the crap out of me, and I coughed to hide my surprise. "Ivy is setting up beside the elevator that will take her down to the basement," he said, grinning because he had made me jump. "I'm going to trip an alarm in the courtyard. Don't go until it trips the second time. Got it?"

"Second alarm, got it," I said, waving his dust away before Susan turned and saw it.

"Soon as you're downstairs, I'll do a flyby for your ID and take the elevator up for Ivy."

It wasn't a bad plan, but I knew the maybes were driving Ivy crazy. "Got it. Second alarm. Go!" I hissed as Susan gave up on the two women and started back, maps smacking her thigh.

Giving me a thumbs-up, Jenks dropped down below the level of the counter and flew off at ankle height, his sparkles making a brief flash against the marble floor.

"Any bets?" Susan leaned against the counter like a tired tourist. I stared at her blankly, and she looked at her watch and added, "If I get out of here before Bull shows up?"

"Ahh . . ." I hedged, and she leaned to look down the hallway and into the Great Hall.

"Damn, they aren't going to wait," she said, dropping back a step. "Barb, I'm going to go snag them. I do *not* want to be sitting here for the next hour. If anyone else comes in, send them down. I'll keep them in the Great Hall until the tour is supposed to start."

I made a face as if I was going to protest, and then an irritating whine of an alarm shrilled into existence. My pulse quickened, and I spun the fake rings on my fingers. "Go," I said, wanting to be out of here. "It's probably nothing." She hesitated, and I added, "You're going to lose them."

Her breath a quick exhale, she reached over the counter and grabbed a tour guide flag. "Thanks. I owe you."

Her heels *click-clacked* away, just as the alarm cut out. "No, thank you," I said dryly, then waved to Frank standing at the opening to the gift shop. He abruptly ducked inside, and I spun my chair to see three men striding importantly through the lobby and toward the café. One was in a suit and tie, one in a security uniform, and the third was maintenance. *Way to go, Jenks!*

"Barb!" the man in the suit exclaimed when we made eye contact, his pace never slowing. "I want to talk to you. Where's Sue?"

I spun my chair nonchalantly. "Tour," I said, scanning the ceiling for pixy dust.

"Don't go anywhere." His head dropped and he barked into a handheld radio, "I want an answer now, not in five minutes!"

Just as they vanished into the corridor, the alarm began again. I smiled at the masculine, PG-13 swearing. Frank was laughing. I could see him shaking through the glass walls.

It was time to go, and I grabbed my shoulder bag and dropped the BACK IN FIVE MINUTES sign on the counter. "Bathroom!" I mouthed to Frank when he noticed, and he nodded and went back to testing out the headphones for the "soothing sounds" display.

Alarm still shrieking, I angled to the employees' restroom, waving to Larry and heading down the cold stairwell to run Barb's card through the reader at the bottom.

Cement walls painted white and a tile floor put down in the 1960s met me, grimed in the corners and looking like they hadn't been washed in five years. Heart pounding, I fingered the doppelgänger charm in my pocket, eager to get rid of it. My heels were noisy, and I passed the break room trying to be quiet when I heard the hum of a microwave.

"Barb!" someone shouted, stopping me cold.

Shit. "Yeah?"

"Bull is looking for you."

I exhaled. "Why do you think I'm down here?"

Whoever it was laughed, and I hustled down the corridor, taking my heels off as I went and stuffing them in my shoulder bag. I had a rough idea where the show was being stored, and I wove through the maze, thankful that Nick had given me the grand tour.

The sound of Jenks's wings slowly became obvious. "How long we got?" I said when he hummed around a corner, taking it tight so his dust made a wide arc.

"Depends how long that alarm stays on," he said, and as if mentioning it had been the trigger, it went off. "Seven minutes," he muttered. "Where's the elven crap?"

"We should have done this at night," I said, as he flew off faster than I could run.

"They have dogs at night!" he said, hovering before a pane of glass for a second before going to the next.

The floors now had carpet squares, and air smelled like lemons instead of tuna fish. We were close, and I fingered Barb's ID. "I like dogs," I said, peeking into the room though Jenks already had. "Dogs and I get along great." Seven minutes? It was going to be close.

"Rache!"

Three doors down, he was dusting heavily, and I jogged forward. Before I even got there, he had darted under the door. I looked past the glass to see long tables covered with artifacts in cases ready for display. My heart pounded.

"Got it!" Jenks sang out. "Run your card!"

Smug, I ran my card, and the door clicked open. Barb wasn't cleared to be down here, but thanks to Jenks, the door's security system was recording the last number that had been used.

"Go," I said as I went in, my fingers already unhooking the lanyard to lighten the load. Jenks snatched it, his flight bobbling as he headed down the hallway to the elevators. I didn't like separating like this, but if all went well, Ivy would join us soon.

"Like clockwork," I said as I shut the door behind him and turned. *Riffletic,* I thought as I scanned the room for the rings. I needed the pair donated by Riffletic. They were perfect, and probably exactly what Riffletic's estate said they were, seeing as I had found two confirmations of it in Trent's books. *Crap, I'd forgotten to take those back this morning.*

I took the doppelgänger charm off, shuddering as I felt the magic leave me. I smiled when I saw the rings were all together in one case, and I scanned the little cards under each one, concentrating on the few that had pairs of rings. Slowly my smile drained away. No Riffletic.

Concerned, I paced through the entire exhibit, thinking that such valuable rings as elven wedding bands might have been given their own case. Statues, books, pictures, and even an ancient tea set, but no more rings.

"Son of a bitch!" I whispered, hearing the sound of soft-soled shoes in the hallway, then pausing when I spotted two of the three tarot cards I'd once seen hanging in Trent's great room. Had the Riffletic family pulled their rings from the show upon hearing I wanted them?

The card reader beeped, and annoyed, I spun to the door. "Where are Riffletic's rings?" I asked Ivy as she came in, then froze when I realized it wasn't Ivy.

A smallish woman in a businesslike skirt and lab coat was standing there, staring at me. Her glasses were thick, and she had a folder in her hand and a sketch of what looked like a gallery. "Who are you?" she said, clearly affronted. "You're not supposed to be down here."

Crap on toast! I thought, scrambling, then decided to play it to the hilt. "I said, where are Riffletic's rings?" I repeated tartly, wishing I had a clipboard or something. A clipboard and a hard hat could get you just about anywhere. "I flew all the way here to pick up some stupid rings, and I don't see them. Who are you?"

Head tilted, the woman eyed me suspiciously. "I'm Marcie. I'm arranging the displays for the show. And Riffletic's rings have already been picked up."

"Well, that's obvious," I said, hand slapping my thigh as if she was being stupid. "If Riffletic's rings are not on display, then the Cumberland estate wants their pieces back as well."

The woman frowned, and I added with a sniff, "There seems to be some question as to the safety of your facility. My God, I got down here with no problem at all."

Marcie looked at her open file folder. "I don't have a record of any Cumberland pieces."

"You lost our rings? What kind of rinky-dink museum are you!"

"We are one of the oldest art museums in the United States," she said hotly. "Don't move." Never taking her eyes off me, she backed up to a landline phone. It looked like it had been down here since they put the carpet squares in.

"Me moving will not be an issue. I'm not leaving until I have the rings in my possession," I said, haughty. *Damn it, Ivy, where are you?* "I can't believe you misplaced them."

"Who did you say you were?" she asked, and we both looked up as the door beeped.

Ivy, I thought in relief, then choked when Nick walked in, cool and calm in a pinstripe gray suit and a blue tie. I almost didn't recognize him with his hair slicked back and his shiny shoes. *Because of him, Ceri and Pierce are dead.* It was all I could do not to crawl over the tables between us. I clenched my teeth when our eyes met and he smiled.

The woman set the receiver back in the cradle. "And who are you?" she asked, pushing her glasses farther up her nose.

He beamed, reaching behind his coat for his wallet. "Nick Sparagmos. FIB," he said, and I couldn't help my bark of laughter. "Thank God you found her," he added, grimacing at me and flipping his wallet open to show an ID. He closed it before Marcie could do more than lean to look, stuffing it away where he'd gotten it from. "Hands in fists on the top of your head," he said to me. "Don't make this hard on yourself."

Why, are we surrounded? I thought sourly, but he was between me and the door. Ku'Sox might drop into him, and then I'd be banned from the museum for blowing it up or setting it on fire, or . . . something. I slid away from the table I was leaning against. "You touch me, and you die, Nick." Damn it, how was I going to get the rings now? Not only were they gone, but if I took my second choice, he'd know and tell Ku'Sox.

The woman looked from me to Nick. "Someone better tell me what's going on," she threatened, and I leaned back, gesturing for Nick to say something, dying to find out, myself.

"This is Le'Arch, the notorious art thief from the United Kingdom," Nick said, pointing at me as he came in. "Have you searched her yet?"

"Oh. My. God," I said, not sure I'd heard him right. "Nick, please tell me you did not just make an anagram of my name. Please. Just please."

His jaw clenched, and he took another step forward. He was almost far enough from the door that I had a good chance of making it through, but without the rings—which were not even here anymore—I was dead anyway. "She has a history of claiming to be agents of big corporations and walking away with priceless artifacts," he said, and the woman's hand came away from the phone.

How long had he been listening at the door, and where in hell were Jenks and Ivy?

Well, Nick wasn't the only one who could tell pretty stories. "Marcie, this jerk is my old boyfriend. He doesn't work for the FIB, and he's been stalking me all week. The man is a thief."

Nick stiffened. "*I'm* a thief?" he said, looking odd in his new clothes as he advanced another step. "I'm not the one stealing ancient elven artifacts to break the ley lines. You are a *menace,* and I'm trying to stop you."

"How dare you blame me for that!" I shouted. "I'm trying to stop him!" His jaw clenched, and I turned to Marcie. The woman hadn't picked up the phone, but she was ready to. "Marcie, I'm sorry," I said, still trying to turn this into a stalker boyfriend issue. "I'm going to file a restraining order as soon as I get out of here. He doesn't work for the FIB, and he's lying to you to get me in trouble with my boss. If I don't get those rings out of here, I'm a dead woman." *True enough.*

Nick made an exasperated sound when Marcie looked at him with doubt, starting to believe me. "Neither of you move."

"Has she taken any pieces yet?" Nick said, but it sounded desperate. "What rings did she ask after?"

Marci's eyes narrowed, her belief swinging back to him. "Riffletic's."

Nick leaned to see the ring case. "There's a pair missing."

"There is not!" I said, affronted, but Marcie had already pulled away from her corner, rushing to look. "No!" I exclaimed when she lowered her head to see and Nick grabbed a heavy vase. It hit the back of her head without breaking, and the woman hung for a heartbeat, eyes wide as she slowly collapsed.

"You son of a bitch!" I said, lunging forward to catch her, my bare feet burning on the carpet squares as I struggled with her weight. "What in hell are you doing? Now it's assault!"

The door beeped, and Nick barely got out of the way as Ivy yanked it open. "I say we return the favor and get the hell out of here," she said as Jenks flew in, sword bared and his dust a dismal blue. Something bad had happened. *Where is Jax?*

I carefully lowered Marcie to the floor, rising up mad enough to plow my fist right between his smiling teeth as Nick backed out of Ivy's easy reach. He was still Ku'Sox's toy. I could tell. "What are you doing down here?" Nick said idly, his head tilted so he could eye a row of artifacts and me at the same time.

Jenks landed on Ivy's shoulder, clearly distressed. "Can we just get out of here?"

But I didn't have the rings yet, and at a loss, I shook my head.

Nick's smile widened. "Don't have what you came for?" he mocked, running a finger on a glass case to leave an obvious mark.

"You got Pierce and Ceri killed," I accused. "How dare you smile at me."

His smile vanished, but I couldn't tell if his sudden contriteness was real or contrived. "I'm sorry about that. I didn't know he was going to kill them."

"He's a psychotic demon!" I shouted, then lowered my voice when Jenks's wings hummed a warning and he darted into the hall. "He doesn't need a reason to kill people, just a reason not to. You are one dumb warlock," I said with a sneer. "Ku'Sox is going to kill you, too."

Nick chuckled, tugging his sleeves down to cover his cuffs. On Trent, it looked good; on him, it looked nervous. "Ku'Sox needs me." Hands on his knees, he leaned over the case of rings. "Mmm. Riffletic rings? I understand they were pulled. Weren't they the elven wedding bands? Seriously?" He straightened. "Better than chastity, I suppose."

Ivy had inched closer, and seeing it, Nick shook his head, stopping her. He still belonged to Ku'Sox, and I didn't want the demon showing up. If we were going to take Nick out, it would have to be fast. But I didn't know if that really mattered anymore. My plan was royally flushed. Ku'Sox wasn't stupid. Three seconds after Nick told him what we were after, he would have it figured out. Maybe I could make that work for me.

"Ku'Sox doesn't need you," I said caustically, and Nick looked up from the display as if I was being stupid. "Or maybe I should say he won't. Thanks to Trent, those Rosewood babies don't need your lame enzymes. The only reason he hasn't eaten you yet is because you're spying on me."

Nick smiled as if giving a benediction. "As I said, he needs me."

"Yeah? For how long?" I said. Clearly distressed, Jenks hovered just outside in the hall at the ceiling. He tapped his wrist like a watch. Ivy wasn't close enough, though. "Maybe you haven't noticed, but I've got an expiration date," I added. "You're going to be deadweight after tomorrow, whatever happens."

Nick frowned, his fingers twitching.

"Didn't think about that, did you, crap for brains?"

His head came up. "You know nothing." He looked at Ivy. "Stop moving, vampire."

Ivy rocked back. "Cut it short or bring him," she said. "We have to go."

"Bring him?" I barked, my chin lifting. Then I said to Nick, "There is no hole deep enough or dark enough to hide you when Ku'Sox decides he's done with you and pulls your plug."

Arms swinging, I headed for the door, figuring he'd get close enough to smack him if he thought I was leaving.

Sure enough, he reached for me, and I let him grab my arm. "We used to be good," he said, eyes angry.

"Yeah? Well, I used to be *stupid*!"

Grabbing his wrist, I spun to put my back to his front, and levered him right over my shoulder. He hit the floor in front of me with a groan, and Ivy was there, her long arm against his neck even though he was out. Jenks flew in at the noise, hovering over us.

"When do you want him to wake up?" she said, and my lip curled.

Jenks's dust was still that depressed blue. "How about never?" he suggested. There was a long tear in his new clothes. *Jax?*

"Ten minutes," I said in disgust, and she let go, shoving him across the narrow walkway to slide into a lower cupboard.

"I like Jenks's idea better," she said as she got up.

"Yeah! What's up, Rache?" Jenks snarled. "You know he doesn't deserve it."

I nodded as I turned back to the rings. "We all have a part to play," I said as I looked over the selection. Time was pressing on me, making me jittery. It couldn't be because Nick was helpless on the floor and I was walking away.

Ivy smelled of darkness and earth as she eased up beside me. "Anything you take he'll know and tell Ku'Sox."

"The ones I really wanted are gone, anyway," I said, wishing I had my cheat sheet, then remembering Marcie had one. "Jenks, check Marcie's sketch there. Who donated the demon slave rings?" Slave rings. This was a mistake. This was a mistake in a big way, but I had to take a huge leap if I was going to survive.

He whistled, his dust a shade brighter as he darted to the woman and leafed through her papers. "Ahh, Cabenoch." He flew up, his dust settling on the velvet background to look like stars on a moonless light. "Cabenoch. That's German, isn't it?"

"It's elvish," I said, finding the rings I wanted. Something in me quivered seeing them there, plain circles of battered metal. They were both tarnished, but one looked as if it had been on a hand that had never seen dirt, and the other had never seen the sun. Slavers. That would work, though it curled my lip thinking about reinvoking them.

"Okay. It's rigged, right?" I said, and Ivy carefully slid the entire box almost entirely off the table. Jenks darted under it, and from the door, Marcie groaned. We had maybe thirty seconds. I didn't want to hit her again. "Jenks?" I prompted, and a wash of depressed blue bathed our feet.

"Standard stuff," he said, not coming out. "I dusted you about ten seconds of electronic memory, so make it fast. Ready?"

I nodded, eyeing the rings I wanted and pulling the fake ones off my finger.

"I still don't see how this is going to help," Ivy griped. "He's going to know the ones you took."

"Just hold it still," I muttered. "Ready, Jenks?"

"On my mark . . . go!" he said, and I opened the lid, feeling a pull of a magnetic field. Breath held, I grabbed the rings, slipping them both on my index finger as I dropped the fake rings in their place. Ivy's eyes widened when I then moved the "donated by" card, then another.

"How long, Jenks?" I said. "Give me a count!"

"Four, three," he said, me moving cards like a con artist on the corner. "Two," he said, and I pulled my hands out, shutting the lid. "One!"

My eyes met Ivy's, and she exhaled. Muscles easily managing the weight, she slid it back onto the table. Jenks flew up, and all three of us looked at the lumps of metal sitting in my hand. They felt as dead as they looked, but something in me quivered. I could bring them back to life. I could make this anew. *Demon slavers.* I shuddered.

"Can we go now?" Jenks said, his dust still that dismal blue, and I nodded, not looking back at Nick as I walked out the door.

Next time I had the chance, he wouldn't be so lucky.

Chapter Twenty-Two

My protection circle hummed with the satisfyingly pure sound that I was identifying with the narrow ley line out back in the graveyard, the bell-like *ting* a spot of beauty in the chaos of sound and abrupt faults every other ley line was spitting out right now. Frustrated, I set the nested slave rings on my palm, and after Jenks's somewhat unenthusiastic thumbs-up, I peeled my aura off my hand, leaving it bare to everything all the way to my wrist.

The steady, ringing *snick, snick, snick* of Ivy sharpening her second-best katana in the corner was a soothing rhythm, but I still felt uneasy as I imagined the thinnest whisper of red aura spilling down my arm, mirroring the shadow of veins to puddle under the rings, rising to gently enfold it and breathe the first hints of life into the cold metal.

"Looking good, Rache."

But it wasn't good, and my heart pounded as I exhaled, empting my mind of everything but the rings. The red had taken, I could feel the cold metal resonating, and I shifted my aura to orange, pinpricks racing over my arms like goose bumps.

Jenks's wings clattered, and my brow furrowed. The sliding sound of Ivy sharpening her blade hesitated, and I stiffened as the orange rose up and over the ring, completely unabsorbed. *Take it, damn it!* But I knew it wasn't going to. I'd been trying all afternoon, and I had never gotten any further than this, and I didn't know why.

"Damn it all to the Turn and back," I muttered, letting the rings drop into my palm and lowering my hand. My full aura raced down my arm, and I shivered, feeling protected again. Jenks's wings slumped, and I shoved the rings into my pocket like a guilty secret.

"If I hadn't done it once, I would have said Pierce made it up," I said sourly as Ivy held her gray length of steel up to the light. "And I don't know why you're sharpening that blade. It's like bringing a knife to a gunfight."

"It's always good to have a backup plan," she said mildly. "And before you say anything, just shut up about it. Jenks and I can keep whatever demons there are at bay while you and Quen do what you need to do."

"I wasn't going to say anything," I said, and her easy motion on the blade hesitated.

"Mmm-hmm." Her tone made it clear she knew I was lying. I'd feel better if they were here and out of harm's way. It was going to be warmer tomorrow night but maybe too cold for Jenks. And Ivy was going to be more of a liability than an asset trying to defend herself against magic. There was a reason even the I.S. didn't send vampires after a witch. I didn't like Quen being out there with me either, but if anyone could help me, it would be him.

"Keep it simple and everything will be fine," Jenks said, and I jumped when a thrown fishhook and line snagged the edge of the counter and Belle's pale, scary face popped up. With an acrobatic flip, she levered herself up and away from the drafts to stand among Trent's library books. I still had to get them back, and I wondered what kind of late fee I might be risking.

Keep it simple, I thought as I reached to tidy Trent's books. Nothing about any of this had been simple. I'd been trying to get these stupid rings to reinvoke since getting back from the museum, all with no results. It was as if something was blocking me. Maybe because the sun was up? Slave rings were foul. Just the idea made me uneasy. And here I was, trying to reinvoke them. For a good reason, I kept telling myself, but did I really want to be the person who believed the end justified the means?

"It will work," I said as I stacked Trent's books with a thump, and the draft blew Belle's spiderweb-like hair back. "You can't lose with a vampire vanguard and a pixy backup."

Ivy glared at me, and I gave her a questioning look until she darted her gaze to Jenks. He was slumped over again, his wings not moving. Damn it! That was supposed to have cheered him up, not remind him of his stupid son! I hadn't known it at the time, but Jenks had found Jax in the back halls and thrashed him soundly so he wouldn't raise the alarm. I was sure his son was okay, but Jenks was depressed.

"Jenks," I pleaded, wiping my hands off on the apron and coming to sit kitty-corner to Ivy, Jenks standing between us. "I'm sorry about what happened with Jax. But I'd be lying if I said I wasn't thankful. It was the difference between walking out of there and being carried."

Jenks's face was frozen in grief and guilt. "I hurt him," he said bitterly. "I tore his wings to shreds. My own son. He won't be able to fly for months, if ever again." A dark pool of black dust spilled off the table for Rex to paw at. "He's my son, even if he is blind, ignorant, and . . ."

His words cut off as his head drooped. Heartache clenched my chest, and I curved my hand around Jenks, wishing I was smaller so that I could give him a hug, and then maybe a shake. "He's been misled," I said softly, and Jenks angrily wiped his face, his hand glowing with a silver dust. "He's your son, Jenks. Whatever happens."

Clearly depressed, Jenks sat down where he was, his legs crossed and his head down. "I don't think *my son* will be spying on us anymore. I scared him. I scared him into believing I'd kill him if he ever came home again."

"Jenks . . ."

"I'm fine," he said with such bile that I knew he wasn't. Head coming up, he flew to the sill, standing beside the overturned water glass and looking out the window with his back to us as he gazed into his garden, shadowed in the coming sunset.

I exchanged a worried look with Ivy. I had no comfort for him, nothing to say.

"He will forgive you."

It had been Ivy who spoke, and Jenks spun, the anger so thick on him that I was glad I hadn't tried to make it better. "What do you know?" he snarled, his wings humming to a transparent brightness, but his feet were nailed to the sill.

Ivy didn't look up, staring at the light glinting on the cool length of steel as she held it up. "I scared someone I loved like that," she said softly. "I was young and stupid. The sex play got out of hand. I cut him deeply and wouldn't stop. I ignored him when he told me no. I carved deeper when he begged me to stop."

The sword dropped, and her head drooped to follow the steel in her hand. "I knew he could take more and that his pain was fleeting. I thought I had a right to correct his assessment of his abilities, but what I was doing was confusing his mental limits with his emotional ones. I was riding high on his fear, and I bled him within an inch of his life."

Only now did she look at Jenks. "He forgave me. Eventually. Jax will, too."

I shifted uneasily, guessing she was talking about Kisten. It sounded about right. Kisten could forgive anything, since he'd done terrible things himself. I thought about that, wondering if only those who did horrible things would ever be able to forgive me. *This had to stop,* I thought, feeling the bump of the rings in my pocket.

"Your son made a serious mistake," Ivy said, and Jenks shuddered. "You beat him, told him he was making an error that was going to end his life, and you told him to walk away before you came back and finished the job. You saved his life. He will forgive you."

Jenks blinked fast, looking like the nineteen-year-old that he was, with all the insecurities and inexperience that that came with. He wanted to believe. I could see it in his brilliantly green eyes. He took a breath to say something, then changed his mind.

I suddenly realized I had to leave. "Ah, I need to make a call," I said, leaning down to slide my scrying mirror out from my cookbooks. "I'll be in the garden," I added, thinking Jenks might open up if I wasn't around. God! We were a messed-up bunch.

"I'll come with you," Belle said, snaking down her rope. "Make s-s-sure the gargoyles-s-s leave you alone."

I looked back as I left, seeing that Jenks had flown to Ivy's monitor. His wings were drooping, and the dust spilling from him was making an oily pattern on the dark screen.

"I left him there, bleeding out. Ivy, he can't fly."

"Neither can Belle, and you can't call her any less a warrior. You saved his life. And perhaps ours. I'm sorry that it was so costly."

I thanked my lucky stars that neither of them said anything else until I grabbed my spring jacket and fled to the back porch. Standing in the cool breath of the coming sunset, I shoved my arms into the thin leather and glumly sat, Belle taking up a position two feet to my right where I probably wouldn't squish her. I set my scrying mirror on my left. The squeak of the cat door was loud, and glowing eyes turned to us from the graveyard when the more mundane sound of the screen door hadn't moved them.

Huddling into my coat, I waved at the gargoyles. I wasn't altogether comfortable out here with them looking at me, but I wanted to interfere with Jenks and Ivy even less. Besides, I really did want to talk to Al. The rings weren't invoking. I knew I could do this since I'd done it before. I just needed the confidence of someone who could see what the hell I was doing with my aura. Jenks was good, but he couldn't hear the lines like a demon.

Rex jumped into my lap, a spot of warmth that I buried my fingers in. The cold damp of the early evening soaked into me as I breathed in the coming night. Low clouds threatened more rain, and last year's leaves rustled in the cold flower beds, mirroring my mood perfectly. Spring cleanup was slower this year now that Jenks was losing kids, going off in pairs and alone to find their way. How did my life get this complex so fast?

"Rachel," Belle lisped as she stood beside me, bow unslung as she watched the gargoyles suspiciously, "do you think Jenks-s-s will find his strength of will again?"

"Yes, of course. He's just having a bad day. He is the strongest person I know. Except for Ivy." My fingers lightly touched Rex as the cat purred, and I wondered if I could beat someone I loved that badly, even if it was for the greater good.

"I often punished fledglings-s-s for risking the nest."

"My mother grounded me a lot," I said, thinking it hadn't done me any harm. It hadn't made me any smarter, either.

"Jenks-s-s shouldn't be hard on himself," Belle said firmly. "He's a warrior."

"Jenks is a gardener in a savage Eden," I said, believing it. He was a savage gardener with a protective streak. Ivy was just as savage, just as protective, when push came to shove. And me? What was I? What choices would I make when the world hung poised on the arc of the pendulum and I was ready to send it in a new direction?

"You will call your demon now for advice?" Belle asked, and I followed her gaze to my scrying mirror.

"I don't know," I said, shifting my feet down a step. "He might not be healed enough."

Again, the silence stretched. "I'm sorry about Ceri," Belle said stiffly. "And Pierce."

I almost smiled. The three of us had killed most of her clan and left her wingless, but perhaps it made more sense to her with her warrior mind-set. "Thank you, Belle."

"They were great warriors. Pierce . . . Jenks tells me you were nearly joined with him."

I nodded, bringing up my second sight. Newt's ley line hung at chest height, a hundred shades of red glowing, mixing, swirling. I desperately wanted to see Pierce there, or even Al. But there was nothing.

"It would have been a good match. You're both strong."

"Perhaps," I said softly. I'd thought I had loved him once, but after the shine of his uniqueness had dulled, I'd come to dislike his loose morals more than I had been attracted to his power and dark strength.

Steadying myself, I reached for my mirror. Reluctantly, slowly, I lifted Rex down and set the heavy glass on my lap instead. I stared into the wine-colored depths in the sunset shadow-light, seeing the roof of the church rising overhead, the steeple distressingly free of Bis. It had been three days. Al should be healed by now.

"Have Jenks and Ivy summon me if I'm not back in two hours," I said, and Belle nodded, swinging up onto Rex for her warmth. I shivered in my jacket, feeling as if I was being watched as I took a last look over the sunset-gloomed garden. *Gargoyles,* I thought.

My way home settled, I closed my eyes and put my hand on the mirror, hoping he was healed. *Al?*

There was only the uncomfortable screeching that the collective had absorbed from the unbalanced line.

Al, I thought again, hope growing since I hadn't gotten a do-not-disturb notice. Just no response. *Algaliarept.*

My eyes closed as the unholy chaos of the collective dissolved into the rushing sound of water or wind, and I felt the lofty sensation of having doubled my mind. Relief coursed through me, and I took a slow breath, sensing green trees, old and damp. I'd found him. I think.

In my thoughts, there was a pool of water among the tree roots, only a few inches deep and looking like glass. The air was moist and warm. I could hear water dripping and smell both moss and fog. There was no wind. No grit, no stink of burnt amber. Dancing over the still water were tiny blue butterflies the size of my thumb. It was a forest pool primeval, the light barely making it through the leaves. On the far side of the stone-and-moss-wreathed pool was a black figure hunched and sitting on the largest smooth boulder, his back to me. Al.

At least . . . I thought it was Al. He didn't look right. *He's dreaming,* I thought, but he must have heard me as he turned, scrabbling to hide whatever he was doing on the rock.

"Al?" I said in our shared dream, remembering having done this once before. I wasn't sure it was him. He was thin—almost malnourished, like a fairy—his skin very dark and his hair a tight curl. He stood, and I realized he had leathery wings draped down over his back like a cloak. His eyes were red-slitted goat eyes, but so wide they looked black. I'd never seen him this thin and spindly, the angular sharpness even in his face, narrowing down to a very small pointy chin. He looked like a creature of the air. Alien.

"Rachel," he said, his voice the same as I remembered, even if it was a shade embarrassed and deeper than it should be for such a slight frame.

Nervous, I focused on his eyes. "Are you okay?" *Is this what demons originally looked like?*

Apparently not hearing my dream thought, Al turned around to look sadly at the rock he'd been sitting on. "I broke it," he said. "They can't leave until I fix him, and if they stay, they're going to die. They need the sun . . . too."

I edged closer, wondering how long this shared dream might last. On the rock was a handful of blue and silver shards as sharp as glass.

"I've been trying to put her back together," Al said, gesturing, "but the pieces don't match, no matter how turned."

"Oh." Okay, this was really weird, but no weirder than the last dream we shared about blue butterflies vanishing into the walls of a maze grown from wheat.

"The edges are torn," he said, gesturing. "I don't remember when I broke it."

I frowned, bending over the mess. "Look, you've got this piece upside down," I said, then jerked when the shard cut me. A drop of my blood glistened on the silver sliver, and then like magic, the splinters just sort of melted together into a whole, the entire butterfly turning red from my blood to look like stained glass.

"Some things can't be fixed," Al said forlornly as I watched the red butterfly flutter her new wings on the rock and then fly up to join her friends.

Al didn't look up from the rock, and I wondered if he was still seeing broken shards where there was now nothing. "Al, you're dreaming," I said, and he brought his eyes up to meet mine. There was an uncomfortable innocence in them, and I started to wish I could back up and start again. "Can you bring me over? I need your help."

His gaze went to the butterflies dancing up through the canopy, blinking in surprise as he looked back at the empty rock. "Sure," he said, clearly preoccupied. "Come on over."

I gasped in pain as the line took me, hearing Al's bellow as everything vanished in a flash of white-hot agony. I didn't understand! It had been three days. He should be healed by now, and I hit the ground hard as reality—or the ever-after, actually—re-formed around me.

My face plowed into the black marble floor of Al's spelling kitchen, and my shoulder gave a twinge as I rolled toward the large circular fire pit with its raised benches. "Ow," I said softly, hearing Al cursing nearby.

It had been a rough landing, but I was here, and with a renewed hope—and embarrassment—I untangled myself and propped myself up on an elbow. My scrying mirror was lying on the floor, and I scooped it up, checking it for cracks before setting in on the bench. The new, ragged hole in the wall gave me pause, Al's bedroom looking gray beyond it—a door into the once doorless room. Apparently he'd wanted in before he could jump a line. A pained sound jerked my attention to the small hearth at the front of the room.

It was lit, and between the shadowy coals and the slate spelling table was a hunched figure on the floor. "Mother pus bucket," Al groaned, throwing back the blanket he had been wrapped in to scowl at me. "I was asleep!" he yelled, his new black eyes glaring as he held his head. "What do you mean by asking me to jump you over here when I was asleep? The lines are all a bloody hell mess! You can't jump without a gargoyle assist, or it bloody hell *hurts*!"

"Really? I had no idea," I said as I sat up, wishing my head would stop throbbing. At least he was healed, though, and I cautiously sat on the hearth across from him, recalling that weird batlike image he had had in his dream and wondering if he remembered it. He was in his robe, not surprising me at all. "Sorry," I said, as he felt his ribs and grimaced. "You okay?"

"Do I look okay?" he griped, and I couldn't help my grin. "Why the hell are you laughing! You think this is funny?"

"No," I said, unable to stop smiling. "I'm just glad you're okay."

He grumbled under his breath, groaning as he reached for a lump of dirt he then threw onto the fire. The stench of burnt amber grew stronger. "I'm assuming you have a reason to be here," he said, watching the fire, not me. "Besides wanting to see me in *pain*."

I scooted closer, wondering if the room was indeed smaller. There wasn't the floor space that I remembered, but maybe the new door would account for it. "I need your help. Dali gave me until Friday to settle with Ku'Sox, but I think he'd rather kill me if he gets the chance."

"I can't imagine *why*," he snarled, hunching into his blanket and looking miserable.

I took a breath. "I can prove Ku'Sox broke my line, but I need—"

He looked at me as my words cut off in guilt. Oh God. They were elven slavers. He wouldn't help me. What was I doing here?

"What do you need . . . Rachel," he said suspiciously.

Licking my lips, I tugged my coat closer. It was unusually cold in here. "Ah, I can prove Ku'Sox broke the line by moving all the imbalance at once to the line in the garden and thereby exposing his curse. But I have to keep him off me until someone comes to look, and that won't happen until I prove I can best him. And to do that, I need help."

Al didn't shift, didn't make a single indication that he heard me. "Black-souled student thinks she can just come anytime she wants," he grumped, reaching back to scratch his shoulders under his blanket. "Were you in my dream?"

"No," I said, and then when his black-eyed stare fell on me, I amended, "Yes. Al, I've got a workable plan. I need help."

He sighed, but if it was because I'd seen his dream or that I had a plan he was sure would fail, I didn't know. "Damn blue butterflies," he whispered, watching the red sparks drift up the chimney. "They don't mean anything. Are you hungry?"

What was it with men trying to feed me all the time? "No. Al—"

"I am," he said, interrupting me as he reached for a covered basket beside the hearth. It was tied with a checkered bow, and I imagined it was from Newt—hopefully on one of her good days. "I've not eaten in weeks, it feels like," he said as he undid the ribbon and looked inside.

"Al, I need your help."

"Oh." His expression fell. "I am *not* eating that. Rachel, this is foul. Come smell this."

"Al!"

Al stopped fussing with the basket, his head down. "I know you want to use my rings. You aren't strong enough to overpower Ku'Sox alone. No one is, not even two demons together. Not three. Five, it took last time, and since only four walked away from the encounter, no one is willing to try again. Especially when there are bribes of mended demon babies with which to escape to the sun in."

"You know?" I said, my surprise quickly vanishing.

He eyed me as if embarrassed. "Of course. I was burned, not lobotomized. My wedding rings are not enough." Pulling them from a pocket, he pushed them around in his palm with a bare finger. "Even if you and I wore them and stood before Ku'Sox, they would not be enough."

I was starting to get mad. Why did I have to do this all by myself? "You've given up!"

A weary slump came over him. "Rachel . . . We made him to be better than us, able to crush an elf warlord on his own. My rings are not enough."

"But I know how to fix the line!" I protested, and he reached up to set his rings on the slate table beside him. "It's not broken, just overloaded. Ku'Sox shoved all the tiny imbalances in your collective lines into mine, making them more than the sum of their energies. Bis and I separated Newt's signature imbalance from that purple sludge and got it back into the line she made."

His eyes widened, and I stifled a shudder at the new blackness of them. "Interesting," he said, tossing another chunk of earth on the flames. "The loss is keyed to individual lines . . . and you separated one?" Settling himself deeper into the flagstones, he seemed to find strength with the fire behind him. "Is this why Newt's room are not shrinking anymore?"

"Probably," I said, wondering if there was a direct connection between the imbalance, the leak, and the missing mass. If so, she wasn't going to like my dumping the imbalance into her line. "That's why Ku'Sox took Bis. But I don't need Bis to move the entire ball of sludge to Newt's line and expose Ku'Sox's curse."

Al's expression twisted. "Whereupon he will descend upon you and—"

"Turn me into a dark spot on the ever-after floor. Yeah," I said, picking at a seam in the floor. "I was hoping that once I proved he did it that maybe some of you might . . . I don't know . . . *help me maybe!*" I shouted, frustrated.

Chuckling, Al resettled himself. "I would, but it will take at least five, not counting you because you don't know squat."

I would have argued with him, but he was right. "Quen will stand with us. And Trent, if we can get him free."

Al stiffened at Trent's name. "Elf magic might prevail where demon can't," he admitted grudgingly. "As much as I'm loath to admit it, Trent would be the better choice." He poked at the fire to send up a flurry of copper-colored sparks. "He's a savage beast with a strong bond to his trickster goddess." His eyes met mine in warning. "Powerful, but chaotic. Untrustworthy."

It wasn't a ringing endorsement, but surprisingly promising, and I eyed him from around my snarling hair. "Are you saying that elf magic is more powerful than demon?"

"I would never *admit* that," he said with a guffaw. "But Ku'Sox knows demon magic. Elf magic, from the old wars? Not so much."

The way he was looking at me made me nervous, and I dropped my eyes.

"Mmm," he grumbled, apparently satisfied. "Demons acting in concert isn't enough. To surpass Ku'Sox, there must be a complete melding of thoughts into one action. My rings only work between demons. There's no way to join an elf soul to a demon."

There is, I thought, suddenly scared to say it. "Ah, that's kind of why I'm here . . ." Heart pounding, I extended my arm and opened my palm, the firelight glinting on the rings.

Al leaned forward in interest, his thick bare fingers brushing against mine as he took the rings. "These are . . . Where did you get these?" he said, his black eyes narrowed as he made a fist around them, hatred pouring from him.

My lips parted. Scared, I fought to keep from backing up. His grip on the rings looked tight enough to crush them. My thought went back to what Quen had said about demons perhaps being slaves first. "The museum. I wanted something else, but they were gone when I got there, and these were—" I gasped when his fist clenched. "Al, no!" I shouted, grabbing his hand and trying to pry open his fingers. "Don't break them! It's all I have! Please!"

He snarled at me, the lines in his square features heavy and ugly. With a grimace, he yanked out of my grip and threw the rings into the corner. My breath came fast, and I lunged after the twin pinging sounds, scrabbling like a spider as I found first one, then the other.

I held them tight to my chest, my back to him as my pulse pounded. He would never help me. Head high, I walked back to the fire with the rings in my shaking hand.

"Elven slavers!" Al growled. "They are ugly, and I have done a lot of ugly, Rachel."

"Ku'Sox is uglier," I said stiffly. "This is what I have. I'm going to use them. If I can hold him off long enough, maybe the rest of you cowards will stand up to him."

"Except the rings are dead." Al's voice was harsh.

I stood before him, the fire warming my shins. I wasn't sure how he was going to react once I told him I could bring them back to life. "I, ah, can reinvoke them."

He looked up at me, a sour anger in the tilt of his head. "No one can reinvoke them."

Sitting down, I scooted until our knees almost touched. "I reinvoked elven silver two days ago with Pierce's help."

Taking up a poker, he jabbed it into the flames. They were slavers. He'd never help me. "So go ask him," Al muttered, clearly not believing me.

"He's dead. Nick helped him escape Newt so he and Ceri could try to kill Ku'Sox."

"Ceridwen?" Al's head snapped up. "What does she have to do with this?"

I suddenly remembered that she'd been with him for a thousand years, that he'd been so careless when replacing her as his familiar that I'd been able to save her life. Looking back, I think he'd done it intentionally. And all this time I'd thought that I'd been more clever than he. God, I was stupid. I think he had loved her.

"Al, I'm sorry," I whispered, kicking myself for not considering that he might feel pain at her loss. "Ku'Sox—"

Al extended a shaky hand to stop my words, his head dropping. "Enough," he said, the hard sound of his voice a band of metal around my heart, squeezing, hurting.

I shifted closer, the scent of burnt amber coming from the fire stinging my eyes. Al had taken a deep breath, and I watched as he slowly exhaled, his hands unclenching. "I'm sorry. I thought you knew. Didn't Newt tell—"

"I said *enough*!"

I hunched into myself, my own grief welling up as I watched him shove his own down, denying its existence. "Al, I need your help," I whispered, and he seemed to become a dark lump before the low flames. "I only have until tomorrow midnight. I've done this before. I don't know why it's not working."

Al's shoulders were slumped under that blanket, and his expression was numb. I wasn't even sure he was listening anymore. "You don't know what you ask."

"It's the only way to make a sure connection between an elf and a demon," I said. "And since no demon will help me . . ."

Al's head turned from the fire. His black eyes bore into me, and I stifled another shudder. "Top shelf," he said flatly. "Behind the books."

I followed his gaze to one of the few open bookcases. Silently I stood and shoved the rings in my front pocket. Feeling his eyes on me, I crossed the room, counting my steps. It was smaller by about a foot. My hands were steady as I stood on tiptoe, one hand on the shelf for balance as I moved three books out of the way, my hand searching blindly in the small space behind them. A jolt went through me as I found the cool, smooth shape of a ring.

"Don't put it on," Al cautioned as my heels came down and I turned with a ring in my hand. It was tiny, almost a pinkie ring. I wondered whose it was, since it wouldn't fit on Al's hand. Unless . . . he was in the shape of that gaunt black bat.

"What is it?" I asked, cold but too wary to come back to the fire.

"Half of a set," he grudgingly said, his eyes down as he snatched it from me, cradling the ring to him as if it were alive. My eyes widened as I realized it was his shackle, his tie to a miserable past. "I want you to see this," he said. "To know what you risk."

"I'm sorry," I said softly as I came forward to sit cross-legged before him again. He was flushed, embarrassed and ashamed to be clearly still tied to it. "Where's the other half?"

Al smiled a savage, ugly smile. "Gone, along with its owner."

My eyes fell. I couldn't look at him. *Al had been a slave?* "Al—"

"I trusted once."

I couldn't say anything, huddled cold before his fire in his shrinking room, failing world.

"You're willing to risk your life," he said, "but what of your soul? What if the master ring falls to someone else? What then? It's only the slave ring that can't be removed by its wearer."

My eyes fell to Al's hands, just visible among the folds of the blanket. He wasn't wearing gloves, and they looked hard and worn. But I had no choice. Miserable and unsure I looked up. "I have to do this."

I couldn't tell what he was thinking. His eyes catching the red glow of the low flames seemed almost normal. "Then why have you failed?"

Oh God. I knew why I'd failed, and I dropped my gaze. "I'm afraid," I whispered, and he smiled. "Damn it, it's not funny!" I shouted. "I'm afraid!"

Still smiling, Al looked at my fingers knotted around one another, but he didn't reach out to touch me. "Do you trust Quen?"

Miserable, I thought of Quen, his morals, his loyalty, his strength of character. Ceri had loved him, and Ray was his entire world. I knew exactly what I would get with Quen, and I nodded. I trusted him.

"Do you trust . . . Trent?" Al said. My head snapped up, and Al bobbed his head at my deer-in-the-headlights expression. "Ahh, there it is," Al said, infuriatingly smug.

"Trent won't ever have access to it," I said quickly.

"Chances are he will. If you trusted him, you could invoke them. Show me what you do to invoke elven . . . silver."

Flustered, I dug the rings out. "I trust him. I do," I asserted, but my stomach clenched, telling me I was lying.

Al shrugged his shoulders, and his blanket fell away. "Then show me."

Fine. Mood sour, I carefully snuggled the smaller ring into the cradle of the larger. Shifting on the hard flagstones, I perched the rings on the tips of the fingers of my left hand, holding it right at eye level between us. One last look at Al, who had fumblingly put on a pair of glasses I could only assume would let him see my aura easier, and I closed my eyes.

God, please help me do this, I thought. *I need to do this.*

Exhaling, I pushed the aura off my hand, feeling it hang about my bent elbow like a shirtsleeve, warm and soft. Al grunted in surprise when I made an odd twist in my head, and my entire aura flashed red. "You layer your aura?" he breathed. "One vibration at a time?"

Nervous, I wondered if showing Al this was such a good idea. The demon was a packrat. No telling what defunct charms he had lying around. But I nodded, not opening my eyes as I sent a tendril of red aura to snake up my arm. I shivered as it skated over my pulse points and crawled up my fingers, twining over the joined rings and thickening. My pulse hammered. This was where it usually all fell apart, and I carefully, slowly, shifted my aura twining about me and the rings to the slightest shade of orange.

"Careful . . ." Al breathed, and my head started to hurt as tiny cracks in the rings showed.

"I can do this," I said through my clenched teeth. I had to do this. I had no choice.

But it was Trent, and I felt tears of frustration prick my eyes and my hand start to shake. He had caged me, hunted me, and made my life hell, even as I had fought to shove down his throat that he was immoral and deserved punishment.

But my breath came out in a sob as I realized I didn't believe that anymore.

I remembered his agonized expression in the ever-after basilica when he begged me to see his people to health, his anger when he pulled Nick off me, his willing sacrifice to endure death and the end of everything he had worked his entire life for—to save one child.

"Rachel," Al whispered, but the tinkle of wild magic plinked through my soul as one whirling eye of a thousand turned and focused on me. Others were drawn, and my courage faltered as they laughed at me for thinking I had any power but the power of choice.

And at that, my conviction grew. Choice. Damn it, I trusted Trent. Damn it all to hell, I trusted him down to my soul—not because I had to, but because I chose to.

Tears rolled down my face, and I shook at the realization. I trusted him, even with my soul. *And he isn't meant for me.*

The wild magic laughed, and it was as if the eyes marked me with the blackness of the night, making me theirs. *I am yours,* I agreed miserably, but it was true, and more important, it was my choice. It always had been.

I shook as the entire rainbow skated over my skin, flashing to a blinding white that sank inside itself to an impenetrable blackness. With an echoing *ping,* the rings reinvoked.

Gasping, I opened my eyes wide to see the rings glowing like glory itself. With a sudden implosion of thought, the making of the rings imprinted on my mind. The degradation that the rings in my shaking hand had once caused echoed through me, the cruelty of the master, the anguish of the slave, the petty bitterness and the savage backlash that ended both lives and broke the rings. It was all there, in the tinkling laughter of wild magic, savagely honest in its cruelty. Lives had been ruined beyond belief with the power contained here, and now it was mine in two tiny bands of hard metal.

"Rachel."

I couldn't look away from the rings. I could feel tears on my cheeks and sense Al—a dark bear of a shadow—hovering before me, his hands outstretched, afraid to touch me.

"Rachel?" It was questioning this time, and I blinked, curving my fingers around the warm metal. They were alive. All I wanted to do was destroy them.

"These are evil," I said, choking back a sob as my aura thickened, pinpricks of energy welling up through me in protection—protection against stuff such as what I had made. And I would trust Trent with this? "These are evil!" I said louder, seeing them through my tears.

My arms hurt, and I jumped as a blanket smelling of Al and burnt amber landed around my shoulders. "You did it," Al said in wonder, and I looked up, shaking. "You trust him?"

"I wish I hadn't." Sniffing, I wiped a hand under my nose. "No wonder you hate elves."

I went to hide them, and Al caught my wrist. Slowly my fingers opened, and he took them, his expression solemn as he held the rings up to the firelight. His glasses were gone, and he held them close, squinting. "How sure are you of his commitment?" he asked, his tone guarded and soft.

I wiped my eyes and held my shaking hand out. The memories of the rings still echoed in me, still coloring my thoughts as I tried to readjust my world. I'd known elves were savage, fighting for their existence under the boot of the demons. I had guessed that the demons were seeking revenge for the elves cursing them into a slow spiral of extinction. But I hadn't realized how deep it went, how convoluted it was, how old.

Shaking the feeling off, I took the rings from him and jammed them away in a pocket, hiding them. I'd use them, and then when done, I'd destroy them. They were tools, and I wouldn't let fear rule me. "It doesn't matter," I said, answering him. "It's the choice I make."

Al sighed and looked into the flames, through them, maybe, at nothing and everything. "Perhaps you should concentrate on saving yourself," he whispered. "Let us all die. We're broken beyond repair."

I thought of Al in his dream, looking nothing like this, more like an elegant bat. Broken? Perhaps, but I had put his butterfly back together with my blood. "I never liked the movie *Titanic*," I said, and he grunted, his gaze sharpening on me. "They both could have gotten on that damn door."

Al smiled, and a weird, kindred sensation filled me. Standing, I took his wedding rings from the mantel and handed them to him. "Don't try to forget her," I said, and his hands closed on them, wonder in his eyes as he looked up at me.

"You don't know what you're asking."

"Yes, I do." I had to leave. The rings were awake, and the sooner I used them, the sooner I could destroy them. "Could you . . . send me home?"

He blinked, then got to his feet with a huge sigh. "My student just reinvoked wild magic, and she can't get herself home?" He laughed, but it fell flat, and I jumped, startled when his thick finger touched my jaw, turning me to make me look at him. "If he betrays you, I will finish what I started with his fingers," he said, and I shivered. "Tell him that."

"I will."

The smooth finish of my scrying mirror slid into my arms, and he backed up, eyes running over me as if it might be the last time he'd ever see me. "We are such cowards," he said softly, and then my breath sucked in as the line took me, my head exploding in pain. I think I passed out, because I didn't remember hitting the hard red cement slab that covered Pierce's grave in my backyard, but that's where Al dropped me.

Sitting up, I rubbed my bruised hip, looking past the silent gargoyles perched around me as I pulled my scrying mirror to me. "Ah, hi," I said as I got up, nervous and stinking of burnt amber. Leathery wings rustled, and red and gold eyes blinked. "I hope I didn't disturb you," I said as I edged onto holy ground, my hands touching the outside of my pockets to be sure I still had everything. I had reinvoked wild magic. Somehow I had done it. I had everything in place.

Tomorrow was going to be a long day.

Chapter Twenty-Three

I could feel gargoyle eyes on me as I began picking my way back to the church, taking the shortest path but giving their hulking shadows as much space as I could. The sun had gone down while I'd been in the ever-after, and I wondered if I had time to take a quick shower to get the stink of burnt amber off me before I started in on some charms. I wasn't sure what would be the most helpful, seeing as Ku'Sox could take anything I could dish out and throw it back to me with four times the power.

"Don't let me down, Trent," I muttered, feeling as vulnerable as new skin. Damn it, why did I have to trust him? My life was a lot easier to understand when I didn't.

Behind me, the gargoyles rumbled like elephants, and I ducked when a shadow arrowed over my head. It was a gargoyle, my first wild hope that it was Bis dying as she did a flip to lose her momentum and land atop a grave marker facing me. I knew she was female because her eyes were yellow and the tuft of fur at the tip of her tail was black instead of white. She was more slender than Bis, too, and had a definite grace to her motions as she resettled her wings.

"I thought you were Bis," I said, trying to cover my surprise.

"I'm Glissando," the young gargoyle said, her ears almost flat to her skull and her higher but gravelly voice rumbling. "Bis's friend."

Uneasy, I flicked my gaze behind her to the church, the glow from the uncurtained windows spilling out into the garden. "I'm sorry," I said as my attention returned to her. "A demon—"

"Took him, yes," Glissando interrupted me, the slant to her golden eyes becoming angry. "His father would like to talk to you."

"He's out there?" I said, voice squeaking, and then I mentally kicked myself. Of course he was out there. Every gargoyle in Cincinnati was in my backyard.

"I'll take you to him," Glissando said, and my pulse pounded. Damn it, how was I going to explain this to him? Why I had put Bis in such danger?

"I should've tried to get ahold of Bis's dad right when it happened," I muttered, and Glissando ruffled her wings in agreement. I slowly turned, wondering which one of the pairs of watching eyes belonged to Bis's dad. What was I going to say to him? Did he know that I was a demon? That Bis was bonded to me? Bis had said he had talked to his dad just last week, but "Hey, Dad! I'm bonded to a demon!" isn't the kind of thing that came up in casual conversation.

Glissando's ears swiveled, catching the sound of Jenks's wings before I did. The irate pixy dripped a weird mix of blue-and-green glowing dust as he arrowed across the damp graveyard. "Oh God, you stink worse than six-week-old pepper piss, Rache," he said as he hovered before me, eyeing Glissando suspiciously. "Everything okay?"

I nodded, my hand touching my pocket where the slave rings sat. I was going to trust Trent with my life. I was an idiot. "I need to talk to Bis's dad," I said, and the pixy's dust flashed a surprised gold.

"Ah, you don't mind if I come along," Jenks said, daring her to protest.

But the cat-size gargoyle lifted her wings and shrugged.

Muttering half-heard comments about the back of an outhouse, Jenks snuggled in behind my hair just under my ear. It was too cold for him to be out here, but I wasn't going to insult him by saying so.

We turned back to the waiting gargoyles, and I flinched. It was one thing to tell yourself that the kid you took in is playing with demons to learn the lines, but another to tell his dad.

"You sure you don't want Ivy?" Jenks asked as Glissando flew past us to land on the next tombstone and blink at us impatiently. "She's bigger than me."

"You saw her sharpening her knives," I said as I picked my way back the same way I came out. "You want *that* out here in the dark with *this*?"

There had to be over two dozen pairs of red or yellow eyes turned our way, glowing in the twilight. Glissando shifted nervously as I passed her, hopping to a marker only a few feet ahead. "Can I talk to you?" she asked, and I hesitated, surprised.

"Sure."

With a small jump, the gargoyle landed on my other shoulder, startling me and making Jenks swear. I braced myself, but there was no echo of the lines in my mind. Bis had bonded with me. His images were the only ones that could reach me now.

"I was hoping Bis would be my life mate," she said, and Jenks made a pained whine.

"Sorry," I said as I followed her pointing finger and shifted my path through the long, wet grass. "I didn't mean—"

"It's okay," she said, interrupting me. "I simply wanted you to know that I've known him all his life. And now they're calling him the world breaker. The one we've been waiting for, who will set the lines ringing to a new song or destroy us completely."

My eyebrows rose. *World breaker?* The gargoyles that I'd seen when I'd popped in had all turned, and with a sinking feeling, I realized that's where we were headed. *Can I make a good first impression or what?* "Glissando . . ." I started, but heavy claws pinched my shoulder, bringing me to silence.

"He's always been just my friend," she said, her voice gruff and yet feminine. "Now?" She hesitated, snuffing. "I mean, can the goyle who spends half his waking moments trying to spit on a bird in flight really be the one who's supposed to change everything?" she finished plaintively, making Jenks snicker. "He's a person, not the savior they all think he is. The stupid half-flat is so noisy he can't catch a pigeon off wing."

Savior? I thought, confused. They thought Bis was something out of their collective foretelling? How come this was the first I was hearing about this? "I'm, ah, trying to get him back."

"Back?" She snorted, and Jenks yelled at her when her tail whipped around my neck for support. "He's learning the line," she said sarcastically. "He can't do anything from here."

She really cared for him, and guilt tightened around me. Damn it, I'd really messed up his life, and now he was in real danger. "Glissando, I really like Bis. He's important to me because he's a member of my family, not because of an old wives' tale. We're going to fix that line. I won't let him down."

The small gargoyle took a deep breath. "Thanks," she said, her head down. "I'll tell them you're coming. That's them, right over there."

She spread her wings behind my head, and I stiffened. "Wait. If they are calling Bis the world breaker, what are they calling me?"

Her tail slipped from around my neck, and her weight shifted. "You're his sword to break it with."

I blinked and gaped after her as she effortlessly took to the air.

"Holy crap!" Jenks exclaimed. "I've been taking rent from the gargoyles' savior?"

I swallowed hard, glumly forcing myself to keep moving forward. "And his sword," I said, thinking it was a lot to put on the kid. "What does that make you?"

"It makes me the landlord!" he said in satisfaction. "Hurry up, will you? It's cold."

Unable to see the humor in it, I inched onto the small patch of unsanctified ground, marked by a red slab of cement and Pierce's grave. Six large gargoyles, male and female, lurked on the surrounding stones, their wings draped over their backs. Behind them, dozens lurked, watching as well. A huge gargoyle was perched on the angel statue, his claws leaving delicate scratches on the angel's face like tears.

Nervous, I scuffed my feet, and his big red eyes narrowed at me. It was obvious they didn't like being this close to the ground, but it put them nearer to the one line in Cincinnati that was humming instead of screaming. "Uh, hi," I said, pulling one hand out of my jeans pocket to give him a little wave, and the rest of them shifted their wings in a leathery hush. *I have two of the world's most powerful rings in my pocket, and I'm in danger of being squished.* "Ah, you must be Bis's father."

"I'm Etude," the gargoyle on the statue said, his vowels grinding together low and deep in his throat. He shifted his claws, and a flake of stone broke from the statue, hitting the cement to shatter. His ears flattening for a second, he flushed a deep black. Suddenly I felt more relaxed, having seen Bis do the same thing when embarrassed.

"Don't worry," I said. "I never liked that statue much. This is Jenks."

Jenks made a burst of dust but stayed on my shoulder. "I'm here to make sure none of you hulks hurt Rachel," he said loudly, and the gargoyles around us murmured, sounding like a distant avalanche. "I'm just warning you, is all," he finished, and I lifted my shoulder to get him to shut up.

"Ah, about me losing Bis in the ever-after—"

"Bis?" the old gargoyle said, and I sighed at the interruption. "Yes. Ah. Can I talk to you?"

"Sure . . ." Confused, I stuffed my hands back in my pockets, not knowing what was going on anymore. This wasn't what I had expected.

"There seems to be some confusion," Etude said, gesturing to the gargoyles surrounding us. "Everyone seems to think Bis is going to do this great thing. But this is my son we're talking about. We all know the mistakes he's made, the errors he sings."

The gargoyles watching nodded, their eyes showing impatience. Not liking their attitude, I cocked a hip. "He's saved my life more than once."

"All I'm saying is that it's a lot to put on someone so young," Bis's dad said. "He's only forty-seven."

"He told me he was fifty!" Jenks exclaimed.

Etude's wings opened, and I backed up in alarm, but he was only making the jump to the flat slab of cement. My expression blanked as he came forward on widely spaced toes. My God. He was huge. I froze, and Jenks darted away when the gargoyle put a sinewy, lightly furred arm over my shoulders, towering over me. "You and I both know that Bis is a good kid, but he's just a kid," he said softly, shifting his wings to block the other gargoyles' sight of us.

Unnerved, I let him move me forward back onto the softer ground and away from the others. "They're calling him the world breaker," I prompted, and Etude snuffed, his pricked ears going flat for a moment. He smelled like an iron bell, and somehow it made my teeth hurt.

"He's my son," he said. "He's bonded to you—a demon. I can see it in your aura. This isn't what I wanted for him. Everyone wants their child to grow up a little better than they are," Etude continued. "Settle down, raise a few goyles. Sing songs that resonate with the universe."

"That's not what I want for my kids," Jenks said.

"I accept his choices," Bis's dad said, far too reasonably to make me comfortable. "Even if it means that he might have to live in the ever-after and never see the stars again."

"I wouldn't make him do that," I protested, and his hand on my shoulder tensed, his claws pinching me for a bare second in warning.

"But you and I both know that Bis is not a great hero. He is a lob-winged klutz."

My mouth dropped open, and I pulled out from under his wing. "Etude, I think you have sold your son short," I said, facing him squarely, not liking that I had to look up at him. He was the size of a small elephant. "Your son, at the tender age of forty-seven, found and pulled my soul out of the ley lines when I had hardly a scrap of aura left to find it." I jabbed a finger up at Etude's bare, well-sculpted chest, and the gargoyle took a step back. "He jumped me to the only person possibly able to keep me alive," I said, following him, chin raised as I got into his face. "He sang me *two* resonances that exist in *one* line so I could repair it!"

"Ah, Rache?" Jenks said, hovering over Etude's shoulder, looking worried.

"That line right there," I said angrily, pointing. "The one that you are all clustered around like it's the last fire on a never-ending night! Right now, Bis is in the ever-after playing patty-cake with a psychotic demon who is trying to destroy the ever-after. He's trying to learn all the lines in an ungodly short amount of time so we can save your fuzzy asses!"

"Rache?" Gargoyles were winging in from all over, their black shadows landing menacingly in a large circle.

"If your son is the world breaker, I'm going to see him through it!" I shouted.

Shaking, I dropped back, suddenly aware that glowing red and gold eyes watching me were backed by strong muscle that could wring dust from a rock like water from a sponge. But I wasn't done yet. "Now you all can stay in my graveyard because I know the lines *suck* right now, and if they are giving me a headache, you must be in agony. But if you *ever* call Bis a lob-winged klutz again, I'm going to hunt you down at noon and chip your ear off!"

"Ah, Rache?" Jenks warbled.

"What do you want, pixy?" I snarled, my knees shaking as I stood with my hands on my hips.

"Never mind."

Etude was eyeing me, his big red eyes assessing, and my arms somehow got tangled up over my middle. I knew it made me look afraid, but I was trying for pissed. I was both. "Perhaps," Etude rumbled, his ears perking forward at me, "my son made a wise decision after all in his choice of weaponry. Can you keep him alive?"

His voice had changed, becoming respectful. I took a breath, hearing it shake as I exhaled. "I intend to," I said softly, believing it. *Everyone wants me to protect someone. Who's going to protect me?* "Down to my last breath."

Etude looked me up and down again. Rising to his full stature, he gestured to someone behind me. I couldn't stop my instinctive half step back, but Etude was smiling a savage black-toothed grin at me when he looked back. "In that case," he said, shifting his wings behind him, "what do you want us to do with these two? We found them skulking about and think they're up to mischief."

"No fairy-farting way!" Jenks exclaimed, and I felt my face flash hot.

"Nick," I said, not surprised, all my bile and anger distilled into that one word. I couldn't help my smirk as I looked at Nick hanging between two gargoyles, his toes inches from the soggy, chill earth. Jax was sitting on the palm of another gargoyle, his wings tattered and his back to us, clearly wishing he was somewhere else. The hand of the gargoyle holding him was radiating a visible gentle heat, and seeing him, Jenks swore loud enough to make his son's shoulders come up to his ears.

I didn't care if Nick could read the emotions on my face. None of what I was feeling was particularly nice: satisfaction, maybe, that we—well, someone, anyway—had caught him; anger that he had slapped me; hatred that he had betrayed Ceri and Pierce to their deaths. That Ivy and I had downed him in the museum was only a minor consolation.

He was here to steal the rings, and I felt my pocket to reassure myself they were still there. Thank God the garden was full of bright eyes tonight. Jenks's wings were turning blue from cold, but he hovered before Nick, looking as ticked as I felt. "Nick, Nick, Nick," I said, hands on my hips. "I wish I could say it was a surprise."

Sullen, Nick grimaced from the pain in his shoulders. His face had a swollen bruise, and I wondered if Ku'Sox had beaten him because he hadn't gotten the rings from us. He said, "Are you going to let me explain, or just assume you know what's going on?"

The corner of my eye twitched. "Hold him," I said curtly. "Keep him on holy ground. Jenks, get a strap, will you?"

"Holy crap!" the pixy said as he realized the danger Nick could turn into, then darted to the church, leaving an unsettlingly thin band of dust to show his path. Hearing his wing hum fade, Jax went scarlet. His wings were tattered beyond belief, but the main lines were undamaged. He'd recover. For all his anger, Jenks had been careful.

The surrounding gargoyles moved their wings, whispering in elephant tones as they chuckled at my precaution. "He won't evade us," Etude said, his voice holding a mocking assurance, and I tapped the line to make every single gargoyle's ears prick.

"That demon I told you about?" I said, pulling in the clean energy and filling my chi. "The one that has Bis? He can drop into this piece of crap like he's an old slipper."

Etude's tail curved up into a question mark, and Nick grunted as the sharp claws holding his shoulder pinched.

"So you don't mind if I strap him, do you?" I added, walking a sodden heel-toe, heel-toe toward Nick over the grass. "Simply being on holy ground won't stop Ku'Sox from taking over Nick. A strap, though, will at least prevent Ku'Sox from using a line if he should feel the need to drop in and see how his *favorite* human is doing. Our agreement to leave me alone aside."

"Ku'Sox isn't possessing me," Nick said, and I shrugged.

"Things change." I stopped before him, feeling confident with my belly full of energy and fifty gargoyles backing me. "Are you telling me you don't *do-o-o-o* that anymore, Nicky baby? Forgive me if I don't believe you." Maybe I shouldn't be so cocky, but I was so angry at Nick that I was beyond caring.

The gargoyles had hoisted him up, giving me the impression of him being crucified. Nick squinted down at me, clearly hurting. "You were right," he said, his words thready from the pain in his back and shoulders. "Ow. I'm here to help. Will you stop hurting me?"

The grinding sound of rocks had to be laughter, and a tiny thrill of anticipation dove through me. *Oh, please . . .* "I'm right, huh?" I said as I cocked my hip. "Right about what? I've said *so* many things about you." *Hurry up, Jenks. I'm no good at monologues.*

Nick's feet twitched, and a gargoyle hissed. "Trent is licking his boots," Nick said, unable to meet my eyes. "You were right. Ku'Sox doesn't need me anymore. I want to help you."

I leaned in, ready to smack his feet away if he tried to kick me. With two gargoyles holding his arms, it might be a really bad life choice. Because of him, Ceri and Pierce were *dead.* My eyes narrowed. "We don't need you either, Nick."

The door to the back of the church slammed into the siding, and I turned, backing up out of Nick's reach. A silver sparkle arrowed to us leaving a bright trail; the time inside had warmed Jenks up as I had hoped. It was too cold for him to be out here. Tomorrow wasn't going to be any better. How was I going to convince him to stay home? He would see through any excuse.

Ivy was behind him, moving fast until she found herself among the hulking shapes and she slowed to a respectful pace. One of her katanas was in her grip, and she lowered the tip, becoming a slow-moving shadow as the gargoyles responded to her with pricked ears.

"Strap the fairy louse," Jenks said as he dropped the flexible band of silver-cored plastic into my hand.

I swung my hair off my shoulder to give Jenks a warm place to land, but he went to Etude instead, looking tiny on the giant's shoulder. A wave of heat was coming off the gargoyle. My eyes went to Nick, and I hesitated. I didn't want to touch him. He might jump me out.

"Allow me," Etude said after Jenks buzzed discreetly into the giant's ear, and I gratefully gave the plastic strip to him. His clawed hands moved dexterously, and with a finger gesture, the two gargoyles holding Nick set his feet on the ground so they could strap his hands before him.

"Thanks," I whispered softly, and Etude's ears flicked back.

Nick grunted, shifting his shoulders in relief as the band tightened over his wrists with a sound that made me shiver. "I understand why you don't trust me."

"Oh, I doubt that." I backed up to where Ivy waited, not trusting him when there was no one ready to rip his arms out of their sockets if he did so much as sneeze. "If you did, you wouldn't be here."

Free of his guards, I looked him over, seeing the wear and tear of living with a demon. His eyes darted. Stubble was thick on his cheeks. The suit was gone, and he was wearing a pair of black jeans, black shirt, dark sneakers, shivering in the cold. Scars covered his neck and wrists and had turned his ear into a soft mess of scar tissue. If I didn't know he'd gotten his scars as a rat in Cincinnati's illegal rat fights, I'd say he was a vampire junkie. Either that, or a brimstone addict. "Where's your suit?" I asked, and his eyes met mine, blue and haunted.

He didn't answer me, and Ivy sidled close, whispering, "Did you get them fixed?"

Nodding, I touched my pocket. "Is that what you came for, Nick-k?" I said, and Ivy's eyes went black. "Trying to buy your way back into Ku'Sox's good graces? Might be expensive. More than a thief like you is willing to pay."

"Ku'Sox will kill me if he sees me again," Nick said, and Ivy sashayed closer, the tip of her sword making a soft hush in the spring-long grass.

"So will we," she murmured.

I couldn't help my smile. She was always so honest with her emotions. It was truly refreshing. Even better, Nick was falling for it. It didn't matter if he was lying to us and Ku'Sox has sent him to sabotage. It didn't even matter if he was telling us the truth and he really wanted to help—which I didn't entertain for a second. What mattered was Nick believed us, that we thought we had the strength to stand up to Ku'Sox. If he believed, Ku'Sox would, too. My ifs were disappearing, and Bis was a freaking world breaker. How could we lose?

I glanced at the church, wondering why none of them had perched on it, clearly a more comfortable place for them than a cold stone a foot off the ground. "Let's go in," I said, shivering in the damp. "Everyone who fits, that is. It's cold out here."

"You want to take Nick inside?" Ivy asked, and Jenks's dust turned an ugly red.

"He's lying," the pixy said, looking severely at Nick and Jax.

I couldn't help my snort. "I know. But it's cold out here. We can do this inside." Leaning toward Ivy, I whispered, "Besides, I want to see how far this goes, and we can't when we're standing around out here in the garden."

"It's going right to Ku'Sox, that's where," Ivy said.

Shifting foot to foot, I winced. "Ivy, I'm cold. Jenks is cold. As soon as Jax gets off that gargoyle's hand, he's going to be cold. Nick is strapped and the risk is minimal. Can we please go inside? I have to save the world tomorrow, and I don't even know what I'm going to wear yet."

Ivy eyed me, then pointed at Nick with her sword. "Move," she said, and Nick blew his breath out in a long sigh before he started walking. Jenks clattered from Etude's shoulder, shedding a thick dust over Nick as he followed him. I hoped he wasn't pixing him. I didn't want to have to deal with a sullen, itchy Nick. A sullen, tricky Nick was bad enough.

Seeing them headed for the church, I turned to the gargoyle who had Jax, hesitating when I realized Etude had taken the pixy and was extending him to me as if he was a gift.

"Thank you," I said as I held out a hand, and Jax made the short, wobbling walk, his head down and clearly ashamed. "For everything," I added, so Etude would know I wasn't just talking about the pixy.

Etude grimaced, his long canines making him look fierce. "Bring Bis home," he said, and then his wing circled around me as if in protection. "He might be the world breaker, but he was my son first."

I looked up at the craggy face, wishing things were different. Al had once told me that the demons were responsible for the beginnings of the gargoyles. They were a young race, nearly as young as witches. We'd been created as magically truncated demons, twisted and lied to until we believed what the elves told us. The gargoyles had been created to serve demons, shaped to the demon's needs. Both smacked me wrong.

"I will," I said, then curved my free hand over Jax when he sat in my palm. "If you'd like to perch on the church, that would be okay."

Etude looked at the steeple. "This is my son's home. I need his permission."

I had no idea what to say, and still holding Jax, I turned away. The gargoyles shifted to let me pass, and I hastened to catch up with Ivy. I could hear Jenks berating Nick long before I reached them, and I hoped he wouldn't be so harsh with Jax. The pixy still hadn't said anything, and I was torn. "You know your dad loves you," I said, not knowing why.

"He has a funny way of showing it," the pixy muttered.

"So do you."

Jax's head came up. "Yes but," he started, then seemed to deflate. "I'm sorry, Ms. Morgan," he said, his long hair shifting to hide his eyes.

I waited another moment, then realizing he wasn't going to say anything more, I curved my fingers around him to try to keep him warm.

"You want me to lock them in my closet?" Ivy said when I caught up, her sword tip never wavering from Nick's kidneys as she stepped over the wall. "It's soundproof."

I hadn't known that, but I shook my head. I didn't know what to do with them, but I was cold, and I wanted to get inside.

"We should just stake them." Jenks darted back to us, and Jax shifted against my fingers. "Right here in the garden. Let the spring fairies make nests in their insides."

That was just nasty, understandable but nasty. I replied, "Not that I want to spend time with Nick, but I'd rather know where he is, wouldn't you?"

Ivy frowned, her concern clear in the porch light as we went up the wooden steps. "He makes one move I don't like, I'm going to give him to Nina to bleed dry, even if it will set her back a week."

It was the best I could hope for, and I hung back on the bottom step as Nick opened the back door and went in, Ivy tight behind him. "Shoes off," I heard her bark, but it was more to put him off balance than to keep the floors clean.

Then again . . . I mused as I came in to find her scowling at Nick, the man leaning against the wall to wedge his shoes off without using his hands. I debated whether to change the zip strip for one encircling one wrist, not two—then decided not to. I was sure he was Ku'Sox's ace in the hole. Otherwise, he'd be dead by now.

"Okay, we're inside. Sit," Ivy said tightly, and Nick dramatically fell into the soft leather sofa to send up a puff of vampire-incense-scented air.

"I came to help!" he protested when she poked her sword tip at him to move down, and I set Jax on the top of the couch so I could take my coat off. It smelled of ever-after, and in a splurge of motion, I tossed it out on the back porch to air out.

"Help?" Ivy leaned forward, stinking of angry vampire, her fangs showing as she gripped his shoulder and put her head right next to his. "You want to help yourself."

She shoved him into the cushions, and Nick flicked a nasty look at me for not stopping her. He was a big boy. He could take care of himself. "I was coming to talk to you when the gargoyles grabbed me," he said. "I was on the front walk. I wanted to tell you I was sorry."

"But you're not." Jenks nearly spat it, his wings transparent as he hovered at eye level.

Nick turned to face me as Ivy pointedly sat in the chair across from him. "I made a mistake. I'm trying to fix things," he said, but his tone was too hat-in-hand.

Jenks laughed bitterly. "So is Rachel. Actually, she's trying to save all the demons and the entire ever-after, so what's your point, crap for brains? Didn't you expect the deranged, freak-of-nature demon to turn on you?"

I didn't like Jax being so close to Nick, and I put my hand down for him to climb on so I could move him to the end table. "I'm sorry, Ms. Rachel," he said as he got on and sat down, tattered wings tickling my palm. I said nothing, mad at all of them as I set him under the table lamp and turned it on to warm him. Still angry, I sat in the chair beside him and snatched up the remote, turning the TV on for any news that would indicate we were in worse trouble than before. Setting the remote clattering onto the end table, I traced my cheek where Nick had slapped me. Not hurting him for the hell of it was harder than I thought it would be.

"I knew you wouldn't believe me," Nick said, and Ivy shoved the coffee table into his shins to get him to shut up. "I want to help."

This time it was belligerent, and Jenks laughed. "Help!" Jenks exclaimed, and Jax hunkered down under the light, his back to his dad and looking miserable. "No fairy-farting way!" he yelled, and his kids who had been hovering vanished. "You are *not* switching sides. You are *lying*! Rache, why are we even listening to this? Nick put the *lie* back in *believe*."

"I don't know," I said listlessly. "Maybe because if he's sitting in front of me, he's not coming behind me with a knife. Besides, there's nothing on TV."

Nick pushed the coffee table away from his knees, and Ivy pushed it back. Clearly at the end of his patience, he tossed the hair from his eyes and held his wrists up, asking to be released. I shook my head, and he lowered his bound hands. "Ku'Sox dying is the only chance I have of surviving this."

"You think?" Jenks said, but I could feel Nick's eyes on me as I watched the news—nothing so far about surface demons at the park, not even a teaser for the end of the broadcast.

"I was mad," Nick continued. "I thought . . ." He hesitated as my teeth clenched. "I was trying to get back at you, okay? It went too far."

My eyes flicked to his, holding. Jenks's wings clattered, and he rose. "Too far?" he said. "Destroying the ever-after and magic to tell your old girlfriend—who doesn't even like you—that you were mad at her was 'too far'?"

I didn't have to say a word. Jenks was doing all my yelling for me. I appreciated it. It freed me up for more important things, like watching the latest insurance commercial. But even so, my anger grew. Because of him, Ray would never know her mother.

"I was wrong," Nick said staring down at the table, his hands in his lap. "You were right."

At that, I couldn't help myself. "I'm the better bet now, huh?"

Relief slipped into his expression as I finally talked to him. "I'm trying to survive."

"Rachel doesn't owe you crap, you lying sack of toad shit," Jenks said.

I put the arches of my feet on the edge of the coffee table. "I don't owe you crap, you lying sack of toad shit." *That* one, I wanted to say.

Nick pressed his thin lips together, his stubble showing strong when he flushed. "Fine. I'll leave."

He shifted forward to stand, getting no more than three inches before Ivy stood, the pointy part of her sword touching his chest. Looking at it, he sank back down. The tension was getting thick. I didn't have a clue what to do with him, much less what I was going to wear tomorrow. "Let him go, Ivy," Jenks said bitterly. "We don't need him."

"He can't go," I said as three of Jax's sisters brought the miserable pixy a blanket. Damn it, he was crying silver tears. I was going to smack Nick into the next dimension for having misled Jax so badly. "He'll run back to Ku'Sox and tell him how I'm going to smear him into demon pâté."

"Is that what you think I'd do?" Nick said, his words clipped. "Go back to Ku'Sox?"

I leaned over the table. "If the crap stinks, wipe your ass."

"I made a mistake!" Nick's gaze was fixed on mine, and his words were precise. "Throw me a goddamned life preserver, will you?"

My eyes went to the low ceiling, remembering thinking that myself so many times before. His mistake had cost Ray her mother. Lucy, too. "Nick? *Shut up.*"

Sullen, he pushed back into the cushions. Jax was staring across the room at Belle. She'd come in and was standing beside Rex at the archway, her bow strung and her expression severe. Rex had been Jax's cat, and I'd give a lot to know what Jax was thinking, both about the cat and that Belle, a fairy, was living under his father's roof.

"Rache, this is dumb," Jenks said, wings going full tilt as he landed on my knee. "Call the I.S. to come pick him up so we can get on with what we have to do."

Standing before Nick, Ivy shrugged, which told me she agreed with Jenks. I thought for a moment, my gaze lingering on Jax, miserable as he huddled under a blanket his mother had made. "I'm not happy about this either," I said, "but the I.S. can't hold him if Ku'Sox can pop him out."

"I told you—" Nick started.

"Shut up!" I snapped, and Jenks dusted a heavy black to pool on the floor. "I used to listen to you, but you lied and I walked." Leaning forward, I caught his eyes and held them. "Tell you what. I'll keep Ku'Sox off you if you stay in the church. That's it."

"Rache . . ." Jenks complained, and I held up a hand. Like I believed for one second that he would stay in the church?

"Set one toe out of it, and I don't care anymore."

Nick exhaled loudly, clearly wanting more. He wasn't getting it.

"I have stuff to do." Heart pounding, I looked at the clock on the cable box. "Excuse me."

Nick's expression became alarmed at the prospect of my leaving him with Ivy, and sure enough, Ivy smiled to show her teeth, her motions slow and sultry as she almost crawled over the couch to sit beside him. "Can I leave you two alone for five minutes?" I asked as I looked down at her, not altogether kidding, and she smiled even wider.

"I want to talk to you," Jenks said, rising up with an aggressive wing clatter.

"Sure," I said, the memory of Jax's tattered wings swimming up. Behind me, I heard Nick tell Ivy to fuck off. Either she would kill him or she wouldn't. To be honest, I was more concerned about what I was going to wear tomorrow than Nick's survival. "How are you doing, Jenks?" I said as went into my room, despairing over finding anything in my closet.

Wings clattering, Jenks landed on my dresser, his gaze on the wall as if he could look through it to see his son. "Peachy damn keen," he grumbled.

I could hear the gargoyles in the garden rumbling like elephants as I shut the door. A feeling of pity swept through me. Ivy was annoyed—but Ivy often was. I was angry—again, understandable. Jenks had parental guilt mixed with a strong streak of protection, and he was having the hardest time. "I'm sorry about Jax," I said as I opened my closet door and shoved everything to one side. Maybe there was something at the back that I'd missed, but the only things there were the clothes my mom hadn't wanted to take with her and were of too high a quality to give away.

Jenks's expression lost its anger, and he sat, slumped on a perfume bottle, wings drooping. "I didn't think I'd have to face Jax again," he said softly, and my heart nearly broke.

"I imagine that's what he's thinking," I said, and Jenks met my eyes. I pulled out a filmy scarf, drawing it through the air and letting it settle on my bed, thinking it might make a good sash. Maybe I should start with the boots and work my way up.

"I just want to . . . smack him," Jenks said, gesturing weakly. "He doesn't know how short life is. He's throwing it away. He could be so much if he'd . . ."

"Come to the dark side?" I said, trying to lighten things up. Jenks was silent, his wings slowly regaining their usual color. *Not the white leather dress. Not the black leather pants.* My fingers trailed reluctantly off my usual leather. I'd be the same person I was before in it—I had to be different to-morrow. I felt different. My clothes should reflect that. I wanted something that said power, and everything I had said power and sex. Maybe Newt had the right idea with her martial-arts outfits and androgynous hairstyles. I wasn't going to shave my head, but something more masculine might get the demons to stop looking at me like I was nothing but a pair of X chro-mosomes.

"Why don't you ask him to come back to the church?" I said as I lin-gered over an off-white linen leisure suit of my mom's from the '70s, the entire era a bastion of post-Turn fashion freak-out. It had bell-bottoms, but it was also form fitting and flowing, the vest showing off my curves with-out screaming sex. In sudden decision, I pulled it into the light. "For good."

"What?"

Draping it across the bed, I kicked off my boots to try it on. "If he's through with Nick, ask Jax to come back. Maybe he's afraid you don't love him."

"Don't love him . . ." Jenks's eyes were wide, and his mouth gaped.

There was a pop of air from the back of the church, both familiar and surprising, and I froze, Jenks and I looking at each other. *Al?* I wondered, and then my heart pounded at Newt's voice screaming Latin. Newt?

Oh God, they'd come for me.

Chapter Twenty-Four

I lurched out of my room, almost tripping on Rex streaking into the front sanctuary, a ribbon of caramel with a frightened sparkling of black pixy dust from one of Jenks's kids over her. Ivy screamed from the kitchen, and I bolted. Jenks was a zizzing light before me, and gripping the edge of the frame, I slid into the kitchen. The cloying scent of burnt amber was so thick, I could almost see it.

"Newt, no!" I exclaimed, and she looked at me, her black eyes lost in madness. She had pinned Ivy to the floor, the butt of her staff at her throat. Ivy was wide-eyed, the blackness of her pupils deep with forever. Terrified, she held the end of the staff, unable to shift it. Jenks darted down with his sword, and I cried out a warning when Newt gestured at him.

Jenks was flung backward, his swearing cutting off when he hit the fridge and slid down.

"Stop!" I cried as I tapped the line, and Newt took a magic-hazed hand from her staff.

It gave Ivy a chance, and she spun out from under the stick, going for her katana. Grimacing, Newt turned back to her, swinging the stick to strike her across the temple. It met Ivy's head with a dull *thwap,* and she collapsed.

Oh God. Ivy!

"Invader!" Belle shouted from the floor, and Newt shifted the aim of the black ball of death in her hand from me to the fairy, the demon's white robes furling elegantly.

"Newt, stop!" I shouted, diving in front of Belle to intercept it. I threw up a protection circle as I lunged, but Newt's magic tore right through, hitting me in the chest as I took the fall, narrowly missing squishing the small woman I'd been trying to protect.

I clenched into a ball, a spasm ripping through me as everything cramped. My feet scrabbled against the floor as I was racked with a curse that felt like it was ripping my spine apart. Newt hauled me up, pinning me to the farm table.

"Don't hurt Newt!" I gasped as Belle trilled like an Amazon warrior. "Belle, stop!"

Newt's black eyes stared into mine, wild and alive. Her color was high, accenting her new, spiky red hair, cut short just at her ears. Her fingers were clenched in my hair as she forced my head back, and her staff was across my neck, pressing me into the table. Clearly something had snapped in her. *Had she remembered something, or forgot?*

"Belle, no!" I cried out as the fairy, poised at the top of the hanging rack, gathered herself to jump on Newt.

"*Immolerate!*" Newt snarled, without even looking back.

A wave of force pushed from her, and I squinted as the air was pressed from my lungs. Belle was gone, and I panicked. I couldn't move my legs, and they felt like they were on fire.

"I have to kill you now," the crazed demon said, and I choked as she pressed into my throat. "And I was doing so well. If I don't, they'll believe that *I'm* responsible for *all of this*!"

"Fine. Great. But don't hurt my friends," I gasped, my hands trying to shove her off me. "Please."

The muscles of her jaw smoothed, and her shoulders eased. "Don't hurt your friends?"

"Please," I wheezed, my grasping fingers brushing the tips of her hair. If it had been an inch longer, I could have pulled her off balance. "My friends. Belle, she's the fairy—she's a great warrior. She protects the pixy children who live here. Jenks needs to be alive to help Ivy. Ivy is trying to live with her guilt. Please don't ruin her. She's so beautiful inside."

The fervor of her eyes diminishing, Newt eased up, clearly confused, and I took a grateful gasp of air. "And help Bis," I said, my hands dropping to her staff, trying to push just an inch more of space between us and failing. My arms, too, felt like they were on fire. "If you have to kill me, will you help Bis? Will you do that for me? He deserves better than to be with Ku'Sox the rest of his life. He's just a baby."

"Bis?"

She was confused, and I forged ahead. "And take Al his chrysalis." My eyes darted to the window. I couldn't see it; the angle was wrong. "It's right there on the sill," I said, wishing she would turn to look. "He thinks he can't love anymore, but I know he can. Tell him he was right. He used to have wings. They were like stretched moonlight. Tell him I'm sorry."

Newt took a step back, her grip falling from me. "You know what we looked like?"

Slowly I sat up against the table and rubbed my throat. Ivy was still out. So was Jenks. Belle was standing guard over him, fierce and determined. I didn't know where Nick was. I didn't care. "I saw the pools of shallow water, the moss green branches overhead," I said, voice ragged. "The fog that muffled and soothed the sun." Newt dropped back another step, her hands loose on her ebony staff, confusion in her eyes. I coughed, sending ribbons of fire to flare and die in my limbs. "The ever-after was a paradise. What happened?"

"We killed it."

I looked up to see Newt lost in a memory.

"Both the elves and us in our war," she said, her grip going white on her staff. "Together we killed the ever-after. They could flee. We were left to wallow in our shared war waste. We make it worse with every curse, but we have no choice. To survive, we must set things even more out of balance."

Somehow I wasn't surprised that the elf-demon war was to blame. "I'm sorry."

Newt's focus sharpened, and her long face grew tight again. "I didn't want to kill you. They made me do it."

"I'm not dead quite yet." Still holding my throat, I slid to the edge of the table and cautiously slipped off. Pinpricks of fire like the stars of returning circulation burst against my skin and vanished. Newt shifted her staff, and I eyed her sourly. Clearly she was having a bad Newt day. "Since when does anyone make you do anything?"

I crouched to feel for a pulse at Ivy's wrist, and Newt's face was ugly when I turned back. "They think I'm plotting with you," she said angrily. "Because I petitioned for time for you. Because my rooms are no longer shrinking. Al has been imprisoned, but I was told to kill you. If I do, they'll not only let me live another day, but they might listen to me."

Al was in jail? Crap on toast, it was down to Quen and me.

"Ku'Sox is at fault," Newt admitted bitterly. "It's easier to blame you. Killing him is impossible. Killing you is merely hard."

That was kind of nice. Killing me being hard, not easy.

Jenks was sitting up and holding his head, wings askew. Belle crouched beside him, whispering in his ear as her eyes never left Newt. "If you kill me," I said, cautiously moving to sit in my chair, "you'll all only live another week, tops." I gestured helplessly. "The reason your rooms aren't shrinking is because I fixed your line. That's why it is the only one that sounds right anymore. If I had Bis, I could fix them all. Can you get him back for me? Now?"

Newt backed up, confusion in her stance and apparently not knowing what to do if I didn't attack her. "No. You make it sound easy, not killing you."

"Easy?" I pushed out Ivy's chair for Newt with my foot and she stared at it in distrust. "It *is* easy. What I've had to do to save you dumb-asses is hard. First I had to figure out a way to fix the line. And when I do, you let Ku'Sox take Bis from me. I somehow find a way to prove Ku'Sox broke it, and then they convince you to kill me before my deadline. And now I not only have to prove Ku'Sox broke my line, but then survive doing so without Al? Without anyone? Ku'Sox wants you all dead. My God, why do you keep believing him?"

Newt glanced at Ivy, then back to me. "We made him. He owes us his life. He's going to bring the demons back to the sun with the demon children he has stolen. You owe us nothing. Why would you help us?"

I honestly don't know. An elbow on the table, I felt my neck. "Ku'Sox is a liar and a psychotic genius. I've had a very bad week, Newt. A very bad week. And to top it off, I don't have anything in my closet that is suitable to wear while saving the world."

"Are you sure?"

Head tilted, I met her eyes. God, I was tired. "You've seen it. Not much has changed since then."

Newt's black eyes narrowed. "No, I mean are you sure that . . ." She hesitated, glancing at Ivy. "Are you sure you can prove Ku'Sox is betraying us, not you?"

A rueful chuckle slipped from me. It must have surprised her, because she backed up almost to the door, her staff held defensively before her. "Given half a chance," I said. "Can you just hold off until tomorrow to kill me? By sunset tomorrow, I can prove all this was Ku'Sox's fault or he will have killed me himself. If we're both around come sunup, you can kill who you want, and we can all get on with our lives."

Newt shook her head mistrustfully. Ivy was starting to come around, and Jenks made a slow, wobbly flight to her, hopefully to tell her to pretend to still be out. "We're losing too much space. It has to be now."

My toes were the only part of me still tingling, and I looked at them. *When did I get a hole in my sock?* "You can't give me one lousy day?"

Slowly, hardly moving, Ivy sat up against the wall, holding her head. I made the finger motion for her to not move, and Jenks whispered it since she couldn't focus yet.

Newt drew herself up, her black eyes flicking over Ivy, not afraid, but assessing. "The leak is too wide. I've run out of room. You and Al, and I myself now, are so far in debt that there's nothing left."

"I've got a bushel basket full of truth," I said as I shifted in my chair to face her square on. "I know what you looked like. I saw the Eden your war destroyed. Ku'Sox knows only what you've shown him, and I'm sorry, Newt, but you've shown him only the present, not your past. You really want him in charge of your future?"

She hesitated, fingers clenching on the staff.

"I know you're afraid," I said, and she barked in laughter.

"Afraid of you!"

"Not of me," I said. "You're afraid of the endless days continuing with no change. You're tired. You think Ku'Sox is how you can let go and still continue on, but look at him. He's not you, he doesn't have your soul. That's why he keeps trying to eat them."

She was listening, and I sat up, trying to look like I knew what I was talking about. "Look at how he's getting past the elven curse. He's stealing babies. He's stealing the wisdom to keep them alive. I broke the curse you put on the elves, and I can damn well break the curse that keeps you stuck in the hell you both made of your paradise. I can free you, Newt. You can finish free of the ever-after as you began it."

Newt swallowed hard. A tear slipped from her, and she wiped it away, shocked. Behind her, pixies were plastered against the window, watching. "We had wings."

I smiled. "You flew between the clouds and the moon."

Her eyes came to me. "It's not a dream."

"No. This? This nothing that you live in?" My hand lifted and fell. "This is the nightmare you made for yourself. Let me wake you up."

Her lungs heaved as she took a deep breath. She looked scared, wild. She might do anything. "Strike me," she said softly, her stick held tight in her grasp.

From the floor by the fridge, Jenks rose up, wings clattering. "Whoa, whoa, whoa!" he said. Newt took a firm stance and pointed the butt of her staff at Ivy as the woman got to her feet, listing but ready to attack.

"Easy!" I shouted, standing up and holding out a hand. "Everyone just take it easy!"

Newt grimaced, and then, as if having a sudden thought, she set the end of her stick on the floor and calmed. "Wait," she said, and Ivy hesitated, ready to jump at her. "Let's find something from your closet for you to wear. *Then* you can strike me."

Totally confused, I blinked. "Why?"

Smiling to scare the bejeebers out of me, she came forward, watching me but keeping that staff of hers between her and Ivy and Jenks. "I need a reason for you to be alive come sunup. I'll tell them you hit me."

Jenks darted into the back room, his swearing dropping like golden apples. Nick was gone, apparently, but I could do nothing as Newt looped an arm in mine and a pulse of magic from her lifted through my hair, shattering the sanctity of the church. Damn it, she'd done it again!

"I can give you until sunrise. Then you will be summoned and you will die," Newt added, making me feel all warm and cozy.

"Tonight?" Jenks yelped as he flew back in, an angry red dust showing his path. "What happened to her four days?" Then he turned to me, his dust almost catching fire. "Rache, we got a problem. Nick ran off."

Newt hesitated at the threshold of the hallway, cautiously testing the sanctity with the butt of her staff. "That little worm of a man?" she said. "He owes me a familiar. Maybe two. I don't remember."

She gestured, and Nick popped into existence on the table beside me. I spun as Trent's books hit the floor, and then Ivy was on him, her eyes dark as she pulled him off and slammed him up against the wall. Dazed, Nick struggled to focus, then breathe when she gave a little squeeze, clearly enjoying herself.

Newt still had her arm in mine as she half turned to watch. Her hair was now my length, and I started. "You're Ivy . . ." the crazy demon said, and Nick coughed violently as Ivy's grip went slack in surprise. "I think I liked you."

Jenks and I exchanged a panicked look, and I turned Newt back to the hallway and away from Ivy. "Ah, let me show you what I've got picked out," I said, almost pulling her into the hall. Behind us, I heard Nick hit the floor with a pained grunt.

Looking over my shoulder at the stove clock, my gut clenched. *Call Quen about the new deadline, pick out my clothes with Newt, keep Ivy from killing Nick. Was I forgetting anything?*

"You have until sunrise," the demon said, looking at the pixies hovering at the top of the hall in the sanctuary as she led me to my closet. "Not because I particularly like you, you understand. I simply can't do all that you charge me with. You're going to have to do that yourself."

Chapter Twenty-Five

There's-s-s a car at the curb," Belle said as she appeared at my open bedroom door, and a jolt went through me. *Quen. Finally.*

"Tell Ivy to stay put. I'll get it," I said when six enthusiastic pixies darted into my room with the same message, all of them chattering loud enough to give me a headache. "Ivy!" I shouted before she could move. "I'll get it. You watch Nick."

I touched the rings in my pocket for reassurance as I shooed everyone out of my room and shut the door behind me. Pace fast, I headed for the sanctuary. Ivy was where I'd left her on the couch, stretched out and dangerously languorous, and I gave Nick a disparaging glance as I passed. "Don't let him move, whatever happens, okay?" I asked Jenks, and he left my shoulder to stand on the coffee table beside Jax. The smaller, tattered pixy shied at the soft clatter of his dad landing, and I hoped that the two of them would start to talk again.

Stomach churning, I went to the door, promising myself that if I lived through this, I was finally going to get a light in the foyer.

"It's Quen!" one of Jenks's kids said in excitement as I undid the bolt to the front door and peeked out into the lamp-lit dark.

Relief filled me as I pushed the heavy oak door open wider in invitation. Quen was getting out of the black beamer parked at the curb, and my face warmed as I remembered him charging me with Trent's safety. And here I was the one asking him to help me. At midnight. On a weekday. To save the world a day ahead of schedule.

His hair slicked back, Quen was wearing all black again and soft-soled shoes. My eyes fell as I remembered the first time I had seen him. He'd looked like a gardener. Perhaps that was what he'd truly like to be.

"How are the girls?" I asked, and he brought his gaze back from where he'd been saying a soft hello to the pixy bucks braving the cold to escort him in. The light on the sign over the door made creases in his face. Or maybe it was the burden of his life balancing on a fine point. It was going to fall one way or the other.

"Doing well," he said, looking taller than usual because I was in my stocking feet. "Ellasbeth is getting to know them." A frown crossed his features. "They're locked in the closet until I get back. Did you have fun raiding the museum today?"

Smiling, I took his sun-weathered hand in mine as he extended it, pulling him into a hug instead. My eyes teared up as I remembered Ceri. The scent of cinnamon and warm wine filled my senses, and Quen took a quick breath to catch his grief. Anger at Nick flared, and I shoved it away. "I appreciate your help," I said, thinking that he smelled different from Trent, dark and warm, not green and warm. I wondered if it was a mark of more maturity or just an individual trait. "Are you sure you want to do this? It's just us. No demon assist."

His lip twitched, and Quen pushed me into the church, his hands heavy on my shoulders. "I'd rather it be that way. The girls will not be safe until this is settled."

From just inside, a pixy girl chanted "Come in! Come in!," and I stepped aside. He slipped past me, and I leaned into the night, looking for any pixy dust before I shut the door.

The latch clicked shut, and I turned toward the warmth and light. I gasped as someone pulled on the line out back, the draw so heavy that my knees almost buckled. Wide-eyed, I watched Ivy spring from the couch. "Quen, no!" she shouted, the dust from Jenks's startled kids sifting down to make her glow.

Heart pounding, I lurched into the sanctuary. Nick was sitting in his chair, hands bound before him, glaring at Quen. Ivy was between them, her face pale as Quen stood ready to fling a black ball of energy at Nick. His expression was terrifying with hatred. He knew Nick was to blame for Ceri's death—and I had let him walk in unawares. *Shit. Could I be more clueless?*

"Quen," I said softly, padding over to him. I reached to touch his arm, and he jerked from me, the curse sparking the air between us.

"Why is this filth alive?" he said, cords showing in his neck.

I put my hand on his arm again, gently tugging. "The gargoyles found him in the garden. He's my present to Al when this is over. You want to sign the card?"

"Tink's titties, I do," Jenks said, his dust a bright silver as he hovered beside me. Ivy was holding her breath. If Quen began throwing curses, Ku'Sox might drop into Nick just to see what was up.

"Quen . . ." I fidgeted nervously. "Al is not at all happy about what happened to Ceri." I couldn't say *dead*. This was as close as I could get without crying. "Until this is over, I want to know where Nick is, tied up in my church with a vampire and pixy guarding him."

Quen's expression pulled up into a hateful mask. "He killed Ceri!"

"Ku'Sox killed Ceri," I said. "Crap for brains here lied to her, knowing it would happen. I'm not going to let him hurt anyone else by allowing him to wander the universe. He's here. Where we can watch him."

With a twang on the line that made me jump, Quen let the curse in his hand dissipate. "He couldn't wander the universe if he was dead, either," he muttered. "You ask a lot, Rachel."

I gave Nick a nasty look—the smug son of a bitch pissed me off. "I know. I'm sorry."

Quen wasn't done yet, though, and Jenks's wings clattered when the man took several steps closer to the thief. "If you move, I will send fire through your spine and explode your brain from the inside."

Eyeing him darkly, Nick opened his mouth, and I gasped as Quen lashed out impossibly fast. Ivy jumped, but he'd only slapped him, and Nick's head was lolling as he struggled to focus. Up in the rafters, the pixies shouted their approval.

"Can I speak to you in private for a moment?" Quen said, dismissing Nick.

Nick was still trying to focus, and I turned to Quen. "I see your magic is back within normal parameters," I said as we headed to the kitchen. Jenks and Jax were inches away from each other. Neither one was dusting heavily in distress. This was good, right?

Quen's pace was slow as we entered the hallway. "Have you eaten yet?" he asked, surprising me. Hesitating at the top of the hall, he turned halfway around. "Is anyone hungry? We have time to eat before we go. I want to talk to everyone, and it might as well be over food."

He wants to eat?

"Pizza, maybe?" Quen said, squinting at Nick.

The pixies in the rafters shouted their agreement, but Ivy's expression said what I was thinking. Pizza sounded awful, and my stomach was already churning. "Sure, okay," I said when she shrugged. Maybe Quen wanted a last supper kind of a thing.

Quen's lips twitched as he glanced at Nick and then away. "Great, can someone else order it? I want to see what Rachel is wearing tonight." He took my elbow, trying to guide me back into motion. "You picked out something nice, right?"

I shivered at how similar his and Trent's speech cadences were. I felt like I was being pushed along, and I didn't like it. "Yes. Newt helped me."

"Newt?" he said, clearly thinking I was joking, and my feet slipped as I stopped to look behind me. Ivy already had the phone, and pixies were shouting out toppings. Jax seemed better, looking at his dad with something other than fear and shame. Nick was sullen as he sulked in the chair holding a tissue to his lip. He wouldn't try to go back to Ku'Sox until the last moment.

"Show me what you're wearing," Quen said, jerking me into my room.

"Hey!" I exclaimed as Quen shut the door behind him.

Arms over his chest, he exhaled in relief. "I see the appeal of living with pixies," he said softly, "but do they ever stop talking?"

"Only when they sleep." Eyeing him, I cocked my hip. "What do you want that you can't ask in front of everyone?"

He compressed his lips and came forward a step. "Can I see the rings?"

Suddenly recognizing the pizza as the distraction he had meant it to be, I nodded. Of course Quen would want to see them, and I reached into my pocket, little pings of energy jolting my burned fingertips. They clinked as they hit his outstretched palm, and his lips parted as he brought them close, nudging them apart with a careful finger. "They're nothing like wedding rings," I said as we looked at them in his creased and calloused palm. "Al recognized them. He almost destroyed them before I reinvoked them."

"Al helped you?" He was close enough for the scent of warm spice rising up between us to remind me of Trent. His fingers twitched as if to keep them for himself, and I stiffened.

"Sort of. And when this is over, we are going to destroy them," I said, suddenly nervous. I took a breath to tell him I had made a bargain with his goddess, then didn't. Trent probably had an arsenal of defunct magic that should stay that way. Besides, it sounded so lame. It had all been in my mind, hadn't it? Al had once said demons could do elf magic but didn't because it was considered beneath them.

Frowning, Quen held up the smallest ring. "I can't believe you managed this," he said quietly, and I was suddenly glad I hadn't told him how I'd done it. They were evil in a way I'd never considered, and I was going to destroy them right after I took care of Ku'Sox. Tonight.

"You need to leave so I can change," I said as I tugged them out of his grip and set both rings on my dresser next to my perfumes.

Quen walked to my dresser, turning his back on me but not leaving. His neck was stiff and his arms were crossed over his chest. I took a breath to tell him to get out, then decided against it. He probably had something else to say he didn't want the pixies knowing. Outside were the low rumbles of gargoyles, and not knowing how good their hearing was, I jerked out the pencil that had been propping the window up. It closed with a snap. Quen jumped, but didn't turn.

"You do know that we likely aren't going to come back," I said, satisfied that he wouldn't turn around. "One elf and a badly trained demon won't be enough."

"I have a duty," he said, and I frowned.

"Sure, make me responsible for Ray losing her father as well as her mother," I said as I got my boots out of the closet and let them clunk to the floor. God, it still hurt. It would for a long time, and my motions to change my clothes grew rough. Quen didn't move, and I thought of Al's opinion that Trent would have a better chance of success than Quen. Getting to him might be a problem.

Quen took up the rings, his silence making me uneasy. "If we fail, do you think Trent can kill him?" he asked as he fingered them, and I kicked my jeans off, feeling vulnerable.

"No." I held up my mom's linen bell-bottoms to me. "It's not so much that I doubt his abilities, but he *is* Ku'Sox's familiar. He's going to be as effective as spit. You can't kill a demon. Ask Newt." *Or Ceri, or Pierce.*

"I can hide your presence from the demons for a short time," Quen said, his back to me. "Perhaps long enough for the ever-after to collapse."

Teeth clenched, I balanced on one foot, then the other as I put my pants on. They were lined in silk, and they felt surprisingly nice. "I'm a demon," I said softly. "If they want me, they summon me. I'm theirs."

"The band of silver you cut off," he started.

"No." I zipped up my pants, swishing back and forth to watch the way they moved. "Thanks for coming out here on such short notice. Apparently I've bankrupted both Al and Newt. Ku'Sox has petitioned that Al be confined, which just leaves us unless you want to take the time to break him out of jail."

Quen took a breath, and I made a noise when he threatened to turn around. "They can't summon you if you wear charmed silver. You could put it on until the ever-after goes and the demons are gone," he said, his neck stiff.

"And then what?" I said, bad tempered. *Is he trying to talk me out of this or see how deep my resolve goes?* Grabbing the hem of my shirt, I pulled it up and over my head. It was cold in just my chemise, and I tossed the tee to the floor. "It never occurred to you that I don't *want* the demons to die out? Maybe I like them, huh? Besides, Ku'Sox is using my line to kill them," I said as I shoved my arms into my top. "I'm partially responsible. You can stay here and watch Nick if you want. Someone needs to."

There was a knock at the door, and I buttoned the vest around me. "Pizza will be here in ten," Ivy said through the door, and then her steps retreated. Ten minutes—a lingering benefit of having been Piscary's scion. That, and Ivy tipped very well.

Distracted, I finished the buttons. "You can turn around now," I said, sitting on my bed to put on my boots.

Quen turned, rings clinking meditatively in his hands as his eyes traveled over me, taking in my choice of clothes. I couldn't tell what he was thinking. It had taken me three days in a car to learn Trent's tells. Quen was a lot harder. "What about Nick?" he asked, his voice flat as the rings shifted from hand to hand.

I stood there, feeling my toes sink into my boots. Shrugging, I took the rings from him and put them in the single vest pocket. "Everything he hears or sees is going right into Ku'Sox's head. I'm counting on it, which is one of the reasons we're going to do it tonight. What happens after tomorrow, I'll deal with tomorrow." Turning to the mirror, I stood beside him, gazing at our reflection and evaluating my new look. I touched my hair, deciding the braid was holding up well enough. "So we good?"

"Just one thing." I turned to him and he tossed his head to the front of the church when the bell gonged. "Don't eat the pizza."

I froze, as he reached for the doorknob. Taking a breath, I jumped into motion, confused. *Don't eat the pizza?* "Quen?" I jerked him to a halt in the hallway. I could hear the pixies in the sanctuary, Jenks berating Nick. "Why not?"

Posture furtive, he winced. "Didn't your father ever tell you not to eat with the elves?"

"Sure, because . . ." I stopped, my eyes narrowed as Quen's smile shifted and became not nice at all. "Because you might forget your life as you drink and make merry," I said, not liking this. It was a forget spell, temporary but effective, and Ivy and Jenks would be *pissed*. "Quen, I'm not going to lie to them."

"Even to save their lives?" Without another word, he strode into the brightly lit sanctuary.

Stupid-ass elves . . . I followed, my stomach churning. This wasn't right, and I felt torn as I stood at the top of the hall and looked over the sanctuary with Ivy's piano, my desk, Kisten's pool table, and the cluster of furniture. Quen was already there among them, looking as if nothing was amiss and he wasn't about to charm them all into forgetfulness. Nick was still sitting in his chair, watching Ivy at the front door taking the pizza and paying the man. Pixies were everywhere, the colored silk and bright voices filling the air. Jax was sitting on the coffee table with Belle, but it looked as if she was talking, not guarding him. There was a cheer when the church door shut out the cold, and Ivy came back to drop the pizza on the coffee table right in front of Nick. *Don't eat the pizza.*

Panicked, I met Ivy's eyes, and she hesitated, eyebrows high. Nick gagged, and the pixies descended, working together to get the box open before diving in to snitch the steaming pineapple. I felt alone and apart in the hallway, unable to shake the feeling that it was just another Thursday night. Pizza, movie, and shocking the token human by eating tomatoes.

Slice of pizza in hand, Ivy eased closer, the diverse but weirdly complementary scents of vampire and pizza flowing over me. "Remember this," she said, smiling sadly as she looked at the chaos.

I couldn't take my eyes from her pizza, torn. "Because it won't ever come again," I finished, guilt tugging at me. I was not going to lie to her. "Don't eat the pizza."

She hesitated. Jenks was watching us, and I made a small finger motion as he oversaw his kids fighting over the crust to get the one with the most sauce. Wings humming, his dust shifted to a brilliant yellow.

"What does everyone want to drink?" I said softly, turning on a heel to vanish into the kitchen. Quen's eyes bore into my back. He couldn't have possibly heard me warn Ivy, but he wasn't oblivious to her alertness, either. My heart pounded. I didn't want my friends dead, but I wouldn't lie to them. Ivy would follow. We could talk in the kitchen. The truth was going to hurt, but a lie would be worse.

"Ivy, can I speak to you and Jenks for a moment?" Quen said, and my pace faltered.

Maybe not . . .

"They're helping me with the drinks," I shouted. "Quen, watch Nick, will you?"

My heart thudded as I walked from the noisy throng, but the kitchen was welcomingly cool, and I put a hand to my face, not sure what I was going to say as they followed me in, clearly curious. Frustrated, I turned my back on the small window over the sink.

"Okay, what the hell is wrong with the Turn-blasted pizza?" Jenks said, an unsure green dust sifting from him like an underwater sunbeam. "I'm starving here!"

I thought about what Quen said, and then how they trusted me, not just to have their back, but to not stab them in it, either. "Quen . . ." I started, then threw my hands up, my heart thudding. "He charmed it. I don't want you coming with Quen and me tonight. *Either of you.* Okay?"

"Oh, but elf boy out there is good enough, huh?" Jenks said, his voice virulent.

He was dusting a silver green I'd never seen before, and I came forward, pleading with my eyes. "Jenks, we both know it's too cold for you. Ivy, as much as I want you there—"

She shook her head, feeling her throat as if remembering how easily Newt had pinned her. "I'm not any help, am I?"

It really wasn't a question, and I felt awful. "You are," I pleaded. "Just . . ."

"Just not tonight," she finished. "It's okay," she said around a sigh, her gaze distant, as if looking at the future. I couldn't tell if she saw me there or not.

"It's not okay," I said softly. "It stinks." Jenks was dusting a sour green in the corner, as far from me as he could get. He looked capable and ready, but I knew he would freeze tonight, and so did he. "This isn't what I wanted," I whispered, and his dust flashed silver, even as he refused to look at me.

"But this is where you are," Ivy said, and my shoulders eased. "Go with Quen. I'll watch Nick. All of us will," she said, her voice hard with warning and Jenks clattered his wings at her. "He'll be here when you get back, dead or alive."

I was smiling, though something was dying in me. "You guys are too good to me."

"Only because you made me so," Ivy said, her eyes glinting with unshed tears.

The weirdest feeling of anticipation filled me, seeing them both there in my kitchen, willing to let me go, knowing that I could do this, and trusting me. "Oh my God," I said, eyes swimming. "You are going to make me cry!" I sniffed, then moved about the kitchen, gathering everything up that I wanted to take—magnetic chalk, pain charms—it wasn't much, and I stifled a swift pang of worry. I snatched my cell phone at the last moment, tucking it in a back pocket after making sure it was on vibrate.

"Ivy!" Quen shouted from the living room. "Get back out here and watch Nick, or I'm going to kill him myself!"

I smiled, giving Ivy a hug as Jenks hovered over both of us. "When I get back, we are all going to go out and do some serious vigilante work."

"Ivy!" Quen bellowed. "I'm counting to three!" He couldn't leave Nick, and he didn't want to trust himself to bring him back to the kitchen.

"Thanks. For everything," I said, and Ivy touched my arm before she turned and left the room. My smile slowly faded as I looked at Jenks, who was dripping an angry dust. It still felt like good-bye, but that was okay now.

"See you at sunrise," he said, then turned, almost flying into Quen, the elf irate stomping into the kitchen.

The two of us alone, Quen stared at me, and I shrugged. "I'm not going to lie to them," I said, and his eyes narrowed.

"They'll follow us," he started, and I shook my head, not looking down the hallway to the bright sanctuary as I patted my pocket to be sure I had the rings and went into the back living room for my coat, hesitating until I remembered I had left it on the porch to air out.

"No, they won't," I said over my shoulder, feeling almost relaxed. Ivy and Jenks would wait for me. I wasn't losing them at all. "You're just mad that you don't have an excuse to do your charm."

"A little, yes," he complained as he followed me out. "Did something happen to the sanctity of your church again?"

My eye twitched. "Newt broke it so she could look in my closet." *Again.*

"Oh."

The night air was almost a slap as I opened the door, the soft breathing of the wind taking me by surprise. My coat was frigid as I jammed my arms into the sleeves, and Quen watched as I shoved everything but my chalk into a pocket. "No splat gun?"

Snapping the chalk in two, I wedged a piece into each boot. "He can burst the charms in the hopper and put me out in three seconds," I said, having downed Lee that way once—before we had come to an understanding. "It's your elven charms that are going to hold him, sweetheart. You up to it?"

"Sweetheart?" he muttered, and I turned to the graveyard with its glowing gargoyle eyes. Feeling good for some reason, I started down the stairs, boots clumping until I realized he wasn't following me. I frowned when he took a small, hourglass-shaped charm from his pocket and hung it on the nail the Christmas wreath had rested on. It was the first level of protection every home, be it Inderland or human, had, but we didn't have one up right now.

"Hey!" I exclaimed when he pulled the pin from the intricately detailed charm made to look like a wineglass pouring into another, and a shimmering wave of gold and black rose. Great leathery wings opened in the graveyard, and I shivered, thinking that it was like the demons of hell had come to life and were here to drag me to eternal torture for betraying my friends.

"You didn't lie to them," Quen said as I fumed. "I'm not going to risk Nick escaping."

My protest faded, and I almost fell off the step trying to see up to the top of the churchwide spell. "How long?" I said, my face cold, and he took my arm and turned me around.

"Sunup. Now: I'm doing this to save Trent. You're doing this to save the world. Yes?"

Sunup. If I didn't have this done by then, it wouldn't matter. Nervous, I stuck out my hand, wishing I had my other coat. This one completely ruined the sophisticated air I'd been going for, but it was hard to sling spells when your muscles were stiff with cold. "Deal."

We shook, and then together we went down the stairs to go around the front for his car. A hulking shape waited just inside the gate, and I gasped, almost running into a gargoyle. "Etude!" I said, flushing. It was obvious we had spelled the church.

"And you wonder why I refused to rest on your church," the gargoyle said, his voice incredibly low but holding a hint of amusement.

"Ah . . ." I stammered. "We, ah, need to get to Loveland Castle," I said, looking behind him at the rows of red and yellow eyes. "Are we too heavy for you, by chance?"

Etude grinned, and I shivered at the long black canines. "No. I don't think you are."

Chapter Twenty-Six

If a horse could jump and never land, it might come close to the feeling of flying atop a gargoyle. My knees hitched over the base of Etude's wings, and I crouched low, the wind beating at me so hard my eyes were mere slits. Glory sang through me, the chill air streaming through my hair in a rushing sensation of silk. It almost felt as if I had wings myself, reading the air currents and leaning with Etude to take advantage of the rising air above massive parking lots and the ribbon of the expressway we now flew over.

My stomach lurched as Etude beat his wings in three quick successive beats, and my legs tightened around him, making him flick his ears back to ensure I was still seated firmly. We'd had some trouble gaining altitude without the usual drop from a church tower that gargoyles were used to, but Etude had managed.

Closing my eyes, I leaned forward until I was almost lying atop him, the wind tearing over my back and my head surprisingly close to his ears. Etude banked suddenly, and my arms sprang around his thick neck. His entire body shook with laughter, but I didn't care. This was beyond description. To fly between the dark earth and the black sky when the waning moon rose was surely the pinnacle of existence: the power, the strength, the unsurpassed beauty. If riding a horse was freedom, this was heaven on earth.

If I survive this, I'm going to mend Belle's wings, I thought, exhaling as Etude shifted and we again came in line with the gargoyle who was carrying Quen. To have had this and lose it would break me. Fairies were made of sterner stuff than I.

Still holding that thought in my mind, I rested my head against Etude's warm neck. Quen looked tense, his brow furrowed as he sat almost upright against the wind atop the equally large gargoyle who had agreed to take him. He was riding him like a horse, probably with a much better seat than I had but creating far more drag.

Quen smiled grimly as I caught his eye. Etude's ear flicked back, changing the air currents racing over me, and my grip loosened when the gargoyle leveled his flight. I looked down to the ribbon of lights on the expressway. Traffic was heavy this time of night. "Do you always follow the expressways?" I called out to Etude, his tufted ears turning to catch my words.

"No." He swiveled his head without changing his flight, one red eye finding me, his deep words seeming to reach me despite the wind ripping past us. "We fly as the arrow, but I'm not sure where Loveland Castle is. Normally I'd follow the resonance of the line there, but it's so discordant right now, it's hard to locate. I had one of the kids at the basilica look up directions online for me."

"Sorry," I said, then grimaced, thinking I needed to stop saying that.

A lumpy shape loomed out of the thin moonlight and dark trees, a ribbon of light trailing beside it where the river was. "There!" I said pointing, and Etude nodded, his ears going flat to his skull when he shifted smoothly to put it directly ahead. The second gargoyle grimaced, looking pained as his wing beats became short and choppy. I couldn't feel the line yet, but clearly they could.

Sorry, I thought, then quashed it.

The river-damp air was cool, and we lost altitude when we left the warm ribbon of the expressway. We circled in the faint starlight. The castle was dark and empty, and the memory of burning into reality here burst against my thoughts with a hint of easily mastered panic. I'd been trying to keep Al from abducting a coven member. That hadn't turned out so well, either.

"Circle once!" Quen shouted, letting go of the gargoyle's shoulder long enough to make a circular motion with his finger. "I'll see if there's any magic down there apart from the line!"

Guilt hit me square on, and I looked down with my second sight. Sure, Quen had a stake in this, but he also had a little girl. *And a dead love to revenge,* I added, resolving to let it go. It would be my strength and his skill that would win or lose it.

My skin prickled at a wave of wild magic, and Etude shuddered, his skin rippling to make me clutch at him. "We're clear!" Quen shouted over the wind. "There's no one down there!"

The gargoyles shifted their wings simultaneously, their quick descent making my eyes widen. My arms went around Etude's neck, and I tried to make his center of gravity as near to normal as possible. His balance shifted, and I gasped as his wings made several strong back beats and he landed. Quen touched the ground an instant later. We were right on the gravelly garden path, or at least I was. Quen was about three feet up past the retaining wall, on the upper garden level.

"That line is ungodly awful," Etude said as I slid off his back, my knees rubbery. The air felt very still after the chill wind of flight, and I followed Etude's pained gaze to my line. That purple sludge was still there, almost glowing in the dark.

"Thank you for getting us here," I said, wiggling my toes to make sure I hadn't lost my magnetic chalk. Quen's gargoyle, looking beaten, was shifting awkwardly from foot to foot, his ears pinned back and his tail wrapped around his feet. Etude was handling it better, but clearly was still uncomfortable. "I'm going to fix the lines as soon as I can," I said, and Etude's ears pricked, an odd rumbling snuffling coming from him. I hoped it was laughter.

My knees were still shaking, and I carefully worked the cramps out. "Go," I said, smiling at him. "Both of you. And tell those back at the church they might want to leave. I'm going to dump all the imbalance there in a few minutes."

Etude leaned toward his friend, low elephant rumbles coming from them. Then the gargoyle who had brought Quen nodded, and with a powerful thrust of his back legs, he pushed off and found the air under his wings. Etude, though, remained. "I'm staying," he said, his red eyes narrowing as he looked at the line. "I want to help my son." Wincing, he turned to me. "I might wait at the castle, though, until needed. Burn my scrollwork, that line is awful."

I gave his thick, huge hand a squeeze of thanks. My guilt over having lost Bis grew, but Etude only smiled a black-toothed grin at me, haunches bunching as he made the short flight to land atop the highest point, his wings curving in around him until he looked like a natural part of the roof. That is, until his eyes caught the faint starlight and glowed a savage blood red.

Wild wisps of hair had escaped my braid, and I smoothed them as Quen jumped to my level, his shoes scuffing the gravel. My knees were *still* shaky, but I didn't think it was because of the flight here anymore. Elven magic was our best bet to keep Ku'Sox off us. I felt like a battery and I didn't like it. "Ready?" I said as I brought out the rings.

"It's making my wisdom teeth vibrate," Quen said as he eyed the line, his wince hard to see in the shadow-light. But he turned to me when the rings clinked, and suddenly the confidence I'd felt in the church vanished. It was more than the fear of Ku'Sox. It was the fear of letting Quen use me like a familiar.

"Perhaps . . ." he said slowly, seeing my reluctance, and I took a fast breath, shoving the smaller worn and dented ring on my finger. I felt nothing from it, and breath held, I extended the ring to him. I trusted Quen. If he betrayed me, Al would kill him.

"Thank you, Quen, for standing with me," I said, and then sucked in my breath as he put the ring on his finger and everything changed.

"Oh God," I whimpered, knees giving way, and Quen reached for me. I jerked out of his reach, stumbling several steps away as I found my balance by myself. His hand touched my shoulder, and I lashed out, driving him away. "Just give me a second!" I shouted, panicked but determined to make this work. My breathing came in short pants as I heard him back up, and only then could I straighten out of my crouch.

"Just give me a second . . ." I said again, still not able to look at him. He was there in my thoughts, and not in a good way. I could sense nothing of his emotions, just a theoretical fingertip on my chi, ready to rip what he wanted from it. And I couldn't stop him. It wasn't like Al's rings at all, where both parties had equal access. These were slavers, and I swallowed hard, trying to get used to it.

The ring around my finger glinted. *Al had endured this for how long?* Slowly I straightened.

"Are you okay?"

My stomach hurt. Nodding, I looked up to the dark skies. "Let's do it."

"Trent was right about you," Quen said, clearly uncomfortable as our strengths became one and our will his alone. "You are . . . strong."

Swell. Eyes down, I wavered, my heart seeming to stutter. Wanting to see the line better, I opened my second sight. Quen's aura shimmered, becoming oppressively clear.

"That is incredible," Quen said as he reached for the retaining wall, a haunted look in his eyes. I wasn't feeling so good, though, and either seeing my fear in my face or reading it in his mind, Quen pushed from the wall. "Are you sure you're okay?" he asked, his hand gripping my arms to steady me in the dark.

It was getting easier to tolerate his touch, and I nodded, head still down. "Yes," I said, spinning the ring on my finger to try to make it feel right. "I can't feel the line. Is there any way you can ease up on your grip?"

"Ah, sorry. How's that?" he said, and I blinked as suddenly the discordant jangle of a hundred imbalances in the line hit me.

"That's better," I said, wincing. Now I could really see. The purple line was extruding a bone-chilling cold, even as the event horizon pulled in energy, the atoms and molecules screaming as they were ripped apart. Even the purple of Ku'Sox's aura shredded to a pale red under its influence. Turning, I looked up at the castle.

"Ready?" I shouted and got a raised wingtip and a rumble in return. "I think that's a yes," I muttered, placing my feet and facing the line squarely. "If this doesn't get Ku'Sox's attention, I don't know what will."

I winced, one eye screwed shut as I pulled the line into my awareness fully and blocked everything else out. The multitude of the imbalances screamed at me, and I tried to gather them up, but they slipped through my thoughts like butterflies. "It's not working," I said, eyes opening up to find Quen hovering close and worried.

"Ah, it might be because of the rings," he said. "We're linked, and I'm not doing anything. I know the general idea, but . . ."

"Oh." Feeling foolish, I faced him, then awkwardly reached out and took his hand. His fingers in mine felt funny, but as I held on, a warm feeling suffused me as his awareness surrounded mine. He didn't mean to be domineering, but he hadn't had much practice sharing.

His breath quickened as he tapped into the line, and together we hesitated, taking in the discordant jangle. *Bubble the line,* I thought, getting no response, then becoming concerned when I wasn't able to do it myself. Either he had a wall up, or the rings only worked one way.

"Quen, can you lighten up? I'm having a hard time holding on to anything," I said, spinning the ring on my finger. There was a little notch in the metal. If I hooked my thumbnail in it just right, I could spin it almost entirely around my finger and catch it again. Horrified, I stopped, somehow knowing that I wasn't the first to spin it like that, around and around.

His fingers spasmed in mine. "My apologies. Try again."

As fast as that, a sensation of the line spiraled through me, heady and strong. I snatched at it, pulling it to me. The howling of the imbalance scraped across my nerves, and realizing just how much Quen had been shielding me from it, I gritted my teeth and sifted through the noise to find a bright gold thread in my mind's eye, a tinge of smut making it almost bearable. This was my original imbalance, and gathering everything up but that, I tuned my aura surrounding it to the imbalance in Newt's line in my garden.

"Sweet mother of God!" Quen exclaimed as the ache in the line and in my head evaporated. I jumped, startled as the bubble of imbalance suddenly vanished. I felt a pull, and I dug my awareness into the present to keep us from sliding to join it. There was a sliding *ping,* and then . . . nothing. The event horizon was gone.

"We did it!" I exclaimed, the pure tone of my line singing through me like icing. I was almost dancing. "Quen, *we did it!*" I shouted again, and Quen let go of my hand, beaming. Before us, the purple sludge was gone from the line. It was humming, in tune with reality—apart from the original imbalance, that is.

The wind from Etude's wings sent my hair flying as he landed behind us on the upraised half of the garden. "The imbalance is at the small line in the churchyard," he said, his deep voice rumbling and his ears slanted parallel with the ground to look like a peeved horse. "I can feel it there, but only because I know where to look."

My elation vanished. We had done it, but it was only half over, and the gargoyles were suffering. They were suffering as I reveled in our accomplishments. "Ku'Sox is going to be pissed."

"That's not the half of it," Ku'Sox's voice said, and I spun. Behind me, Etude began to hiss, sounding like a train making long, powerful huffs. Quen stiffened, stepping before me.

"Congratulations . . ." the demon drawled, taking in my pale clothes and Quen's black attire. "Now you're dead."

"Down!" I cried, pulling on the clean purity of the line before me.

Ku'Sox's black spell raced toward us, shedding silver sparkles. The line in my mental grip slipped through my fingers like silk, and I scrambled for it, my mouth gaping. I could do nothing. *What in hell?*

Quen's circle saved us, and both of us fell to our knees as Ku'Sox's spell imploded on its surface, lighting the area in a flash of lightning.

The line! I thought, unable to find it in my light-stunned vision, and then my panic turned to anger. It was Quen. "Quit hogging the line!" I shouted, ignoring Quen's offered hand as he tried to help me up. Etude had jumped between us and Ku'Sox, stalking back and forth with his wings half open. He looked far more menacing than when Bis did it.

Ku'Sox hesitated, his features pressed as he reassessed everything while I got to my feet. Quen stood staunchly beside me, tall and unbowed and smelling of crushed grass and wine.

"An unbound gargoyle?" Ku'Sox said, the disgust in his voice obvious as he watched Etude. "What do you hope to accomplish there?"

"You kidnapped his son!" I said, then elbowed Quen in the ribs. The line had gone slippery. "Let go of the line, damn it," I muttered, then I filled my chi when he did. "We need to work on this sharing thing," I said, and he grimaced.

I dared a look at the line humming clean behind Ku'Sox. "Your sludge is out of the line," I said boldly. "It was your aura signature on the curse that broke it. Give me Bis and Trent, and I might not press charges."

Ku'Sox smiled, and I couldn't help my shiver. "In a moment," he said, smile fading as Etude paced between us. "It *looks* clean, and I don't sense any . . . trickery. What *have* you done, Rachel? You can't have fixed it. You moved it, but where? Curious."

I stiffened as he looked to the sky then took one sharply angled step sideways into my line like it was a river. "You lose!" I shouted, adrenaline pouring into me, and Quen caught my shoulder to keep me from striding forward. "I'm calling Dali. Your ass is mine, and you will admit you broke it!"

"I . . . don't think . . . so." Ku'Sox was in the line, tasting it, almost, making sure it was truly clean. It was. I could guarantee it.

"Your aura signature is at the bottom of that sludge line!" I asserted, and Ku'Sox laughed.

"Perhaps, but I don't see a sludge line."

"That's because I got rid of it!" I shouted, and then I fell back, my folly falling on me. I'd moved all the imbalance, yes, and his curse with it. Until I got all the imbalances where they belonged, no one would be able to see his curse. Damn it! Couldn't I catch a single Turn-blessed break?

"Tell me how you did it," Ku'Sox said, seeming to be genuinely curious. "You couldn't have destroyed it. You put it somewhere, holding it in your chi perhaps? Is that why you stole a pair of elven rings?" He simpered at Quen. "Needed some help holding that much slop?"

My head hurt, and I lifted my chin. I didn't think he knew which rings we had, or he would be more aggressive. That I hadn't proved he was responsible for the event horizon was infuriating, but if we couldn't prove we were stronger than him, it wouldn't matter. *Cowards! Why am I helping them?*

"I wonder," Ku'Sox said, standing in my line and soaking it in, bathing in energy. "Can you defend yourself while hiding all that imbalance?"

Etude's ears pricked in alarm, and I stiffened, imagining a circle around Quen and me. Ku'Sox shifted, and my eyes widened. I reached for the ley line, shouting *"Rhombus!"* only to fall to a knee, fumbling for the line running through my fingers like sand.

Quen pushed out, and I ducked as the sparkles of his thrown energy lit the dark. I could feel the line flowing through me, running into him. I was adding to Quen's defense, but I might as well have been a cat with the help I was being.

Etude roared, his hands grasping as he lunged at Ku'Sox. "No!" I cried out, but Ku'Sox shouted a satisfied-sounding word, and Etude was flung back, flipping head over tail, headed for . . . us.

"Rachel!" Quen cried, jerking me out of the way as Etude crashed into the retaining wall. Rocks and dirt sifted down over him. I shook off Quen's hand and ran to him, brushing the dirt from his huge, pushed-in face. The gargoyle was breathing, but out cold.

"Quen?" I stammered, looking up at him. His lips were pressed together hard, but his anger wasn't at me as he helped me up. I didn't think it was directed at Ku'Sox, either, who was advancing slowly. We were up shit creek, and I didn't even see the "if" that got us there. The rings were not working well. Quen was way outclassed.

"You're not holding the imbalance," Ku'Sox said, curious now. It was the only thing keeping him from hammering us into the ground. "Who is? Is it Newt?"

I am wearing a slave ring . . . echoed in my head, and I looked at my hand in horror. *What have I done to myself?*

"No, not Newt," Ku'Sox mocked, misunderstanding the look of terror I knew I was now wearing. "You're all alone at last, Rachel. It took me longer than I thought to get you isolated. Everyone *likes* you."

I am wearing a slave ring!

Ku'Sox threw something at us, and Quen knocked it away. I hid behind him, unable to think, to comprehend. I had to get this thing off!

"She's not alone," Quen said, and Ku'Sox laughed.

"You?" Ku'Sox stopped eight feet back, not trusting my fear, I think. "You don't count," he said lightly, looking at his nails. "They're letting us fight it out, even if they do like her best. Isn't that nice? They want the strongest parent possible for the next generation." He smoothed his clothes in satisfaction. "That would be me."

Letting us fight it out? Yeah, that sounded about right. We were making enough noise in the ley lines to pique the interest of the most sedentary demon, and the chicken squirts hadn't shown up yet. That didn't bother me as much as the fact that I couldn't get the ring off my pinkie. Scared, I leaned to Quen's ear. "I want the ring off."

"I know. You can't tap a line worth the salt in your veins. I'm sorry," he said, and then I cowered as I felt a huge tug on me and Quen's bubble flashed into existence, glittering a fabulous green before it faded. "If we take them off now, we will die. The only reason my circle is holding him is because it's made with both our strengths."

Crap on toast, he was right, and I stood beside him, not knowing what I could do to make this better. I knew the demons were watching. Why didn't they help us? "You're insane!" I shouted, knowing they were listening. Besides, Etude was stirring, and I didn't want him taken out before he recovered.

"My state of mind is not the issue here!" Ku'Sox shouted, his face red even in the faint light. "It is about strength!"

"It's about adaptability and resources, and all you are is psychotic! You can't fix psychotic!" I yelled back as Etude staggered to his feet, a low rumble of his anger flowing about me as his wings opened and funneled the sound forward. His growl resonated through me, and I swallowed hard.

With a crack of stone, Etude pulled a chunk of wall away and threw it over our heads. Ku'Sox swore, deflecting it to thud into the thick grass.

"Quen, take my ring off!" I exclaimed, tugging at Quen's coat as I felt a huge pull through me. It was Quen, prepping a spell, and I let it flow, knowing I could do nothing wearing this stupid band of silver.

Looking magnificent, Quen threw a ball of black-hazed energy at Ku'Sox. The harried demon deflected it within a breath of contact, and it went whizzing into the river, lighting the bottom of the trees in an eerie glow. Etude was tossing great clods of earth at Ku'Sox, darting from the ground to the air to make a difficult target.

"Quen!" I shouted as the man ran for Ku'Sox, his fist swollen with a green haze. "No!" I shouted as Etude and Quen descended upon Ku'Sox together. Etude's rock fell harmlessly to the side as Ku'Sox sidestepped it, but Quen's blow landed, the man's fist plowing into Ku'Sox's face to make the demon scream and fall back.

Teeth clenched, I lunged forward to pull Quen away before Ku'Sox could retaliate. Fire licked the soles of my feet as we ran, and we were both picked up and flung into the grass, the distance muting Ku'Sox's last curse. My face planted into the clover, and I sat up fast, spitting dirt. Nearby, Etude was shaking his head, a tear in one wing bleeding slowly. Beside me, Quen slowly sat up, his hand touching his lip. "Damn." Quen licked his bleeding lip, almost smiling as he looked back at Ku'Sox, lost under a thick black sheet of ever-after. "Think he gave up?"

"No! He's turning into a bird to eat us!" I shoved my hand into Quen's face. "Take the ring off. Take it off now!"

Quen's face was guilty. "I can't," he said flatly as he got up.

"The hell you can't!" I tugged him around to look at me. "I can't tap a line worth crap. You admitted it yourself. And I can't get the ring off!" *Oh God. Had Al been right?*

"I told you, the only reason we are doing so well is because of your strength and my skill. If I take it off, your strength won't keep us alive."

"Maybe you didn't notice," I said, pointing to the cocoon Ku'Sox was in, "but we're not doing so hot right now!"

Quen's jaw clenched. The misshapen form inside was growing larger, and like watching a chick develop, I saw Ku'Sox's legs thin and lengthen, his arms grow into wings, his head mutate until a wicked, long beak formed.

"Etude, go!" I shouted, waving him off as Ku'Sox punched through the shell of ever-after, screaming a harsh, ugly call that echoed against the trees. "He's going to eat you!" I exclaimed, heartsick when the gargoyle beat heavily into the air, his silhouette a darker blackness against the night sky. Ku'Sox was already his size and still growing.

"My God, Trent was right," Quen said in awe, and I rounded on him.

"Yeah, he's a big badass stork that eats people. Quen, we have a problem!"

Awestruck, Quen watched Ku'Sox flap his wings and croak, daring Etude to attack. "We can circle him. Now's our chance."

"Circle him? It won't stand," I started, and Quen's attention came back to me.

"It will if we work together."

I could not believe this. "We tried that," I said, hunching when the breeze from Ku'Sox's wings flattened my hair. "I want the ring off, and I want it off now!" I reached for his hand to take his ring and use it to take mine off, and Quen jerked away from me.

Shocked, I stared, three feet between us. *No. Not Quen.*

Above us, Etude and Ku'Sox met in a clash of talons and wings. Jerking, I watched as Etude tried to bite the back of Ku'Sox's neck, and they fell, wings beating madly. Descending slowly, they crashed into the trees at the far end of the clearing. They were down.

My heart was pounding as I looked at Quen, hand extended. "Give me your ring."

Taking my shoulders, he spun me around to the fight. "We can do this."

Distrust blossomed in me. *Do this, and I give you your freedom.* I'd seen that in the history books before. Ku'Sox screamed, his black shadow rising up from the trees. Etude was bellowing from the woods, so he was still alive. Ku'Sox was coming right for us, his wings making the air shake, and yet Quen still stood, a green haze about his closed fist.

"Get down!" I shouted, ducking to crouch next to the retaining wall as Ku'Sox swooped over us, his huge claws reaching. The memory of seeing pixies slip down his throat rose up, and I cowered, the wall pressing into me. Fire lanced my shoulder, and I screamed.

"*Immuluate!*" Quen shouted, and I choked as the line raced through me, making the new rip in my shoulder burn like lava.

And then Ku'Sox was gone, swinging around for another strike. Hand clasped to my shoulder, I stood, watching his dark shape against the sky. He was playing with us.

"Rachel! Are you okay?"

I looked at Quen sourly as his enthusiasm paled. It was all I could do to not yell at him that no, I was not okay. "Fine," I said, pushing at the edges of the cut and seeing very little blood.

"Maybe you're right," Quen said as we watched Ku'Sox turn and come back like a deadly pendulum. And then he brightened. "The line!" he said suddenly. "You can jump them. At least to the one in the garden. You can jump us both."

My eyebrows rose. "You want me to jump a line? Carrying you? That's what got us into this in the first place."

"Down!" Quen said, his hand on my shoulder, and we flattened as Ku'Sox buzzed us again. I think he was enjoying himself, but he wheeled sharply, landing twenty feet away, wings outstretched and bill snapping loudly.

"You can do it," Quen said. "If we're sharing mental space, you can carry me. You know the signature. You just dumped the imbalance there. Even if Ku'Sox follows us, the gargoyles will help."

Perhaps long enough for me to sit on him and make him take the slaver ring off. Beyond him, Ku'Sox snapped his beak and strode forward. I nodded—burning to death in the lines was better than being eaten.

"Keep him off us," I said as he took my hands and nodded. "And try not to hog the line!" I shouted, feeling it strengthen around me.

Ku'Sox hesitated, head cocked as I tapped the line and my hair started to float. Letting out a murderous caw, he began to run, guessing our intent.

"Now!" Quen shouted, and I bubbled us, shifting the hue and sound of it to that of the line ten feet away. I knew it by heart now, and it was easy.

I heard Ku'Sox scream in defeat as the beauty of the line took us, and the swirling warmth of the line washed the ugliness of the grove away. Everything went silver in my mind. Quen snapped a bubble around his thoughts, making me wonder how often he'd traveled the lines before.

Home, I thought, recalling the harsh jangle of the chaos I'd made of the line in the garden. It was a mass of orange, blue, black, and red, and though I could see it in my mind, I couldn't shift the resonance.

Home! I thought again, starting to panic. The damn slavery ring was interfering. *Quen, help me tune the bubble to match my aura!* I cried out, but he couldn't hear me, and I couldn't leave him there.

Quen! I tried again, and a cool/warm thought slid into mine with the bright sparkle of butterfly wings.

Got you! came Bis's cheerful thought, and with a shimmer, Quen's and my auras flashed to a strident purple.

I was real. Stumbling, I sucked in a huge gulp of air, shocked when my boots skittered across electric-light-lit tile, not the starlit red slab of cement I was aiming for. I looked up, hearing a groan as Quen hit the floor behind me a second later.

My face became cold, and Trent turned, his rolling chair making a clicking sound as he cocked his head at my battle-dirty clothes and tangled hair.

"This isn't my garden," I whispered, and Trent's smile chilled me to my core.

Chapter Twenty-Seven

Trent stood, a hard eagerness obvious on his blond-stubbled, tired-looking face. Fear slid through me, and I hid my hand with the ring behind me. Quen could give him the master ring and, with it, me. Trent would be the most powerful elf in generations. He could save his people. Why would he ever take it off?

"I didn't expect you until tomorrow," Trent said as he swooped to us, his lab coat billowing behind him.

"The deadline was moved," Quen said. "Sa'han, you were right. This isn't working."

"Obviously. If it was, you wouldn't be here."

He was reaching for me, and I pulled away, standing before he could help me.

"I got you!" Bis almost sang, and my heart sank. We had left Etude alone with that monster. "I snagged you. Right. Out. Of. The. Line!" he crowed, his wings spread and his red eyes sparkling in the fluorescent light. "I'm go-o-od. I'm go-o-od. I'm so bad I'm go-o-od," he sang, doing one of Jenks's hip wiggles, his tail curved over his head and wings spread wide.

I had just left Etude there, and I fought with the desire to go back. Beyond the thick plate glass, the babies slept, the light dim and making the glass somewhat reflective. Trent was gesturing sharply as he and Quen talked in hushed whispers, and I didn't like the chagrined expression that Quen was now wearing. Al was right. I was a fool.

My hands were shaking, and I leaned against a counter, wondering if I was going to throw up. Ku'Sox would figure out where we'd gone eventually. The slaver glinted on my finger, and I wanted it off. "Thanks, Bis," I said when the adolescent gargoyle finished his well-deserved "happy dance" and dropped to the counter, his claws scraping. His smile was wide, and I didn't know how I was going to tell him about his dad. Taking a breath, I whispered, "Your dad is a wonder."

Bis's ears pricked, and the hair on the end of his tail stood straight up. "You saw him?"

I nodded. "He came to the church, then helped keep Ku'Sox off us at the castle. We left him there, but Ku'Sox was after us, not him. I think he'll be okay." *God, please let him be okay.* A baby was crying, and I turned to the nursery windows. The woman was furtively weaving her way to the cradle—as if she'd be punished. "Bis, start jumping the babies and women out of here." I was down to salvage, but I knew getting their children back would mean the end of a nightmare for a handful of families. At least, until their children started doing demon magic, hosts to Ku'Sox's favorites.

Bis took to the air in little hops. "You bet. Where do you want them? Trent's place?"

I was going to say the church, but if Bis knew the line in Trent's office . . .

"My office?" Trent exclaimed, and I pushed myself up from the counter, angry. His hands were in the pockets of his lab coat. Quen's were behind his back. I didn't know who had the ring, and suddenly it was really important.

"The church's garden is full of pained gargoyles right now," I said as Bis crawled on the ceiling into the nursery. *Oh God, what if Ku'Sox was there now? Looking for us?* "I want the ring off, and I want it off now." Neither one of them said anything, and I stiffened. "Did you hear me?"

"Yes, of course," Trent said, but neither one of them was moving. "Can it wait until we get out of here? Apparently you and Quen working together is the only way you survived this long. It would be foolish to halve our strength until we are sure we can afford it."

"Survived!" I blurted. "That's the word for it. This isn't working! We need to go!"

Trent jerked into motion, rolling his chair across the lab to a bank of cabinets. Maybe I should just cut my finger off. I didn't really need ten fingers, did I? Trent got along okay with less than that. "I'm not leaving until the infants are gone," Trent said, rummaging in a drawer. "And until they are, the rings stay on." His gaze went to the blood seeping from the scratch Ku'Sox had given me, and I tugged the torn fabric to cover it.

I glared at Quen, feeling betrayed. "Soon as they're out of here, the ring comes off." But neither one of them said anything, and I headed for Trent, hands clenched. "And then it comes off!" I said again. "I am not going to be your battery to try to kill Ku'Sox. Understand?"

"Yes, of course." Glancing at Bis, Trent stood, his hands full of bandages and ointment he'd taken from the drawer. "Sit, you're injured."

"My arm is fine!" I said, glancing behind me to see only seven, then six babies left. Trent had dropped his head, and then it hit me. I wasn't the only slave here. "How much can you do?" I asked Trent, and his lips twitched. "I mean, are you like his slave slave, or do you still have free will?"

Trent glanced at Quen. "Ah, as long as Ku'Sox isn't paying me any attention, I have my will. And when he makes one mistake, he's going to die."

He was looking at my hand, and suddenly my warning flags tripped. Ashen, I hid my hands and looked between Quen and Trent. There hadn't been enough time in that hushed conversation for Quen to bring Trent all the way up to speed. "You knew I reinvoked the slavers," I said, and Trent seemed to freeze. "How? Did you have Quen pull Riffletic's rings to force me to reinvoke these . . . *slave rings*! So you could use me to kill Ku'Sox?"

Quen's eye twitched, and Trent reached for me. "No, well, fight maybe," he said, his eyes pleading. "You've got it backward, but they're the only way to even hope to make a strong enough bond between demon and elf. I was afraid if I told you, you would have said no."

"I put this on because I trusted you! And you forced this decision on me?" I jerked away from Quen. My hand was in a fist, slaver gold glinting between my knuckles. *You tricky little bastards, what have you done?* I thought, glaring at Quen, then shifted my eyes to the glass behind him. It was shining with a red, rosy glow.

Suddenly the room flashed white, a muffled explosion making the glass tremble. I gasped, falling to my knees when it cracked. Trent went for the floor as Quen spun. A boom of sound shook the air, and the glass shattered inward.

Quen was flung back, arms flailing as he hit the tile a second before the safety glass pattered down on him. Crouched and head covered, I was struck by shards. Babies were crying, at least three, maybe more.

"Where are you taking them, you little swamp rat!" Ku'Sox shouted, and I felt a tug as Bis popped another baby to safety. Ku'Sox didn't know Quen and I were here, and my heart pounded. Shit. Who had the ring? Trent or Quen? Ku'Sox owned Trent. Would he own me by default too?

Quen shifted, and glass slid from him. The faint tinkling went unnoticed as Ku'Sox shouted at Bis. Thumps and pops were coming in through the broken window, and I peeked over the shattered edge of the window frame. Bis was swooping madly, his face alight and his sparse hair bristled. He was enjoying himself, but I was scared to death for him.

"Hey!" I shouted, standing up, and Ku'Sox spun, the demon actually looking surprised for one—blessed—moment.

Black teeth showing in a grin, Bis used the distraction to pop another baby to safety.

Ku'Sox glanced at the gargoyle, then back to me. Looking grim, he walked toward us, snatching a wailing infant from his crib by his leg, his blue blanket falling to the floor. "I don't know if you are incredibly stupid or incredibly clever," he said, carelessly dangling the screaming baby upside down. "Are you seeking a way to implicate me in your . . . foolhardy attempt to destroy the ever-after, or just really, really stupid?"

"I'd go for incredibly clever," I said, then yanked on the line as his free hand clenched, turning a violent black before he threw a curse at me.

"Now!" Trent shouted, and I felt a twin tug on the line as both Quen and Trent threw up a bubble. Ku'Sox's energy tore through both of them, bouncing off my smaller bubble. Black and gold shimmered like oil as Ku'Sox's magic slammed into mine. I gasped when my hold on the line faltered, then held firm. Ku'Sox's magic hung, stuck as it tried to burn through, and I panicked, not knowing what to do. It was better—my hold on the line was firm. I didn't think anyone was wearing the ring. I could do this. I could fight back.

"*Eram pere!*" I shouted, exploding my bubble out. It took Ku'Sox's magic with it, slamming it into the ceiling to rain down like evil pixy dust.

Trent tripped on something and went down, hand reaching for a counter. "Bis!" I shouted as the gargoyle darted to the last screaming infant as Ku'Sox ducked. "We have to go!"

Trent pulled himself up, tall and proud. "*Digitorum percussion,*" he intoned, the heavy black in his hand growing darker, his golden aura racing over it to make it glow. My eyes widened as he pulled back, aiming for Ku'Sox. I could feel him pull on the line, he was so desperate. But he was aiming for Ku'Sox.

My God. The baby. "Trent, no!" I cried, and I lunged for him. Quen's foot tripped me, and I plowed into Trent, grabbing him about the knees instead of his middle where I'd intended.

We went down, my teeth clenching as we hit the floor. Trent cried out in anger as his magic went wild, slipping from his hand to roll into a bank of machines. I ducked as it hit, sparks flying as machinery suddenly vanished, replaced by the smell of ozone and twisted metal.

Shouting, Quen launched himself at Ku'Sox. The two of them went down in a tangle of arms and billowing fabric. Twin bursts of aura-tinted magic flared, and then Quen was flung back, sliding to a halt against the machines, his expression showing his pain and one hand clenched into a fist against his chest.

"What are you doing!" Trent shouted at me, pushing me off him as he stood, and I backed up onto my knees before spinning to face Ku'Sox.

"You might hurt the baby!" I yelled back at him, hunched and ready for the next attack.

"That child is already dead!" Trent shouted, furious.

"Put the baby down!" I exclaimed at Ku'Sox, moving to stand between him and everyone behind me. I didn't know how I was going to stop him, but I was having a much easier time now that I was a slave with no master. *Can I trust him?* asked a small voice inside me, and I ached at the coming betrayal.

"This child?" Ku'Sox said, swinging the screaming baby like pendulum, tossing him into the air to land in his arms. Behind him, Bis tensed, too far away to snatch him to safety. His eyes went behind me. "*Dolore adficere*," Ku'Sox whispered, his fingers moving.

I tensed, but all Ku'Sox did was smile as the child in his arms wailed even louder, hardly able to breathe.

Fire suddenly erupted against my back, thought-stealing pain radiating out from my spine. I couldn't breathe, and I collapsed to the floor, my fingers scrabbling behind me to find what it was. The heat spread to my hands, and I cried out, pulling them to my front to see that they were covered in a burning, golden-hued aura—burning me from the outside in. Ku'Sox's curse had come from Trent.

"*Valeo*," I gasped to counter it, flooding my mind with a numbing cold, sucking in the air as I heard Ku'Sox laugh and the baby scream. His shoes were crunching on glass, and fear gave me the strength to force my head up, seeing him past my strands of hair. Heart pounding, I scuttled backward. Quen was struggling to stop Trent. Trent had hit me. He had cursed me. But by his frustrated, pained expression, he hadn't done it by choice. My God, Ku'Sox was nuts. He was laughing, knowing full well I'd rip his head off if I could. But maybe he knew I'd never get even half a chance.

"This is not me!" Trent shouted, his face creased and sweat darkening his hair as he shoved Quen off him. "It's *not* me!" he said again, grunting with the effort to keep his hand from rising. His eyes widened in a sudden fear. "Flee, Rachel . . ."

"Sa'han!" Quen cried out, ducking behind a bubble when Trent threw another spell. It was aimed at me, and I threw up a circle, but my reaction was too slow and it tore through it, the spell hitting me square on before my barrier could fully form.

Pain crawled over me like ants, skittering from my chest and working its way through me, and I screamed. If it reached my mind, I was dead. "*Valeo*," I sobbed again, curled on the floor within my bubble, shaking as the pinpricks faded and died.

"Interesting," Ku'Sox said, that baby still wailing in his arms as he sat on the broken window frame and crossed his ankles to watch. "Do that one again. I want to know if she can do it any faster."

"Damn it all to hell!" I shouted at Trent as I looked up, seeing Ku'Sox's frown; he was not entirely pleased that I could counter that one. "You do that again, and I'll smack you!" I said to Trent as I trembled with adrenaline.

"I can't help it," he rasped through gritted teeth, and then he dropped to one knee, groaning as he fought whatever Ku'Sox was making him do next.

"Yeah, well, sorry then," I said, gathering my will. "*Alta quies simillima mort!*" I shouted, flinging half of the curse at Trent, holding the rest in my palm, burning. The curse tore through my bubble, absorbing it and pulling it over and around me like a dirty shirt. It smacked into Trent, and the man went down, his neck nothing but cords of muscle. He gave one spasm, then lay still, his chest rising and falling peacefully.

"You struck him!" Quen said, clearly shocked.

"He hit me first," I said, then flicked the rest of the charm at Ku'Sox.

The demon deflected it with a hasty pop. I knew it wouldn't land, but at least he had stopped laughing. Trent lay unconscious. It wouldn't last long, and I got up, hurting, tired, and pissed. Flee, Trent had said. It sounded like a good idea. If Bis could snatch us from a ley line, then he could by God jump us out as he had the babies.

"Rachel?" Bis said, looking scared as he landed beside me on the rolling chair. "He's got the only baby left."

"I'll get him," I said as I stood up and tugged my shirt straight. "Get Quen and Trent out of here. Catch me when I jump." If Trent wasn't here, then he couldn't try to kill Ku'Sox using me to do it.

"No!" Quen said, arm up to fend Bis off, and then they were gone.

I took a deep breath, glad Quen was safe. If Bis didn't come back for Trent or me, then I'd die happy. Ray would *not* grow up without her father.

"Give me that baby," I said, shaking as I listed to one side, and Ku'Sox took his pinkie from the now quiet child, charmed to sleep with a curse.

"One step closer, and I squeeze," he said, smiling down at the sleeping infant.

I froze as Trent stirred behind him. "You want me, not him."

Ku'Sox raised an eyebrow. "Offering to take his place? But I already have you. Come sunup, I will be pleading to the collective to spare your life. And they will give you to me because otherwise, I'll kill them all and they know it."

"Not unless I kill you first." Maybe Trent had the right idea after all.

Bis popped into existence, right on top of Trent, and I jerked. "You will regret this, little rat!" Ku'Sox shouted, and I flung up a bubble around them as Bis popped Trent out. Ku'Sox's magic winged into the nursery, quiet and empty. "Enough!" Ku'Sox shouted, throwing the baby from him as if the infant were trash.

"No!" I shoved myself into motion, arms outstretched as the baby screamed in fear. I hit the floor front first, eyes closed from the impact and stretching forward. My hands were empty. An awful thump echoed through me, and I curled up in heartache. I had jumped too short. I had missed. Knowing what I'd find, I opened my eyes, tears blinding me as I gathered up the silent, limp baby and stood, my knees shaking in anger.

"You will behave, Rachel, or you learn obedience from the back of my hand," Ku'Sox seethed.

The baby was dead, and I held him, rocking him and aching inside. "Now you've done it," I said, voice low and threatening. Trent had been right. The baby had been dead the moment Nick had stolen him. "You will account for yourself," I intoned, shaking as I felt a tweak on my thoughts.

"Who will force me? You?" Ku'Sox snarled, his hand reaching for me hazed with power dripping to hiss on the floor.

The lines echoed in my head as Bis landed on my shoulder, and I gasped when their jagged existence flooded my mind.

"No!" Ku'Sox screamed, but it was too late, and I sobbed as the line took me, the harsh caw of the demon replaced with the howling discord of the broken lines. I deserved the ragged edges cutting at my soul. It was only because of the baby that I bubbled my thoughts against their burning haze as I wept.

Chapter Twenty-Eight

R*achel?*
I thought it odd that a kid who had skin as hard as stone had thoughts as soft as silk, and they slid into mine without resistance. Depressed, I gathered my awareness, not wanting Bis to know how broken I felt, listening to the line screaming around us with a curious detachment.

Rachel, can you bubble this resonance for me? he said meekly, and I let him further into my mind, aching as the line seemed to burn and shift to a harsh orange-green glitter with sparkles. *If we can set this song in the line we're going to, then it won't hurt so bad.*

Bis was in pain, and that galvanized me. Sealing my heartache behind a thick wall, I sent my thoughts deeper into the chaos of the ever-after, finding the resonance he colored for me and bubbling it.

Shift us to this . . . Bis prompted, showing me a shimmery gray and green.

Mentally rocking myself, I did. A ping of rightness went through me. It was as if a tiny wail softly subsided, finding peace in the storm streaming around me. Hesitating in my misery, I caught back a sob, remembering the baby in my arms. *Bis?*

Bis's emotion next to mine was clearer, and he sighed. *Thank you, it will be easier to jump now.* He hesitated, then added, *Sorry about the headache.*

Headache? I questioned him, then suddenly found myself struggling for air. We'd been in the line too long, and I clawed for a way out. There was a pop and a push, and I stumbled, taking a huge gasp of air as I found myself in reality, the screaming of the line replaced by the crying of a handful of angry babies.

Sure enough, my head was throbbing, and I looked down at the little boy in my arms, my hope crushed when I found him silent and pale. He was so perfect, but no longer really here. I looked up, feeling nauseated as I tried to take in more air than I possibly could. We were in Trent's office, and I stumbled out of the line, staggering to fall into one of the chairs before the desk.

From behind his desk, Trent watched me as he dodged the cotton ball of antiseptic Quen was trying to dab on a scrape across Trent's forehead. An office girl I didn't recognize went from baby to baby, assessing and giving instructions to a few people, clearly office personnel, drafted into nursemaid duty. One by one, the babies were being taken out.

"Thank you, Bis," I said when he hopped to perch on the back of the chair behind me. "Your dad will be so proud of you."

So thin a line between alive and not. How could I have just left Etude there?

The wood creaked as Bis shifted his grip. "I'm sorry," he said, meaning the baby still in my arms, and I closed my eyes, feeling the tears begin to slip down.

It was Quen who came forward, kneeling beside me as he took in the little boy's silence and pallor. "Rachel . . ."

I blinked fast, eyes opening at his light touch on my arm. "He threw him to the ground," I said, the room suddenly silent as the last of the babies were taken out and the door shut. "I tried to get there, but I was too far away, and . . ." I couldn't say the rest, my head pounding as I held someone else's child and grieved, rocking back and forth.

Quen's touch on my shoulder was light, almost not there. "Give him to me."

"Why!" I raged suddenly, and his expression shifted to one of pity.

"Let me take him," he said, reaching carefully to make sure his head wouldn't loll. "Give him to me. *Please*, Rachel."

Crying, I let Quen take him. Moving painfully, he got to his feet and carefully passed the baby to another secretary. Someone handed me a box of tissues, and I snatched it, feeling like a wimp. I should be stronger. I didn't know that little boy, but he had been important, and now he was gone—someone's child who had been lost, found, and lost again.

Quen stood beside me as I sat in that chair and cried as the room slowly became quiet. "I know you're hurting, but thank you for bringing Trent home."

Wiping my eyes, I looked up, sealing the pain away for later if I survived this. I couldn't tell what Trent was thinking. That I should be stronger, maybe. I hated it when he was right. "How long until he finds us?" I asked Bis, and he shrugged, wingtips touching above his head.

"Soon." Quen glanced at Trent as if he needed his permission. "Bis fixed the line, and when Ku'Sox finishes his tantrum and realizes it, he will come investigate."

"Sorry," Bis grumbled, and I reached to touch his foot in reassurance, getting a flash of the jangle of lines. "The line hurt, and now it doesn't."

"Bis tells me that his family kept Ku'Sox from damaging the church, but the spell I put on it is gone," Quen added. "And Nick. Ivy and Jenks are fine."

I shrugged, not caring—about Nick, not Ivy and Jenks. The fact that the gargoyles had fought to protect those I loved was more than I could ever repay.

"We should leave," Trent said, standing up behind his desk and taking his lab coat off.

"Where to, Sa'han?" Quen said, and I did nothing, staring at nothing as Trent began to pace. Behind him, his fish swam in a smaller tank, and I watched them listlessly. I wasn't sure who had the master ring, but I knew they wouldn't volunteer to take mine off until they felt safe, and every time I asked and they said no, I felt another part of me die. There was no such thing as safe. When Ku'Sox was dead? When the demons were gone? When the vampire threat was nulled?

"Not you, just Bis and I need to leave," I said, and Trent spun on a heel to give me an incredulous look. "Now," I said, lurching to my feet and sourly waving off Quen when he tried to steady me. His finger was bare. "If Bis and I can fix another line, it will give Ku'Sox somewhere else to look."

"I'm coming with you." Trent was at his desk, his motions quick as he jotted notes.

"No, you're not." If I wasn't so angry about being tricked into reinvoking the slavers, I would have laughed at the stupidity of the situation. *Couldn't you be wrong at least once, Al?* "You'll curse me every time Ku'Sox shows up."

"I can't stay here." Trent flexed his arm as if it was in pain as he paused in his writing. "Besides, it wasn't me who threw the curse at you. It was Ku'Sox."

I sniffed, pushing the edges of my torn shirt together. "Well, it was me who threw that curse at you. Do it again, and I'll knock you flat on your ass so hard you won't get up for a week—ring or no ring."

Trent jerked, his eyes meeting mine from under his bangs. "About that . . ."

Oh God. Here it came. The excuse for me to keep it on, just for a little bit longer.

There was a soft knock, and Quen sprang forward to take the cart of water bottles an aide came in with. "We should keep him with us," Quen said as he took it and all but pushed the man back out. "Otherwise, Ku'Sox will keep using him against us."

I was suddenly a hundred times more thirsty. Keeping Trent with Bis and me would work as long as we stayed a step ahead of him, but why risk it? "I don't remember including you on this private excursion, Quen," I said as I strode to the cart and took a bottle. Damn elves thought they ruled the world. *I trusted you,* I thought, angry as I cracked the seal on one of the waters, downing half of it in one go. It was perfectly chilled, just enough to be cold but not enough to shock me, slipping down smooth as if it were from the fountain of life. Wiping my mouth, I looked at the label. KALAMACK SPRINGS. Figures.

"I trusted you," I accused, pointing with the half-empty bottle, and guilt poured off Quen, adding to my anger. "I trusted both of you!" I shouted, and Trent came out from behind his desk.

"You will not be mad at Quen," he said calmly, jerking to a halt when I pointed at him to keep his distance. "This isn't his fault. I told him to remove the Riffletic rings so you would go for the slavers instead."

"Son of a bitch . . ." I whispered, feeling the ring heavy on my finger. "This just keeps getting better and better."

"It was the only way you'd reinvoke them!" he said loudly. "Rachel, it's my only chance of getting out from under Ku'Sox's boot."

"What, so you can kill him?" I yelled, and Bis dug his claws deeper into the back of the chair, clearly upset.

"No." His face scrunched up in embarrassment, and he glanced from Quen to me. "Rachel, the slavers work both ways."

Confused, I set the water bottle down. "Excuse me?"

Quen cleared his throat, his voice cutting off as Trent raised his hand.

"Shut up, Quen," he muttered, shocking me. "I should have listened to my gut and included her in my decision from the first. We tried it your way, and it failed miserably. She isn't a tool. If she was, it would have worked."

"W-what . . ." I stammered as he dug in his pocket, and my pulse hammered as he jiggled what had to be the master ring.

"I'm sorry, Rachel," he said as he took my wrist, lifting my hand to slide the master ring over the slaver. "I should have trusted you."

"Damn right you—" My voice cut off as the rings touched. A wash of heat flooded through me, and Bis opened his wings and made an odd burble of sound, clearly happy.

Still holding my hand, Trent shifted his grip to become more gentle, less possessive. I looked at my hand, seeing two rings on my finger. I was hardly breathing when Trent easily slid both the rings off.

"I'd rather be your slave than Ku'Sox's," Trent said, and I wavered where I stood as he put both rings in my hand and curled my fingers over them.

Shocked, I looked up at him, seeing in his downcast expression his regret, his embarrassment, and his anger at himself. My distrust wavered, threatening to break apart like fog under the heat of truth. I needed to listen with my heart, not my hurt feelings.

"Sa'han," Quen pleaded, and Trent frowned as he turned away. Bis, though, beamed, the tip of his tail quivering.

"I was wrong," Trent said, and a flash of righteous hurt lit through me.

"Damn right you were wrong!"

"I should have told you."

The rings felt warm in my hand, and I clenched my fist tighter. "I know!"

Trent looked up, leaning slightly to keep his weight off his one foot. He looked tired, fatigued, and the barest hint of relief colored his eyes. "If I had a plan that included slavers, I should have told you so you could have made a more informed decision as to which rings you were going to reinvoke."

There was a lump in my throat, and I swallowed hard. He was becoming what his people needed, and I wasn't part of that—except perhaps at the fringes, where a demon always was. "And?" I prompted, voice shaking.

"And I'm sorry," he said, the tiniest hint of pleading hidden behind his calm voice ringing through me. "I'll do better next time."

Next time?

He reached across the small space between us, and as Quen quietly voiced his protest with a dramatic sigh, Trent turned my fist over and opened it up. His touch was warm on my wrist, and then my palm as he nudged the smaller slave ring from the other and . . . slipped it over his pinkie.

"Trent, no!" I said, reaching out, but he hid his hand behind his back, his eyes daring me to try to take it. "What are you doing?"

Determination tightened the corners of his mouth, and he stood poised as if surprised that nothing had changed. But then it wouldn't until someone claimed the master ring. Quen's head was down, and I wondered if this was Trent's perverted way of saying he was sorry. That if I could take being a slave, he could, too.

"We need to try it again," Trent said, and I closed my hand when he reached for the master ring.

"I'm not putting that thing on," I said, face hot as I backed away. "Even if it is the dominant one. It's foul. It needs to be destroyed."

"I couldn't agree with you more." Trent's confidence was a thin shadow. He was scared. I could see it, and still he came forward and pulled my arm out from behind me. "But if you dominate me with the old, very wild magic that you rekindled, Ku'Sox can't force me to be his familiar."

Quen dropped into a chair, his head in his hands. Hesitating, I squinted at Trent, gauging his resolve in the slant of his eyes. My fingers twitched, and I let him open my palm. "Really?"

"I think so. That was my first idea. Quen wanted to try it the other way first. It was the only way he would arrange for Riffletic's rings to be pulled. That was a bad idea. That, and not including you in my—*our*—decision."

I shivered as he touched my shoulder, his other hand still cradling mine with the ring. *Was he serious, or just trying to make me not so mad at him?*

"You are not a tool, Rachel. I've never thought of you that way."

I broke eye contact, staring at the ring instead. "You should have told me," I said, only realizing now that I'd forgiven him already. I was so stupid. But he was right. Al had said Trent was the better match. With Trent's help, I could do this. *We* could do this.

His hand fell from me, and Trent took the suit jacket that Quen stoically handed him. "Yes, I know," he said as he let it drop and took up the lab coat instead.

I felt Bis move before he shifted a wing, and I stood waiting when he made the short hop to me, landing upon my shoulder, his tail curving across my back and up under my arm. It was a far more secure position than around my neck, and I let the awful horror of the lines race through me. There was a hint of purity in them, and it gave me hope.

"Where to?" Trent asked, and I slipped the master ring onto my finger.

Trent's knees buckled, and both Quen and I reached for him. "My God!" Trent gasped, as he caught himself against the desk, a hand to his forehead.

"Sorry," I whispered, trying to be as innocuous and undemanding as I could. Bis's tail tightened, and I wondered if some of it might be the lines, though he'd felt them through Bis before.

Eyes watering, Trent gestured for Quen to back off. "The lines are . . . indescribably awful," Trent managed, pulling himself to his full height, looking shaken but undeterred.

"That's why the gargoyles are upset," I said as I linked my arm in his, and he started. "If you don't like it, you can bubble your thoughts. You think it's bad now, you should have heard it before Bis fixed your line."

"Can we go?" Bis almost whined. "The sooner we fix another, the better I'll feel."

I took a deep breath and nodded my farewell to Quen. The sun would be up far too soon. I had to finish it by then. "Then by all means, let's go."

And we were gone.

Chapter Twenty-Nine

Swirling, howling colors of noise beat at me as I floundered in a wide river of energy. It was so thick I could hardly think. Fatigue pulled at me. It was getting harder to keep myself intact. *Bis?* I thought, searching for something familiar, and his presence joined mine, a solid, soothing gray.

Trent? I thought, and Bis brought to me his emotions of determination, surprise, and awe of the strength we were surrounded by. He was with us, but quiet, trying to take it in.

Find this! Bis's thoughts were laced with exhaustion, and I fastened on his low impressions of green, gold, and brown, swirling with a harsh slash of red and black. I fumbled through the jumbled imbalances, picking threads and bundling them until I matched what Bis was showing me, which was complex with incredibly high and low sensations. I vaguely felt the drive to breathe, felt the pain of oxygen starvation creeping up on me, making my thoughts slow.

Got it! I thought, panicking when I found Bis struggling. This would be a lot easier if we didn't have to do this on the run. *Bis, where does it go?* I thought as I bubbled the imbalance. *Where does it go!*

His thoughts whispered in mine, singing a color I felt I should recognize. I tuned the bubble holding the imbalance to it, and with a ping of sensation I felt Trent notice, it was gone. A pure note joined the howling energy, ringing in the sound of hope.

Wrenching us together, I shifted the circle surrounding us to the taint of the imbalance I'd just replaced, feeling reality swirl and coalesce. The imbalance made each ley line unique—the key flaw that made traveling them possible.

I gasped as my air-starved lungs became real and expanded, pulling in the acidic taste of burnt amber. Face-first, I plowed into the red dirt, my eyes squinted shut and my elbows taking most of the impact. There was a pained grunt and sliding of rock, and I guessed Trent had made it. The wind was gritty and the sky was dark. Sitting up, I rubbed my chin and spit the dirt out. "Bis?" I croaked, realizing we were in the ever-after. "Shouldn't this be getting easier?"

Bis was a hunched shadow next to me. "I thought the ever-after might hide us a little longer," he said, his red eyes on the sky, the moon, half full and waning, just rising over the broken horizon. "He will find us soon. There's not as much to damage here if he does."

What he meant was fewer people as potential hostages, and I rose, extending a hand to help Trent up. He shook his head and refused, head bowed as he sat on the ruined earth and tried to catch his breath. Bis was getting the job done, but he clearly lacked finesse. Rubbing my scraped elbow, I looked out over a huge drop-off. Turning, I saw a large valley filled with slumps of rock; the edges had a red sheen from the moon, which showed their outlines facing the east. I made a slow circuit, recognizing where we were when I saw the shallow depressions and the broken bridge across it.

"Eden Park?" I asked Bis. "Whose line is this?"

Bis shifted his clawed feet nervously, jumping onto a rock that was probably mirrored in reality by the statue of Romulus and Remus and the wolf. "The only demon who isn't gunning for us," he said. "Al's."

My feet shifted in the dirt, and I looked down, thinking there should be something to differentiate this from everything else. We were standing on the very spot where I'd made my pact with Al to be his student if I could have Trent as my familiar. And there Trent was, coughing at my feet, wearing a ring that made him my slave. *Slaves could be freed, though.*

As if sensing my emotions of regret and inevitability, Trent wiped the grit from his eyes. "I'm sorry," he said as he stood gracefully, the red rock staining his lab coat like blood.

"For what?" Head down, I dragged my foot around us in a circle, rude but effective—my thoughts waiting for the twinge that would mean we were found.

"The sacrifices I asked of you."

Surprised, I looked him up and down. "I'm not the one wearing the slave ring. Besides, I'd be content if I could get an apology for you slamming my head into a tombstone and choking me half to death," I said, twisting the master ring on my finger. Either he knew me better than I thought, or he was getting far more through the rings than I'd gotten from Quen.

His half smile made something in me twist. "Then I apologize."

"And I accept," I said, tucking a rank strand of hair back. "It never happened. Thank you for saving the babies. That was important to me."

His expression went blank. Silent, Trent put his hands on his hips and scanned the brightening skies, squinting.

He isn't telling me something. My nose wrinkled at the stench and gritty wind, remembering when we'd walked from the church to the basilica in the ever-after. There were no surface demons here now, and I wondered where they were. "It's awful," I said softly. "It used to be woods, springs, and fog. All of it, the entire ever-after."

Trent's attention fell to me. "How do you know?"

I shrugged. "I eavesdropped on one of Al's dreams. I think I know what they used to look like, too." My head turned. "They were the slaves of elves once, weren't they? And they rebelled. Got the best of you."

His expression went empty. "Rumor has it."

"And you tried to destroy them."

Trent took a slow breath. I could feel Bis paying attention. "I wouldn't argue with that."

"And now you're helping me save them."

Nodding, he smiled with half his mouth again. "My goal was to save you, but yes, I suppose I'm saving them as well."

Bis jerked. An instant later, I felt it too. Someone was coming. With three wing flaps, Bis was on my shoulder, the healed line singing. I pulled heavily on Al's line, and it hummed through me, drowning out the damage we had yet to repair in other lines. Trent's head came up in shock, feeling it as well.

"Okay, time to see if these rings were worth lying to me about," I said, putting my back to Trent's and readying myself.

"Time to see if you're as good as I think you are," Trent whispered, and I blinked as he raised a circle with the line I had drawn in the dirt. The energy didn't exactly flow through me, but I felt it as keenly as if it had. In my mind, whispers of spells I'd never heard of breathed and glowed with the sound of distant music. My lips parted in awe. Trent's magic. And if I was seeing his internal spell book, he was probably seeing mine.

Along with his wisdom came Trent's desire for Ku'Sox's end. His anger and hatred flooded me, almost sending me down. Trent was driven, and through the rings, I saw the depths of depravity that Ku'Sox subjected him to, what he had casually threatened his child with, and the extent Trent would go to in order to stop him. His emotions joined mine, Ku'Sox becoming ugly and sordid in our shared view as our comparisons made a more perfect picture of his broken, lacking soul. My eyes welled, and Bis touched my cheek in concern.

Trent turned to me, shock in his eyes. It was as if I'd never truly seen him, and it shook me to my core. I blinked fast, wanting to touch him but afraid.

With a pop of air, Ku'Sox was abruptly standing between us and the rising moon. Snarling, he took two running steps, throwing a black ball of hate like a pitcher. I stiffened, still lost in Trent's mind. Ku'Sox hardly seemed to matter compared to the depth of connection the rings could foster. I'd felt nothing like this when Quen had worn them.

Trent looked to Ku'Sox. At the last moment, I pulled deeply on the line Trent and I were connected to, feeling our circle strengthen. Our shared emotion about Ku'Sox—neither entirely his, entirely mine, or entirely real—echoed through us as we stood unbowed as Ku'Sox's magic sped forward, shedding silver sparkles like pixy dust, the very air hissing from the assault.

It hit our barrier with a shower of energy, lighting the inside of our circle with a black haze. Bis's tail tightened, and I heard in Trent's and my mind, the drums of his wild magic. They blended with the humming purity of Al's line—and grew strong. There was no hesitation in Trent's abilities as there had been between Quen and me, and a small part of me wondered why.

"No monologue," I taunted as Ku'Sox took in his lack of result. "I like that."

"I'm going to eat you from the inside out, Rachel Mariana Morgan," Ku'Sox intoned, his hunched form circling us like a big black cat.

His words iced through me, and Trent shuddered.

"Rachel?" Bis warbled, and I turned to follow Ku'Sox, backing up a step at Trent's clenched jaw and pained expression. Ku'Sox was trying to use him.

"Fight it!" I said, grabbing his upper arms. "Trent, you can say no!"

"No, he can't," Ku'Sox mocked, flinging his coat out of his way as he stalked closer, breathing on our bubble to make the black run to him. "*Dolore adficere . . .* Do it, slave!"

Trent shuddered under my grip. The music in his mind faltered, the rushing sound of the line in mine grew loud as Bis's tail tightened. "I am yours," Trent gasped through clenched teeth, and my hand sprang from him, thinking I was betrayed. Trent fell to a knee, looking up at me, pleading. "I. Am. Yours. Claim me, Rachel! Damn your morals and *claim me!*"

Breath held, I spun to look at Ku'Sox, my hand falling to touch Trent's shoulder. "Mine!" I shouted, feeling Bis's weight light on my shoulder and the slave rings burn between us. I fastened on the wild music, remembering the rings' creation, the ugly promise of domination they held, and I claimed it. Black filth roared in as the rings found their purpose and came truly alive—smut for this ancient magic of stream and wood, song and deviltry. "He's *mine!*" I shouted again, and Trent's head snapped up, his eyes wild as my will dominated him.

Fear slid through me, but the music had grown stronger, not less, and Trent panted, blood leaking from his nose. I didn't know if I had him or not. "You're bleeding," I said, wiping it away with my scarf. His eyes met mine at the soft touch, and a chime seemed to shake the ley line, realigning the universe.

He was mine.

"No!" Ku'Sox raged, hammering on our bubble.

Trent was mine, and scared out of my socks, I extended a hand to help him rise. I was responsible for him, and I didn't want to be. Was this what Trent felt for his people? He was stronger than I.

"You can back off now," he panted, and I hastily lifted my domination from his thoughts until Trent sighed in relief. "Thank you."

"Sorry."

"You will not take him from me!" Ku'Sox raged. "I will eat all that you hold dear, I will swallow the sun. I will burn the moon!"

Making a pair of horns with his pinkie and thumb, Trent showed Ku'Sox the back of his hand.

Ku'Sox's eyes widened at the ancient elven insult. With a cry of outrage, he slammed his foot into our circle, bouncing back and screaming when it repelled him with a burst of ozone-tainted energy. "Mine!" he screamed like child in a tantrum.

"Not anymore," I whispered, wondering if we should jump out. We were kind of stuck in this circle. The half-moon was rising. If I remembered right, it would be almost straight overhead at sunrise. We had hours to finish this, or Newt would kill me herself.

"Perhaps we should circle him?" Trent suggested, and I wiped my palms on my pants.

"Good idea," I said, wanting to leave our circle as much as I'd want to jump into a bath of ice. "Pound him into the earth. It's elven charms he doesn't know. After you."

Trent looked at me, and it was all I could do but not laugh for crying. He had the drive, I had the strength, and neither of us had the skill. What in hell had Al been talking about?

"I'll go," Bis said, and I reached out after him, cursing my hesitation.

"Bis, no!" I shouted, his tail a whisper across my neck, and then he was through our bubble, darting madly to evade Ku'Sox's thrown charms.

"Hey!" I cried, and Trent dove through the bubble as well, rolling to a stop behind a slump of rock. I was surprised that the circle around me hadn't fallen. Perhaps the slave rings enabled us to share the same energy fields.

My head snapped up as wild magic coursed through me and Trent threw a charm. *"Adsimulo calefacio!"* I shouted, sending my own curse hot on the heels of Trent's.

Bis flipped in midair to avoid Ku'Sox's strike, his wings gray in the moonlight. Trent's spell hit the demon's raised shield, and the hazy black shattered with the sound of glass. Unhurt, Ku'Sox turned, his eyes widening as my incoming curse hit him square in the chest.

"Yes!" Trent exclaimed, elated as Ku'Sox was thrown back, an ugly gold and black crawling over him, making his back arch. But I wasn't so confident, and I pulled heavily on the line, stockpiling energy until my head hurt and Bis's hair stood on end as he landed on a crag of stone.

"Again!" Trent shouted, his face grim, and together we struck.

Ku'Sox jerked, a haze covering him for an instant as he jumped out of the way, and our combined curses hit the empty ground and exploded, light seeming to splinter and fly.

I ducked, throwing myself behind a rock as our curse flew like shrapnel. Fire burned in my mind, and I rose up, horrified. Trent had taken refuge under a bubble, and since our broken curse held his aura, the energy tore right through it.

He was down, his lab coat filthy with rock, the gritty wind shifting his hair about his closed eyes. But he breathed.

"Rachel! There!" Bis shouted, pointing, and I spun, my breath catching as I saw Ku'Sox leaning against a boulder the size of a small car. The demon smiled, hurt but alive.

"This is only making your sunrise harder, love," he said, and I ran to Trent. I could feel Bis following above.

I slid to a stop, my mind delving deep into Trent's, running the counter curses before the damage could seep in any further. Trent came to with a snort, jolted to full awareness by my stinging mental slap. The rings made it possible. "Perhaps I shouldn't have done that," Trent said, and I helped him up again, dragging him back into our uninvoked circle.

"You can't kill me. Therefore, I win."

Ku'Sox's words echoed over the dead earth between us, chilling me. Light glowed from the crater that Trent's and my magic had made, and in the slashes of angry light, Ku'Sox smiled, shadows making him harsh. "You can't kill me, even with your elf *slave*," he said, the rock sliding from under his feet as he stood. "The collective won't help you. And you—are—dead."

Bis landed upon Trent, and the lines echoed in my mind. "I'll jump you out," the kid said, but both of us shook our heads. It ended here. It ended now.

"*Dali-i-i-i!*" Ku'Sox screamed at the rising moon. "Newt! Show yourselves, you cowards!" His head dropping, he looked at me with savage eyes from under his hanging hair, clearly shaken from the curse that had landed on him. "I will talk to you, you poltroons . . ."

"Stand up," I said, poking Trent in the ribs to make him jump. "Fix your hair, will you? You look a mess."

"Look who's talking," Trent said, even as he ran a hand through his hair to arrange it, his missing fingers obvious.

We both stiffened as the energy in the lines shifted. Nearly where the sun would rise in a scant four hours, a round, squat demon misted into existence, tired and slack-faced. "Is it done?" Dali said, facing Ku'Sox and taking in his ragged appearance. "Fix the damned line before there's nothing left and we're all . . ." He hesitated, breathing the air as if he could smell me. Or maybe he was smelling Trent. He reeked of cinnamon and wine, almost covering up the stench of burnt amber.

"She's alive?" he exclaimed, spinning to us, his expression shocked. "You're alive!"

"I'm alive," I said, breathing hard. *For the moment.*

"For the moment," Ku'Sox muttered, echoing my thought, frowning as Newt misted into existence beside Dali, wearing exactly the same thing I was. Al slumped at her feet, and my heart leaped until I saw the chains about his wrists and the downcast slouch to his shoulders.

"Of course she's alive," Newt said, and Al's head snapped up, his fervent eyes finding mine and tension pulling him straight. "She's Al's wonder child," the demon finished lightly, smacking Al to make him glower at the ass-backward praise.

"Al . . ." I breathed, elated, and Trent stared at me. In my mind, Trent's hatred for the demon rose up, anger for his missing fingers, his fear for having been helpless. It joined my memories of Al's awkwardly given kindnesses when none was expected, and then my pity for the loss of his wife, his life, his love, being forced to live in a hole in the ground, an under-standing found, a respect granted unasked, vulnerable and fragile.

"Al?" Trent said, and I blinked, not comfortable having shared that with him.

"I-I . . ." I stammered, then shut my mouth, unable to explain. Al was cruel, vindictive, angry, elegant, powerful. He gave me strength, he gave me wisdom, not only about magic, but about myself. He was a lot like Trent, only harsher around the edges.

Sensing my emotions, Trent turned away, head down and grimy hair shifting in the gritty wind. "I will never understand you. How can you for-give so easily?"

"Yeah? Well, that's what's going to save both our asses," I said, hoping it was a prophecy, not a prayer.

"Take her!" Ku'Sox shouted. "Finish her!"

Heart pounding, I shifted my feet to find solid earth beneath the scree. My will strengthened our circle, and I felt Trent do the same, wild magic seeping up from the earth to send darts of gold through the black smut crawling over the barrier. "What's the matter, Ku'Sox?" I mocked when Dali and Newt exchanged worried glances. "Since when do you need any-one's help? I though this was between you and me? How come you called them? Can't do it yourself?"

"You are hiding behind a *stinking elf*!" he snarled, gesturing wildly.

"He smells quite nice," I shouted back, making Bis giggle. "And it's not hiding, it's using my resources to the fullest! You can use Nick if you want."

Ku'Sox's eye twitched. Next to me, Trent lifted his chin. "I stand with Rachel to fix the ever-after," he said quietly, making a sharp contrast to Ku'Sox's loudmouthed bullying. "I stand to save the demons. What do you stand for, Ku'Sox Sha-Ku'ru?"

Trent held up his mutilated hand, his ring glinting. Newt leaned to see and Al winced, dragged behind her as she came forward a step. "Al. Where did you get a working set of slavers?" she asked, and then she blinked in what had to be shock. "They're using them backward! Is that even possi-ble?"

Al slowly got to his feet, saying, "Apparently. And I didn't give them to her, she made them herself."

"No wonder she was able to strike me down," Newt said smugly, but I didn't think anyone believed her.

Ku'Sox limped forward. "You're not going to help me finish her? She's using an *elf*!"

"So?" Dali said, gesturing. "This is your issue. Your word against hers. If you can't best her, then maybe she is right, and you are—wrong?"

"She ran away!" Ku'Sox said, gesturing, and I stiffened as I felt another demon show up. He was on the outskirts, listening. "It proves she's at fault! I'd take her down now, but she's grown inventive."

"I think you mean powerful," Newt said slyly, jerking Al closer to make his chains clink.

Dali crossed his arms, looking more confident as several more demons misted in beside the first. "Why should I help you? She fixed my line. My rooms won't be shrinking when the sun comes up."

"But she was the one who broke them!" Ku'Sox glanced nervously at the accumulating demons between us and the waning moon.

"Did she?" Dali's head tilted, and the demons popping in one by one discussed.

Breath held, I did a mental count. Dali's line was the one running through Trent's compound? I looked at Trent, seeing his pale face as he figured it out as well. On my shoulder, Bis squirmed. He'd chosen what lines we jumped to with precision—mine, Newt's, Dali's . . . and Al's?

"You are blind fools!" Ku'Sox paced in the fading light from Trent's and my last joined magic. "If she doesn't die before the sun rises and the energy tide shifts, you will lose too much, and the ever-after will fall regardless of whose lines get fixed."

"Then *kill* her and let's get on with it," Newt said, making Al scowl at her pleasant smile. "I tried already, and she hit me."

"Hey, would any of you mind if I go take care of a few things and get back to you in about an hour?" I said loudly, then ducked when Ku'Sox sent a token shot of energy at us.

It hit the barrier and was absorbed cleanly, making the surrounding demons buzz with interest.

Trent leaned close, whispering, "I think it's funny how they keep trying to kill you when all you want to do is save them."

"Happens to me all the time," I said wryly, and he chuckled.

"Me too."

A feeling of shared kinship darted through me, lighting both our thoughts, and Bis seemed to warm.

"I need your help," Ku'Sox growled, pacing forward. "I can't best her when she's with an elf. The sun will be up soon, and by then it will be too late."

The demons behind Dali didn't like that, but Newt was undeterred. "Perhaps Rachel can."

We had to get this done, and get it done now. Trent had the drive to kill Ku'Sox. I had the power, but neither of us had the skill to best a demon taught the arts of war. Blinking, I brought my head up, finding Al waiting, a devious smile on his face, his bound hands held out to me. *Al did.* My eyes went to his hands, and his gloves misted out of existence to show his wedding rings. Perhaps the three of us could actually do something.

"We need Al," I whispered as Ku'Sox paced up and down, raging at us.

"Don't be foolish. We can't even get to him," Trent muttered back.

"They aren't going to help him," I said, looking to the east and fidgeting. "They won't help us. We need to forcibly take him."

Trent frowned as Ku'Sox grandstanded, claiming another twelve hours of negative energy pressure would put the mass of the ever-after under a viable threshold. "We need Al," I said again, and this time, Trent turned to me, his eyes flicking up to Bis's as the gargoyle bobbed his head. "We can't overpower Ku'Sox without the knowledge Al has. We need him!"

An ugly expression came over Trent, and I got into his face, mad. "Get over it, Trent!" I hissed, taking his arm. "You used me, and now I'm calling it in! What kind of world do you want your children to grow up in? One where they fear demons, or one where they understand them?"

Trent jerked away, angry and unwilling. Behind him, I could see Al waiting. "I am yours," Trent said sullenly, and I swear, I saw Al's lips move in tandem, his expression elated.

"Let's get him!" Bis shouted, and I staggered as he sprang from me, our circle bobbling for a moment as he punched through, spinning madly to avoid Ku'Sox's sudden curses.

"Bis!" I cried, feeling the broken glory of the lines vanish. Then I bolted to Al while Ku'Sox was staring at the sky. I knew Trent would get my back, and I felt him gather a spell, flinging it madly in the hopes of scoring on the distracted demon.

A thunderous boom behind me sent me stumbling, and I crashed into Newt. We went down, me on top of her. "Sorry!" I cheerfully cried as I grabbed my fist and swung my elbow into the side of her head. It met with a thump and my arm went numb. Breath hissing, I got off her, scrambling to find Al and drag him away. I'd broken three boards with that move before, and Newt was down—for a moment at least.

"Oh, you're going to pay for that, itchy witch," Al said, beaming at me, and I sketched a fast circle around us, catching quick glimpses of exploding fireballs and demons in white robes scrambling to find cover.

"Hey, if I'm going to get blamed for hitting her, I'm going to hit her," I said. "Are you okay? Can you tap the lines?" In my mind, elven spells were unwinding, wild magic singing through me. It was as if I was in two places at once, and the adrenaline pounded through me. My head was high, and I breathed deep. When Trent spelled, he sang.

"Circle, circle!" Al shouted, and I ducked, deflecting a black ball of something.

"Not until Trent gets here," I said, seeing Bis swooping around to drop another rock on Ku'Sox. I fumbled at Al's bindings. They were simple cords, but my fingers hummed when I touched them. Clearly they were spelled.

"He's wearing the slaver, yes?" Al said, grabbing my hands and yanking me out of the path of another spell. "He'll get through. Your energies resonate as one."

My fingers on the knot hesitated. *Ivy. Could I save Ivy with this?*

"Look out!" Al shouted, shoving me backward, and I fell, my breath knocked out of me.

Al was standing over me, shouting to the skies, and fingers scrabbling, I reached out for the circle I'd scraped in the dirt, still not having breathed. *Rhombus,* I thought, getting a slip of air in, and Al jumped back, narrowly avoiding getting left outside. Dizzy, I looked up. Newt was laughing so hard she couldn't breathe, blood leaking from her ear as she sat on the ground and scooted backward to sit against a large rock.

"See!" she crowed, pointing. "I told you she hit me!"

Shaky, I sat up, moving a stone out from under my backside. Dali, too, was watching, standing in the middle of everything with his hands on his hips and a frown on his face as if nothing could touch him. Trent was ducking behind rocks as Ku'Sox pulverized them, each jump moving him closer. Trent's charms were circling in my head, filling me with the need to do something, wild and demanding, drawing on me as needed to supplement his strength.

The demons weren't helping. They weren't hindering, either. Only the strongest could ensure the demons' continued existence. I wanted it to be me.

"Trent!" I shouted, and he sprang for us. Ku'Sox took aim, then flinched when Bis dropped a rock on him. Snarling, the demon shifted his attention to Bis.

"No!" I shouted, helpless.

Bis spun, headed for the shelter of my bubble. Under him, Trent pounded over the rocks. Ku'Sox snarled, eyes on the sky as he wound up. Fixed on Bis, he didn't see Dali stick his foot out, and the demon face-planted into the dusty stones.

Okay, maybe they had a favorite here, after all.

"Oh, sorry," Dali said, getting between us and Ku'Sox to help the demon up, brushing him off and getting in his line of sight until Bis back-winged into the bubble, landing on my shoulder, his red eyes wide in excitement.

Trent was a moment behind, slipping through the protection bubble and sliding to a sudden, awkward halt inches from Al—far too close. Al smiled down at him with his thick, blocky teeth, and Trent smiled right back, more than a hint of deviltry in his green, green eyes. Trent was humming, and my thoughts hummed with him. I was alive with him, and it was glorious. Indescribable.

Trent's eyes met mine, and we both flushed.

Behind him, a rock exploded as Ku'Sox's discarded magic rolled into a rock. The watching demons complained loudly, and I felt a dozen protection circles go up.

"Yes, yes, slave rings have a silver lining," Al grumped, holding his bound hands out. "If you two are done mooning over each other, I could use some assistance."

I started, and Bis giggled from my shoulder.

"They are charmed," Al said loftily, as Trent touched them and a strand of wild magic spun through my mind. The curse holding Al quavered, resisted . . . and finally fell when I gave Trent's magic a push.

"Mar-r-r-rvelous," Al drawled, a dangerous light entering his eyes as he turned to the east, to Ku'Sox. His thick hands clenched, and my skin prickled at the energy he drew in from his line atop the valley overlooking the dead city. "You work well together. Good to know."

"Do we jump?" Bis asked, riding the high of the innocent.

I looked over the flat plain below us, seeing the world spread out, dim and red under the rising moon. It felt right that here, at the top of the world, it would end.

"We fight," I said, and Al chuckled, low and long.

Ku'Sox was pacing, his form low and hunched as he watched us in our bubble.

"Wear my ring," Al said, his glove gone as he held out one of his wedding bands. I didn't think he'd ever wear them again.

Trent reached for it, and Al closed his fist. "Rachel is the fulcrum upon which all things will shift tonight. You, Trent are bound to her. She and I are bound together. Only Rachel can focus both our strengths. An elf's drive for justice, a demon's lifetime of skills, and Rachel's strength."

I swallowed hard, flinching at a spark of energy cascading over our bubble. Al and I wearing his wedding rings? Now that I knew what they really were, it held an entirely different feeling.

"I'm okay with that," Trent said, and a slow smile curved over Al's face.

Al looked at Trent for a moment as he remembered something, then his eyes rose to mine. "I never thought I'd work with an elf—again," he said, and he slipped his ring on my finger.

I wavered as his energy mixed with mine, Bis hissing as the strength of both men seeped deep, reading their own surprise as they found common ground within me. "Can I survive this?" I said, meaning to be flippant, but finding I really wanted to know. I was humming, overly full and both of them demanding I do something. It was too much. I looked past our bubble to see Newt standing next to Dali, watching without a hint of emotion showing.

"Prince of the elves, eh?" Al said as his heavy hand took my elbow and shifted me to look east.

"Yup," Trent said, and I shivered as his music fell through my mind. I knew what to do with it. I had only to speak.

"And you are the world breaker," Al said to Bis, and the gargoyle's grip on me tightened.

"No!" he exclaimed, delighted. "Really?"

"And I'm your sword," I added. I had once been Trent's sword, too, when he was on his elf quest.

"You still are," Trent whispered, reading my mind through the bond of the rings.

I sighed. "And what am I to you, Al?"

"My maid," he said brightly. "Shall we do this?"

I let the bubble fall. We would meet the next day free, or dead.

Ku'Sox snarled at us, and I thought he looked like a dog. "The moon is rising! Rachel, face me and die!"

"Quite right!" Al said. "Make war when the moon rises. Make love when it sets." He winked at me, and I gathered the line to me. "Ku'Sox, you slimy little worm! *Now* you will see what a demon is!"

"By the Goddess!" Trent cried as my knees collapsed and I fell, the serpent of black magic unwinding from my head. The power of the demon bands was twofold, not just each of us having our strength combined, but instinctively knowing what the other was doing. It was beautiful. It made us deadly. It was an ancient war machine. The rings were made for this. And now we had access to the weapons vault.

Chapter Thirty

U p! Stand up!" Trent muttered, his tight grip on my arm pulling me upright. Dazed, I felt Trent steady me as Al metaphorically cleared his throat, opening up his arsenal of black charms stored in the collective more than five thousand years ago during the bloody war between his people and Trent's.

Ugly black monstrosities rose and fell in my mind, charms to mutilate, break, and destroy by playing upon the base desires, guilt, and fears of another. It was numbing, and I felt the alien desire to crush rise up in me. Al's presence was smothering.

I leaned on Trent and opened my mind to him.

With a whimper, we both fell as Al's bearing sucked in Trent. "Stand up!" Al demanded, and we did, overshadowed and panting. It was getting easier to bear. "We have a worm to crush!" Al cried out, his eyes alight with the promise of vengeance.

"I'm okay," I said softly, then lifted my chin, accepting who I was and the history of those who came before me. I may not have written these hideous expressions of hate, but I understood them, even as I shuddered at their monstrosity.

Ku'Sox didn't have a clue or a prayer.

"Ku'Sox Sha-Ku'ru!" Al shouted, his voice echoing back from the broken earth. "Come forth and die!"

I took a deep breath as the painful, unharmonious jangle of lines merged into the collective. I felt Trent's awe, and with the imaginary sound of sliding bolts and echoing thumps, an ugly curse grew as if rising from the depths. Al's chanting pulled it into being, and I felt my face go ashen. It would do unspeakable damage, destroying Ku'Sox from his mind out, burning with endless fire and crushing his soul to nothing. That such things were possible seemed the worst kind of punishment.

"*Terga et pectora telis transfigitur!*" Al proclaimed, pushing out with both hands.

Trent jerked, and the energy of the spell pulled through me, burning my brain. The curse sped to Ku'Sox, unseen with a faint distortion as if the very air was recoiling from it.

Trent touched my arm, and I followed his gaze to the black haze coming at us. "Incoming!" I cried, and Al shoved me from him.

I fell on Trent, the ground slamming into us. A shimmer of a protection circle rose up, pulled into being by one or all of us. Al's charm nicked the edge of Ku'Sox's own circle, making an ear-numbing scream as it ricocheted to pinwheel erratically into a tall tower of rock.

I propped myself up on an elbow, jaw dropping when the mountain took the hit and collapsed inward, sucking into a loud bang that echoed to the black horizon.

"I'm not taking the smut for that," Trent whispered, inches away as the demons watching applauded. We got up, shaken as we looked across the space to see that Ku'Sox was staggering but upright, grim faced and determined.

"You don't really think water made the Grand Canyon, did you?" Al smirked. His circle fell as he flicked a ball of energy at Ku'Sox. The demons watching grudgingly applauded when Ku'Sox just as easily absorbed it.

"Throwing stones at each other is getting us nowhere," Trent said, his expression more annoyed than anything else as he tugged his lab coat straight.

"And apparently the ever-after has an expiration date?" I prompted, looking at the east.

Al sighed dramatically. "You have a better idea?" he said, slipping into our bubble to sidestep Ku'Sox's next attack. It hit with a muffled thump to make the earth tremble, and our circle quivered.

Trent frowned. "I do. Listen," he said, and my eyes opened as wild magic blossomed in my thoughts. With the memory of drums and wildly dancing lithesome shapes, I felt Trent's magic spill into me. It tingled to my fingers, and Al gasped. My hands clenched so I wouldn't move as the foreign memory of an intoxicated swaying to a greater will filled me. It was magic from the elven war, magic that demons had never been able to best.

I felt Al's stark terror melt into understanding, but Trent was lost to it, pulling everything to him, shaping it with no thought other than to build. I could feel the power growing with the strength of the sun, the certainty of the tides. A wing-lidded eye opened, purple and stark. It found me, and I shook.

"Bind it," Al whispered. "Rachel, bind it! It's wild magic! I can't!"

But I could. The wild magic had acknowledged me. I owed it, and it would see me through so I could pay my debt. With the energy of the lines, I wove a resonance about Trent's charm, binding it in a form that would find the one it was intended for and no other.

"Now," I whispered, feeling it grow. "Now!" I shouted, severing Trent from the magic and shoving it at Al.

"*Ex cathedra!*" Al shouted to give our curse strength, and Ku'Sox cried out as it blew through his circle unimpeded. Ku'Sox fell to the earth, the elven curse crawling over him like a thousand green snakes, eating his aura, his magic. In my mind, I heard a chiming laugh.

"Bind him!" Trent called out, springing forward through our joined auras as if he had done this a thousand times before, and perhaps in his mind, he had. "He has no magic, but he can still run!"

I ran for the unmoving slump of fabric, not wanting Ku'Sox to turn into a bird and eat us, but I slid to a stop when Al popped into existence right over him. Expression harsh, he put a foot on Ku'Sox's neck and leaned over him.

Trent was beside me. I could feel the auras of the surrounding demons, hear their harsh cries for revenge, taste their desire on the gritty wind. My heart pounded, and I watched as Al's face twisted and he bore down, choking Ku'Sox with his foot. Elven magic had downed him, and I felt a growing fear in the demons, even as they urged Ku'Sox's end.

Appalled, I watched as Ku'Sox pushed at Al's foot, pounding at his leg, his face becoming red as he arched his back and struggled.

"You were a mistake!" Al exclaimed, and Newt's androgynous form shoved another aside so she could see. Dali was beside her, and they served as stone-faced witnesses as they killed one of their own. "You were a mistake . . ." Al said again as Ku'Sox struggled, his fingers clawing Al's leg until they bled.

"Trial!" Ku'Sox rasped, his eyes fastening on Dali's.

I fixed my horrified gaze on Dali, seeing the demon clench his teeth. *Could he claim that?*

"Trial! I have a right . . ." he choked out, hardly audible over the surrounding din.

Dali grimaced and bent his head toward Newt's. "I think he said trial."

Al's teeth showed, and he bore down harder. Someone jostled me forward, and Trent pulled me back before I fell.

"I did!" Ku'Sox got out. "I have a right for a trial by demon!"

"He dies!" Trent shouted, his desire flowing through me by way of the slavers. "Now!"

I looked to the east, frightened when the angry mob of demons at my back began to subside into frustrated mutterings. "We don't have time for a trial!"

But Al was moving his foot.

"Al! You want them to put him in jail?" I shouted, and his eyes met mine, shocking me with their hatred. It would have been better if Trent's spell would have killed Ku'Sox directly, but elves apparently liked their prisoners alive.

"No." Al backed up a step, Ku'Sox lying between him and Newt and Dali. "I want to fucking kill him. Slow had been my intent, but fast would have been acceptable."

Ku'Sox was smiling wickedly as he sat up, scooting backward into the surrounding demons when Al made motions to kick him. "I'm a demon," he said, his voice smoothing out as found his aplomb. "I have a right to a trial."

"Let go of me!" Newt cried, wiggling in Dali's grip. "Let go! I will kill him myself if you are all too *afraid,* and then you can put me on trial!" she shouted.

"Be still, Newt!" Dali exclaimed, but the haze in her eyes scared me, even as I wanted to see an end to Ku'Sox.

"Ah, I have an idea," Trent said softly, his voice both musical and hard. "That is, if you are willing to listen to an elf. The one whose magic caught him."

I turned to Trent, wanting to protest that it had taken all three of us to catch him, but I held my tongue when I saw the harsh light in his eyes, the chilling bone-hard expression of dealing out a harsh death. I'd seen it once aimed at me, and I'd almost died.

Newt jerked from Dali, breathless as she faced us, Ku'Sox slowly getting up between us. "I'll hear the elf," she said bitterly.

"An elf?" a demon from the back called. "We should kill him, too."

There was a muttering agreement, and I stiffened. Trent's chin lifted. The wind shifted his stringy hair in the moonlight, and Trent said, "If he was a thief in my house, his actions stealing the space I claim, the air I breathe, I would do a trial by Hunt."

A chill lifted through me. Trent wouldn't meet my eyes as he stared at Dali. Al was shifting foot to foot, and a murmur of discontent was rising around us like a hot wind. "You would hunt him down?" a demon at the front of the circle said. "As an animal? As your ilk did before we beat you off?"

It was true, then. The demons had been the slaves of elves before the tables had been turned. My new alliance between the elves and demons was falling apart before it could even form, and my heart pounded. On my shoulder, Bis tightened his grip, promising a quick escape, but I didn't want to escape. I wanted justice. I wanted . . . the Hunt?

"I think it's a good idea," I said, my palms going sweaty as the memory of hate swirling in the demons landed on me.

"As they hunted us!" someone cried out, and Al winced. "Like animals!"

I stiffened when someone pushed me, and I stepped into Ku'Sox's space. "Yes. Yes!" I said again, louder, and they quieted. "Like animals. And you proved them wrong."

They shut up, and I turned to look at them, finding all eyes on me. "You are *demons*," I said forcefully, "not animals, and the elves stand at the brink of *extinction* from the force of your correction. Is it not enough?"

Trent stood unrepentant in his lab coat. He could have been in a T-shirt and flip-flops, and he still would have looked noble—proud, determined, harsh, and taking the blame of an entire people that came before him.

"Let me go," Ku'Sox said, his voice oily. "I'm a demon. I deserve a trial, not by some perverted elf tradition, but by my peers."

I looked at him as a scuffling arose from the unsure demons ringing him; then I walked over to stand before him, my hands on my hips. "But you're not a demon, Ku'Sox," I said, smiling beatifically. A sense of satisfaction grew within me. "Every demon here, every demon still alive has been a slave, has been hunted, even me. And you have not. You have *never* felt the anger of being made powerless, controlled, bought and sold." I stood, speaking now to those around me. "You have not," I said softly. "You have not felt the unfair lash, been pissed upon by those who call you animal, underling, an object." Al was thinking. They all were, and my stomach quivered.

"I think you need to *be* a demon before you can claim the right to a trial as one," I finished, and Ku'Sox scoffed.

"You want us to let him go!" someone shouted. "He nearly destroyed the ever-after!"

I held up a hand. "You all nearly destroyed the ever-after by your cowardice. I can fix the lines with Bis. You've seen it. Ask your gargoyles. They've taught him the resonance of your lines. The proper resonance, not this jagged purity. I can have them whole by sunup. And I say, yes, let him go, but as you once were, not as you are now."

The soft hum of decisions-yet-unmade started, and turning back to Ku'Sox, I reached out in my mind for Trent and Al. This was going to take all my finesse, and I didn't have a clue how to do it. It would take wild magic to fix it to him, and ancient demon wisdom to find it.

You want to do what to him? I heard an echo in my mind, the shock of understanding tagging the masculine emotion as Al's.

Like this, I said, eyes closing as a shimmer of my aura fell over Ku'Sox, tainted red from the ever-after. Ku'Sox stiffened, and as the memory of wild magic spun around and around in my head with the sound of fluttering wings, I showed Al a vision that he had shown me, a figure somewhat small, black as midnight, long fingers and toes, leathery wings, stretched like moonbeams. He would have an angular face, and wide black eyes, like Newt and Al now had. There would be long eyelashes, a small mouth, and whiskers, like a cat.

Al wove the charms at my direction, his shock and amazement making his attention skip and jump in mine. "My God!" whispered a voice, and I opened my eyes as the last of the charm melted away to leave Ku'Sox blinking up at us with large black eyes, looking exactly like I'd seen Al in his dream of blue butterflies.

"I had wings," someone breathed. "I remember they shone in the sun and how cool they felt in the sand."

"Black nails," another said.

"I remember the taste of clouds," came a voice from the back, soft and full of wonder. "Stardust in my ears."

"What have you done?" Ku'Sox said, putting a hand to his throat when it came out in a mild, soft hiss. "What have you done to me?"

My head was down as I tried to separate myself from the spell, curse, whatever. Trent's original curse denying Ku'Sox magic still held true, and he was helpless. He was a demon, the original form before mothers changed their children to make them stronger—into tools of war, images of man so well suited for it.

"Rachel?" Trent said, jerking me from my thoughts.

"I saw it in a dream of Al's," I said, looking up to see the wonder and awe in the faces around me. "Did I get it right?"

Trent shook his head in confusion, gazing at Ku'Sox as he tried to move, almost falling until he used his wing as support. "I have no idea."

"Let me go!" Ku'Sox cried, his wings opening in alarm, and they all shifted back, stepping on toes and shoving those behind them until we stood in a wide space open to the night sky, ringed by silent demons. Newt was crying silent tears, trapped in a memory.

"Let him go," I said, and all eyes came back to me as Ku'Sox felt his face in panic and tried to find his balance. "I say he has no right to claim demon law because he isn't one. We hunt. If he runs far and fast enough, he can live with the memory of being hunted, of being a demon. He will deserve to live. But if he is caught . . ." I hesitated, seeing understanding trickle through them, reigniting their bloodlust. "If he's caught, then kill him like the animal he is."

"I am not an animal!" Ku'Sox cried out, his voice high as the demons cheered their approval.

"Yes, you are, dear boy," Newt said, her cheeks wet as she came forward to help him find his balance. "I say that the elf, ah, that Trenton, has an excellent idea. Let Ku'Sox go."

Ku'Sox tensed to jump up and away, and he was mobbed, beaten down. I backed up into Trent, and he held me in front of him, his grip warm and his breath coming over my shoulder as they dragged Ku'Sox up and spread his wings wide so he couldn't move.

"Say you we hunt?" Dali shouted, and I winced at their shouts, fisted hands in the air.

Ku'Sox struggled, blood running in little rivulets from where they gripped too hard. "You can't do this to me!" he rasped, his black eyes wide in fear. "I am a god!"

Newt came forward. "But we can, love," she said, giving him a small kiss on his furry face. "Fly fast."

"No!" he shouted, his word whistling in fear, and they let him go.

I ducked as he was away, his wings beating the ground as he surged into the air. Sounding like a dove, he whistled into the night sky. My heart thudded as I watched him go, his gray shadow quickly going faint.

"He's getting away!" someone shouted, and Bis flapped his wings for their attention.

"I can find him," the little gargoyle said as he took to the air, and I was proud of him for having lost his fear.

Al sidled up to me, leaning to mutter, "I hope you know what you're doing. He's going to be the devil to catch again."

Ku'Sox's shadow dwindled and vanished into moonlight. Clusters of demons were watching as well, discussing the best way to follow—giving him a generous head start but clearly eager to be away. "He was impossible to catch before only because you didn't stand up to him," I said softly, my gaze lingering upon Bis, sporting in the air over them, spiraling in his joy of flight. *The gargoyles . . .*

At my other side, Trent was frowning, still watching the sky. "We need mounts for a hunt. I'm not going to run after him."

I turned to Al, seeing he had the same idea I had. "Winged mounts," the demon said, and I nodded as he took a huge breath, and shouted, "Tre-e-e-ebl-l-l-le!"

Trent drew back in awe as Al's gargoyle popped into existence right before us, looking as large as Etude, but thinner. She lashed her black-tipped tail and winked at Bis wheeling above her. "I'll thank you for getting your demon to fix his holy-ass's line," she said brightly to Bis, her ears flat to her skull and making Al scowl. "How about the rest of them? It still sounds like hell out there."

"Working on it," Bis said breathlessly as he landed on my shoulder, and I sealed my thoughts off so I wouldn't have to deal with the screaming line just yet.

Demons had noticed, and like a fantasy flick gone wild, dragonlike shapes were popping in everywhere, enthusiastic gargoyles eager for a chance to pay back some of the misery they had endured for the last week. I backed up into Trent as Al swung atop Treble, the gargoyle shivering as she rose easily up into the air before dropping back down. Wings were unfolding everywhere, yellow and red eyes swirling with an eagerness to be away. Shouts echoed, and I paled. Ku'Sox didn't have a chance.

"Go! Go!" Newt cried atop a gray-faced, wrinkled gargoyle, and the behemoth rose up on two legs, wings stretching to show a patchwork of scars. His expression savage, he gnashed his black teeth and vaulted into the night.

Others followed, and I hid my face as the dust flew. The noise peaked and dwindled, and I looked up as they rose in a great spiral, cutting between me and the stars.

"They will find him," Trent said, and I turned, my scuff sounding loud in the sudden hush. Behind him, Al waited with Treble, hungry to be gone. Trent's face held resolute emptiness. He had wanted to go, needed to see an end, needed to be a part of it. And he had been excluded. We needed one more mount.

"Bis?" I said, and the little gargoyle's eyes blinked.

"I'll get my dad," he said and vanished before I could tell him his father was likely lying broken next to the Loveland ley line. My shoulders sagged with guilt, and I thought of Ivy and Jenks. Why did I always leave such a huge amount of collateral damage? Maybe I should have taken the shame of simply killing Ku'Sox in his sleep.

"Having second thoughts, itchy witch?" Al said as Treble dug her claws into the earth to leave great gouging divots.

I took a breath to answer, my head jerking up along with Al's as a great shape sprang into existence above us in the empty night sky. "Etude!" I cried out, and he waved, great gaping holes in his wings looking painful as he spiraled down, Bis darting energetically around him.

"Mother pus bucket, he's a big one," Al said, making Treble blush a deep black.

"You're alive!" I cried out, elated as he landed.

Bis alighted on his dad's shoulder, looking proud. "My dad fought Ku'Sox!" he crowed. "They're singing about him already!"

Etude snuck a glance at Treble, his gaze lingering on Al perched on her back. "I'm glad you're alive as well," he said, a heavy hand touching my shoulder to make me feel small. "My boy is safe. If you ever need anything—"

"She needs a mount," Al said, interrupting him. "We are hunting the breaker of the lines. Interested?"

Etude stiffened, his eyes flicking to the sky. "Is that what I hear? Yes, I'd gladly take a pound of flesh for the pain we've endured. Rachel? Don't mind my wings, I can still fly. We can be on them in moments. They are blazing a trail even humans can see and tremble at."

Trent's jaw clenched, and he looked at the sky.

"Not me," I said, looking at Trent. "Take him."

Shocked, Trent turned. "Me?"

I shrugged, ignoring Al's heavy sigh to get on with it. "This is your kind of thing," I said, remembering the baying of dogs and the fear. Maybe I was with my kin after all. "I've got stuff to do. Lines to fix."

Etude nodded, looking disappointed as Trent seemed to grow three inches taller, eagerly accepting Etude's helping hand to sit astride him. Then, unexpectedly, he leaned back down and extended a hand for me.

"This is your kind of thing, too," he said, his eyes glowing with his need to ride, to chase, to hunt. "You can fix the lines later."

"No," I said, then slapped at Treble's hands as she grabbed me about the waist and plopped me behind Trent. "Hey! Wait!" I shouted, then screamed as Etude jumped into the air, his wings beating fiercely. My arms flashed around Trent, and I could have smacked him for his laugh. A wash of ever-after coated us, an echo of a healing spell ringing in my head as Al mended Etude's wings. Etude rumbled his thanks, then stole Treble's wind, earning a screech and a mock dive from her.

"They went this way, Rachel!" Bis said, his words ripped away with the black, gritty wind beating against me. My hands were about Trent's waist, the warmth of his body blocking most of the wind as I peered around him, looking for a red smear of magic. I could smell the ringing of an iron bell, and the warm scent of cinnamon, all washing over me in a cascading sensation of heat.

With a tweak on my awareness, Treble winked out of existence, diving into a line on the wing. My breath caught, and feeling Bis enfold us, the force of the wind vanished, replaced with the howling energy of a line.

And then reality was back, and we were diving into Cincinnati. Lights of buses and cars flashed as the chill air of the coming dawn pulled through my hair. Exalting in it, I spread my arms and held on with my legs to let the air brush the stink of burnt amber from me.

I felt Al's sudden emotion flair, feeling it echoed in Trent. He stiffened before me, and I looked, first at Al and Treble flying close by, and then to the city we were approaching. Cincinnati was beautiful with lights, green with spring, the sounds from her muted as the dawn approached and nightwalkers looked to the sky and stared at the weaving magic of red racing through the city buildings.

We had found them, and Treble cried out. The warbling call for battle was answered, and I shivered, remembering hearing the dogs bay for me. Still distant but closing, a red ribbon of magic iced the pack of demons on their winged mounts, chasing a fleeting shadow of gray, running for his life. Darting between buildings, rising and falling wildly, he flew, the demons tight behind, glorying in the chase.

"Look!" I called as the glowing Hunt flowed through the center of the city and Ku'Sox vanished into a ley line. But instead of following as they had through Al's line, the demons rose up in a huge arc like leaves in the wind coming up against a wall, scattering into chaos.

"They don't know where he went!" Bis shouted, his red eyes catching the streetlight as he swooped at my elbow. "Follow me!"

He dove toward the ground, and I shrieked as Etude followed, Al tight behind.

We slammed into the ley line, vanishing into chaos. Bis found me, throwing a resonance into my thoughts. Through the rings, Al watched and Trent marveled as I wove a circle around it, capturing the imbalance and tuning it to the university's ley line.

We burst into existence in the ever-after, a stream of howling demons following us as we fought for altitude, dodging broken shells of buildings. Ku'Sox was just ahead, and the demons surged after him, screaming their vengeance, red magic streaming behind them. It was truly the Wild Hunt, and I would be lying if I said it didn't scare the crap out of me.

On Ku'Sox fled, and on we followed, hounding him, following him through line after line as he tried to shake us like a fox traveling down a river. We sped through reality, causing fear and awe among those who saw us, a red smear of magic howling against the stars, rising in the heat from the buildings and dropping over the cool woods. Over the ever-after we tore, sending up gouts of red dust as we followed dead rivers and empty lakes, scoured by the gritty wind. We followed until Bis grew exhausted from mending the lines and rode in his father's arms and I slumped behind Trent, weary and heartsick. This was not me. I didn't thirst for vengeance, even vengeance justly earned. I did not demand blood for blood. I did this to live without fear. I wanted an end to it.

Still, each line we mended gave the gargoyles strength until they were reaching for Ku'Sox's wings, the purity of the lines a harsh contrast to the demons' base desire for death. Then Etude's weight shifted, and I realized we were landing.

"What?" I said, pulling my head up from Trent's back where I'd been hiding, wishing it was over.

"He's gone to ground!" Trent shouted, pointing, and I looked at the dusty red earth, brightening in the coming sunrise. Demons were sliding from the backs of their gargoyles, clustered about a small pile of rock. Slowly Etude spiraled down. The noise of the earth strengthened, and my stomach twisted. This was the end.

Etude found a place, his wings closing the instant his feet lightly touched the ground. Trent slid from him easily, and I slowly followed. My hand on Trent's shoulder, I stumbled after him, pushing through the demons and gargoyles to find Ku'Sox's hole.

"We'll never get him out of there," I said, looking at the brightening sky. Already the black of the hazy sky was turning to a faint pink, and the gritty wind was picking up. I didn't know where we were—all places were the same in the ever-after.

"Or maybe we will," I said again as I realized the gargoyles, though weary from flight, were tearing great gaping holes in the earth. Like organized terriers, they dug great chunks of dirt, tossing them to the side as if they were pillows to shatter into smaller chunks.

I blanched at Trent's anticipation. He stood waiting, elated and riding the high of the chase and looking forward to the grisly end. He felt my eyes on him, and he looked up. "It was a good Hunt," he said, and the demons who heard him agreed, their gaze holding a new respect.

A call went up, and the stones quit falling upward from the hole. A muffled boom shifted the earth, and a handful of demons dropped into the craggy entrance. I leaned forward, Trent beside me. Something oily slid through my thoughts, and I shuddered. Al was the only one not looking down into the hole. He was looking at me, and I quailed.

"We have him!" came up a call, and those of us at the edge backed up. "We have him! And his familiar, too!"

Nick? I shivered, my arms going around me as the demons crawled up from the hole, their gargoyles leading the way to help them. Two sodden thumps hit the dirt, and the watching demons went quiet. Only one of the captives breathed.

"Nick?" I said, and the man's eyes found mine, widening.

"Rachel!" he said, then fell back when someone shoved him down. He hit the dead body of Ku'Sox and recoiled, horrified as he tried to move away from the alien-looking shape. Ku'Sox's wings were broken in several places, and his head was tilted at a sickening angle, his neck snapped through. He was dead, but I felt nothing, numb.

"We found them grappling," a demon I didn't recognize said. "I don't know if we killed Ku'Sox or his familiar."

My eyes widened and my knees wobbled as I realized what had happened. Was that Ku'Sox dead before me, or Nick—Ku'Sox changing their forms in order to survive?

"Rachel, it's me!" he said, rising up only to get shoved down again. "Tell them it's me! I never meant to hurt you! Please!"

The demon holding a staff to his chest shrugged. "Well?" the demon asked me. "You know him best. Is it Ku'Sox or his familiar?"

I edged past Trent, feeling every stone under my foot, every gust of gritty wind in my snarled hair. Weary, I came to a halt before the downed figure, seeing the emotion behind his eyes, the wrinkles just starting at the corners, the stubble glinting red in the rising sun. It looked the same as when I had left Nick at midnight.

Reaching out, I touched his face, rubbing a bit of blood off his cheek, feeling it between my fingers, remembering Nick's smile that turned into betrayal, not once, twice, but three times. Was this Nick or Ku'Sox?

"Rachel," he whispered, begging. "Tell them it's me."

My heart beat, and my lungs emptied. Ceri was gone. Pierce. But what hurt the most was that two girls would grow up not knowing Ceri's proud strength, how her compassion blended with a brutal justice, and that she had loved them with the depth of her soul.

"Rachel!" he screamed, terror making his face lined. "You told me that you would keep me safe!"

I leaned in, smelling the fear in his sweat under the stink of burnt amber. "You left the church," I breathed, and he jerked away from me.

Trent's light touch on my elbow shocked through me, and I spun. "It's Nick," he said to me, his desperate expression the last thing I'd ever expected.

I know it's Nick! I screamed in my thoughts, but I didn't want it to be. If

I said it was Ku'Sox, they would rip him apart. I wanted him dead. I wanted him gone. How could I let him feel the sun and joy when he was why Ceri and Pierce were dead?

Trent stepped forward, the demons silently watching. "You know it's him."

"He should be dead!" I shouted, and he nodded, his eyes closing in a strength-gathering blink. "He is slime! He's everything I despise. He's hurt you, he's hurt me, and he has lied to me too many times. He doesn't deserve to walk away from this!"

Nick pulled himself together, shaking as he looked up at me whispering, "Please."

Trent shoved a toe at him to be quiet, then took my hands to draw my attention to himself instead. On our fingers, the slavers glinted blood red in the coming sunrise. "You're right," he said, and Nick whimpered. "But let him live. Not for him. For me."

"For you!" I jerked out of his grip, falling back into Al. His thick hand fell on my shoulder, and I pulled myself straight.

Jaw clenching, Trent followed me. Nick cowered behind him, the torn remains of Ku'Sox steaming beside him in the cold wind. "For me," he said, but his voice was too soft for it to be him wanting to take his revenge on Nick alone. "I want . . ." he said, then hesitated, taking a breath of air and lifting his chin. "I want one pure thing in my life," he said loudly, his voice ringing in the red-tinted air. "I want one thing I can point to and say, 'That is good, and it's a part of me.'"

My heart thudded and my eyes teared up. He thought I was good? I couldn't speak as Trent took my hands and pulled me a step from Al, and I shivered as the demon's touch fell away. "I want," he said softly, "you to keep what you can of the person you want to be. Don't sacrifice it for this." Lip curling, he gave Nick a sidelong, dismissive glance. "Don't let your desire for revenge give him the power to make you what you don't want to be."

"It's hard," I said, and the demons around me began to shuffle, eager to be gone.

But he smiled and tucked a strand of hair behind my ear. "Of course it is. If it was easy, everyone would do it."

Newt pushed the dead carcass of Ku'Sox into the hole with her foot, and Nick scrabbled away from the edge. "Well?"

It hurt to say it, but I took a breath and looked straight up. Trent's fingers were clasped in mine. "It's Nick," I said, then danced back when Nick cried out, reaching for me.

As one, the demons groaned. Al's shoulders slumped, and then his eyes narrowed. "I say we still kill him," he muttered, reaching, and Newt slammed her staff down between them.

"I claim him!" she shouted, swinging her staff in a wide circle, and they fell back, used to her outbursts. Trent pulled me out of the way, and I watched Newt almost crouch over Nick, her robes covering his feet. "He's mine! He's mine by rights! His actions cost me a familiar, and I claim him!"

"No!" Nick cried out, his hand reaching for me. "Rachel! Please!"

Her head tilted, Newt waited, one eye almost slitted shut as she looked at me. I nodded, and the demon laughed, hauling him up and giving him a shake. "Go wait for me," she intoned, and he stared, panting in fear. She gave him a shove, and he stumbled, vanishing as she flung him to her rooms. I thought of him landing in the mockery of my kitchen, and a tiny part of me felt the first hints of justice.

I jumped when Al's hand landed on my shoulder again. "He will be dead in a week," the demon murmured, his ash-scented breath tickling my ear.

But I knew Nick. He was too ugly to die.

The sound of Newt's staff scraping on the stones was loud as she came forward to us. Demons were vanishing with their gargoyles in pairs and groups, and the bite of windblown rock blew about my feet, rising. I closed my eyes when it reached my face, and my hair began to stream behind me. I didn't know what was going to happen tomorrow. Maybe I could take a day off.

"It was an excellent Hunt," Trent said, and my eyes flew open to see him extending his hand to Dali. "I am Trenton Aloysius Kalamack. I am not my ancestor."

Dali looked at it, then Trent. "No, you are not," he said, his hand unmoving. "But you come from the same place."

Trent's hand slowly dropped, and he inclined his head in understanding. "Perhaps later."

Dali backed up a step, his eyes touching mine and Al's. "I need to think on this." A coating of ever-after shimmered over him, leaving the clear air of morning empty of him.

Newt sighed. "And so it circles," she said, her black eyes coming to meet mine as the sun spilled over the rim of the ever-after, turning me a blood red. "It looks as if I won't be killing you this morning, Rachel. You have been given a reprieve."

Nodding, I pulled the slaver ring off my finger and handed it to Trent. The two demons winced as Trent removed his slave ring, silent as he handed them back to me. They were mine again, and I could destroy them.

I was alive, but what color was my soul?

Chapter Thirty-One

There was no moon as I followed Trent down the soft sawdust path of his private gardens. It was silent but for the sighing of the wind in the tender new leaves, and I could smell the cedar the path was made from. Small ferns laced the path, tiny because they'd been above the earth for only a few weeks, but I knew that by the end of the summer they'd be nearly as high as my knees.

"I appreciate you coming out," Trent said, a few steps ahead of me, looking comfortable in his black pants and gray shirt, his tie loose about his neck and no coat on against the slight chill. "I have a clear schedule, but showing up at your church after midnight isn't prudent."

I thought of the news vans and nodded. "It's not like I have anything on my plate," I said, staring up at the dark branches as my steps slowed. No, it had been very quiet the last week. Most days it was just Jenks and me knocking about in the church—Ivy was spending a lot of time with Nina, trying to bring her back from the brink. I'd gotten a lot done in the garden, but I was bored to tears. When Trent had asked me to come over when I'd called to tell him I had the curse to mend his hand ready, I'd jumped at the chance. But I was more than a little curious as to why we hadn't done it in his office or private apartments. Maybe he wanted to make s'mores? I could smell a wood fire somewhere.

"Business still slow?" he asked, holding a dogwood branch heavy with last night's rain out of the way.

"Nonexistent, but Al is keeping me busy." I had to force myself to move forward to duck under the branch, and I didn't know why. It wasn't Trent. He had been professional if somewhat quiet when he'd met me at the kitchen entrance at the underground garage. I'd never even seen the upstairs apartments, having gone immediately to Trent's secondary office on the ground floor, and out into the gardens from there. It was nearing midnight and the public offices were deserted.

Water spotted my shoulder when Trent let the branch go. A flower drifted down, and I kept it, feeling as if it had been a gift. Trent led the way. The lamp in his hand swung, sending beams of light into the wet leaves. I shivered, then stopped dead in my tracks when the path forked. To the right was a narrow nothing, to the left, well-manicured sawdust. Trent continued on down the right path, and I wavered, feeling the need to keep moving.

"Trent," I said, actually two steps down the wrong path. Confusion and nausea rose up, and I stopped, unable to go back. *What in hell?*

"Oh. Sorry." Motions sharp, Trent came back and took my hand, pulling me back to the smaller path. "There's a ward."

His fingers in mine were warm, and my head came up. The nausea vanished, and I took a deep breath. "To keep people out?" I guessed, feeling funny as he led me up the narrow, crooked path as if I were a reluctant child. My breath came in a quick heave, and panic took me. Almost laughing, Trent gave a quick yank, jerking me forward another step.

I stumbled, gasping as a wave of energy passed over my aura. Wild magic sang in my veins, setting my heart to thumping, and then I was through. Halting, I turned to look over my shoulder. The main house was surprisingly close. Jenks and I had probably been within a stone's throw of the ward when we had burgled Trent's office, and we'd never known.

"The ward only hits you when you try to force your way in," Trent said. "Otherwise, you'd never notice it. At all."

Breathless, I pulled my hand from his. "You made it?" I said, and he turned away.

"My mother did." His pace slower, Trent wove a path through the tall bushes. I could see a little roof up ahead, but little else. "She made the ward, the spelling hut, and pretty much everything in it."

The path opened up, and I stopped beside him as he lifted the lantern high. There in the soft glow of a candle was a small house made of stone and shingled with cedar. Moss grew on the roof, and the door was painted red. It felt abandoned, but the glow of firelight flickered on the inside of the windows, and smoke drifted up from the chimney. Clearly he'd been out here earlier tonight.

"I found it shortly after she died," he said, a faint smile quirking his lips. "Made it into my own place to avoid Jonathan. It's only been recently that I've been using it to spell in. It's remarkably secure. I thought you might like to see it." He lowered the lamp and I followed him to the wide slate stone that served as a threshold.

There was no lock, and Trent simply pushed the door open. "Come on in," he said as he went in before me and set the lamp on the small table beside the door. His back was to me as I hiked my shoulder bag up and sent my gaze over everything to find it neat and tidy. It was one room, the walls covered in shelves holding ley line equipment, books, and pictures in frames. Two comfortable chairs were pulled up before the small fire on a knee-high hearth, and another beside one of the small windows. A cot was half hidden behind a tapestry hanging from the ceiling. All in all, it was a nice getaway, having none of the gadgetry I'd come to associate with Trent, but all his gardener earthiness that showed itself only in his orchid gardens.

"I've not been here in weeks," he said as I relaxed in the smoke-scented warmth. "Except for earlier tonight, of course. It's been quiet since Quen took the girls and Ellasbeth home."

My head came up. "I can't believe you let her have them," I said, feeling his depression. "Even if it is short term. You love those girls! Ellasbeth is such a, ah . . ."

I caught my words as Trent took my coat and hung it on a hook behind the door. "Bitch?" he said, shocking me. "It was either that or invite her to stay here, and I'm not ready for that." His finger twitched, and I bit back my advice to tell her to take a hike. I knew he was going to marry her at some point. Everyone wanted it. Expected it.

"They'll be back in April, and Quen is with them, in the meantime. We're doing monthly exchanges until they get older, and then we can start stretching it out."

He was trying to hide his distress, but I could see right through it as he went to the fading fire and crouched before it. "For now, I get them half the time, Ellasbeth the other." His motions stirring the coals slowed. "I never knew what silence was before. I go to the office, come back to an empty apartment, go back to the office or the stables." He looked up. "I hope you don't mind, but I don't feel so alone out here. Fewer reminders."

I nodded, understanding. It still hurt that Ceri was gone. I could only imagine how quiet his apartments were with no one there but the many reminders of her and the girls. The warmth of the place was seeping into me, and I came forward, liking the old wooden planks and the dusty red woven rug. "Sorry."

Trent set the poker back and dropped a small birch log on the coals. The bark flared and was gone. "Quen will see they're safe and that Ellasbeth doesn't warp them too badly. I've got my spells to work on until then. And business, of course."

Hands in his pockets, he looked over the small hut, and I could see the long days stretching before him. That the girls were gone wasn't exactly what I had been sorry about.

I scuffed the last of the dirt from my feet, not knowing what to do. Trent made a neutral smile and excused himself to go to the small counter set under a dark window. There was a teapot that made me think of Ceri, and I wasn't surprised when Trent's reaching hands hesitated. Shoulders stiffening, he drew it closer and took the lid off and looked inside. "You want some coffee?" he said as I faced the fire to give him some privacy. "I've got some decent instant."

"Only if you want some." I went to the shelves, drawn by a tiny birch bark canoe that I recognized from camp. A trophy with a horse on it was tucked behind it, and a hand-drawn picture of a flower behind that: memories. There was a half-burned birthday candle, a blue-jay feather, and a dusty stalk of wheat tucked into a wide-mouthed handmade pot, again from camp. I frowned, feeling as if I recognized it. *Would my fin-*

gerprint match the one in the glaze? I wondered, afraid to bring it closer and see.

Uncomfortable, I sent my fingers to trace the spines of the books, a combination of classic literature and world history. The room smelled like magic, the cedar mixing with the scent of cinnamon and ozone. My aura tingled, and I slipped into my second sight long enough to see that the tail end of the line that stretched from his public office to his private one nicked the edge of the little hut. There was a circle there, made of something that glittered black. Beside it was what I had to call a shrine.

Curious, I went to investigate, smiling when I saw a black-and-white photo of his mother tucked beside a lit candle and a small fingerbowl of fragrant ash. On sudden impulse, I set the flower I had found beside the candle. My fingers brushed the candle as I pulled back, and my head jerked up at the wash of warm sparkles that numbed it. Faint in my thoughts, wild magic burbled and laughed, and I curled my fingers under.

"She's beautiful," I said, looking at the photo with my hands behind my back.

"You can pick it up."

The soft sounds of his making coffee were pleasant in the extreme. I tentatively reached for it, finding the ornate silver frame surprisingly heavy. It wasn't sparking wild magic, so I took it to the fire to see it better, dropping my bag on the floor and sitting on the edge of the seat to tilt the photo to the light.

Trent's mother was smiling, squinting at the wind that had taken a wayward strand of her long hair. Behind her was a mountain I didn't recognize. Beside her, looking just as wild and free, was Ellasbeth's mother. There were flowers in their hair, and deviltry in their eyes. I'd guess it was taken before they had come to Cincinnati. I wondered who'd snapped the picture. I found my lips curving up to smile back at them. "You have her face," I said softly, then flushed.

Trent noisily put the lid on the teapot. Bringing it to the fire, he set it on the hearth. There was a kettle in his other hand, moisture beading up on it as he set it on a hook and shoved it over the flames. "It's going to take a while. There is no electricity out here."

"I'm in no hurry." No electricity meant no way in or out when a circle was set. This was more than a getaway; it was a spelling fortress. I suddenly realized Trent's eyes were on the photo, and I stretched to set it back on the small table beside the candle. "Do you bring people here often?"

Trent sat gingerly down in the other chair. His eyes roved over the room, trying to see it as I might be. "Not often, no."

Not ever, maybe, by the looks of it, and I waited for more, grimacing when it became obvious there wasn't any. "Ah, so are you ready for the curse?" I said, and his breathing hesitated a bare instant.

"If you are."

He was annoyingly short-answered tonight, his mood closed and somewhat stiff, but seeing as I was going to curse him, I didn't blame him—even if the curse was going to fix his hand. I'd stirred it myself under Al's eye, and I'd admit that I was more than a little nervous.

Trent slid back into the chair as I lifted my bag onto my lap and dug inside for my scrying mirror. My fingertips tingled as I found it, cramping up as I brought it out and set it on my knees. I had prepped the curse over the course of the week, storing it in Al's private space in the collective. All I would have to do was tap a line, find the collective, and say the magic words to access it. "If this doesn't work . . ." I started, and Trent waved me to silence.

"Rachel, you turned Winona back into a human guise. You can repair my fingers."

I wasn't so confident, and I settled back, then scooted forward, the scrying mirror making my knees ache with the magic taking notice of where I was. Like a slime mold after the sun, it stretched and dove for the tiny sliver of line that ran not five feet away.

"It shouldn't hurt," I added, feeling my fingers slip as I started to sweat. "If it does, just say the words of invocation again, and it will reverse as long as it hasn't sealed yet. Okay?"

He nodded, and his jaw tightened.

I took a breath. Exhaling, I gently reached for a line, my fingers jerking on the glass as it spilled into me with an icy suddenness. The lines had been painfully sharp since I'd dove through all of them, almost as if their clarity had improved a hundredfold. The glass hummed with a myriad of conversations, whispers on the edge of my awareness, drops and swells of power as demons went about their daily grind of fighting boredom. The collective felt warm, peaceful for once, and I felt my eyes slip shut as the heat of the fire mixed with the blanket of spent adrenaline still holding the collective in a muzzy contentment. Oh, if only it could last.

Leaving the puddled warmth behind, I willed a small part of my thoughts into Al's storeroom, shocked when my muscles seemed to lose their focus. A heavy lassitude filled me, and I wondered if Al was asleep. I'd never encountered this when storing or accessing spells in Al's private space before. The way the collective was set up was that private curses were stored in private spaces, and public curses were stored where everyone could access them, be they the stuff to get rid of warts or entire species. Use a public curse, and you took on the smut for its creation—plus whatever smut the maker tacked on to it. It was how some demons tried to get rid of their smut, a dubious attempt at best.

"Here," I said brusquely, feeling dizzy as I held out my hand across the space between us. "I didn't want to risk making a charm tailored to you specifically in case the identifying factor could be used against you, so I need to touch you to focus the curse."

"Does it have to be my right hand?" he asked, and I blinked, trying to focus on him. I felt half drunk—without the mild euphoria.

"It can be your foot, for all that it matters," I said, and he scooted forward, slipping his left hand into mine. It was cold, and I gripped it tighter. "*Non sum qualis eram,*" I said to access the proper curse, one hand in his, the other on the mirror.

I stiffened as the energy spilled up through me, shaking off the smut of the curses around it and shining with a dull gleam in my mind. *I pay the cost for this,* I thought, wondering how I got to this point: willingly taking the smut for a curse to help Trent. Warm and chattering through my synapses like water around rocks, the curse sped from my mind to my chi, pulling energy along behind it until it dove through my hand and into Trent.

His hand spasmed, clenching hard enough on mine to hurt.

"It's done," I said, and he let go, holding his right hand up to the flickering firelight. My shoulders eased as I saw five fingers there, five perfect fingers. Exhaling, I flopped back into my chair, relieved. I'd used a modified healing curse to set his body back to the DNA sample stored in the collective, a memento of his time as a familiar. It would have all the tweaking that his father had done, not only preserving his life but extending it.

As well as fixing his hand, I thought, pleased that I could do this one thing. It was good to be whole and unscarred.

And then I looked up at him and paled. *Oh no.*

The pleasure in Trent's expression hesitated as he saw my face. "What?"

My mouth opened as I stared at his ears, but I didn't quite know how to tell him, and my face warmed. His ears were pointed, just like Lucy's and Ray's. Shit, I thought that his dad had fixed them by tinkering with his DNA, not cropping them like a Doberman.

"Um . . ." I started, then jumped when the silver bell hanging suspended above the fireplace made a single beautiful peal of sound.

Trent looked up, startled, and then we both flung ourselves backward from the heavy burst of burnt-amber-tainted air that exploded on the hearth. I gasped as Al popped into the room. Shrinking backward, I pulled my legs up onto the chair. Trent had stood, shoving his chair back nearly three feet as the demon in his crushed green velvet coat all but rolled into the fire, arms and legs askew.

"Al!" I shouted when he came to a grunting halt. Then I cried, "Al!" in a panic. "You're on fire!"

His sleeve flaming, he sat up, blinking from behind his blue-tinted glasses sitting halfway off his face. "Oh, look at that," he slurred as he set a black bottle down to pat at his arm. "I am on fire."

"Get him out of here, Rachel," Trent said in a bad temper as he stood to the side, his expression lost in the shadows. "This is intolerable."

I winced, glancing at Al when he began to giggle at the flames he was making dance on his fingertips. "I'm sorry," I said as I unfolded myself from the chair, really meaning it. "There's no reason for him to show up." I turned to Al. "Al, you need to leave. Now."

But the damage had already been done. And it wasn't like I had a say in the matter.

"Don't want to go . . ." the demon slurred as he took a swig from the bottle and scooted to lean against the rock next to the firebox, his knees pulled up and his head thrown back. "I heard you tap a line, and I came for a visit. It's so quiet. There's no one about, no parties, no one to flay, to torture." He blinked, as if seeing the ceiling for the first time. "Where am I?"

I glanced at Trent now moving quietly through the room, gathering things up and shoving them into drawers. The candle at the shrine was out. "Oh my God," I said, peering closer at Al. "You're drunk!"

Trent shoved a tiny window open in anger, and Al raised his bottle in salute. "No, I'm not," he protested. Then . . . "Wait, I am. Yes. I am drunk. You have no idea how hard it was to get to this mar-r-rvelous state of disconnection." Wavering, he looked past me to an open cupboard. "Oh, look, there's more."

As I watched helplessly, Al staggered upright, stumbling to a rack holding six bottles of white wine I hadn't noticed before. At a loss, I turned back to Trent, immediately seeing his ears.

"This is elf wine!" Al announced loudly, and Trent frowned. "Oh, Rachel, this stuff is toxic. Knock you on your ass. Where are we?"

"Somewhere you shouldn't be," I said, frustrated. Trent had opened up to me, showed me something important and fragile to him, and I go and bring Al into it. That it was an accident didn't mean anything. My gut hurt, and seeing my scrying mirror, I scooped it up and held it up to Trent so he could see himself.

Trent frowned at his red-tinted reflection. Then his eyes went wide and he grabbed the mirror from me, holding it closer, tilting his head to see. In the corner, Al began to laugh uproariously, the bottle of elf wine lighter than when he had taken it. "She gave you your ears back, little elf!" he said, and I cringed. The night had started out so nice, too.

"I'm sorry," I said, miserable. "I thought that your ears were changed at the cellular level, genetically stunted. I didn't know they had been surgically altered."

"Pointy ears. Pointy-eared devil," Al said as Trent held the mirror with one hand and felt his ear with the other. "This is good," he added, squinting at the bottle. "Ha! It's your label."

I couldn't tell what Trent was thinking, and I cringed when he finally met my eyes. "I can change them back . . ."

"No, this is fine." He took a last look, then handed the mirror to me. "Um . . . I like it."

He was lying, and I hunched miserably into myself. From the corner, Al said, "Want me to cut them for you?"

"No!" Trent exclaimed, then shifted on his feet nervously. "This is good," he said as if trying to convince himself. "Ray and Lucy have natural ears. It's fitting that I do, too."

"You sure?"

He looked a little ill, but he was smiling. "Yes, I'm sure. Thank you."

One foot cocked behind the other, Al leaned heavily on the counter and belched. "At least your hair will stop falling into your eyes with those huge wings of yours."

I stiffened. "They are not huge," I said crossly. "Trent, don't listen to him. They're just right. Seriously, I can fix them," I said, reaching to touch them.

Trent's hand on my wrist stopped me. "I like them," he said, and I froze. Letting go, he retreated to his chair, sitting down and unlacing his dress shoe.

"What are you doing now?" Al questioned, listing heavily as he tucked another one of those bottles under his arm and staggered for the cot half hidden behind a curtain. "Seeing if your circumcision is gone? It is."

My expression went blank, and Trent hesitated, a silk sock in his hand as he felt the underside of his big toe. He looked at me, and I put a hand to my mouth, face flaming. "Oh. My. God. Trent. I'm sorry." Crap on toast, could I screw this up any more?

"Um," Trent said, clearly at a loss.

"Call me tomorrow," Al said seriously, pointing at him with a bottle as he reclined on the cot. "I've got a curse that will take care of that."

"Ah, I had a scar on my big toe," Trent said, his thoughts clearly scattered. "It rubbed sometimes." He put his sock back on, the firelight making the creases in his forehead obvious.

"Unless you like the snake in a turtleneck look," Al said, and I hung my head and massaged my temples. "Ceri did. But she was earthy in her desires. Delightful little animal she was."

Al went suddenly still, his breath rattling as if he was in pain. *Ceri.*

Suddenly I understood. That was why he was drunk. But it didn't excuse Al's presence. "I'm so sorry," I whispered, mortified. "I didn't think—"

"She called it my purse of delight," Al was saying to the ceiling, flopped back on the cot until only his legs showed beyond the curtain, one foot on the cot, the other draped down onto the floor. A little sob came from him. "I should have freed her. I should have freed her . . ."

Trent had turned away, his steps long as he strode to the wine rack. "Rachel, have you tried my family label?" he asked, almost frantic as he searched for a corkscrew. "It's fairly palatable for having been grown at this latitude. My father shoved a few more genes into a species or two for better sugar production." Hands shaking, he poured white wine into a glass, downing it in one go. If I didn't know him better, I would say he was babbling.

This was going really well, and I glumly sat back down on the raised hearth, my elbows on my knees and my head in my hands. The kettle had begun to steam, and I pushed it off the fire. I didn't feel like coffee, and by the looks of it, neither did Trent. From behind the curtain, Al was either singing or crying. I couldn't tell. Asking him to jump out probably wasn't a good idea.

The clink of glasses brought my head up, and I wasn't surprised when Trent gingerly sat next to me, setting the glasses on the hearth between us and filling them both. "He misses Ceri," I said softly, to which Trent nodded, his own eyes filled with a private heartache.

"Miss that little bitch?" Al said, the curtain fluttering as he tried to get up. Arm waving, he managed it, his eyes haunted. His next words were lost when he saw the twin glasses, one of which Trent was handing to me. His heartache deepened, and he held his bottle high. "Yes, a toast to Ceri." His bottle sloshed as he shook it. "You were a most exceptional familiar." His arm dropped, and for a moment, there was silence. "I should have freed you, Ceridwen. Perhaps you would have sung to me again if I had."

I thought of Al's blue butterflies, and I set my drink down untasted. The last thing I needed was to add a headache to this. "I'm sorry, Al," I said, my eyes welling up.

"She was a familiar, nothing more," he slurred, swinging the bottle. "Why should I care?" But it was clear he did. "Miss her? Ha!" he cried.

"That elf woman was useless! Hardly able to warm my coffee in the morning. Pierce did a better job of keeping to my schedule. I wouldn't take her back even if I *could* get that damned resurrection curse to work." His head drooped, and I hoped he would pass out soon. "She was forever waking me up in the morning, crashing the cupboard doors. The bitch."

Beside me, Trent seemed to start. "She did that to me as well, every time I tried to sleep in on the weekends. Then she'd smile at me as if she didn't know she'd woken me."

"Crashing about," Al said, gesturing with the bottle. "Making more noise than a box of squirrels. She did it on *purpose,* I tell you. On *purpose!*"

Trent shook his head as we watched Al begin to become unconscious. "The woman could stomp like an elephant," Trent said softly, leaning to whisper in my ear and make me shiver. "Quen threatened to smack her."

"Yes, thrash her," Al said, slumping back against the wall. "But she always had my coffee and toast to distract me." His expression became serious. "You cannot thrash the person who makes you coffee. It's a rule somewhere." Blinking, Al slumped against the wall, his hair pushing up behind him. "It was a sad day when she stopped singing. You can't keep a caged bird. No matter how beautiful she is. Maybe if I had freed her. But she would have left me. This is hell, you know? My rooms are so quiet."

I shifted on the raised hearth to build the fire up. I had a feeling we might be here for a while, and this was the only light source besides Trent's lantern in the window.

Trent took a sip of his wine, a brief flash of worry crossing him. "Mine, too," Trent barely breathed, his sadness obvious.

Al jerked forward in a sudden movement, and Trent started. "That is intolerable!" Al said, his feet flat on the floor and gesturing with his bottle before taking another gulp. "You must put yourself into the collective immediately so that we may converse!"

Poker in hand, I half turned, shocked. Trent, too, looked uneasy. "Ah, no. No, thank you."

Head violently shaking back and forth, Al scooted forward on the cot. "Nonsense! We already have the wine. Rachel, fetch my yew stylus. It will take a moment."

My head came up at the slippery pull on the ley line, and Al frowned as things started popping into reality and falling to the floor. "I need to tell you the circumcision curse if nothing else," he slurred, blinking at the small vial of camphor that appeared in his fingers.

"Al." I jumped at the dull crack of an empty scrying mirror hitting the ground inches from my foot, then ducked when the demon threw a bag of sand from him in disgust. "Al!" I shouted. "Knock it off! He doesn't want to be in the collective!"

"I'm flattered," Trent said with a false calm, the fire flicking eerily behind him, "but I don't think the rest will appreciate it. Would you like another bottle of wine?"

I wondered if he was trying to get him drunk enough to pass out until the sun rose, seeing as Al showed no sign of leaving. Sure enough, his mouth on the bottle, Al nodded. "You helped kill Ku'Sox," he said when he came up for air. "You don't think they remember that? You can handle being in the collective." He reached eagerly for the bottle Trent was extending.

"I'm not worried about handling it. I think they wouldn't approve," Trent said.

"Fiddlesticks," Al said, then cleared his throat. "*A-dap-erire . . .*" he intoned carefully, and I checked to see that my zipper was up when the cork flew out of the bottle. He might be drunk, but he still had control, and it was right where it belonged. "Elves used to be part of the collective," Al said as he winced at the first harsh swallow. "Just because there haven't been any for the last five thousand years doesn't mean it can't be done. You can access the old curses then. Protect yourself. You're going to need it. The old ways are ending. Embrace the new. Elves and demons living together." He blinked. "Oh God. We're all going to die."

Standing beside the cot, Trent took the empty bottle from Al. "No. Thank you, but no."

"Here." Al reached out for the cracked scrying mirror, and I handed it to him, wishing he would go to sleep. "Draw the figures, elf man. Draw it. Pick a name. We can use your marvelous wine. Ceri, be useful and go fetch some salt."

My heart clenched, but kneeling beside the fire as I was, I didn't question why he'd called me that. "Go to sleep, Al," I said, my own sorrow rising.

"You want to be prince of the elves or not?" Al said, wavering where he sat. "Royalty always conversed with demons before they were wed. It's tradition. It's how I tricked Ceri into loving me. You're not married, are you? On the side, perhaps? In Montana?"

Trent grimaced. "I need to think up a good name. I promise when I get a good name that no one can think of, I will. Why don't you rest for a minute?"

Al delicately belched, and sighing heavily, he leaned back into the shadows until his black eyes glowed from the dark. "Capital idea. Good idea. Clever, clever elf. We will wait. You pick out a name, then call me."

The fire snapped, and then from the cot came a long, rattling snore. Trent cautiously tried to take the bottle from Al, giving up when it began to glow. Leaving it in Al's grip, he turned to me and shrugged. "I think he's out."

"I am so sorry." Embarrassed, I got up from the fire and began to collect the stuff that Al had popped in from his kitchen. "I had no idea he'd feel the curse, much less come and see what I was doing."

Trent handed me the bag of sand. "He probably has never dealt with grief," he said, and I set it with the rest.

"Too much of it, rather. He was married once. Only the demons who knew how to love survived the making of the ever-after."

Shocked, Trent looked from me to Al and back again. "I didn't know that."

A long snore came from behind the curtain, and a soft mumble. Trent sat down in his chair, clearly reluctant to leave Al here alone. "Do you think he can resurrect Ceri? I've tried."

My chest hurt, and I sat in the chair next to him where we could both watch the fire and Al both. "No. I've tried several times, too. Pierce as well. They've moved on. I'm happy for them, but it hurts." I hadn't been able to summon my father or Kisten, either.

Trent was rubbing his new pinkie with his thumb in introspection. "Quen will be hurting for a long time. That's why I insisted he go with the girls. And as a buffer for Ellasbeth."

Hearing more in that statement than he was saying, I turned to him. "How about you?"

"Me?" He looked at the bottle in Al's grip, then topped off his glass with the bottle on the hearth between us. "I'm not the one Ceri loved," he said, but I could hear his regret. I waved off his offer to refill my untouched glass, and when I remained silent, he added, "I liked her, but I didn't love her. She was . . . too proud to love me. Distant."

"And you need someone more earthy," I said, only half kidding.

Al snorted. There was a clunk, and the wine bottle rolled out from behind the curtain. It sloshed to a halt at Trent's foot, and he reached for it. "A little spontaneity would be nice," he said, touching my foot by accident when he set Al's bottle next to ours. "I already miss her and her elegant demands and flashing indignity. You couldn't tell the woman no."

"Not that . . ." Al mumbled in his sleep. "He's going to need that later . . ."

"I'm angry at her unnecessary death. It hurts seeing Quen grieve and know it's partially my fault," Trent added, his jaw tight and his gaze unfocused. The scent of cinnamon was rising, mixing with the scent of burnt amber and woodsmoke. It almost made the burnt amber smell nice. "I'm sorry for this," Trent said softly. "I'm sorry for everything."

This wasn't like Trent at all, but I wasn't surprised to see it. I was upset about Ceri and Pierce, but I hadn't been planning on a life with either of them as Trent had with Ceri—in some disjointed, separate fashion. Alone. He had always planned on being alone, but never this apart. Even with Ellasbeth, he would be alone. I felt bad for him. It wasn't fair. None of it.

"It wasn't your fault," I said, shifting to look at him. There wasn't much space between us, but it seemed uncrossable.

"Maybe someday I'll believe you," he said, his brow furrowed in the firelight. "Rachel, I asked you here tonight for more than getting my fingers back."

Panic slid through me. "What?"

He grimaced, clearly annoyed that Al was snoring in the corner. "We could've done this anywhere, but I wanted you to see me, to see this," he said, gesturing at the room. "I wanted you to know where I came from, what I am under the choices I make."

My heart pounded. "What did you do?" I asked, terrified, almost.

Exhaling, he looked at his watch, the crystal catching the light to make time vanish. Then he scared me even more when he drank his glass dry and filled it again. "I made a big mistake by not telling you why I thought the slavers were the better choice."

"I know," I interrupted, and his brow furrowed.

"By the Goddess, will you shut up?" he said, and from behind the curtain, Al mumbled something. A little rocking horse with wings popped into existence, crashing into the ceiling before falling to the floor to quiver and go still.

"Listen to me," he said, and I swallowed my words. "The Rosewood babies are going to start dying next week," he said, and my breath caught. "If nothing changes, by this time next month, you and Lee will again be the only survivors of the Rosewood syndrome."

"But you fixed them!" I said, appalled.

"Yes and no," Trent said after he topped his glass off again. "I had to fix their genome to ensure Ku'Sox would hold to his end of the bargain and not harm Lucy, but I worked in a small error that wouldn't express itself until it was replicated sufficiently. I couldn't risk that he would get his way if he killed me."

Horrified, I stared at him. He met my gaze levelly. "You killed them. The babies," I whispered, and he shook his head.

"Not yet."

"What do you mean, 'not yet'?" Feeling betrayed, I stood. "Trent, they are all someone's child!" I exclaimed, and Al snorted in his sleep, mumbling.

Trent looked up, agitated. "I mean, not yet. Rachel, the world isn't ready for them."

I cocked my hip, the fire warm behind me. "When is the world ever ready for change, Trent? When?"

Setting his glass down, Trent eyed me, bitter resignation behind his frustration. "What will happen if they live? HAPA knows they exist. The only reason you survived was because you can defend yourself. You want me to give the children to the demons to raise?"

He stood, and I dropped back as he began to pace. "Or perhaps you want me to hide them and their families? I could do it. But you know the demons will find them, and one by one, a demon wanting to see the sun and escape the ever-after will either steal them outright or take over their bodies." Eyes flashing, he pointed at me, his hand wrapped around a wine-glass. "I will *not* allow a parent to love a child who is murdering his pets and performing ghastly magic, not wanting to believe that their child died five years ago and they are raising a five-thousand-year-old sadistic demon until their child's neural pathways are developed enough to work the lines. *They are not meant to be.*" Frustrated, he turned to the window, taking an angry drink, the firelight flickering on him.

From the cot, not a sound escaped, but I didn't care if Al was listening. "But they are here," I said softly, grasping his arm so he would look at me. "Trent. They are."

Trent shook his head even as he met my eyes. "I thought you might say that. If it was up to me, I'd choose the hard path with the easy ending, not the easy path with the hard end."

I drew back. "What do you mean, it's not up to you?"

Taking a last drink, Trent set his empty glass on the windowsill. Exhaling, he scrubbed his face with a hand, hesitating to look at his five perfect fingers. "What would you choose?"

The fervent emotion in his gaze as his eyes met mine scared me. "Me?"

"I want you to decide," he said, looking a little unsteady. "Not because it impacts your species, but because I want you there with me."

My heart pounded. I didn't know what he meant. He wanted me there with him?

Stumbling slightly, he went to sit on the raised hearth, snagging a new bottle on the way. "If you make the decision, you have to be there to help me with the fallout," he said, working the corkscrew with a professional flair. "Either they die naturally, or I continue the cure and the twenty-year battle to hide them until they can defend themselves."

The cork came out with a pop, and he looked at his glass, halfway across the room on the sill.

Shocked, I stared at him. He wanted me to decide? He wanted me . . . to make a decision that he would have to live by?

Giving up, he drank right from the bottle. "I don't want to be alone anymore, Rachel," he said. "And if you make the choice, you have to help me see it through."

"I want them to live," I said softly, and he slumped, his disgust obvious when his bottle clinked against the floor. "What, you asked my opinion, and that's it. You're not going back now that it wasn't anything you wanted to hear."

"No." Trent eyed me sourly. "It would be easier the other way."

Smirking, I crossed the room and sat down beside him. Taking the bottle he handed me, I poured a swallow in my glass. "If it was easy—"

"Everyone would do it," he finished, clinking his bottle to my glass and downing a swig.

"What about Ellasbeth?" I said, my expansive mood hesitating.

Trent didn't look at me. "What about her?"

I thought of the distasteful woman, on a plane to the West Coast right now, but she'd be back, worming her way into elven politics. "Aren't you supposed to be getting married to her?"

Drawing away, he looked sideways at me. The fire was warm on our backs, and his focus was starting to go distant. "This is a business arrangement. Nothing more."

"Well, that's what I thought," I said quickly, and from behind the curtain, Al started to snore. "But she doesn't like me."

"So?"

I thought about that for a moment. "You are drunk," I said as he tried to get the bottle to balance on the rim of its base.

His eyes came to mine. "I am not," he said, and I caught it as it began to tip. "But I will be before the night ends."

I took another sip, actually tasting it this time. I'd have a migraine in about an hour, but I didn't care. "You know, the last time we shared a bottle, you wiped the top off," Trent said.

"Red pop?" I guessed, smiling at a memory, and he nodded.

"You remember. Are the rings gone?"

I swung the bottle between my knees, and my gaze slid to Al snoring behind the curtain. "Al and I destroyed them," I said. "Melted them so they couldn't be reinvoked. You have a problem with that?"

Trent shook his head and reached for the bottle. "No. It was nice being able to reach your thoughts, though. You have nice thoughts."

A smile curved my lips up, and I leaned away so I could see him better. "You *are* drunk."

"I am not drunk." He shifted closer, and I didn't mind. "I'm bored out of my mind."

I took another sip. "This is good," I said, and he acknowledged it gracefully. "I know what you mean about the quiet," I went on. "Jenks's kids are scattering. He'll be down to six kids by fall. Ivy is spending most of her time with Nina. I'm starting to think about finding a new apartment somewhere with Jenks."

"Really?"

I shrugged and passed the bottle to him. "I don't know. I like it at the church, but things have changed. If I wasn't there, Ivy might ask Nina to move in. One vampire in the church is okay, two is asking for trouble. Even for a demon."

Trent set the bottle aside, almost out of his reach. "You don't think you could handle it?"

Thinking about what Cormel had said, I shrugged. "Oh, sure, but people talk."

"They do, don't they," Trent said around a sigh, and my thoughts turned to Ellasbeth. *Seriously? He could do better than that.* "Nick was too scruffy for you, even when he wasn't a demon toady," he said then, surprising me. "Marshal didn't have enough chutzpah to keep up with the elegance you're capable of. Pierce was a first-generation model in a six-g world—novel, but really how far would you get before the software crashed the system? Kisten . . ." Trent's fingers shifted in agitation. "Kisten was an interesting choice."

The reminder of Pierce hurt, but it felt good to think of him and smile. "You're critiquing my ex-boyfriends?"

He made a small noise of agreement. "I like people. Most of the time I can figure them out. You don't make any sense. What are you looking for, Rachel?"

Drawing my knees up, I rocked back and forth before the fire. "I don't know. Someone smart, powerful, who doesn't take crap from anyone. Who are you looking for?"

Trent raised a hand in protest, scooting an inch or two from me. "No, no, no. I'm not going to play this game."

"Hey, you started it. Give. Just pretend we're in camp."

"Someone funny, capable, sexy."

To balance out his strict life. "I didn't bring looks into it. How like a man."

Trent chuckled. "This is my list, not yours. Someone who won't see lovers in the shadows when I'm late for an appointment. Someone who can break a schedule and a nail and not worry about it, but still look good in a dress and not be late for everything."

I looked across the room, seeing nothing. "I want someone who will let me do my job without talking me out of it. Maybe give me a gun for my birthday once in a while."

"Someone not afraid of the money, the press," Trent said. "Someone who won't get caught in the trap that money makes."

"Someone who can do his own magic so he could survive the mess of my life," I finished, getting depressed.

"You live in a church, I live in a prison." Trent became silent.

"It would never work between us," I said, thinking we had strayed onto dangerous ground.

From the cot, Al snorted in his sleep, mumbled about pie, and went silent.

"You're great to work with, Rachel, but we have nothing in common."

Reassured, I let go of my knees and stretched them out, palms on the warm hearth beside me. "That's what I'm saying. You live in a big house, I live in a church." *And yet I am sitting in his little playhouse drinking wine.*

"We don't know any of the same people."

I reached across him for the wine, stretching as I thought of the mayor, the demons, Rynn Cormel. "We don't go in the same circles at all," I said as I leaned back and took a swallow. But I had fit in at the casino boat and his parties.

"People would talk," he said softly, and I set the empty bottle down. The firelight had turned his hair as red as mine. "Which is a shame. I like working closely with you. God, why is it so hard to tell you that? I compliment people all the time on their work ethics. Rachel, I like working with you. You're fast and inventive, and not always looking for direction."

This was going somewhere I wasn't sure I liked. "Trent," I started, glancing at the curtain when Al choked on his own spit and then began to snore again.

"No, let me finish," he said, a hand going firmly down on the stone between us. "Do you know how tiring it gets? 'Mr. Kalamack, should we do this, or that? Have you weighed all the factors, Mr. Kalamack?' Even Quen hesitates, and it drives me batty."

"Sorry."

"You, on the other hand, just go and do what you think needs to be done. If I can't keep up, you don't care. I like that. I'm glad you're going to help me with the Rosewood demons."

"Yeah," I said, wondering if he had any more of that wine stashed somewhere. "That's what you say now, but wait until they start playing with the ley lines."

"My God, you have beautiful hair in the firelight," he said softly, and I blinked. "It's like your thoughts, all cinnamon and wild untamed. I've always liked your hair."

I froze when he reached out and touched it, my breath slipping from me when his fingers grazed my neck. Slowly I reached up and took his hand, bringing it down. "Okay, we need to get you inside, Mr. Kalamack," I said, thinking that he had had way too much to be comfortable saying what he was, doing what he was. "Come on, stand up. I'll stay here with Al so he doesn't steal the picture of your mom."

I stood, still holding his hand and gently pulling him up with me. A part of me wanted this, but the smarter, wiser part knew it was a mistake.

"I am not drunk," Trent said firmly, standing before me without a waver to his stance. "I don't need to be drunk to say you have nice hair."

A flutter lifted through me, and I shoved it away.

"And I do not want to go back to my apartments," he said. "I want to go for coffee. Al isn't going to wake up." His eyes were on mine, and my heart pounded when he let them drop to my lips. "I am not drunk."

"I wouldn't care if you were."

Trent's arms were around me, and they felt right. "No, I want you to know that I do not need to be drunk to kiss you."

"Um . . ." I started, heart pounding more when he leaned in, slowly, hesitantly, stopping just shy of my lips. All I had to do was lift my chin. Breath held, I did.

With a gentle pressure, our lips met. His hands slipped more firmly about me, and I held myself back, not afraid, but wanting to feel everything slowly as I leaned in, tasting the wine on him, feeling the warmth of his body pressing into mine, breathing in our scents that were mingling and changing with the warmth. My hands rose to find his hair, and I relaxed into him as the silky strands brushed through my fingers. I wanted more, and I leaned into him as our lips moved against each other.

I pushed him off balance, and he took a step back, our lips parting even as he pulled me to him closer yet as I stumbled forward into him. The rush of the kiss pounded through me, and I stared at him, breathless, seeing in his eyes that he was not drunk. He was stone-cold sober, and it scared me. "Why did you do that?" I whispered.

He half smiled and tucked a strand of hair behind my ear. "I don't know," he said, his grip on me becoming more sure. "But I'm going to do it again."

Oh God, yes, I thought, and then he pulled me into him. The tingle of the nearby line danced at the edge of my awareness, and as his hands hinted at rising up to find my breasts, I loosened my hold on the energy in my chi to send a dart of energy balancing between us, hinting at more.

Trent's lips on mine hesitated, then became more demanding. Passion ran through me. Heart pounding, I jerked as his back found the wall. It was intoxicating, and realizing I wanted to reach behind his waistband, I stopped.

Breathless, I backed up from him. The warmth from his lips slowly cooled. My lungs heaved, and I stared at him, not as shocked as I thought I would be. "This isn't going to work," I said, scared. "You're going to get married to Ellasbeth and be what everyone needs you to be."

He reached out and slowly pulled me to him. Tense, I stood as he ran a hand through my hair. My eyes closing, I tilted my head to feel his fingers on my face. Reaching up, I took his hand in mine, leaving a kiss in his palm as I curved his fingers around it and lowered his hand between us.

"Yes, I know," he said, coming closer until our hands pressed between both of us, and I trembled as he kissed my cheek. My passion pulled to the breaking point, I opened my eyes as I felt him draw away. I wanted this, but I knew better.

"You want to go for a coffee?" he said, shocking me. "The-men-who-don't-belong might be there, or a demon catching a cup of caffeine. I hear they will give a lot for a good cup of Joe. Al isn't going to wake up until long after sunrise."

Slowly my pounding heart began to ease. "Or maybe we can just talk."

Trent smiled. "We can try," he said, taking up the lantern and opening the door.

Cool night air spilled in, but it did nothing to dampen the memory of his hands on me, touching my skin, bringing tingles to life, bringing me to life.

"What are the chances that nothing is going to happen?" he said as I followed him onto the slate threshold and passed it. "You attract trouble, Rachel Morgan."

Looking at him standing beside me in the darkness, I had to agree.